Palmetto Rose

Palmetto Rose

A TIPSY COLLINS NOVEL

STEPHANIE ALEXANDER

Design and Distribution by Bublish, Inc.
Cover Art by Caroline Staley

ISBN: 978-1-647045-01-2 (Paperback)
ISBN: 978-1-647045-00-5 (eBook)

One need not be a chamber to be haunted,
One need not be a house;
The brain has corridors surpassing
Material place.

—Emily Dickinson

And the day came when the risk to remain tight in a bud was more
painful than the risk it took to blossom.

—Anaïs Nin, Risk

Anyone who strolls the blocks of downtown Charleston surrounding the City Market will run into friendly young men selling rosebuds made from sweetgrass fronds, otherwise known as palmetto roses. Gullah-Geechee artisans use the blossoms to embellish their baskets and wreaths, or sell them by the bunch or as single blossoms. According to a local legend, ladies gave palmetto roses to their soldier-sweethearts as safety talismans during the Civil War. There's no authority to back up this speculation, and given that the roses originated with and have always been the sole creation of Gullah-Geechee artisans, that story is probably another romanticism of an Old Charleston that never was, but a pretty tale, just the same.

Chapter 1

Tipsy Collins had learned a lot about life and death since her marriage ended. Life lessons come with the territory for anyone with the misfortune—or good fortune, depending on your point of view—to experience divorce. Tipsy gleaned her unusual perspective on death, however, from those who were uniquely in the know. No one understands death better than the dead themselves.

She spent a lifetime avoiding ghosts, but when the universe threw her the ultimate supernatural curve ball, she had no choice but to face them. Fortunately, Jane and Henry Mott, the ghosts she discovered haunting her house in the Old Village of Mount Pleasant when she moved in two years ago, turned out to be fountains of insight, not only about the nuts and bolts of ghostly existence, but about Tipsy's own life. Then last summer, she found another unanticipated reason to keep her nose in ghostly business—financial salvation. Her involvement with the late John Huger and Ivy More Brewton had earned her fifty thousand dollars, additional valuable lessons, and more knowledge of supernatural mechanics.

These days, she was finally mastering the strange power that had dogged her since childhood. She'd learned to manage the physical and emotional strain of interacting with spirits. She knew how to set ghosts free from hauntings and how to spot an intergenerational curse. As a bonus, she understood ghosts were people, too, with their own feelings and stories. One of her *best friends* was a ghost. Based on her recent experience with divorce and dating, a dead male bestie seemed a better option than a living male significant other.

Henry Mott had declared himself her supernatural guardian, and refused to leave her house even when Jane moved on. He lingered in her life like an overprotective memory. Don't get the wrong idea—Tipsy *loved* her some Henry. He was the ghostly version of the brother she never had. Still, on days like that May afternoon eight months after she freed John and Ivy from their haunting, he drove her batshit nuts.

Tipsy was completing a sale at the Good Queen Bess Art Gallery on Queen Street in downtown Charleston, her best friend Shelby's family business, where she served as salesperson and resident artist. With Shelby at home with her newborn daughter, Tipsy had picked up extra hours at the GQB. *Extra*, meaning open-to-close, five days a week.

Unfortunately, longer hours didn't equate to a big paycheck. While she squeezed in personal work at the GQB, every hour spent manning the gallery was an hour *not* spent on a painting. Still, even if her paycheck wasn't impressive, it consistently appeared in her bank account every two weeks. The idea of relying on the fickle whims of art buyers terrified her.

She'd soon have available space on the gallery wall, so her inspiration and her paintbrushes needed to start hustling. A Missouri tourist was purchasing one of Tipsy's paintings after visiting the GQB five times in the past two days. The woman had peered from underneath the floppy straw hat she'd purchased at the City Market in an attempt to blend with the locals. She confessed she'd never bought a piece of original artwork, but Tipsy's piece hooked her. Tipsy wanted to lock in the sale before she changed her mind.

Henry hovered around her like a giant invisible mosquito as she tried to arrange shipping. "Will Shelby find another salesman soon?" he asked. "Spending so much time at the gallery exhausts me."

"Your zip code again?" Tipsy asked Madame Missouri. "I didn't catch it."

Henry mused away in her ear. "Is it better to say saleswoman? Saleslady? Sales-gal? I can't follow what's acceptable."

"Probably sales*person*," muttered Tipsy.

"Pardon?" Madame Missouri tapped her credit card against the desk.

"Sorry. Talking to myself." With Henry metaphorically breathing down her neck, she forgot herself and spoke to him aloud. *Henry!* she said in her mind. *Back off! I'm trying to work here!*

"*Excuse me*," said Henry. "I'm merely making conversation."

I'll lose the sale if this woman thinks I'm crazy.

"People love crazy artists. If you're a known lunatic, you'll sell more paintings." He whistled a jaunty tune and retreated to the gallery window.

Madame Missouri ran her fingers over the shiny surface of the painting, a detail of a palmetto rose. "I realize why I *must have* this painting, Ms. Collins. I could almost pluck the rose off the canvas."

Creative inspiration had struck after Tipsy visited Mrs. Green, a sweetgrass artisan Shelby befriended years ago, at the City Market. The GQB displayed Mrs. Green's more complicated creations, and Shelby purchased palmetto roses as favors for special exhibitions. Tipsy had restocked their rose supply, returned to the gallery, and set her basket on the front desk. As she started to walk to the bathroom, her always wandering eyes noted the individuality of each rose. Like real flowers, each had a distinct shape and slight variations in color. She chose one rose among many, and her mental camera clicked. The swirling green and beige blossom created a whirlpool for the eye. She painted it against a black background, and added gold leaf for sparkly effect. Shelby had hung it in the window ten days ago, and it had already found a new home.

Tipsy stood and opened one of the cabinets behind the desk. She retrieved two palmetto roses from a larger sweetgrass basket. Each distinctive faux flower had a long yellowish stem capped by an intricately woven sweetgrass rosebud. "Some bonus art left over from our last exhibit," she said, as she handed them to Madame Missouri.

"Pretty. Did these come from the Market?"

"Yes. We buy them from Mrs. Green. She's been selling her baskets there forever."

"So these are authentic?"

"All the roses are authentic. The Gullah-Geechee people don't teach their sweetgrass artforms to anyone outside their community."

She frowned. "That seems selfish."

"It's hardly selfish to keep something for themselves, when the white folks have always had everything in Charleston," said Henry, with a disdainful sniff.

How twenty-first century of you, Mr. Mott, said Tipsy, in her mind. As always, Henry exasperated her, then redeemed himself minutes later.

Tipsy wrapped up the sale and hustled Madame Missouri out the door. She entered the sale information into the computer, tidied up the desk, and turned off the lights. It was closing time on a Wednesday evening. Her three children were with her ex-husband, Ayers Lee Collins, IV, until Sunday afternoon. He'd taken an extra night to make up custodial time he lost during a recent fishing tournament. Her extended kid-free weekend loomed before her, in all its potentially productive glory. She would zip across the Ravenel Bridge and spend the remaining daylight hours painting on her front porch.

"I'm gonna head out, Henry. Work on the heron commission painting."

"A bird in a painting is worth two in the bush," he said.

"Birds have to be on the canvas before it's worth anything. You should go, too. Your edges are fuzzy." Henry could only leave Tipsy's house for about thirty minutes before the house reeled him in again.

"Will you be safe walking to your car?"

Tipsy smiled as she stuffed a box of chocolate-covered almonds and some charcoal pencils into her purse. She pointed at her casual floral romper and flat sandals. "Yup. I'm dressed to power walk. Besides, it's not near dark—"

The bell over the front door *clink-clonked* its annoyance and Henry disappeared like a lightbulb blinking off. Tipsy expected Shelby, who loved to barge in and out as if the door had done her a personal wrong. She turned to greet her oldest friend, but instead, a newer one confronted her.

"Hey, lady! What's happening?" Sullivan's Island's middle-aged glamour queen, Pamella Brewton, crossed the threshold like she was stepping onto a runway. She wore black Louboutin pumps and the skinniest of skinny jeans. Her sleeveless white turtleneck elongated her already graceful neck. She'd twisted her dark hair into a facelift-inducing topknot, revealing gold dangly earrings in the shape of palmetto bugs, Charleston's notorious oversized flying cockroaches. "How's my favorite *clairvoyant artiste*?"

"Hey, Pammy," said Tipsy, as she wrestled her own wavy, chocolate-y brown hair into a ponytail. "I'm good, but keep it down with the *clairvoyant artiste* business."

Another voice spoke up in Tipsy's mind. Her Granna, who had raised her and passed on her own psychic abilities along with her big gray eyes. To Tipsy's eternal gratitude, whatever made them this way allowed them to chat in Tipsy's head, although Granna had long since passed on.

Ah, Miss Pamella. Subtle as a donkey kick in the rear end.

I agree, replied Tipsy. *Like Henry, she's maddeningly lovable.*

Pammy's bright green eyes twinkled. "Aren't you over the whole *my amazing supernatural powers are top secret* thing?"

"I'm not keeping such a tight rein on that secret, but I'm not letting it run off at a full gallop, either."

"But I'm allowed to tell someone under *certain circumstances*."

"Certain circumstances that will never happen." Tipsy slung her purse over her shoulder. "Unless someone needs a house ghost-busted and is willing to pay big bucks, it's on the DL."

"I *happen* to have a friend whose circumstances meet your criteria. Someone who makes me look positively *impoverished*."

"No way. Who? How? Where is the—"

"Kid-free tonight, right?"

"Right. I'm going home to work. I got some tall, skinny, feathery friends to paint."

"Big Bird can wait, lady. We're heading to the psych ward."

———+×+———

Accessing the medical university's inpatient psychiatric unit isn't like strolling into Publix to pick up fried chicken. When they were denied entry, Pamella texted her rich friend with the ghost problem and asked her to meet them outside. Tipsy and Pamella waited on a bench in the psychiatric hospital's courtyard. Tipsy sipped from her water bottle, while Pammy drank from her omnipresent Yeti cup. Unlike her sauvignon blanc soaked days of problematic boozing, Pammy's Yeti contained Coke Zero.

Pamella had recently celebrated eight months of sobriety. She and her husband, Doug, lived a healthy, alcohol-free, empty-nester life in her family's cottage on Sullivan's. They'd accumulated three wiener dog puppies and named them Cinnamon, Sugar, and Nutmeg. Tipsy anticipated a Ginger would soon join the pack. Maybe an Allspice, or a Garlic. The whole family, human and canine, walked miles on the beach and lived off organic food. Pammy knitted sweaters for the dogs. Given their Zen vibes, their free time, and their surplus income, Pammy and Doug might open a yoga studio or a juice bar.

"Nutmeg doesn't like thunderstorms, so I'm taking her to a doggie therapist who specializes in anxiety—"

"How about you give me the scoop," said Tipsy.

"He's certified by the International College of Animal Psychology—"

"I mean about your friend with the ghost."

"Oh, right. Me and my ADD—"

"Yup. Squirrel on cocaine."

"Jillian Porcher Yates is her name. She's like five years older than me. Her parents were friendly with my father—you know how it is downtown. Everyone knows everyone. She moved to California for college. I didn't see her for years. She returned to town not long ago—"

"Pamella!" A petite woman waved from down the sidewalk. She walked as fast as her short legs could carry her, a miniature soldier on parade. She wore dark cropped jeans, a delicate pink cashmere sweater, and pink ballet flats on her tiny feet. Her diamond earrings sparkled like flashing high beams. A severe ponytail kept her blonde hair out of her face. With no noticeable boob job, she didn't *quite* qualify as a Charleston Dress Code Blonde, Baby Boomer Edition.

Pamella stood, so Tipsy followed her. Even with Tipsy's flat sandals, they were two WNBA players looming over a cheerleader. Pammy grabbed the woman and hugged her. "Jilly! You *poor* thing."

"Hey, Pammy." With her pretty but pinched face, Jillian looked like she ran marathons and lived on lettuce.

Pamella introduced Tipsy, and then waved at the bench. "Sit, y'all. Any news on Sophie?"

Tipsy and Pamella sat on either side of Jillian like marble bookends holding up a skinny paperback. "She's sleeping," said Jillian. "They're trying to keep her calm."

"Sophie is Jillian's daughter. She's a student at the College of Charleston. Or she *was* a student. She…can I say it?"

"Better you than me," said Jillian. "It's tacky to cry in front of strangers."

"Sophie had a total *mental breakdown*, bless her heart."

Jillian sucked air through her nostrils, as if to sniff up escaping tears.

"Jeez," said Tipsy. "What happened?"

"She *just lost* it," said Pamella, as she rummaged through her handbag for a tissue. "Screamed the roof off the house. Trashed her bedroom. Punched out a few windows. Threw a chair over the piazza railing. Crazier than a high raccoon rolling around a meth lab in broad daylight."

Jillian took Pammy's tissue. She squeezed her button nose, as if stopping up a drain.

"How awful." Tipsy tentatively touched Jillian's shoulder. "I have three children. My son, Ayers, is ten and my twins, Mary Pratt and Olivia Grace, are eight. You must be so worried."

"It's difficult, but I hope you can help us." Jillian's years in California had softened her Southern accent, but hints remained in drawn out vowels, as unintentionally elongated as a poorly sewn hem. "I'll make it worth your while."

She retrieved a lipstick from her logo-covered leather handbag. Louis Vuitton? Chanel? Hermes? Didn't make a difference to Tipsy, since she'd never contemplated purchasing one.

"Why don't you explain what's going on first," said Tipsy.

"I didn't raise her this way," said Jillian, as she coated her lips in bubble gum pink. "I was the chief financial officer of a fortune five hundred company. A blonde, Southern woman in finance. You have to be tough. Her two older sisters…one graduated from Berkeley's law school and the other just finished her orthopedic surgery residency."

"Wow. Impressive." The family's professional background seemed irrelevant to Sophie's mental breakdown, but Tipsy had to respond somehow.

"I'm saying we're *strong women*. But Sophie…she's different. I should start at the beginning."

"Pammy said you recently moved back to town after a long stint on the West Coast?"

Jillian smiled for the first time. "Yes. I met my husband, Dan, at Stanford. He was a true finance geek. Started a hedge fund with a couple friends."

She said it like her husband had joined a garage band. "I have a basic idea of what those companies do," said Tipsy. *I think it involves billions, Granna.*

"We settled in the Bay Area. Didn't get back to Charleston for *years* at a time. Dan traveled a lot. I had an equally intense career, and we had our two older girls. My father and sister had both passed away and my mother was…*difficult*. I didn't want my children around her."

"I have one of those mothers, so no judgment," said Tipsy.

"We tried for a third baby, but no luck. Then Sophie came along when I was forty. A *wonderful* surprise. You can imagine how we all doted on her, but she was a challenging child. I suppose all parents have one."

Tipsy considered her daughter Mary Pratt, who emerged from the womb screaming for attention and never stopped. "True. My daughter M.P. never met a crisis she didn't start or exacerbate."

"Sophie, too, but there was more. *Unnaturally* more. She was painfully timid with anyone outside our family. So standoffish, the other children at school stopped talking to her, but she didn't care. She sat in her room all day, talking to herself and her toys. She chatted with the empty air in public. She'd cling to me like a baby kangaroo trying to climb back into Mama's pouch. Sometimes she laughed at nothing. People *stared*."

"Ah," said Tipsy. "I see."

Granna spoke up. *Sounds familiar.*

"When I asked her about it, she offered the most *specific* descriptions. A barefoot boy with blonde curls. A woman in a long princess dress. A man with moccasins and feathers in his hair. I thought she had a wild imagination, but she insisted they were real."

The ever-subtle Pamella poked Tipsy. "You *seeeeee*."

"And she was *so sad*. It's not *normal* for a child to be constantly sad. Poor baby. It broke my heart. Then…" Another pause and a nose plug. "Dan died of cancer when she was ten. A brain tumor. Three months between diagnosis and…the end."

Tipsy started to commiserate, but Jillian rushed on as if turning the page on a terrible plot twist. "Sophie was so distraught, I pulled her out of school. I hired tutors. Took her to psychiatrists and therapists. During middle school, she became…reclusive. Even threatened suicide."

"Such a difficult age," said Pammy. "It's looming on your horizon, Tipsy."

"Don't remind me," said Tipsy, who had tortured Granna with her middle school melodrama. Karma would surely smack her three times over with her own kids.

"We got her on the right medications and she finally got a grip as a teenager," said Jillian. "As if she understood no one else saw what she saw, and she stopped talking about it."

Tipsy nodded and thought of Henry. He'd had no one to help him understand his supernatural talents, either. He suffered a similarly lonely childhood until he learned to ignore ghosts.

"I reenrolled her in school in tenth grade and she seemed to turn a corner. She had friends, played tennis, and made good grades. I was beyond relieved. Then I got the news that my mother, Betsy Porcher, had Alzheimer's. We have no other family, and I felt guilty for keeping my girls from her. Sophie and I came home for a visit. She fell in love with Charleston. She adores my mother's house. She loved my mother herself. *BeeBee* this, *BeeBee* that."

"I was close to my grandmother, too."

"It's easier to be a grandmother than a mother. Besides, the doddering, senile version of my mother was an improvement on the version I remember. Sophie wanted to attend the College of Charleston. It's not Stanford, or even Berkeley, but I agreed. I want her to be happy."

"That's what every mother wants," said Tipsy.

"Every *good* mother," said Pammy, whose mother had abandoned her as an infant and died in prison after murdering someone.

"I'm no Mother Goose, but I do the best I can. I agreed to C of C, and I also agreed to move home and take care of BeeBee. Just like that, I was retired. Things went well the first semester. Sophie lived in the dorm, but she visited us. She joined a sorority. Dealing with Mama was hard, but I managed. Reconnected with old friends and got involved in a bit of local charity work—"

"*A bit?*" interjected Pamella. "Ha! She's been doling out her time and cash all over town. Lowcountry Food Bank. Historic Charleston Foundation. Cooper Hall Alumna Foundation. The Gibbes." She poked Tipsy again at the mention of the Gibbes Museum, Charleston's grandest art repository. "She's an *art lover*, too."

"If you have my kind of money, you can either work yourself to death accumulating more, or spend your time giving it away," said Jillian. "I kept busy, but I also watched over Sophie from afar. Then in January, Mama died suddenly of a heart attack. Now I'm dealing with her estate. Trying to figure out what to do with the house. Sophie begged me to keep it, but I haven't decided. I *love* that place. It's like a fairytale castle, but it's a huge old house, with huge old problems. Much more than I need, especially when Sophie is supposed to be in college."

"But she's *not* in college at the moment?" asked Tipsy.

"Correct. She took my mother's death hard, but I thought she'd be okay. Then about three months ago, she started spending more time at Mama's house, and less time at school. She constantly complained about headaches, stomachaches, and exhaustion, but she wouldn't talk about anything. She seemed depressed and agitated. I caught her talking to herself like she did as a child. I was *terrified*."

"Can I tell her about Catherine?" asked Pammy.

Jillian gripped her nose for dear life, but she shrugged, and Pamella went on. "Jillian's mentally ill sister was institutionalized on and off for years. She passed away young. Y'all were teenagers, right?"

"She was sixteen. I was seventeen. Schizophrenia can run in families. I'm *so worried* for Sophie."

Perhaps schizophrenia isn't the problem in this gene pool, said Granna.

"She planned a spring break trip with her sorority, but she cancelled. Hibernated in her bedroom at my mother's house. Her sisters visited, but she wouldn't talk to them, either. After spring break, she dropped out of school and moved into Mama's house."

"That's when she *really* got bad, right?" asked Pamella.

"Yes. So moody and weepy, but she denied anything was wrong. I caught her throwing up in the bathroom, and she lost a lot of weight. I thought she had an eating disorder, or she'd gotten herself into an abusive relationship. Maybe met some nutjob online."

"It happens," said Pamella. "I met a man on Bumble who claimed to be a fifty-five-year-old lawyer but turned out to be an eighty-year-old creep living in his son's garage—"

"So what happened next?" asked Tipsy, before Pamella steered the conversation off a cliff.

"Two days ago, she had an appointment with her psychiatrist. She hemmed and hawed about getting dressed. I kept harping at her and she got hysterical. Before I knew it, we were running late and she was madder than a box of frogs. I went downstairs to put stuff in the car, but when I came back up, I heard her talking to herself in her room. I walked in, and she's standing there like a zombie." Jillian's mouth hung open and her eyes bugged out.

"How did you handle it?" asked Tipsy, although she could guess. She'd had her share of explosions as she tried to get her kids out the door.

"I said, *Sophie Yates! We have to go!* She jerked out of it like I just—" Jillian smacked her own cheek. "—and started yelling about how I don't understand her. Then she spilled it. Said she's been seeing ghosts her whole life, and my mother's house is haunted. She said she's been… interacting…with a *dead person.*"

"What did you say?"

"I lost my temper. I admit it. *You get your butt in the car, go to your appointment, and listen to your doctors!* Then she really shot off the deep end. I didn't know what else to do, so I called 911. The EMS people brought her here."

"So Sophie is…a clairvoyant? She can see ghosts?"

"If it's *truly* possible, then I suppose she can. Can you see them?"

Tipsy hesitated, since old habits about the dead die even harder. "I…basically—"

"She can," said Pamella. "She freed my Meemaw Ivy from haunting my cottage. She even befriended her. Tipsy has *lots* of ghostly friends. She knows some of Charleston's most distinguished dead citizens!"

"That's a stretch. I don't know Denmark Vessey, or any founding fathers." Tipsy touched Jillian's knee. "Did she say anything about the ghost?"

"Only that she's there. Or *he's* there. Hell! I don't know. But if she's telling the truth, that would drive anyone insane. Living with ghosts *cannot* be good for your mental health."

"It depends on the person, and the ghosts, but it can take a toll on your *physical* health. If she's never lived with ghosts, that explains the headaches and the fatigue and the throwing up."

"What a relief. At least she's not bulimic."

"Did your sister—what was her name?"

"Catherine. Catherine Rose."

"Like you said, things can run in families. This kind of *thing*, too. Did Catherine ever talk about ghosts?"

"It was so long ago, but…" Jillian squinted, as if peering into her own memory, and then shook her head. "She didn't say much that made sense. Especially the last few years."

"I take it you'd like me to get rid of the ghost?"

"Can you?"

"Let me explain the basics—"

"If you tell me too much about how it works, I may go crazy myself. Just get it done."

"Okay, but…it's complicated. I spent months working on my last mysteries. It's also not guaranteed. But I can help Sophie learn how to manage it, at the very least."

"I'd much prefer a complete exorcism, so we better get started. The doctors are already talking about releasing her. How can I return her to a house that's infested with dead lunatics?"

"Y'all can stay with me on Sullivan's," said Pamela.

"You're sweet, Pammy, but I have workers in and out constantly. It's a nightmare. Pamella told me how much she paid you—"

"Oh, that. Right." Hedge fund or not, Tipsy didn't want to scare her off. Not many people would hand over fifty-k on something they didn't believe in yesterday. "She was really generous—"

"I'll double it. One hundred thousand."

Tipsy about fell out when Pamella offered her fifty-k last summer. This time, she was as floored as her Daddy passed out on Granna's linoleum after a bender.

Close your barn door before you catch a few horseflies, said Granna, and Tipsy shut her gaping mouth. *People pay divorce lawyers and real estate agents that kind of money. You're offering an even more specialized service!*

"Will that work for you?" asked Jillian, with a hint of impatience.

"Yes. That's great."

"This is my daughter we're talking about. It's chump change."

Hahahaha! Chump change? Good lord!

Keep cool, said Granna. *Act like bush fund gazillionaires offer you six-figure gigs every day.*

Granna's linguistic flubs were as bad as Henry's, as if she'd passed away a hundred years ago, not roughly twenty. *Hedge, Granna. Not bush. Hedge fund—*

"*Nothing* is more important to me than Sophie's well-being. I can't believe I'm saying this, but it's a deal." Jillian got to her tiny feet. "Want to meet Soph? I assume you don't have anything else planned this evening."

Tipsy's plan to work on her commission grudgingly gave up its prime spot on her schedule. Her herons would remain in the bush—or the hedge, *hardy-har-har*—and not in her hand. "Sure. And no. This will be top priority."

"I have to go. Doug is golfing and the Spice Girls have been alone too long." Pamella kissed Tipsy's cheek when they stood. "Told you she was rich," she whispered.

"See you, Pammy. Thanks for connecting us."

"You better get going." Pamella pointed at Jillian's back. "Your new boss is waiting."

Tipsy followed Jillian as she speed-marched toward the hospital's entrance with her Louis-Chanel banging against her hip.

Your new boss is a drill sergeant, said Granna.

What have I gotten myself into?

When Granna didn't have an answer, she usually stayed quiet. As Tipsy followed Jillian into the psych hospital for the commencement of her third supernatural mystery in two years, Granna's silence spoke volumes.

Tipsy peered over Jillian's head into a sterile hospital room. She made out the shape of a young woman, asleep in the bed. Jillian crept into the room and beckoned Tipsy after her. She leaned over her daughter and brushed her hair off her forehead. Sophie stirred and turned away from her mother's hand.

"There's another chair," said Jillian.

The extra chair let out a sputtering honk as Tipsy dragged it across the tile floor. "Yikes. Sorry," she said, as Sophie rolled toward them.

The smudgy black remains of her last eyeliner application melded with the dark purplish circles under Sophie's hazel eyes. She'd twisted her thick, dark blonde hair into a saggy bun. She had delicate features, and a splattering of freckles across her nose. Probably quite pretty in healthier times, but her hollow cheeks were like deflated balloons and her collarbones protruded.

"*Sophie Rose.*" Jillian spoke louder than necessary, as if her daughter had pulled a Van Gogh and cut off her ears.

"Your sister was Catherine Rose, right?" whispered Tipsy.

Jillian nodded. "A bunch of roses in my family. My mother was Betsy Rose. I'm Jillian Rose. My sister, Catherine Rose. I kept up the tradition with my girls." She cleared her throat. "Soph. Sweets. This is Miss Collins. She's here to…uh…"

Tipsy stepped in. "Hey, Sophie. I'm Tipsy. How are you feeling?"

Sophie rolled over again and presented them with her back.

"Sophie Rose *Yates.* Stop it. I want you to talk to Tipsy."

"I've already talked to the shrinks," said Sophie.

"I'm not a shrink."

"Therapist?"

"Nope."

"Some sort of nurse?"

"Negative. That's your third strike. You got a bonus guess?"

Sophie didn't reply. Jillian pinched her own nose again. "Please. Please just—"

"Maybe I should talk to her alone?"

"Fine. Why not?" Jillian held up her phone. "Text me when you're finished."

Tipsy gave Jillian her number and Jillian started typing. Tipsy's phone dinged as she walked out the door. She read the message. JILLIAN YATES. SOPHIE'S MOTHER. $100K.

As if you'll forget, said Granna.

What now, Granna? You got through to me in my disgruntled teenage years.

Sometimes. Other times, I struck out. I suggest talking to Sophie like she's a younger version of yourself.

Hmmm. What had Tipsy wanted most as a teenager? Compassion. Lack of judgment. To be taken seriously.

"I promise," said Tipsy. "I'm no mental health professional. I'm an artist."

"So now I'm doing art therapy."

"I wouldn't know where to start with therapy, art or no art. I heard your mom is an art lover. Do *you* like art?"

"I guess. But I can't draw."

"Lots of art forms don't have anything to do with drawing. I'm sorry you feel so bad. Sounds like you've been through a lot the past couple days."

"What do you want?" asked Sophie, over her shoulder.

"Your mom thought you'd like to talk with me because we have something in common."

"I *just said* I can barely draw a stick figure."

"Not that. She told me about the ghosts."

"She doesn't *believe me* about the ghosts."

"She does now. She knows I see them, too."

Sophie half turned, and presented Tipsy with her pretty profile. "You're kidding," she said. "Or lying."

"Neither."

"Prove it."

"I don't know how to prove it since there's no ghosts around—"

Sophie rolled over again.

"Okay. Hold on." Tipsy searched for a convincing example. "When I was little, I saw a boy in my church. He wore short pants with suspenders and this, like, newsboy cap. He looked about seven years old. When I first noticed him, he seemed older than me. Then I kept getting older, but he stayed the same age."

"Huh. Go on."

"Sometimes I talked to him, and my grandmother—my Granna—made me stop because folks would think my marbles ran out my ears and rolled into the storm drains. I still waved to him sometimes, because he seemed so lonely. Granna got ticked off when I acknowledged him."

Sophie finally faced Tipsy. She tucked her hand under her cheek. "Your grandmother believed you?"

"Yes. She saw spirits, too."

"If she wanted you to avoid them, you must stay away from graveyards. So many ghosts wandering around those places."

Tipsy smiled, sensing a test. "Nah. Superstitious BS because the living fear everything associated with death. I *do* know one ghost in a graveyard, but he happened to die there. Ghosts haunt the place where they died."

Sophie's left eye twitched. "I'm listening."

"I'd like to listen to *you*. Can you tell me about the ghost in your house?"

"Will you tell my mother?"

"She hopes I can help you sort out this supernatural stuff, but… from one clairvoyant to another, I'm honestly interested. My house is haunted, too, so I know how stressful it is. When I first moved in, living with ghosts literally made me sick. Interacting with them exhausted me. I got terrible headaches and sometimes I threw up."

"Seriously? That happened to me, too."

"If you're gonna be a clairvoyant in Charleston, you'll probably end up living with a ghost eventually. It's an old city by American standards. Our houses hold a lot of history, and some of it isn't pleasant. But it *can* be managed. The ghost in my house has become a good friend."

"What's the deal with your ghost?"

"That's a long story, and I'm here to talk about *your* ghost. Do you talk to her? Or him?"

She shifted uncomfortably. "Yeah. I talk to him."

"So it's a guy?"

"Yeah."

"Only him? I mean, are they any other ghosts in your house? Some houses have multiple hauntings."

She shook her head.

"Do you know anything about him?"

"I guess."

This is like pulling teeth from a grumpy sloth, Granna. "Okay....so this dead guy—"

"I tried to ignore him at first...but now we're friends." She scowled, on the defensive for no discernible reason. "It's not *that* weird. You're friends with *your* ghost."

"I didn't say it's weird. I'm all for ignoring the random ghosts we see around town. But like I said, if you live with one, you have to deal with it. Tell me about him. What's his name?"

She squirmed again. "Thomas."

"When did he die?"

"A long ass time ago."

"If y'all are friends, I figured he'd told you—"

"I don't want to talk about this. It's, like, sad. Thinking about my dead friend who is stuck in my house forever. I have a headache. I already feel like shit in general."

"Physically, or emotionally?"

"Both. *Hello.* I'm in the psych ward."

"Right. What do you and Thomas talk about?"

"*Stuff.* Ghostly stuff, mostly. It's nice to talk to someone who, like, gets it."

"Now you can talk to me, too. Since talking to Thomas makes you upset—"

"It's not his fault. I'm…in a bad place."

"Your mom told me you've been struggling. She seemed to think the ghost is the problem."

She rolled her eyes. "Of course it doesn't have anything to do with *her*. Or the rest of my life."

"What's going on with the rest of your life?"

"Just…stress. School. My family."

"I heard your father passed away when you were a child, and then your grandmother this winter."

"Yeah. It was sad when BeeBee died. But Dad passed a long time ago. Mom thinks I should be, like, *over* it."

"I bet she misses him, too. Seems like she cares a lot about her family. Especially you. She's super worried. She said you haven't wanted to talk to her lately."

"I'm sick of her treating me like a fragile glass doll." She snorted. "I did crack the other day."

"She hopes I can help you. Someone who understands."

"How much is she paying you?"

Tipsy paused, taken aback.

"Don't tell me," said Sophie, with a dismissive wave. "My mother solves all her problems with money. At least you don't think I'm crazy, like everyone else does."

"I don't know you well enough to know whether you're crazy or not."

Sophie stared at the ceiling. Her eyes shone with unshed tears. "I'm tired."

"We don't have to talk anymore."

"If you can see ghosts, can you do me a favor? Can you go to BeeBee's house and find Thomas? Tell him I'll be back soon."

"Sure. I'll try."

"I don't want him to think I just, like, left without saying goodbye."

"I'll go by the house, and you can text or call me anytime. I'm happy to talk about this stuff."

"Maybe." Sophie gave Tipsy her number and Tipsy sent a text. TIPSY COLLINS. FELLOW CLAIRVOYANT. She added a ghost emoji to lighten things up.

Given Sophie's concern for this Thomas guy, Tipsy texted Jillian, too. I THINK I MADE SOME PROGRESS. DON'T TELL SOPHIE I'M TRYING TO MAKE THOMAS MOVE ON, AT LEAST FOR NOW. SHE SEEMS PRETTY FRAGILE, AND IT MIGHT UPSET HER.

"Great. We'll talk soon." Better to let the girl decide she wanted to talk than force the issue. "I'll let you rest. Get in touch anytime."

"'Kay. Bye…Tipsy."

As she walked to the door, Tipsy vowed to remember today's conversation when her own daughters' adolescent moodiness reared its histrionic head. Surely Mary Pratt would be first. She'd walked and talked before O-Liv. She'd be first to decide no one understood her.

Sophie Yates wasn't friendly, but she was having a hard time. Still, Tipsy made some progress down the long road to the Fortress of Teenage Angst. A moat remained to be crossed, but at least the tower was in sight.

———◆✕◆———

"Ma'am?" A blonde nurse waited outside Sophie's door. "Are you Ms. Collins?"

"That's me." Tipsy followed the nurse down the hall.

"Mrs. Yates left, but she wants you to speak with her daughter's physician. She gave Doctor Brandt permission to answer any questions you have."

Tipsy's stomach did a floppy twist, like a lanky child trying to learn to summersault. "Did you say Doctor Brandt?"

"Tipsy?"

She turned at the sound of her name. The summersault turned into an uncoordinated cartwheel. Scott Brandt stood in an alcove beside a Coke machine.

OMG. My hot ex-in-law.

Here we go again. Ayers's new wife's ex-husband is no relation to you. Keep it that way.

Tipsy ignored Granna. She smiled at the tall, handsome man with deep blue eyes, dark hair, and a short beard. "Hey, Scott. How random, meeting you here."

He smiled back. "It *is* the psychiatric hospital, and I am a psychiatrist."

"Guess it is, and you are."

"Great to see you."

"Good to see you, too."

"Y'all *know* each other?" The nurse said, with a swiping glance from Tipsy's feet to her forehead.

"We do." Scott chuckled. "It's kind of complicated."

The nurse muttered a goodbye, then power walked down the hall. Probably racing to the nurses' breakroom to spread this interesting development in good-looking, single Scott Brandt's life.

"I haven't seen you in months," said Scott.

"Not since Jump Zone," said Tipsy, in reference to his son Tristan's birthday party. "My kids were wiped out and went to bed early that night, so thanks."

"Once again proving the benefits of a good trampoline bounce," he said, in reference to their first conversation. "What was the word?"

"Cathartic, right?"

"Soporific as well, apparently."

Damnnnnnn. That good vocabulary again. Good lord, Granna!

Hmph. A brainy man is attractive.

"How's your painting?" she asked. Not long after she met him on Ayers's driveway, Scott had stopped by the GQB on a day she wasn't working. He bought a Tipsy Collins original—a landscape of the marsh behind Pamella's Sullivan's Island house at sunset—and texted her a photo of the painting in his dining room. Despite Granna's misgivings, she kind of hoped his support of her work would give them an excuse to chat. She thanked him, but he went silent after one text exchange.

She'd seen him a couple times at kids' functions. He always waved and smiled, but that was about it.

"It's great, thanks," he replied.

"That question sounded silly. Like the painting has its own feelings."

"Paintings might not have their own feelings, but that particular painting gives *me* feelings."

"What kind of feelings?"

"Peaceful ones. Not always easy to come by in this post-divorce life."

"Don't I know it. The painting *process* makes *me* feel peaceful, so I'm glad I can share some of my tranquility."

"Thanks for easing my burden."

His eyes were very blue. Tipsy's stomach did a haphazard gymnastics floor routine in her midsection. She led the conversation in a more clinical direction. "You're treating Sophie?"

"Yes. She's not ready to go home yet, but I believe we can manage her depression and anxiety. Mrs. Yates asked me to speak with you about her. Mind if I ask why? Don't see a lot of artists hanging around here."

Tipsy remembered Henry's observation about mentally disturbed creatives. "I figured this place would be full of eccentric artists."

"Unfortunately, we have more homeless schizophrenics than artistic genius schizophrenics."

"Do you think Sophie has schizophrenia?"

"There's a family history, but she's an interesting case. Her thoughts are organized and she's not presenting with paranoia. Nothing more about the delusions she confessed to her mother during the incident. I see more signs of major depression than psychosis. She's nineteen and she's lucid. We can't force the issue. I'm in a holding pattern. Her mother wants her to stay in the hospital as long as possible."

"Not surprising. She's in maternal protective overdrive."

"I know, but this isn't a long-term facility. Difficult conversations with Mama Bear are in my future. She strikes me as someone who isn't used to hearing no."

"I think you're right. You must be good at analyzing people."

"I analyze everyone. Comes with the territory." He leaned on the Coke machine. "But back to my question about you…"

She seized on Sophie's suggestion. "I'm going to do art therapy with her."

"Didn't know that was your thing."

"My…uh…career is taking me in different directions."

"You have any other questions?"

"Not now. This situation is intense, and I just got involved. I need to think about it, if I'm being honest."

"If we're both trying to help her, that's the best way to be. You… still have my number?"

"Yes. You still have mine?"

"Yeah. Feel free to text me if you have any more questions about her." He shoved his hands in his pockets. "This might be *too* honest, but since I have the opportunity…I thought about texting you after Tristan's birthday party, but my life was a little complic—"

"Dr. Brandt?" The blonde nurse was back. "The ER is calling you about an admission."

He removed his phone from his pocket. "Sorry. I forgot to turn on vibrate."

"Sure," said the nurse, but from her pursed lips, she thought he was ignoring the vibrations in his pocket.

Something else is vibrating in those pants, said Granna.

A snorting laugh escaped Tipsy as the disgruntled nurse left again. Scott's fledgling smile widened. "I gotta return the ER's call, but first, tell me what's funny."

"Who knows? Maybe I'm hearing voices."

"Text me about that, too." He raised his phone as another call came through.

"Go on. Take it." Tipsy backed away and then turned around. She made it halfway down the hall before curiosity made her peek over her shoulder.

On the day she met Scott Brandt, he'd looked up from his phone as she drove away from him. He'd waved, and she'd given him a clumsy waving reply as she yanked on her steering wheel. This time, he didn't *need* to look up before he waved. He still hadn't answered the phone. It hung by his side, flashing its annoyance at his neglect.

Scott was watching her. *Staring* at her, with that bemused smile. Their eyes locked, and although it was even sillier than asking after the emotions of a landscape painting, she felt as if his blue gaze had gravity. Like he was pulling her back down the hallway.

This time, she waved first. He waved back, and then took his call.

Chapter 2

Olivia Grace and Mary Pratt needed posterboards and markers for an end-of-the year school project, and naturally, Big Ayers had neither. Tipsy swung into Office Depot on the way home, picked up the requisite artsy stuff, and drove to Ayers's new house off Long Point Road. She slowed as she passed his former residence—the pretty coastal cottage that was also *her* old house. The new owners had planted palmetto trees on either side of the front door. A jogging stroller sat on the front porch. Tipsy had kept her own jogger in the same spot.

She parked in front of Ayers's new place, a nouveau farmhouse encircled by a one-story wraparound porch with trendy wire railings. It had white board-and-batten siding, no shutters, and a drive-under garage. A black privacy fence encircled the back yard. According to the kids, Ayers was putting in a pool.

No. Not just Ayers. *They* were putting in a pool. Ayers and Kate, his new wife. Scott's *ex-wife*.

Tipsy texted Little Ayers, since the girls didn't have phones yet. HEY BUDDY! PLEASE ASK THE GIRLS TO COME GET THIS STUFF. CAN YOU HELP THEM SO I CAN SAY HI? ☺

LITTLE AYERS: SURE MOM WERE COMING IN A MINUTE IM ABOUT TO BEAT THIS LEVEL ON MARIO CART

Little Ayers cared little for proper punctuation in his text messages, but since he was only ten, she didn't begrudge him. His generation paid no attention to dotting their *i*'s, crossing their *t*'s, or correct use of semicolons. At least he didn't replace the respective proper words with *U* and *R* and *4* the way his father did. That's where Tipsy drew the line, grammatically speaking.

When the front door opened, her identical twin daughters, Mary Pratt and Olivia Grace, ran down the front steps on long, coltish legs. Their curly brown ponytails bounced in time with their gangly limbs. True to form, a unicorn capered under a rainbow on O-Liv's yellow tee-shirt. Mary Pratt, on the other hand, wore a black tank top emblazoned with red rhinestones that spelled out *HOLLA!*

Tipsy got out of her Tahoe and opened the hatch. "Hey, y'all! The art fairy has arrived!"

"Hey, Mom!" said M.P.

"Mama-Mia!" Only Olivia Grace still consistently called Tipsy *mama*, but she'd added some flair to the endearment. *Mama-Mia. Mama-jama. Mamacita.* Once she referred to Tipsy as *Hot Mama*, but Tipsy nipped that one in the bud.

"How was school?" asked Tipsy, as she gave out hugs.

"S'okay," said M.P. "Now you'll ask if we learned anything."

"Did you?"

"Not much," said O-Liv. "Bo-*ring*, like usual!"

Tipsy offered them a posterboard. "Your South Carolina group projects should be fun. Did y'all decide on a topic?"

"Ms. Ryder said we can be our own group. Just us, together. Our project will be about sweetgrass baskets," said M.P.

"That's a great topic. I'll ask Mrs. Green—Miss Shelby buys baskets and roses from her—to talk to y'all."

"Hey, Mom," said Little Ayers, as he clumped down the stairs. He was barefoot and wore a VANS skateboarding tee-shirt. He flipped his shaggy blond hair out of his eyes. He, too, was growing like a dandelion in rich soil. Tall and skinny, with a fluffy mop on top. "Is my skateboard helmet in the truck?"

She found Ayers's sticker covered helmet in the backseat. He'd taken up skateboarding with a vengeance; part of his hero worship of Scott and Kate's son Tristan, an avid skateboarder. He practiced in the driveway at her house for hours. The racket from his kick-flips and one-eighties and ollies sounded like someone chopping down trees with a blunt ax. "You going to the skate park with Tristan this weekend?"

"Yup," he said, as he took the helmet. Mary Pratt held the posterboards, and O-Liv had a bag of fresh markers and letter decals.

They chatted for a few minutes, and then Tipsy let them off the hook. "Y'all get to it. You must have homework." She ruffled Little A's hair. "And Mario Cart levels to beat."

She kissed them again, and they ran up the stairs. Best to get going. Watching them walk into a house that wasn't hers never got easier. A gruff voice spoke over her shoulder as she opened the Tahoe's door. "You got a minute?"

She turned with her hand still on the door handle. Big Ayers walked across the driveway toward her. He wasn't wearing his usual baseball cap, so she took in the latest recession of his hairline. He'd lost a lot of weight over the past year, and was in surprisingly good shape. The beer-bellied days following the collapse of their marriage were behind him. Sharp angles had reemerged on his face, and his big brown spaniel's eyes were clear and bright and framed in thick curling lashes. Notwithstanding his slowly retreating hair, she grudgingly recalled his youthful handsomeness.

"Sure," she said, despite the eternal trepidation his presence wrought in her. "What's up?"

"How's it going?"

"Good, thanks."

"You selling a lot of paintings?"

"Yup. Business is rolling."

"Maybe I'll stop by the GQB and see if y'all have anything for our living room wall. Give me a chance to say hi to Shelby."

"Sure." Ayers hadn't mentioned Shelby or the GQB in years.

"You should think about painting fulltime. You were damn productive back in the day. Bet you'll make more money if you're busting out your own paintings instead of selling other people's stuff."

"Hopefully I'll get there soon." Ironic for Ayers to give her career advice, since he'd never listened to her suggestions about his own professional life. Besides, they both knew he screwed her out of alimony during their divorce litigation. He paid less in monthly child support than the state guidelines required, as the amount was set during his financial low point, when Tipsy had been wracked by guilt over the divorce. Let's not forget the substantial savings he'd lost in a sketchy land deal. She hadn't even gotten the settlement money he owed her. If she had financial issues, Ayers had exacerbated them.

She set such frustrating and pointless thoughts aside. The sooner he said what he needed to say, the sooner she'd get out of there. "Do you want to talk about the kids?"

"Yeah. *Sort of.* Not really."

Tipsy's right eyebrow crept up her forehead. To her surprise, Ayers smiled. "I know that look. I'm babbling. I...wanted to ask you something."

"Okay. Shoot."

"Did I...always think I was right?"

Now both eyebrows were up. "When we were married?"

He nodded.

"Ah, Ayers. I don't want to fight—"

"I'm not trying to fight. I'm serious. This *is* about the kids, because I don't want them to hear arguing in the house. You and me didn't fight much."

"Are you saying you and Kate are arguing?"

Words exploded out of his mouth like an auctioneer on a tight deadline. "Yeah. A *lot.* I don't know *what* to do about it. Nothing I do is right. If I try to talk to her about anything, she gets mad. I start out being frustrated with *her* about something, but she ends up pissed at *me*, and I'm apologizing. She's even mad at me when I keep quiet. I don't know what I did wrong most of the time. She gives me the silent treatment for hours. Sometimes days. She says I think I'm right about everything, but she makes me feel like *anything* I say about *anything* is wrong."

Maybe his weight loss didn't come from watching his carbs. Nothing like stress to kill the appetite.

Ayers is confiding in me about his problems with his new wife. What the actual f-bomb, Granna?

He don't have anyone else. He's not going to confide in his hunting buddies in the deer stand.

What about Mimi? His own sister would be more appropriate. Good lord.

Before Granna could reply, Ayers said, "It's probably weird for me to talk about this—"

But it is about the kids, Tipsy. If they're having issues, better for you to understand what's going on.

"—but you know me better than anyone else."

Tipsy collected her nerve. "Can I be blunt? You won't get pissed?"

"Blunt, yeah. Pissed, no."

"Yes. You *do* think you're right all the time."

"Oh…*kay.*"

"Look, I *hate* fighting, Ayers. I avoid conflict if at all possible. For most of our marriage, I was too compliant. I didn't rock the boat, because I wanted a peaceful ride for the kids."

His jaw worked, but he didn't scream in her face. "Hmmm."

"Maybe Kate isn't afraid of conflict. Maybe she's *also* the kind of person who always thinks *she's* right."

She envisioned tires bouncing over potholes in Ayers's head. "Shit," he muttered.

"But you were never one for the silent treatment. I always knew *why* you were mad—" Since he said he wanted bluntness, Tipsy chomped on that bullet, despite her fear of his reaction. "—even if I didn't understand your anger, or thought you were out of line. You rage, then you get over it. Sometimes within a few minutes. If she's more inclined to fester, y'all better address it."

He looked up the stairs behind him. Tipsy saw trepidation in *his* eyes. Ayers Lee Collins, IV, nervous about what awaited him in his own house.

If that ain't karma, said Granna.

"Y'all thought about counseling?" asked Tipsy.

"Huh? Oh. We're not at that point yet." He swiped a hand across his mouth. "I better go inside. If she sees us talking for longer than the time it takes to get a homework update, there'll be hell to pay. She'd be jealous of me talking to my own mother."

"Yikes. Sorry."

"Thanks for talking with me about it."

"No problem. You're right to worry about fighting in front of the kids. Please try to—"

"I got this, Tipsy. Don't get all *worked up*." Ayers could only maintain his cool for so long. "I got enough to deal with in there. I just…*damnit*. Calm down—"

"I *am* calm—"

"I'll talk to you later." He turned and stomped toward the house. "You have…a nice night!"

That's his way of apologizing for biting my head off. Why are men constantly telling women to calm down?

Because they don't have control over their own selves. They're—what is it called? Projectors.

I think you mean projecting, but Ayers does like to shine blinding light on his own opinions. What a strange day, Granna. New ghost project. Hundred-k. Run into Scott Brandt. Ayers seeking my opinion about his glowing personality. Wonder what will happen next?

This time, Granna answered, but with another question. *Why don't you go home to your haunted house and find out?*

Tipsy got in an hour of painting on the front porch before darkness set in. Henry rarely bugged her when she was working, but he appeared like a detached shadow as she washed her brushes under the garden spigot.

"I've been dying to ask—"

"Too late for that," said Tipsy.

"Very funny. Did Pamella truly have a ghost-removal commission for you?"

Tipsy lay the wet brushes on a towel and picked up her unfinished painting. Two great blue herons with entwined necks stood out against solid black. So many people wanted these stark backgrounds these days. Tipsy *liked* the contrast, but with the pressure on to produce more work, she also appreciated the simplicity. Great blue herons weren't really blue. These birds would eventually be many graduated shades of purplish gray, and her intensely detailed rendering hadn't made it past their black and white heads, orangish beaks, and beady yellow eyes. Minimalist backgrounds saved time.

"Can you get the door?"

Henry waved one hand and the front door opened. Tipsy walked through the doorway, only to be confronted by Henry standing in the foyer. "Well?" he asked.

"Give me a minute to get cleaned up. I'll meet you on the sofa."

Tipsy set the canvas on the dining room table, put away the rest of her supplies, and clipped up the stairs to her bedroom. If Henry's pacing and toe-tapping made a sound, she would have heard it on the second floor. She washed her face, applied nighttime moisturizers, and changed into a pair of taco-print pajama pants. She yanked a maroon College of Charleston tee-shirt over her head. Shelby bought it for her as a joke. C of C's mascot is a cougar—the stark white letters across the shirt read *COUGAR MOM*.

By the time she joined Henry in the family room, he looked about to burst with curiosity. Before he exploded like Slimer from *Ghostbusters*, she told him everything she knew about her latest supernatural project—Sophie Rose, her mental breakdown, Jillian's hundred-k. Even the sudden appearance of Scott Brandt. "So...I texted Jillian. Asked her to dig up anything relevant in their house's history. The house is on Legare Street."

"Ah. If South Battery sings Charleston's song like an operatic tenor, Legare Street hums it like a beloved lullaby. Of all the beautiful streets in Charleston, that thoroughfare surely has the most stories. Hidden behind the highest walls and the oldest names."

"I'm excited to check it out," she said. "Like all old Charleston ladies, the late Mrs. Porcher's own house fascinated her. She researched the place at the South Carolina Historical Society before she lost her mind. Jillian promised to look through her mother's notebooks for anyone named *Thomas*. I'll visit tomorrow. Try to find him and see how crazy he is."

"Remember how John talked to the palmetto bugs, and Ivy tried to impale you with an umbrella?"

She nodded. She'd never forget John's hysterical palavering with the local vermin, nor Ivy's enraged, skyward propulsion of a heavy patio umbrella. "Neither of them cooperated at first. *You* weren't exactly agreeable yourself when you realized I wanted to free you from this haunting. When I started doing this...*work*...I figured every ghost would go leaping headfirst into the next life if given the chance. No such luck."

"Some of us have reasons to delay. Fear. Anger. Love. It's a good idea to keep your motives to yourself until you've assessed the situation."

"Agreed. I told Jillian to keep Sophie Rose in the dark, too. She likes this Thomas guy, even if living with him is making her sick and contributed to her mental breakdown." She sighed. "I hope Thomas isn't totally insane. I have a *psychiatrist* involved in this mystery, but I can't ask Dr. Brandt to evaluate a ghost."

"Isn't Dr. Brandt the man you and Shelby describe as hotter than an—"

"—August day in hell." Tipsy's phone rang and she held it up. "Speaking of the new mommy."

"We have a mystery to address, and you prefer chitchat."

"I've told you everything. Shelby might need me."

"She *needs* you to gossip with her," said Henry, but he settled into the sofa's corner like a semi-transparent, irritable accent pillow.

Tipsy answered the FaceTime call. Three weeks after giving birth, Shelby was still deflating, a balloon with a slow leak. Tipsy took in her beloved, slightly puffy face, messily braided blonde hair, uncharacteristic lack of makeup, and too-tight BROCo tee-shirt. Shelby prided herself on her perky bustiness, but her swollen boobs were the size of late summer watermelons.

"Hey! Where's Baby Lottie?" asked Tipsy.

"Asleep on Bryan's chest." Shelby pointed at her gigantic tatas. "*My* chest needed a break."

"Hey, Tips!" Lindsey, Tipsy's other bestie, appeared in the frame.

Tipsy leaned toward the phone. "Linds! How did you escape?"

Lindsey's own new baby was only about eight weeks old. "Shelby had a hankering for something sweet. I had a hankering to get the hell out of my house for an hour. I hit Harris Teeter for strawberry ice cream. Left Baby Paul with his daddy and his big sister."

Shelby held up a bowl of pinkish ice cream and shoveled a heaping spoonful into her mouth. "Heavenly," she muttered around her spoon.

"How's P.D. coming along with Daddy duty?" Tipsy asked Lindsey.

Lindsey rolled her eyes. "Emma loves being a big sister. She's more help than P.D., and she's only twelve. That's what happens when a man has his first child as he's approaching forty."

"Ugh. Don't say that," said Shelby. "Brian is thirty-nine."

"What-*ever*," said Lindsey. "Brian is the baby whisperer. You're *so* lucky."

"I *am* so lucky." Shelby's lip trembled.

Tipsy remembered those new baby days, when every part of her body ached and her racing hormones turned her into a fountain. As if sensing tears, Lindsey rerouted the subject. "What's up with you, Tips?"

"Not much. If I knew y'all were partying, I would have joined in."

"It's so hard for us to get together these days," said Linds. "I can't even remember our last happy hour."

"*I remember*," said Shelby, as if reminiscing about fond childhood memories. "Two-dollar domestics. Half-priced appetizers. Sunset over Shem Creek."

"Y'all want some man gossip?" asked Tipsy, before Shelby burst into tears over cheap nachos.

"Bring it!" said Lindsey. "Although I don't want to *touch* a man ever again. Thanks, but no thanks." She held up her fingers in a cross, as if warding off the devil and his penis-wielding henchmen.

"What does *that* mean?" asked Shelby.

Lindsey vaguely gestured to her nether regions. "I got another week before the doc gives me the go ahead to…ahem… *go ahead.* Tipsy knows how unpleasant the first attempt can be. Like giving birth all over—"

Shelby's eyes were bugging out of her head, so Tipsy cut in. "I saw Dr. Scott Brandt today."

Her comment drew Shelby and Lindsey's attention away from Lindsey's out-of-commission lady parts. Shelby spoke around a mouthful of Ben & Jerry's. "Where?"

"Uh…" Tipsy didn't want to acknowledge hanging around the psych ward. The girls might think *she'd* had the mental breakdown. "I ran into him downtown. We caught up for a few minutes and it was…ah…" She also didn't want to come off like a delusional romantic ninny.

"Is he still dating that woman?" asked Lindsey.

"What woman?"

"I didn't tell you? Well…I hear so much gossip, I forget half of it."

"Friend fail!" said Shelby. "You *forgot to mention* gossip about Tipsy's hot ex-in-law? The one she has a major crush on—"

"*Paaaah.*" Tipsy snorted like a disingenuous horse. "I don't have a *crush* on him. But since we're on the topic…what did you hear?"

"I can't remember who told me—" Lindsey grimaced. "Oh. Yes, I do."

"Let me guess," said Tipsy. "Julia talked your ear off while you were getting a facial."

Lindsey nodded at the reference to Tipsy's ex-boyfriend's *current* girlfriend. Will Garrison started dating Julia, a twenty-seven-year-old aesthetician, mere weeks after dumping Tipsy on her ass.

"We avoid talking about *Wulia* in our circle of trust," said Shelby, "but that chick has fingers on the pounding pulse of the Mount Pleasant rumor mill. Now you *have* to tell us."

"Hmmm…How did we make the connection? Oh, yes. She told a story about a hairdresser who got fired from the salon. She drank too much wine at a promotional brunch, then got in a screaming match when a customer complained about her brassy highlights. Turns out the Hellraising Highlighter was dating Scott Brandt."

"No way," said Shelby. "Dr. Brandt, dating someone who gets into public catfights?"

"I got into a public catfight last summer," said Tipsy, in reference to an infamous night at The Windjammer on the Isle of Palms.

"That was self-defense. Your claws came out because Kim Nowak came at you first."

"I *am* surprised Scott would be wrapped up in that kind of thing." Tipsy imagined Scott Brandt as too dignified for such Charleston dating scene drama. Although, she'd thought herself above it, too. The night of the Windjammer Incident, she got more drama than the Academy Awards.

"I'm sure it was him," said Lindsey. "The Hellraising Highlighter called him that night. He picked her up from the salon and Julia saw him practically throw her over his shoulder and drag her out of there. Do you think he's still with her?"

"I have no idea. We didn't talk about our personal lives."

As if on cue, Tipsy's phone dinged and a name appeared over Lindsey's head. SCOTT BRANDT.

Tipsy's heart smacked against her chest like a deftly served tennis ball. "Holy shit," she whispered.

"What?" asked Shelby.

"Hold on." She minimized the FaceTime call and swiped over his text.

HEY THERE. IT'S SCOTT. GREAT TO SEE YOU TODAY. SOPHIE SEEMED PERKIER AFTER TALKING TO YOU, SO THANKS FOR WHATEVER MAGIC YOU WORKED! ON A SEPARATE NOTE, HOW ARE YOUR KIDS DOING AT THE NEW HOUSE? I'M A LITTLE WORRIED. I GET THE SENSE THINGS ARE TENSE, BUT KATE AND I DON'T

COMMUNICATE WELL. IF YOU DON'T WANT TO TALK ABOUT IT, I UNDERSTAND. HOPE YOU'RE HAVING A PEACEFUL NIGHT.

She flipped back to FaceTime. "Y'all…Scott Brandt texted me."

"Sister! Eeek! Eeeeeeek!" Shelby would have been equally enthused if Tipsy got a text from Brad Pitt. "What did he say? Tell, tell, tell!"

Tipsy minimized the call and read the text out loud. With a flick of her finger, Shelby filled the screen again. "Oooooh!" said Shelby. "He wants to *talk to you about the kids*. Or…*does he?*"

Lindsey took the phone from Shelby. "Be careful, Tipsy. If he doesn't get along with his ex-wife, he may be digging for information. He'll drag you into his family court debacle. Next thing you know, you're served with a subpoena. You'll have to spill the tea in a legal sense."

"He doesn't seem like—"

"Don't put *anything* in writing!"

"Okay. I get it."

Lindsey scowled. "He's hot, but I would *not* go there. You and Ayers are getting along these days. Plus, it's just…*weird* to get involved with your ex-in-law."

"It's not *that* weird," said Shelby. "Tipsy is an above average gal. There are many single men in this town, but being above average *naturally* reduces your selection pool."

"Dr. Brandt is dating the Hellraising Highlighter. Who says he's looking for above average?"

"Y'all," said Tipsy. "Stop bickering. It's only a text. We're acting like we're in middle school, Shelby."

"So what? Eighth grade was a fabulous year for me."

Lindsey looked at her phone. "Speaking of men texting…P.D. cleaned up a blowout diaper. He thinks he deserves a poop-swiping *medal*, bless his heart. I gotta go." She leaned around Shelby again. "Just be careful, Tips. I warned you about Clarice Andrews, right?"

Tipsy refocused on Shelby when Lindsey disappeared. "She's right about Clarice."

Lindsey had advised Tipsy to avoid Clarice, a notorious playboy, last summer. Tipsy hadn't followed her wise counsel, and got herself reamed out by a member of Clarice's harem during the Windjammer Incident. Instead of the Hellraising Highlighter, she got Revenge of the Real Estate Agent.

"*Text him*, sister," said Shelby. "Your dry spell is coming up on its one year anniversary."

"Thanks for reminding me."

"You say you're okay being single—"

"I *am* okay."

"But you gotta admit it's kind of boring."

"Better bored than crying my eyeballs out over another fool with good hair and buff biceps. If Scott is dating some wacko, I don't want to jab an ornery bull with a cattle prod."

"She'd be a cow, not a bull."

"Cows can still have horns."

"*Everybody* makes dating mistakes. I dated plenty of wackos. In addition to Clarice, you had Ayers, and Will, and don't forget Saint Dave—"

"Running through *that* list of winners won't make me eager to add to it."

Shelby smirked. "I give you twenty-four hours, max. The curiosity will be too much for you."

Tipsy opened her mouth to deny it, but Shelby was right. She was a cat on her deathbed.

"Congrats on selling the palmetto rose painting, by the way," said Shelby. "You got a new piece for the gallery?"

"Not yet. Finishing a commission right now. I have ideas for new pieces. Just need more time and a few more arms."

"I'll hire someone soon and you can cut back at the GQB."

"No huge rush. You need me."

"But like you said, *you* need painting time."

"I also need a regular paycheck."

"You can make more from selling a big painting than you make in a month working for me."

Now Shelby was a career coach, like Ayers. "I know, but—"

"Besides, if you're going to break out of the Charleston market, you *need* to make the jump to full-time painting. I love working with you. I can count on you and you obviously know your art. Customers love you. But I can't be responsible for stifling the career of my own best friend."

"Let's get you through the newborn stage, okay?"

They chatted about Baby Lottie's sleep patterns for a few minutes, but thoughts of her stagnant professional evolution distracted Tipsy. Shelby's husband, Brian, appeared behind her and rubbed her shoulders. "Can I reclaim this mama for the evening? Lottie's snoozing in her bouncy seat."

Shelby looked up at her hubby like he was the Archangel Gabriel. Calm, steady Brian Callahan from Connecticut managed Shelby's post-pregnancy emotions, cravings, and aches and pains like a therapist crossed with a midwife. Tipsy smiled as she said goodnight to both of them.

Once they disconnected, she reread Scott Brandt's texts. As she opened the text box to consider her reply, Henry spoke up from the end of the couch. "Are you going to heed Miss Lindsey's advice?"

"Oh, gosh. You're still here, Henry. Sorry. We tend to blab on when we get going." Tipsy set down her phone. "I don't know. On one hand, Ayers will most likely lose his shit if he finds out I spoke with Scott about the dynamics at his house. Scott dating some whack-a-doo runs another red flag up the pole. Hand number two, I haven't met *one man* who even *vaguely* interested me since Will ditched me and the Clarice debacle. If I avoid every degree of Kevin Bacon, I'll be alone forever."

"Despite my love of a good metaphor, I can't imagine how Irishmen and breakfast meat are relevant."

"It means everyone is connected to everyone around here."

"Ah, I see. My friend, there are always multiple hands with you. You're intellectually ambidextrous."

"Thanks, I think." She shrugged. "I would like to, you know, *feel him out*—"

"Is that phase similar to *breaking up* or *hanging out?*"

"It means I'd like to understand what he wants."

"Then I don't see the harm in feeling him up."

She chuckled. "It's a little early for that."

"I'm saying there's no harm in sending a few texters."

I still don't think it's a good idea. Big Ayers won't take kindly to it.

He doesn't have to know, Granna. Just a few texters, like Henry said.

Frankly, those last words are about as famous as Rhett Butler's lack of giving a damn.

"Of course," said Henry, "the choice is yours."

Granna and Henry spoke over each other, like the voices of her conscience sitting on her shoulders. She wasn't sure who was the angel and who was the devil.

Chapter 3

Since she didn't have to drop the kids off for school, Tipsy got up before 6:00am, went to the gym, came home, showered, gathered her canvas and supplies, and arrived at the GQB before 9:00am to get in an hour of painting. She was determined to tackle the heron commission and free up time for new paintings. She wouldn't be able to concentrate if she didn't attend to her text messages—her texters, as Henry called them. After she set up her easel, she picked up her phone.

First, a texter to Big Ayers about the kids' weekend activities. Even on Ayers's weekends, the children's increasingly hectic schedules required parenting teamwork. Thankfully, they'd managed to communicate reasonably well this school year. REMINDER: LITTLE A HAS LACROSSE PRACTICE THIS EVENING AT 5PM. SATURDAY MORNING HE HAS A GAME AT 10AM AND THE GIRLS HAVE VOLLEYBALL CLINIC FROM 9:00-10:30AM. LET ME KNOW HOW YOU WANT TO DIVIDE AND CONQUER. BUSY WEEKEND!

Next, she replied to Jillian Yates's messages and confirmed she'd stop by her house on Legare Street after work. She felt nervous and excited about searching Jillian's historic mansion for a new ghost. Pamella's cottage was adorable, and her own house oozed Victorian charm, but any house on Legare Street was guaranteed to impress. Given such a house's long history, its ghosts should be equally interesting.

Finally, she reread Scott Brandt's text message for the tenth time. She typed and deleted and typed again, before finally reviewing her own message. HEY, IT WAS NICE TO SEE YOU, TOO. HOW IS SOPHIE THIS MORNING? I'M VISITING HER FAMILY'S HOUSE TODAY. AS TO YOUR OTHER QUESTION, I'M WILLING TO TALK ABOUT THE KIDS, BUT SINCE WE'RE BEING HONEST, I DON'T WANT TO PUT ANYTHING IN WRITING. IF YOU'D LIKE TO CALL ME, THAT WOULD BE FINE.

She hit send, silenced the phone, set an alarm for quarter to ten, and started painting. When the alarm sounded, she prepped the gallery for opening. She swept, adjusted the lighting, and flipped the door sign from *Closed* to *Open* before allowing herself to check her phone. Scott had replied within minutes of her text, but she forced herself to prioritize the practical. She read Ayers's message. EVERY WEEKEND IS BUSY THESE DAYS. I'LL TAKE LITTLE A 2 LAX SATURDAY MORNING IF U CAN GET THE GIRLS 2 VBALL

SURE, NO PROBLEM!

Ayers's typing bubble appeared. GOOD DEAL. THX

Despite that relatively congenial exchange's reminder of what she risked by communicating with Scott, she swiped on his name.

SCOTT: GOOD MORNING! I'M HAPPY TO TALK ON THE PHONE, OR WE COULD MEET FOR COFFEE.

Tipsy paused a moment before replying. Admittedly, it was a short moment.

TIPSY: OKAY. WHAT'S YOUR SCHEDULE LOOK LIKE? NEXT WEEK I'LL BE PRETTY BUSY WITH THE KIDS.

His typing bubble lit up immediately. MY KIDS ARE WITH KATE THIS WEEKEND SO I ASSUME YOURS ARE WITH AYERS. YOU HAVE ANY FREE TIME THE NEXT FEW DAYS?

Between her best friends having new babies and her lack of male suitors, she didn't have much going on. She didn't want to acknowledge her lackluster social life, so she replied: I CAN DO SUNDAY MORNING. UNLESS YOU'RE A CHURCH GUY.

A subtle test. Tipsy didn't have anything against those who regularly attended church. More higher power to them. Unfortunately, in Mount Pleasant, the churchiest-churchgoers were often the most morally suspect.

SCOTT: SUNDAY WORKS. NAH. I'M A CHRISTMAS AND EASTER CATHOLIC. HOW ABOUT YOU?

TIPSY: CHRISTMAS AND EASTER, WHEREVER I HAPPEN TO END UP. MY GRANDMOTHER'S CHURCH HAD NO SPECIFIC DENOMINATION. She hit send, then added a bit of humor. THERE MAY HAVE BEEN SOME SNAKE HANDLERS UP IN THAT JOINT.

SCOTT: HAHA. THERE WERE A FEW OF THOSE IN MY HOMETOWN OF CRABTREE, TENNESSEE, OUTSIDE JOHNSON CITY. WHERE DID YOU GROW UP?

TIPSY: CRABTREE, TN? SOUNDS LIKE THE BOOMING METROPOLIS WHERE I WAS RAISED. MARTINVILLE, SOUTH CAROLINA.

SCOTT: I'LL HAVE TO PULL OUT MY MAP FOR THAT ONE. SORRY TO RUN, BUT I HAVE TO SEE PATIENTS!

TIPSY: NO PROBLEM. TEXT ME SUNDAY MORNING WITH A TIME/LOCATION FOR COFFEE.

SCOTT: ABSOLUTELY. ☺

"Shit," she whispered, but she smiled as she said it.

So much for a little texting, said Granna. *You're already meeting him for coffee.*

It's just to talk about the kids.

Uh, huh. What about the current peaceful state of affairs between you and the father of your children?

I can't give Scott any details, Granna. All I can say is that he's right. Things are tense over there.

Tipsy stood and walked to the gallery door. One of her own paintings sat on an easel in the window facing Queen Street. Another closeup study. Meticulously detailed sunflowers seemed to turn toward her, as if curious about their creator's state of mind. Or maybe they were taunting her. With the palmetto rose gone, they were lonely and demanding company.

The half-finished painting of the two herons sat on its own easel beside the front desk. Their necks, like intertwining water slides, should be covered in a million feathers. Nearly as many sinews on their gray legs. Each feather and scale required a brush stroke. Each brush stroke required seconds of time. She'd already sold the herons, but the buyer's deposit wouldn't do the work for her. She had to finish one job and move on to the next.

Even as she mentally mixed shades of blueish-purplish-gray, other painting ideas percolated in her head. She rummaged through her mental file cabinet. The Ravenel Bridge's gray underbelly, as she'd seen it from P.D.'s boat last fall. The swooping white steel suspension cables against the fiercely blue October sky. Choppy harbor whitecaps. Undulating rainbows magically viewed through tossing sea spray. For a lesser artist, the perspective would be impossible. Tipsy's internal camera had captured, saved, and framed it all with one click.

Or a little girl in a pink gingham dress, fascinated by a guitar player's plaintive version of *Carolina in My Mind*. A scene from her girls' night with Pammy last summer at Debordieu Colony. The child's blonde pigtails, pudgy tummy, and bare feet had contrasted with the hippy musician's rangy form and grizzled, graying beard. She'd stared at him with wide blue eyes. Tipsy had sketched that lovely beachside scene, but she hadn't found time to finalize the drawing, let alone start painting.

She couldn't forget the palomino draft horse she'd recently befriended. His driver stopped near the corner of Queen and State as part of his carriage tour of the French Quarter. He gave the tourists his spiel about the historic buildings and the local art scene while the horse swished his stubby tail and chewed his bit. Whenever Tipsy walked past the gallery window, the horse's ears pricked, and he looked her in the eye through the glass. He seemed so intelligently curious that she asked permission to give him an apple. The driver affectionately said, "I usually don't let people touch him, but Ol' Creamsicle likes you."

Tipsy had given Creamsicle his treat, and she swore the horse winked at her. Charleston's carriage companies rescued most of their animals. Many were former Amish farm workers. Huge, gentle creatures. If not for the opportunity to do the comparably easy work of chauffeuring tourists through the historic district, they'd end up in slaughterhouses. She wondered what that old boy had seen through his appraising eyes before he entered into semiretirement.

Her camera had clicked, and the painting laid itself out in her mind. Creamsicle's velvety pinkish muzzle, those big liquid brown eyes, and his shaggy white forelock. The cascading purple and red pansies in the window boxes of the house behind him. His wry, inquisitive expression. She would paint Creamsicle as the individual, emotional being she instinctively knew him to be.

So many paintings, so little time. The herons had to come first, before architectural monuments, adorable children, or good Ol' Creamsicle. Certainly before risky electronic flirtation with an attractive doctor. The gallery was empty, so she returned to the waltzing birdies. She sashayed from one heron to the other, her paint brush pirouetting over the canvas. Still, Scott Brandt lingered in her consciousness, as if waiting for a space to open on her dance card.

Tipsy anticipated limited parking on Legare Street, so she rode Shelby's office bike down State Street to Broad, and turned right. She passed the Blind Tiger Pub and multiple musty old law firms. She slowed at the intersection of Broad and Meeting, where the former city hall, the county courthouse complex, the federal courthouse and old post office, and St. Michael's Episcopal Church formed a cluster of local, state, federal, and ecclesiastical institutions known as the Four Corners of Law. She whizzed by the art deco sign for the classic clothier Berlin's (*Since 1883*), a slew of grandiose private homes, and the brownstone edifice of the Cathedral of St. John the Baptist.

She took a left on Legare Street and pedaled toward the harbor. With each rotation of the tires, the houses were larger and the ivy-covered, brick and stone walls were taller. Like Henry, Tipsy had long favored the quiet mystery of Legare Street over South Battery's touristy bustle. In the early days of her marriage, when Tipsy and Ayers lived on Society Street in the Ansonborough neighborhood, her jogging loop included a mid-run slow down on Legare. Even then, with her limited knowledge of Charleston's quirky culture, she sensed Legare Street smugly enjoyed its own hidden beauty and worked hard to preserve it. Many stone and brick walls encased downtown Charleston's estates, but none matched the majesty—or the intimidation factor—of Legare Street. Some were twelve feet tall and topped with iron spikes. Ornate iron gates begrudgingly allowed passersby a peek at opulently furnished piazzas and into English style gardens. The famed Sword Gate House even took its name from its gate—two intricately hewn iron spears crossed by a broadsword.

Oak and magnolia trees shook hands across the street with their spidery, leafy fingers. Their tunneling roots raised cement mountain chains on the street and sidewalk, making for a bumpy bike ride. She noted the descending house numbers, dismounted near the corner of Legare and Gibbes Streets, and found the correct address. A placard hung on the chipped brick and stucco wall.

The Doctor Bonneau House
Circa 1805

The Bonneau family immigrated to Charleston from Périgueux, in the Dordogne region of southwestern France, following the 1685 revocation of the Edict of Nantes. A classic example of Charleston stucco design, this house takes its name from Dr. Rene Bonneau (1830-1880), a noted Civil War field surgeon. He gained the nickname "Dr. Legbone" as it was said that his impressive physical stature allowed him to cut through a femur bone with only a few swipes of his saw. Dr. Bonneau married renowned local beauty Agnes Barre, who died in childbirth during the War. Dr. Bonneau returned to Charleston, where he resided in this house and continued practicing medicine until his death.

Of all the history attached to a place like this, how charming to include the late owner's proclivity for detaching limbs. *I'm relieved we're not searching for Dr. Legbone, Granna.*

Nothing unusual about a man going by his middle name. Might still be the Thomas we're looking for.

Ugh. Let's hope not. I want another ten-k if I'm exorcising a hulking amputation expert.

She peered through the requisite ornamental iron gate, across a sand and gravel driveway and a wide lawn. The estate's smaller structures included rectangular brick servants' quarters, a brick carriage house that served as a garage, and a slowly collapsing glass greenhouse.

The four-story pink stucco main house had black shutters, white piazzas, and four brick chimneys. It sat toward the rear of the several-acre property, a modest debutante waiting to be introduced. Some of these old houses had basement levels of sorts, and therefore steep staircases and raised entryways, but the Bonneau House's first floor piazza and main entrance sat at ground level. Two other piazzas topped the first. Eight dormers along the roofline were sets of curious eyes, peering nosily over the neighbors' walls.

Tipsy pressed the button on the intercom and it buzzed under her fingers. She expected Jillian to answer and ask her to identify herself, but the intercom *click-clicked* and the lock mechanism released. Such an aged gate should be squeaky, but it smoothly slid open as if recently doused in WD-40. She walked her bike onto the property and leaned it against the wall's interior side. A bumblebee flew out of the ivy and landed on the handlebars. Its legs and antennae waved; a fat, fuzzy welcome wagon.

She examined the expansive grounds. An ancient oak tree grew in the far corner. Its heaviest, longest limbs rested on the ground. Cables attached to the surrounding walls and other branches held the whole woody creature together, as if it were in traction. A taller, slimmer, equally timeworn magnolia held court in the corner closer to Legare Street. The two trees were an arboreal Laurel and Hardy, or Lurch and Cousin It.

A black Mercedes sedan and a red Jeep Wrangler with a College of Charleston sticker on the rear windshield were parked near the garage, beside two white contractor's vans, stacks of paving stones, a large appliance box, and an industrial strength pressure washer. The house looked freshly painted and a dark blue rectangular swimming pool glowed beside the servants' quarters. Still, several centuries of wear and tear were like deep wrinkles resisting a hefty dose of Botox. Dented gutters had semi-detached from the garage roof and she detected dry rot under the eaves. Dead boxy hedges had turned into crispy botanical corpses. A pineapple fountain surrounded by scraggly rose bushes stood in the middle of the driveway, but the dry, cracked bowl and surrounding weeds told her it had burbled its last burble years ago. A few pink and red and white blossoms leaned toward the fountain as if searching for moisture.

Once Tipsy completed her gawking appraisal, she walked toward the house. Sand and gravel scrunched under her feet with a sound like grinding teeth. Her long skirt kicked up dust, and sneaky pebbles lodged between her toes. As she approached, Jillian called to her through the open door. "Come on in."

Tipsy shuffled her feet to extricate lingering pebbles and walked up four steps to the piazza. Jillian had decorated in typical Charleston style, with a Charleston green joggling board and wicker furniture with striped cushions. The pygmy palms and flowering annuals in the planters and window boxes looked fresh and frisky, as if Jillian only tended to foliage within arm's reach. The piazza had a haint blue ceiling, once again proving that color had no effect on restless spirits.

Jillian stood in the foyer with a stack of mail. She wore a tennis skirt and a tight red Lululemon top. Sweat glistened on her temples, but her lipstick was firmly in place. "Hurry up now," she said. "So much to accomplish today, including sorting out Mama's latest bills. Amazing how they keep coming even after she's passed."

"Sorry about my ogling. This place is as pretty as I imagined."

"It's not as pretty when you're maintaining it. My mother couldn't keep up for the past ten years. I've been making improvements. Painted the exterior. Regraded the driveway. Put in the pool. I thought it would be fun for Sophie, but…" She pinched her nose. "Working on some rewiring now. New HVAC system and roof are next."

The scuffed wooden floors creaked as Tipsy crossed the threshold. Despite the lavender candle burning on the ornate sideboard, the place smelled like old wood and dusty carpets. She gazed up into the staircase, like the swirling interior of a nautilus shell, all the way to the fourth floor. A crystal chandelier dangled above her head on worn, precarious wiring. Hopefully the electrician would address that issue, but in the meantime, Tipsy stepped out from under it.

Jillian led her across multiple Oriental rugs and through a formal sitting room decorated with delicate antique furniture. Next, a dining room with seating for twenty, copious brass candelabras, and another unstable chandelier. They entered a narrow galley kitchen at the rear of the house. It must have been renovated twenty years ago, when dark cabinetry and granite were all the rage. Despite the dimness, a breakfast table beside a bay window and a brick fireplace made it cozy.

"If I stay here," said Jillian, as she opened the fridge, "this kitchen is the next upgrade. So gloomy, and uncivilized to live without an island. I have sweet tea or pomegranate juice. I can make you a kale and spinach smoothie, or there's bourbon in the butler's closet if that's your thing."

With that California-meets-Carolina beverage selection, Tipsy stayed close to home. "Sweet tea is fine. Any updates on Sophie coming home?"

"Thankfully she's staying through the weekend." Jillian retrieved Tipsy's tea and directed her to the kitchen table. "Dr. Brandt has been so kind and understanding. He said y'all know each other?"

"Yes. His ex-wife and my ex-husband are married. He's my *ex-in-law*." She waited for Jillian to laugh, but she didn't seem to have much of a sense of humor.

"Apparently she's improved since she spoke to you."

"I'm sure she feels better knowing someone believes her."

"Right."

Her terse answer made Tipsy rush to spit out her own foot. "I don't blame you for not believing her. What sane adult believes in ghosts?"

Jillian didn't reply. She retrieved a notepad from the counter and flipped a few pages. "I went through Mama's notebooks. About went cross-eyed reading her writing, but I think I found him. Thomas Rene Bonneau. Born, 1863. Died, 1883. He inherited the house from his father—"

"Dr. Legbone?"

"You must have read the placard outside. Thomas inherited the house from Rene when Rene passed away."

"Interesting. His mother must have been Agnes Barre, *renowned local beauty who died in childbirth*. Anything else about him?"

"Nope. He died, and the house sold about a year later. It was a boarding house when he owned it, and for most of the last century. My parents bought it when we upgraded from our old house on Church Street in the late 1970s."

"Boarding house makes sense. Hard to keep up a house like this for a single family today, much less after the Civil War when everyone struggled to survive. So…Thomas Bonneau. About twenty years old. A decent start."

"If you say so. By the way, I spoke to my accountant about the best way to handle your payment. Since you're an artist, I'm going to take you on as a *home design consultant*. Pamella showed me the paintings she commissioned, and your website. My personal taste runs toward modern art, but your work is pretty damn amazing."

Over the years, Tipsy had gotten better at accepting compliments. "Thank you," she said.

"Since you're my new home design consultant, you might as well design something."

"A painting? Do you have something in mind?"

"Actually, yes. Come with me."

Tipsy followed Jillian through the kitchen and the pantry into a small guest bedroom. Two canvases leaned against the bed, backside forward, as if hiding their faces. "My mother's friend painted these portraits of me and my sister," said Jillian. "I *literally* can't stand them."

She flipped the canvases. Each painting depicted a stiff teenage girl in a white dress. One blonde, one auburn-haired. They sat on plain wooden chairs against a smeary gray background. The subjects must have been pretty young women, but the paintings were amateur at best. Terrible depth and perspective. Flat, distorted features. Harsh brushstrokes.

"I can see *why* you can't stand them."

"They hung in the dining room for decades. It upset Mama, but I took them down when I moved in. I promised her I'd commission a new painting of my sister. If you're already helping me out, I can keep my promise." She pointed at the girl with the reddish hair. "This is Catherine. Only her. I don't need a painting of myself."

"Sure. I'm happy to." Happy might be a stretch. Tipsy enjoyed painting, no matter the assignment. But a piece for Jillian would stand between Tipsy and the Ravenel Bridge, the little girl and the guitarist, and Creamsicle. *Damn those herons,* she thought, as she pictured their judgmental yellow eyes. *I have to finish that painting!*

"I'll pull some photos of Catherine for you. Now, do you want to look around the house? See if you can…find this… Thomas?"

"Sure. It's best for me to walk around alone. Ghosts often sense me, and they come out. He might not if you're around."

"Okay. I have those bills to tackle. I'll be on the second floor piazza if you need me."

"Is there any place I should avoid?"

"Nope. You have free rein. By the way, there are some old photos in my father's study. Stuff he found in the attic when we moved into the house."

"Cool. Any chance one of them is Thomas?"

"Don't know who any of them are, but some of them are from that era."

That era. So far, she counted Henry and Jane's murder as her earliest mystery. This one threw her another forty years into the past. As she went further back in time, the chances of finding anyone with useful information decreased. The thought did nothing for her confidence, but she wouldn't worry about such particulars until she found Thomas Bonneau. No point putting the cart before the Creamsicle.

Tipsy was huffing and puffing by the time she got to the fourth floor. Beside the attic, she found a simple bedroom with slanted ceilings, where Jillian had stored the lonely remnants of Betsy "BeeBee" Porcher's later years. She'd stacked clear plastic bins of clothes and old ladies' shoes on the bed. On the floor, two canes, a pile of photo albums and cookbooks, and a box full of old-fashioned hair curlers. She'd seen no indication Betsy haunted the house, but she closed the door softly on her way out, as if a slamming door might disturb her.

Five bedrooms on the third floor contained ornately carved marble fireplaces with empty grates. Four were stuffed with fussy late twentieth-century country decor. Quilted bedding, rocking chairs, and drawings of bonneted geese and smiling frogs. Only Sophie's room had been recently remodeled. Her four-poster bed dripped with gold beaded curtains, and a black bedspread covered hot pink sheets. She'd piled old stuffed animals on the pillows. A MacBook sat on a white desk beside a door that opened to the piazza. Tipsy reviewed the framed photos on the desk. A round-faced, adorable blonde girl with a mustachioed man who must have been her late father. Another of Jillian, Sophie, and her two blonde sisters. Several photos of sorority girls in green and purple shirts. Tipsy recognized the colors of Kappa Zeta, the sorority she belonged to at the University of South Carolina. In the recent photos, Sophie had full cheeks and bright eyes. She grinned in her KZ bid day tee-shirt, just as pretty as Tipsy had predicted.

Sophie had decorated the black marble fireplace with white lights. Tipsy inhaled the conflicting sweet scents of sea breeze candles and fruity body spray. Nothing about the room screamed *unstable young adult clairvoyant*, so she walked downstairs to the second floor. She peered into Betsy Porcher's huge, abandoned bedroom suite. Across the hall, she found another large bedroom. Several designer handbags and some tennis gear revealed it as Jillian's room. In both rooms, red and gold décor and lush velvet and satin fabrics made her think of Buckingham Palace. Stiff, snooty men with George Washington-style hairdos glared at her from faded portraits. Tipsy couldn't imagine getting undressed under the condescending gaze of those bewigged patriarchs.

She returned to the first floor. In a library-turned-family room, reading material took up most of the built-in bookshelves, but Jillian had added a modern sectional sofa and hung a huge flat screen television over another opulent fireplace. Copies of *Charleston Magazine* and *Garden and Gun* sat on a sleek, modern coffee table. The most boring room in the house.

Tipsy was nearing the end of her tour, and no Thomas, but the final closed door on the far end of the library must lead to the study. She listened to her own footfalls and the floor's constant creaking as she approached the closed door, but when she touched the doorknob, she heard…*whistling*. The chipper tune spoke of upright pianos and raucous saloons. When she cracked the door, cold air wafted up her arm.

She stepped into a small, cramped room. Ledgers, magazines, and maps sat on a wide, intricately carved wooden desk. Dusty liquor bottles and etched glass tumblers waited patiently on a brass drink caddy. She'd need pliers to extract one of the leatherbound books crammed onto more built-in bookshelves.

A man leaned against the bay window overlooking the gardens. Heavy gold drapes framed him, as if he'd stepped onstage at the Globe Theater. At under six feet tall with a slight build, he would have seemed small beside Henry, who was at least a head taller and had a lanky, broad-shouldered frame. When compared to John Huger, who could have chosen between the NBA and the NFL, this guy was minute.

He wore a dark shirt and a dark overcoat, black trousers and broken-in lace-up boots. He had the deathly pallor common to ghosts, with full reddish lips and piercing dark eyes. His wavy black hair tumbled over his forehead, and true to his nineteenth-century origins, he had longish sideburns. A hint of babyishness in his handsome face, as if he hadn't grown into his full glory before he died.

"My *stars* and garters," he said in a singsong voice, as he crossed his legs at the ankle. "I got a visitor."

His jocular greeting took Tipsy aback, but these days, a ghost would not unnerve her. He couldn't be any more dangerous than Ivy More Brewton, whose hissy fits turned tree limbs into projectiles.

She nonchalantly approached the shelf and ran her fingers along the fading old lettering on the books' red, blue, and green spines. True to Jillian's word, framed daguerreotypes and grainy black and white photos sat on one shelf: a wedding party, an old man with a long white beard, three laughing boys in the garden, a white baby on a solemn black woman's lap. Two oval portraits graced the mantle, a blonde woman holding an ornamental fan and a pretty raven-haired lady with squiggly 1850s curls.

"Kitty got your tongue, ma'am?" asked the young man.

"No, sir." Tipsy faced him. "Waiting for you to make a proper introduction."

"My apologies! My name is Thomas. Sometimes called Tom, although no one calls me much of anything anymore." He smiled. "Thomas Bonneau, at your service."

Bingo, said Granna. *Now play it cool, sugar.*

"You must be related to Doctor Rene Bonneau."

"How'd you know about Ol' Doc Legbone?"

"There's a sign beside the gate. This place is called the Doctor Bonneau House."

"My dear father would appreciate that. And you are?"

"Tipsy Collins. Nice to meet you."

"Tipsy! You are most welcome in my humble home. As you can imagine, conversations are long in coming for the likes of me."

All Tipsy's ghostly friends had the Old Charleston accent, a unique—and nearly extinct—manner of speaking. The musical drawls of Henry, Jane, and John Huger eschewed single syllables and final consonants. Twelve months in a *ye-ah.* Row the *bo-ut* across the *Cup-pah Riv-a.* They shared their *fath-as'* wisdom and put *sup-pa* on the table.

Thomas Bonneau's even thicker accent had sprouted in rich antebellum soil, a congealed stew to their hearty soups. It had French hints and traces of a Caribbean lilt. The wealthy white man's version of a Gullah-Geechee accent.

"You've had a conversation partner lately," said Tipsy.

"You mean the *chah-min* Miss Sophie?"

Charming was a stretch, but the psych ward could wear the charm out of anyone, much less a moody, frustrated teenager. "I haven't seen that side of her yet, but we just met. She said y'all are friends."

"As the saying may go, charming is as charming does." He reached into his overcoat and scratched his chest. Watching him—fidgeting and bundled up in a stuffy room on a late spring afternoon—made Tipsy feel claustrophobic. His pale hand drifted to his neck and he itched around under his collar. "What else did my friend say?"

"Not much. She gave me the basic parameters of your haunting. Your name, you died a long time ago, and you're a solo haunting—"

"Solo haunting?"

"You're the only ghost in this house."

"Ah. This all sounds very official."

"I've investigated a few hauntings. Developed a checklist."

"How is Sophie? She didn't seem in top form when she left the house."

"Nope. She's in the psych ward resting up after a nervous breakdown."

Thomas took only two steps, but his slithering ghostly locomotion carried him to her side. Most ghosts she'd met had a unique scent, but she detected nothing particular. Unless the study's mildewy odor originated from his person as much as the antique books and musty draperies.

"Sick ward?" he asked, and scratched his hair.

"*Psych* ward. Like, a lunatic asylum."

"Oh, *no*. In my day, when a family needed to be rid of a hysterical woman, she'd be tossed lickety-split into one of those terrible places."

"Thankfully for Sophie, it's not your day. She's there to get help, not be warehoused."

"I hate to be nosy, but I overheard the ruckus—"

"Overheard the ruckus, or participated in it?"

"Pardon?"

"Sophie's mother heard her talking to someone before she…got hysterical. Someone her mother couldn't see."

"I was there, but only because Sophie called for me. Jillian thundered in and they argued, and I never had the chance to understand Sophie's distress. It broke my heart listening to mother and daughter rail at each other so!"

"You look about as heartbroken as a happy face emoji. In fact, you're *oddly* chipper."

"I'm not familiar with that particular modernism, but I take your meaning. Must I be morose because I'm dead?"

"Death usually throws a damper on one's outlook—"

"You know what they say about lemons and lemonade."

"Life gave you a bushel of lemons and left out the sugar. Death at a young age."

"It's true. I'm but a *lad* of twenty."

"You *look* twenty, but you're the oldest ghost I've met so far."

"I'm vintage '63. Smack in the middle of the War Between the States."

"The *Civil War*."

"That's what they're calling it these days? Eh. War is anything but civil."

"If your father was away amputating limbs, how'd you…come about?"

"Given my existence, my father obviously managed to visit. My mother died giving birth to me. According to Father, I killed her with my overly large head."

"That's not a fair assessment. Women died in childbirth all the time—"

"True, but *also* according to my father, their babies usually died with them. Me and my large head had the nerve to survive. By the time the war ended and my father came home for good, I was past two years old, and my mother nearly the same in the grave."

"How terrible." Tipsy meant both the facts and the insinuation that Thomas grew up thinking he killed his own mother.

"It doesn't get better!" Thomas scratched his cheek and grinned, as if he couldn't wait to lay his sad tale on her. "Only me, Dr. Legbone, and the servants in this house for years! My father was a *very* busy man. He didn't have much time for me, and then he died when I was seventeen! Thus leaving me quite alone in the world!" Tipsy's mind put excited exclamation marks at the end of his statements.

"Sounds like you had a rough childhood."

"Yes, yes. All terribly tragic, but I preferred the lonely days. When my father was home, be endlessly reminded me of the unfortunate size of my head. He knocked me upside that same noggin if I got in his way."

"What a jerk. Then you passed away so young. I've heard some sad life stories from ghosts. Yours is up there."

"The good die young, as the saying goes. And thus, I am as I have always been...and always will be."

A bunch of existential blah-blah-blah. This is when he loses it, Granna, even if he seems as reasonable as Abraham Lincoln delivering the Gettysburg Address.

But Thomas smiled brightly. "I found the fountain of youth! All things considered, a charmed existence!"

He's the happiest ghost I've ever seen, said Granna. *Don't strike me as someone who will be eager to move on.*

All the more reason to keep him in the dark about my intent to make him mosey down that path.

"Sophie is supposed to come home soon," she said, "but when she freaked out—er, got hysterical—she told her mother she sees ghosts, and this house is haunted. Jillian is hesitant to bring her back here."

He scratched at his thigh through his thick pants. "Then it's a good thing you made my acquaintance. You can assure all involved I have no ill intentions."

"I'll tell Jillian, but not sure it will make a—"

"Miss Tipsy. What danger do I pose to Sophie in my depleted state? Besides, I cherish every long-awaited opportunity to palaver, and like she said, we're *friends.* You do believe me, *don't* you?"

He looked at her with beseeching eyes. Clear, intelligent, and so damn *earnest.*

"I hate for you to think poorly of me," he said. "I hope you and I can be friends, too."

He looked like he might cry if she didn't agree with him. His intense dark eyes pulled at her heart. If he suggested she open the study window, climb out, strip naked, and do the Running Man down Legare Street, she might consider it.

Tipsy, snap out of it.

"Something wrong, Miss Tipsy?" he asked.

"No. Nothing's wrong. By the way, when I saw Sophie, she asked me to find you. Let you know she's…ah…doing okay, and she'll be home soon."

"Kind of her to think of me. She's a sweet girl." He raked his nails down his neck. He would have drawn blood, if he had any left.

Tipsy backed toward the door, and he slid after her. Even for a ghost, his legs didn't move much. Every spirit had ghostly quirks. Thomas slid around as if standing on Little A's hoverboard and scratched like a flea-ridden puppy.

"Must you leave? We're just getting to know one another."

"Yeah. I've got—"

"Do come back. A friend of Sophie's is a friend of mine."

She backed into the doorknob, twisted it, and stuck one leg through the open door. "I'll see you when Sophie comes home. Have a nice…uh, day."

She stepped into the family room and slammed the door behind her. *Thanks for the wake-up call, Granna. He sucked me in for a minute with those eyes.*

You're welcome, sugar. He's a handsome young—old—whatever—man. What else do you think?

In addition to being handsome, he's different. Never met such an enthusiastic ghost. I have the urge to discuss this with Henry.

One unusual spirit may understand another.

Let's get out of here before Jillian asks questions. Not sure what to make of that interaction yet. Tipsy tiptoed across the squeaky floor toward the front door.

"Are you *certain* you believe me?"

"Shit!" She tried to stop herself, but she had one foot in front of the other. Thomas Bonneau was only six inches from her, and she stepped through him.

—•✕•—

When Tipsy's foot hits the ground, she's standing on the same floor, in another century. She shakes her head to dissipate the yellow lights that always obscure her vision at the beginning of these time hops. She's beside the fireplace in the Bonneau House's cramped study. A candle-laden chandelier hangs over a different desk. Similar books line the bookshelves. A cabinet with glass doors houses dark blue apothecary bottles and archaic medical instruments. An engraved placard hunkers in a layer of dust on the desk, as if it hasn't been moved in years. R.M. Bonneau, Doctor of Medicine.

Thomas Bonneau sits in the chair with his boots propped up on the desk. He appears about the age of his ghostly self. He's not as deathly pale as he is in Tipsy's when, but he's fair-skinned and rosy cheeked. His dark hair tumbles over his head in messy waves. Paper and bottles of ink crowd the desk, but he's not working. He stares out the window like Lord Byron, as the sun wafts through the foggy glass and casts shadows on his elegant features.

He certainly doesn't resemble the broad-shouldered man in the daguerreotype on the desk. Tipsy would have noticed this photo on the shelf back in her own when, so it must have been lost to time. Spindly handwriting along the bottom of the image identifies the hulking man in the photo. Doc. R.M. Bonneau. 1860. *In the black and white photo, Dr. Bonneau's light blue eyes remind Tipsy of a Weimaraner; an intense, silver-eyed hunting dog. He wears a Confederate uniform, but a medical bag lays across his lap instead of a musket. Given the huge hand resting on his thigh, he could remove a limb or two and not break a sweat.*

"Lookee here," says Tipsy, since Thomas can't hear her. "I've seen you before, ma'am." Another frame holds a photo of a slim, raven-haired woman

58

in an off-the-shoulder, hoop-skirted gown—the same photo sits on the mantel in Tipsy's when. Her skin is alabaster; her waist, wasplike. She has a long neck and elven features, like a lovely, black-eyed fairy. The resemblance between Agnes Barre Bonneau and her son is uncanny. Thomas is a mama's boy, even if she died before he had a chance to know her.

The door opens, and a buxom young woman enters. She looks to be a few years younger than Thomas. Her blonde hair is piled atop of her head in loopy swirls and she has short, straight bangs. Her features are steady and even. The kind of face where no one attribute attracts attention or praise, but the overall effect pleases. The Victorian version of the girl next door. A Post-Antebellum Charleston Dress Code Blonde.

She wears a light blue dress with a high, tight collar. Between her cinched corset, long, fitted sleeves, and the collar's chokehold, Tipsy wonders how she can breathe. Even the embroidered ivy vines creeping around her bodice appear suffocatingly tight.

"Hello, Mr. Bonneau. Thank you for inviting me."

Thomas smiles, as if he's posing for a portrait and must hold the position, lest his features be smeared for all eternity. His body turns toward her, but he keeps staring out the window, like he's maintaining eye contact with a prettier girl on the other side.

Once his head catches up with the rest of him, he says, "You're most welcome here, Patty. Dr. Legbone would never forgive me if I left his old friend's daughter to fend for herself in the marsh. How was the trip from the islands? Wadmalaw, was it?"

"Edisto, sir. Long, but we had no trouble."

"Wonderful. Shall we discuss your new position over a cup of tea?" Patty opens her mouth, but before a sound escapes, Thomas barks, "Rachel! Tea in the library."

"Sir," says an affirmative voice from beyond the door.

Thomas opens the study door for Patty and follows her through it. There's something of his fluid supernatural propulsion in his languid glide, like he may spin around and moonwalk into the library. A middle-aged black woman lays out tea cups on the decorative table between two elegant but threadbare chairs near the fireplace. She hands a cup and saucer to Patty, who thanks her. "Y'all want a fire, Mr. Thomas?"

"No, Rachel. Tea will keep us plenty warm." He waves at her. "You go on, now."

Rachel leaves them to it. Patty sits primly on the edge of a worn settee, like the spindly couch might collapse under her. From her goggle eyes peering over the teacup, landing on her ass isn't her only fear. The room intimidates her, from the uptight furnishings to the long-nosed Bonneau relatives that sneer at her from oil portraits. She makes eye contact with a painting of Thomas's lovely mother. A benevolent half-smile touches Agnes's lips. She's the only person in the house who won't judge Patty harshly.

"So! Patty," Thomas says, as he swoops in for a tea cup.

Patty grabs the armrest, as if to hold the sofa in place. Tea sloshes over her cup and dribbles on her skirt.

Thomas gives her a napkin. "Relax, honey. You're jumpier than a one-legged rooster."

Given Tipsy's basic understanding of Victorian formality, Thomas's use of that endearment strikes her as ballsy. Patty's face flames, as if to make up for the lack of fire in the hearth. "Forgive me. Never been in a house like this one, sir."

"Heaven forbid! Enough of this sir *and* Mr. Bonneau. *We're the same age, aren't we?"*

"I'm nearly seventeen."

"And I'm just past nineteen. Tuck your sirs away in your apron. It's Thomas. Or even better, Tom."

"I'll try to remember... Tom." She sets the teacup on the table and dabs at the tea stain on her dress.

"Speaking of aprons, your father's letter said you have a talent for sewing. You sew that costume yourself?"

"I did. When my daddy fell ill, he insisted I take a little coin and sew something nice for myself. So's I'd be a walking advertisement for my abilities."

"Can you sew men's clothing?"

"I can. Sewed Daddy's shirts and trousers myself. Did all the mending."

"I only take on male boarders. I questioned the wisdom of bringing on a young woman like yourself. I run an upstanding establishment, but you know how men are."

"How are they, sir—Tom?"

He chuckles. "Never mind. The truth is, I need a feminine hand to help me run this place. When I got your father's letter, asking me if I had any work for you, it seemed a turn of fortune for both of us. When did he pass away?"

"About three weeks ago."

"And your mother?"

"Three years gone now. It's been hard times on the islands since the war. Not enough to eat. Water is poor. I had brothers and sisters. A few of 'em. But I'm the only one made it past twelve. When my last little brother passed, my mama went and gave up. She stopped eating what little we had. Caught a fever and heaven called her right quickly."

"Terrible. You have no other family?"

She shakes her head. "Daddy hoped he'd see me wed before he passed, but consumption took him quicker than we expected."

"He said you ran the household after your mother died. You must have been quite young."

"I was. But I'm not afraid of hard work, in the garden or the kitchen. Or behind a desk. Daddy taught me to write and cipher."

"You've been sent to me from heaven." He winks. "There anything you can't do?"

She either doesn't catch the wink, or doesn't understand it. "Not that I can reckon. I do fine work, too. Ladies' work. Embroidery and the like, if any of the gentlemen need handkerchiefs." She stands and digs in her little satchel. "See here? I made these."

She gives him a handkerchief. Tipsy leans over his shoulder and squints at the finely stitched initials. Patty points at the letters. "That's my father, J.L., Jr." She retrieves another hankie. This one features a monogram—P.M.L.— and embroidered flowers. "Here's my own initials."

"These are fine indeed," says Thomas. "Can you make a few for me?"

She squirms with pride, or embarrassment, or both. "Cert'ly. T.B.? Do you have a middle name?"

"Rene. After my dear departed father."

"Daddy always said, if it weren't for Rene Bonneau swiping off his arm, he'd never have made it home. He held your father so dear."

"Nothing bonds two men like an amputation."

"He called Dr. Bonneau a giant among men, but his admiration went beyond the doctor's physical stature. He spoke often of his serene nature and his compassion for the men he treated."

"Serene and compassionate. Huh. Interesting." He turns away from her and strums all ten fingers on the mantle. "Let me see. What else do you need to know? Rachel puts dinner out at noon and supper on the table at half past six. But if you're to be the housekeeper, you may adjust as you see fit."

"I'll see how I get on with Rachel before I start changing things. Don't want to ruffle the feathers of a loyal hen. I'll make this house run smooth as a silk necktie. I promise."

"I'm sure you will, and I'll be grateful. As they say, a man's home is his castle, and I'll have peace in my realm. Nothing like venturing into the wide world outside these walls for merriment and amusement and fine conversation, and returning to the tranquility of my own house."

"You're a fortunate man."

"I am, aren't I?" The clock behind them strikes noon. "Look at the time! I need extra pocket money for those new handkerchiefs. I should go while the going is good."

"Go where?" She touches a finger to her lips, hushing herself. "Not that it's my place to ask."

"It's not, but you need to understand how things work around this place, and that includes how I work. Or, in Dr. Legbone's opinion, how I don't work. My father hoped I'd attend the medical university like himself, and my grandfather, but I'm rather squeamish. So I earn my coin in other ways."

"From the boarders paying their keep?"

Thomas answers with his own question. "You are a nosy little Nelly, aren't you?"

His blasé voice doesn't give away his feelings, but it's a passive aggressive comment. Tipsy waits to feel his annoyance. A hint of irritation. Maybe defensiveness, if he has something to hide.

She gets nothing.

Odd, since the memory maker's emotions are always magnified in these visions. She usually sees unpleasant memories, so she usually experiences secondhand unpleasant feelings. But Thomas Bonneau's emotions reveal nothing more to Tipsy than his snide comment reveals to Patty.

She mumbles apologies as he checks his reflection in an octagonal mirror hanging on the wall near the door. He shakes out his hair and smiles, as if checking for bits of food in his teeth. He looks at Patty's reflection behind him. She shudders and dabs her cheeks with her father's old hanky.

"Now, Patty. Are those tears?"

She wipes maniacally. "I'm real sorry for being nosy. My daddy always said I talk too much for a girl."

"He sounds like a wise man. It's more becoming for a woman to listen. You want to catch a husband someday, don't you?"

"Of...course."

"I'll help you practice listening, since I tend to run on myself!"

She opens her mouth to respond, then shuts it, as if she's already putting her new listening skills to good use. She nods instead.

His voice softens. "I know what it's like to be alone in the world, but you got to buck up."

"I suppose you do *understand. Orphans, both of us." His solidarity seems to fortify her.*

"Dry those tears. You'll be safe here, and you have God given skills to offer." He laughs. "More than I can say for myself!"

Patty smiles for the first time. "I'm sure you have much to offer, Tom."

"There are givers and there are takers, as they say. Which one are you, honey?"

"They? Who—" Her smile falters, as if she isn't sure what he wants to hear. "I can't say I know yet."

"You come straight to me at any time if there's a problem around here."
He points at the grandfather clock in the corner. "I take that back. Not any
time. *I keep late hours and I don't enjoy early wake ups. I'm like a bat!"*

She giggles, clearly enchanted. "You'd make a very big bat."

"Speaking of bats, your room is close to the attic."

"Are there bats in there?"

*"We try to keep ahead of them, but a few always sneak inside and set
up camp. Then there are the stinging critters. Sometimes those feisty fellows
meander into the hallways. Don't want you to step on Bumble Bill or Willy
Wasp in the middle of the night."*

*"Goodness. Thank you for warning me. Somehow, in all my days on the
farm, I've never been stung."*

*"It's quite painful, and you can't know how you'll tolerate it. In my
childhood, I stepped on a single honeybee and my throat swelled like a frying
sausage." He reaches into his pocket and removes a handkerchief. "When
you've rested and had something to eat, why not practice my initials on this?"*

She takes the blank white cloth from him. "T.R.B."

"Yes, that's right—and yours were?"

"P.M.L."

"Let me guess," he says, as he backs toward the door. "Patricia Mary."

"Close. Patience Mary."

Chapter 4

Tipsy opened her front door and dumped her purse on the foyer sideboard. A quick look in the hallway mirror served as a reminder of her relative seclusion. Lately, she'd spent all her free time painting. Responsible behavior? Yes. Lucrative results? Hopefully. Sunkissed glow? Negative. Despite the late May heat, her skin was only a few shades darker than Henry's. She called out to him. "Henry! Hey, Mott! You around?"

He swam into existence in the mirror, standing behind her. "Now you want to talk. Perhaps you'll interrupt me by taking a face-phone from Shelby and Lindsey."

She turned to face him. "Face *Time*. Come now, Mr. Mott. Petty jealousy is below you."

"Petty jealousy led me to detest John Huger for over a century."

"That's ancient history. You're a new man."

"To the contrary. I'm a very old man."

"Not as old as Thomas Bonneau!" Tipsy removed her sandals, wiped the bottoms of her still sandy feet, and beckoned him into the living room. She flopped on the sofa, tucked her long legs underneath her, and covered her toes with her flowy skirt. She told Henry about her conversation with Thomas, including the memory of him chatting with the blonde woman, Patty. "From what I learned today, our boy Thomas had a tragic life, even for those tragic times."

"And what of his manner?"

"Now that's a whole different bucket of fish bait. His manner was... really... *nice*."

"You speak as if being nice is a bad thing.'

"No, but... he was so *friendly*. No ghost has ever been so pleasant during an initial convo."

"I wasn't *un-nice* when we first met."

"You weren't outwardly mean or rude, but you were...off."

"Here we go again. *Off* what?"

"Off your rocker. You *and* Jane. As for y'all's *manner*...plain miserable, both of you. Every ghost I've met over the past couple years has been unhappy. Lonely. Sad. Frustrated. Regretful. This guy was *upbeat*. Lighthearted. Oozing positivity. I waited for him to say something wacky, but it was just pleasant chit-chat. Like he might ask me to play cards over a shot of bourbon."

"What of the memory?"

"He was equally congenial to this woman Patty, who came to help him run his house. If the memory showed her to me, she must be important. He clearly loved his house, and his house intimated the hell out of her. She seemed sheltered and innocent. He's handsome and charming and a bit rakish."

"Sounds like a recipe for a torrid romance."

"That could be where it's heading." She turned on the table lamp behind her head. "Another weird thing. Remember how we pick up the feelings of the person...uh...hosting the memory?"

"Oh, yes," said Henry. "Ivy and Camden's awful emotions in their memories made me feel like I might slide back into insanity."

"Same. But I didn't get anything from Thomas. No feelings, bad or good."

"It doesn't sound like an emotionally charged memory. A casual meeting between employer and new help, correct?"

"Yeah. Maybe that's it. Did you know any Bonneaus?"

"I can't say I remember the name."

Tipsy described the placard outside the house and what Jillian and Thomas had told her about the Bonneau family. "So they call it the *Doctor Bonneau House.*"

"I feel one has to have a certain disposition to remove arms and legs as a profession."

"Especially during the Civil War. That must have been hell. I can't imagine the gruesome things he saw. Not the best mindset to have when embarking upon single parenthood. It sounds like he was hard on Thomas. Beat on him. Gave him guilt trips about his mother dying in childbirth."

"I don't remember any Bonneaus at St. Philip's, or among the families I knew from St. Michael's. *Bonneau* is as French as Robinette and Huger. Perhaps you'll find information at the Huguenot Church."

"Good idea. The Huguenot Church's graveyard isn't big compared to St. Philip's. I'll swing in there tomorrow after work. Maybe the answers will be spelled out on his tombstone. Some life and death stories are. That would be amazing." She sunk into the pillows and stared at the ceiling. "But everything in my life is complicated. Why should my latest ghostly mystery be any different?"

"I remember you telling Wi-yum Garrison that complications come with being an adult."

She watched a few cobwebs dangling from the gently spinning fan, like strands of hair escaping a ponytail. "I know, and I stand by that statement. I don't want Will's kind of simple, but it would be nice for *something* to fall into place without me having to kick, scream, and claw for it." She stood and stretched. "Anyway, thanks for talking to me, but it's painting time. I have *got* to make progress on the damn heron commission."

"I'll leave you to your bird watching, ma'am." He disappeared, and given the rumbling thunder, Tipsy set up her canvas in the living room. She painted for two hours while a summer storm raged around her house, until her arm stiffened and her brain felt like congealing grits. She stretched, checked her phone, and swiped over a text from Shelby.

SHELBY: OMGGGGGG...I WENT BY THE GALLERY TO PICK UP SOME FILES AND THE AC IS OUT AGAIN. IT'S LIKE AN OVEN IN THERE ALREADY AND IT'S SUPPOSED TO BE ALMOST 90 TOMORROW.

TIPSY: YIKES! WHAT'S THE PLAN?

SHELBY: HVAC GUY IS COMING IN THE MORNING. WHY DON'T YOU TAKE THE DAY OFF? I HAVE TO BE THERE. BRIAN CAN WORK FROM HOME AND LOTTIE'S TAKING A BOTTLE.

"What do y'all think about a little extra TLC tomorrow?" Tipsy asked the herons. They glared at her. "No need to speak up. I can see it on your faces." She sent Shelby a text. SURE! I CAN USE THE EXTRA PAINTING TIME. HOPE IT'S A SIMPLE FIX!

Her paycheck would be smaller, but she'd be a day closer to finishing the herons, and she could squeeze in a visit with *T.R. Bonneau, Doctor of…Nothing.*

SHELBY: ME TOO, BUT THAT SYSTEM IS HOBBLING AROUND ON A TERMITE INFESTED PEG LEG. I'M GOING TO HAVE TO LAY OUT THE CASH FOR A NEW UNIT SOONER OR LATER.

Tipsy responded with a couple appropriate emojis: a sweaty face, a sad face, and a dollar bill with wings. Given her aching arm and the gift of extra time tomorrow, she cleaned up and retreated to her bedroom, where she donned her *COUGAR MOM* tee-shirt and a pair of unsexy cotton underwear. She was fixing to lay on her bed and watch Netflix— another exciting single lady evening—but she checked her phone first.

To her surprise, she had a text from Scott. HEY THERE. HAPPY THURSDAY. FYI, YOU CAN TEXT OR CALL ME IF ANYTHING COMES UP WITH THE AYERS/KATE SITUATION. OR ANYTHING IN GENERAL. WORKWEEK IS WIPING ME OUT AND I'M SITTING ON MY COUCH TRYING TO PUMP MYSELF UP FOR THE FRIDAY PUSH. SO... HERE IF YOU WANT TO CHAT. ☺

Thunder grumbled in the distance, as if disappointed it had retreated just as things got interesting. She typed a reply. HI THERE TO YOU TOO. NOTHING NEW FROM AYERS/KATE LAND, BUT I'LL LET YOU KNOW IF I HEAR ANYTHING. I'M HOME, TOO. CRAZY WORK WEEK PLUS ALL THE KIDS' END OF THE SCHOOL YEAR STUFF. I HAVE TO TAKE ADVANTAGE OF EVERY SECOND OF KID FREE TIME, SO I'M STILL EXHAUSTED EVEN WHEN I DON'T HAVE THEM! CATCH-22.

SCOTT: DO YOU HAVE THE KIDS MOST OF THE TIME?

TIPSY: YES. ABOUT 70/30. HOW ABOUT YOU?

SCOTT: OFFICIALLY, I HAVE THEM 30. SHE HAS 70. I WANTED MORE TIME, BUT SHE DOUBLED DOWN ON EVERY OTHER WEEKEND. MY ATTORNEY ADVISED ME TO WAIT IT OUT. SHE FIGURED ONCE THE STRESS OF SINGLE PARENTING KICKED IN, KATE WOULD OFFER ME EXTRA TIME. SHE DOES. WE'RE PROBABLY CLOSE TO 50/50 NOWADAYS.

TIPSY: I GET IT. I WISH AYERS WOULD TAKE A LITTLE MORE TIME, BUT HE'S PREOCCUPIED WITH HUNTING AND FISHING.

SCOTT: I DON'T HUNT. ONLY FISH IF SOMEONE TAKES ME ON A CHARTER. BUT MY JOB IS DEMANDING. IT WOULD BE HARD FOR ME TO HAVE 50/50 ALL THE TIME, BUT I TAKE WHATEVER SHE'LL GIVE ME THAT I CAN WORK AROUND.

TIPSY: YOU MIGHT BE THE ONLY GUY IN CHARLESTON WHO DOES NOT HUNT OR FISH!

SCOTT: I WAS RAISED IN TENNESSEE, SO YOU'D THINK I'D BE INTO HUNTING. OR BASS FISHING. BUT IT WAS ONLY ME AND MY MOM MOST OF MY LIFE, SO I NEVER REALLY LEARNED. PLUS THIS SOUNDS CHEESY BUT I LIKED WATCHING THE DEER BEHIND MY HOUSE WHEN I WAS A KID. DIDN'T SEE ANY REASON TO KILL THEM.

TIPSY: THAT'S NOT CHEESY. IT'S SWEET. She didn't want to scare him off by bringing up his personal life, but curiosity overwhelmed her. CAN I ASK YOU A QUESTION?

SCOTT: SHOOT.

TIPSY: WHY ARE YOU SO CHATTY ALL THE SUDDEN?

SCOTT: THAT'S A LONG STORY. I WAS IN A PRETTY BAD EMOTIONAL STATE WHEN YOU MET ME. THE DIVORCE WAS INEVITABLE, BUT STILL HARD. THEN I GOT MYSELF INVOLVED IN A "SITUATION" THAT DRAGGED ON FOR WAY TOO LONG.

He must be referring to the Hellraising Highlighter. TIPSY: I HAD A "SITUATION," TOO. A FRIEND ONCE TOLD ME EVERYONE NEEDS A DYSFUNCTIONAL RELATIONSHIP POST-DIVORCE. ☺

SCOTT: I CHECKED THAT BOX. THESE DAYS I'M IN A BETTER PLACE. GETTING USED TO THE DIVORCE DYNAMIC. GOT OUT OF THE "SITUATION"... IT SEEMED FORTUITOUS YOU TURNED UP AT THE HOSPITAL. I'VE THOUGHT ABOUT YOU. I LOOK AT YOUR PAINTING EVERY DAY.

She considered asking more about his latent disfunction, but decided to focus on the fact that she'd crossed his mind a time or two. No need to play coy if he was putting it all out there. Kind of exciting to put herself out there, too, even via text. I'VE THOUGHT ABOUT YOU, TOO. GREAT MINDS, RIGHT?

SCOTT: THEY DO THINK ALIKE ☺ SO HOW'S POST-DIVORCE LIFE TREATING YOU THESE DAYS?

With that, a strange floodgate opened. Tipsy and Scott spent the next three hours texting. She gleaned more intimate details about Scott via text in a few hours than she had learned about Will in a month of dating him. Scott was three years older than Tipsy—ALL THE SUDDEN I'M STARING DOWN THE BIG 4-0—and his father died in a car accident when he was four. His mother, a middle school science teacher, raised him on her own in a tiny town outside of Johnson City, in East Tennessee—MY MOTHER IS THE STRONGEST PERSON I KNOW. I'M A MAMA'S BOY AND PROUD OF IT—He got a scholarship to the University of Tennessee, and then another scholarship to Vanderbilt University's medical school. His mother moved to Nashville when he went off to college and she remarried—SUCH A RELIEF TO SEE HER SETTLED AFTER ALL THOSE YEARS OF STRUGGLING—and he was close to his stepfather, a country music executive. He called himself a late bloomer—I WAS A SOCIALLY AWKWARD DORK UNTIL MED SCHOOL—who married Kate, his first real girlfriend.

He asked Tipsy tons of questions about herself, and she fired off her own small town Appalachian background. Her flaky mother, her alcoholic father. Granna—MY ROCK OF AGES. WITHOUT HER I WOULD HAVE ENDED UP IN FOSTER CARE—who passed away a couple months before she headed off to college on her own scholarship. Her marriage to Ayers—I WASN'T A COMPLETE DORK, BUT I WAS AS NAÏVE AS CINDERELLA AT HER FIRST BALL—and her struggles fitting in with his family. The years after she had children when she couldn't paint a thing—LIKE MY INTERNAL CREATIVE WI-FI DISCONNECTED, SO I KEPT TRYING THE WRONG PASSWORD UNTIL I GOT LOCKED OUT.

It wasn't just the typical logistical stuff about life—it was the cause and effect, the feelings and the fallout. Her typing fingers weren't fast enough to keep up with everything she wanted to say. She finally checked the time.

TIPSY: THIS IS CRAZY, BUT IT'S PAST ONE.

SCOTT: WE MADE IT PAST MIDNIGHT, AND THE SPELL DIDN'T WEAR OFF ☺

TIPSY: MY BALLGOWN HAS TURNED INTO AN OLD TEE-SHIRT AND A MESSY BUN.

SCOTT: SINCE I AM A GENTLEMAN, I WILL NOT COMMENT ON WHAT I IMAGINE TO BE THE STATE OF YOUR ATTIRE.

The innuendo made her cheeks burn in the best way. TIPSY: HAHA, SILLY. YOUR IMAGINATION MIGHT BE DISAPPOINTED.

SCOTT: I DOUBT IT. BUT I'LL HAVE CARPAL TUNNEL TOMORROW FROM ALL THIS TYPING.

TIPSY: ME TOO.

SCOTT: SOOO...WE'RE SUPPOSED TO TALK ABOUT THE KIDS. BUT I'D ALSO JUST LIKE TO TALK. IF YOU'RE AVAILABLE, CAN OUR COFFEE CHAT TURN INTO DINNER TOMORROW NIGHT?

She didn't think twice this time before responding. YES. I'D LIKE THAT.

SCOTT: AWESOME. ANY PLACE YOU WANT TO GO? OR AVOID, HAHA?

TIPSY: LET'S AVOID SHEM CREEK. TOO MUCH OF A SCENE. OTHERWISE, I'M UP FOR WHATEVER.

SCOTT: SAY NO MORE RE: SHEM CREEK. I'LL COME UP WITH SOMETHING.

TIPSY: SOUNDS GREAT. GOODNIGHT, SCOTT. IT WAS REALLY NICE CHATTING WITH YOU.

SCOTT: SERIOUSLY. BEST CONVO I'VE HAD IN AGES. TEXT OR OTHERWISE.

TIPSY: NIGHT ☺

SCOTT: SWEET DREAMS.

Tipsy hadn't stayed up so late in a month of Sunday Fundays, but their flirty text marathon left her keyed up, and it took an hour for her to fall asleep. Once her jitters transitioned to tremors of exhaustion, her subconscious mind presented her with an image of Jane, Henry's wife, on her front porch. In her dream, Jane wasn't pale and cavern-eyed. She wore a pink cashmere sweater and pink ballet flats, à la Jillian Yates, instead of her gauzy lavender dress and bare feet. Tipsy woke to echoes of Jane's hearty laughter. For the hundredth time since Jane moved on almost two years ago, she longed to confide in her ghostly girlfriend.

She lay in bed wondering what her dream self said to make Jane laugh. Maybe something about her crush on Scott Brandt. No use denying it anymore. If it looks like a duck, swims like a duck, and quacks like a duck, it's a crush.

He's finer than pearl buttons on a satin dress, Jane. Sexier than a silk chemise. I'm absorbing up his pheromones like a biscuit sopping up gravy.

Jane would have no idea what pheromones were, but she'd get a kick out of Tipsy's quacking anyway.

Tipsy looked at her phone. It was just past six on a Friday morning. No kids. No GQB. She'd snoozed for less than five hours, but she felt wide awake. She got up, donned running clothes, and hit the streets of the Old Village. She hadn't had so much on her mind in ages, and a run always provided clarity.

Priority *numero uno*, Miss Sophie Rose. She wasn't sure what to make of Thomas Bonneau, but the stress of living with him wasn't doing Sophie right. Her thinness and the dark caverns under her eyes worried Tipsy, to say nothing of her depression and anxiety. She'd love to ask Scott for his medical opinion, but she couldn't tell him that Sophie's malaise stemmed from her interactions with a guy who lived through Reconstruction.

Sophie hadn't reached out yet, so Tipsy sent a simple HOW'S IT GOING text before her run. As she jogged down Pitt Street, she reviewed her plan. Paint for a few hours before hitting the Huguenot cemetery, then the Bonneau House to chat with Thomas. Maybe she'd luck out and discover how to send him on his way in record time.

If he *wanted* to go. Even if she discovered how he died, it would still be his choice to move on. |He seemed pretty damn content with his lot.

Next, her mind returned to Scott. *Text* life wasn't *real* life, but she'd never exchanged such personal messages with a man, like swapping diary entries. She could reread them and glean details that would have gone in one ear and out the other in a regular conversation. Such solid background information would make their date less awkward.

So it's a date? asked Granna. *This is a bad idea, Tipsy. Ayers will—*

He doesn't have to know. Shelby made a good point. I haven't dated anyone since Clarice last summer. I've taken time to be on my own and figure things out.

Lindsey made a better point. Yes, he's smart and handsome and seems oddly—how do y'all say it? Smart about feelings?

Emotionally intelligent.

Yes. Surely there's another man in town who isn't an emotional doofus, who also isn't likely to make your ex-husband take you back to court.

I'm worried about how Ayers will react, too. But Shelby was also right about the fishies in the sea. Most of them are too toxic for consumption.

Suit yourself. Granna retreated in a pique. Tipsy picked up the pace, as if to outrun Granna's judgment. They rarely argued, and grudging silence with someone who exists in your own head is no fun. Still, her heart insisted she meet up with Scott.

Maybe the loneliness she'd proudly managed for months—or the chemical reaction she experienced the first time she saw Scott on Ayers's old driveway—were driving her heart. Her pulse picked up and her heartbeat thumped against her temples, reminding her that her head and her heart were ultimately connected. Despite the intriguing nature of these unexpected interactions with Scott, her head wouldn't let her heart forget the agony she'd gone through with Will. Or Big Ayers, for that matter. At thirty-six, she didn't have a great track record when it came to choosing men.

Her phone vibrated against her leg, and she smiled as she remembered Granna's comment about the vibrations in Scott's pants. She slowed to a walk, pulled out the phone, and despite the conflicting messages emanating from her skull and her chest, her smile became a grin when she saw Scott's name.

Scott: Good morning! I'm really looking forward to this evening. Hope your Friday is starting off great.

Tipsy: Me too! And so far, so good.

That's how things were playing out, from her interactions with Scott to Ayers's lack of knowledge of the same. So far, so good. She'd run with it, literally and figuratively. She started jogging again.

⬩✕⬩

Tipsy usually avoided the vicinity of her workplace on days off, but with the French Huguenot Church a block from the GQB, she had no choice. She scored an elusive spot in front of the gallery, beside the HVAC truck. Heat wafted through the propped open door. She peeked inside, but didn't see Shelby, so she didn't feel too bad for avoiding that inferno.

The sunflowers in her painting glowered at her through the window. Shelby often honored Tipsy's work with such prominent placement, and not just because of their friendship. The paintings' unidentifiable charisma had lured many potential buyers into the gallery. They drew innocent artistic bystanders into Tipsy's imaginary world, like the palmetto rose painting had sucked Madame Missouri into its optical whirlpool.

She hadn't provided the sunflowers with company, so they were still lonely. No one was around, so she approached the glass. "I'm working on it. Keep your petals on," she whispered.

She walked down Queen toward the pink church, a Gothic Revival masterpiece with cathedral-style windows and at least a dozen pointy pinnacles, encircled by a short iron fence. The dark caps on each spire reminded her of witches' fingernails. The church was solemnly European yet whimsically Caribbean, like Thomas Bonneau's accent in architectural form. She paused to read the sign on the exterior wall. The congregation was founded around 1685. The current building, circa 1845. It wasn't as large as St. Philip's, St. Michael's, or the Catholic Cathedral, but the original aristocratic French parishioners had fled Louis XIV's righteous papist wrath and its accompanying persecution. Perhaps they preferred to keep a low theological profile. The church's tallest spire subtly poked the Holy City's famously steepled skyline like an unassuming nose in the air.

Tipsy found the gate and entered the oddly cozy graveyard. She wandered the rows of monuments, and as expected, she found interesting backstories on the legible markers. Fear made the Huguenots uproot their families, board rickety boats, and sail across the uncaring ocean. The concept of America would have been a foreign fairytale to the seventeenth-century French, whose own country was the envy of the western world. Upon arrival, Charlestowne must have seemed like a lawless, disease-ridden backwater village. The engraved stones, with their references to sickness and wars and brutally short lifespans, reiterated that Tipsy had twenty-first-century problems.

The graves were closer together than the ones in the St. Philip's graveyard. Some stones had toppled backward in granite and slate swoons. Others split under the conflicting pressure of driving rain and harsh sunlight, or sunk into the dirt like the deceased were pulling their own memories down with them. She stopped before a six-foot-tall memorial that reminded her of a miniature Washington Monument. Two cracked sarcophaguses and several smaller stones gathered around the central edifice like weary parishioners awaiting a repetitive sermon. Tipsy stepped over the short marble border wall, traced the embossed *B* on the obelisk with one finger, and read the names in front of her.

Doctor Rene Bonneau
1830-1880
Agnes Barre Bonneau
1839-1863

She walked around the monument and read the names on each face, before turning to the sarcophagi and the simpler headstones. More Bonneaus. Perhaps Thomas's grandparents, uncles, aunts, or cousins. The smallest markers revealed only initials and years. *B.B., 1825,* and *L.B., 1840.* Little stones for tiny people who had lived their entire lives in a single year.

She crouched to brush grass away from the collapsed stones and attempted to discern their disjointed messages. When she stood, she pressed her thumbs into the small of her aching back.

He's not here.

Granna spoke up for the first time since their morning tiff. *Seems odd. This family prayed together, and stayed together.*

Maybe I missed him somehow.

She wandered the rows for thirty more minutes, but unless Thomas Bonneau had changed his name, he wasn't in the cemetery with his twenty-odd relations. Deflated, she returned to her truck. She drove toward Broad Street, and the glowing pink monolith of the Bonneau house.

It looks like a giant tipped-over Pepto-Bismol bottle, said Granna, as Tipsy parked in front of the house.

Totally. Tipsy was eager to put the tension behind them. *An enormous cattywampus antacid container.*

Jillian wasn't home, so Tipsy punched in the entry code and pushed the gate. It slid open agreeably, but this time it let out a tiny squeak, as if it recognized her and felt comfortable speaking up. The gravel and sand driveway once again wreaked havoc on her home pedicure. When she stepped onto the piazza, she slipped off her flip-flops and swiped at the bottoms of her feet to dislodge irritating rocks. She had just squiggled her toes back into her flops when Thomas Bonneau spoke up.

"Miss Jilly went to the market."

Tipsy's eyes followed the sound of his voice toward the joggling board. He sat on the board with his legs splayed out before him and his hands laced behind his head. Azalea bushes bloomed on the other side of the piazza railing. He looked like an angel reclining on the edge of a pink and green cloud. An *overdressed* angel. Just looking at his overcoat added a layer to Tipsy's extant sweatiness.

He ran a finger through the blossoms poking between the railings. "I visited Richmond once, in the springtime. Up north, azalea bushes burn brighter, but they burn out fast and go back to sleep. Our azaleas are awake for months, so they take their time blooming."

Tipsy sat on the opposite end of the board. "Richmond is up north, huh?"

"To me it was. My northernmost exposure to the wide world."

"You call her Jilly? Sophie's mother."

He nodded and scratched his cheek. "Her own mother called her Jilly. Her father, too. And her sister."

"Catherine Rose, right? Jillian said she died young. Even younger than you."

"Yes. She only lived in this house for about a year before she passed."

"Was Catherine like Sophie?"

"Yes. Her parents were always sending her off to some special hospital. Never seemed to help her much, poor child."

"I mean, was she a *seer*? Like *me* and Sophie?"

Thomas gave his chest a good scratch. "She always talked to people her family couldn't see, but she aimed her diatribe at those trapped in her own head, not stuck in purgatory. I suppose it's *possible* Catherine was a seer, but she saw so many *other things*, one hallucination blended into another. A sad, lonely creature."

Tipsy sought a way to ask Thomas about the memory she'd seen without giving it away. "*You* must have been lonely in this big house after your father died."

He shrugged. "The house was always buzzing. Boarders coming and going. We had the same maids for years. Rachel and Susan. And Drake, who did the manly jobs around the place."

"So…managing the house kept you busy?"

"It was too much for me, what with my other…pursuits. I employed a housekeeper the last year or so. Patty was her name. The daughter of my father's late friend. A simple country girl. One of those thick, hardy creatures. Surprisingly competent, until she got too big for her bonnet, as they might say. She forgot her place. You know how it is with help."

"Nope, I don't. I'm a one woman show." Tipsy waited for more, but he didn't offer it. She subtly switched topics. "Do you know how *you* died?"

"Why would I dwell on such unpleasant things?"

"Just curious. Maybe you heard about it over the years."

"The house passed out of the family after I died. No one left who cared to speak about me."

"Jillian told me it remained a boarding house after you passed away."

He nodded. "The boarding house years were more interesting than the family eras. I gathered all manner of news from the boarders, even if I couldn't speak with them. A few seers like yourself passed through. Fascinating English fellow spent a month here during one of the great wars. He kept me abreast of the goings on in the world. Particularly about that odious German fellow. Heinz, was it?"

"You must mean Hitler. The Second World War."

"Sad times, those. How is Sophie? Is she coming home soon?"

"Not sure. Jillian may move her into a hotel. She's too fragile to have her supernatural abilities in her face."

"Jilly must be anxious for her to return, and I hate for that poor girl to be in limbo because of me. I'll have to stay away from her. She won't even see my pallid, smiling visage welcoming her home."

"Look. You seem like a nice guy, but I don't know you. Neither does Jillian. You clearly enjoy talking to living people. Maybe the temptation would be too much for you."

"All I can give is my word." Scritch, scratch.

"I want to give you the benefit of the doubt. I hope your intentions are good, but there are a lot of selfish people out there. Alive and dead."

"Fair enough. Thank you for being honest. But I hope y'all don't punish Sophie Rose for my presence. I want nothing more than to spend eternity on this porch, watching the slow bloom of the azaleas."

He seemed so *reasonable*. Tipsy almost asked to touch him and send him on to wherever ghosts went, but reasonableness aside, he was also the supernatural version of an overheated pig in cool mud. With no indication he'd help her to help him, she had only one way to get information. The time for finagling was upon her, but whenever she went on a trip down a ghost's memory lane, she briefly lost consciousness, although she'd gotten better at staying upright. During her last peek into Thomas's mind, she woke on her knees, as if she'd tripped over him. Still, Thomas needed to equate her *lights out* with a good old-fashioned swoon.

Head rush, said Granna. *You have 'em all the time since you don't drink enough water.*

Tipsy looked down at her own bare leg. On a whim, she smacked her thigh. "A spider!" She jumped to her feet and grabbed the sides of her head. "Whoa. I got up too fast. I feel…lightheaded."

"You should drink some water," said Thomas.

"I've heard that before." She wobbled in Thomas's direction and braced herself. She needed to plop her butt into the perfect spot. Touch him, without tipping headfirst off the joggling board.

She took two steps back, one to the right, and braced herself. She sat on Thomas Bonneau's lap.

—————◆✕◆—————

Tipsy blinks, but when the flashing yellow lights clear, it's still dark. She splays her hands before her face, and the outline of her fingers slowly sharpens. A halfmoon casts a bluish glow over the cobblestones under her feet. Her ghostly friends emit a similar luminosity in the dark. Perhaps the moon is dead, too.

The cobblestones mean she's somewhere in downtown Charleston, so she peers around for a familiar landmark. Smallish, boxy houses line the street, and the German Fire Company building is on her left. She recognizes the relatively nondescript but notorious Pink House by its flamingo-colored walls, black shutters, and reddish gambrel-tiled roof. One of the oldest buildings in town, it once served as a tavern and a brothel. If she remembers correctly, Chalmers Street was the heart of Charleston's old red-light district.

Movement on the stoop of a gray house catches her eye. A man and a woman are framed in the light of the open doorway. It must be unusually cold, because she can see their breath. Before the closing door eclipses the cheery firelight emanating from the house, Tipsy recognizes Thomas Bonneau's dark hair and refined profile.

Thomas takes the woman's hand and tugs her down a few stairs to the street. Tipsy can't make out her features, but her reddish hair looks to be a bad 1800's dye job. She wears a low-cut red dress and a lacy black shawl over her shoulders, like a gypsy crossed with a grieving widow.

The woman misses the last step, stumbles, and falls against Thomas. He's got on dark clothes—perhaps his black overcoat—but she can't be sure. It's too much dark on dark, with no contrast.

"Watch the stones, Ginger," he says. "That's my clumsy girl."

Ginger—if that's her real name—giggles. "I'm as suuuuure footed as…a mule. A…big, ol' clippity-cloppity mule."

Given her slurred speech, she's drunk. She's also outside with Thomas, with no chaperone, after dark. She's not a South of Broad society type.

Red dress, red-light district, *thinks Tipsy.*

"Where we going?" she asks. "Tom, where?"

"Somewhere that rascal James Drayton can't bother us."

She laughs. "Jamie Drayton is an old…friend."

"I thought I was your only friend these days."

"'Course you are. But should I be rude to my old friends? Let's go back inside—"

"No. I want to take a stroll."

She lags behind him. "You're fussing at me, but you have an unmarried woman…living in your house."

"Patience? What about her?"

"She's young and pretty."

"Young, yes. Pretty…debatable." He leads her toward the intersection of Chalmers and State Street, and takes a left. Lumpy cobblestones become flat dirt, but the woman stumbles anyway.

"I'm tired and it's cold," she whines, and tries to back up. "I want to go back."

He mutters something Tipsy can't hear, and the woman says, "Stop being cross, Tommy."

Thomas's reply is still unintelligible. Tipsy trots after them, hoping to get closer. If he's fussing and cross, she should get some emotions from him. Maybe enough to help her figure out what's happening in this weird memory.

They duck down Unity Alley, a narrow brick and stone passageway connecting State and East Bay Street. George Washington himself once took his leisure at McCrady's Tavern and Long Room, and in Tipsy's when, a revamped version of Mr. McCrady's historic restaurant is squished into that narrow space. In this time, the buildings appear to be rough-and-tumble warehouses. They jostle against one another, as if to avoid falling into the alleyway. Wisteria branches crisscross the sliver of open sky, and the ivy-covered walls beside Thomas and his lady friend press in like overgrown hedges in a garden maze.

They momentarily disappear into the alley's skinny canyon. When Tipsy catches up, her eyes must readjust to the lack of moonlight. Ginger huddles against the wall, like she might be sick. Thomas pulls her upright. She's talking, but Tipsy can't make out her mumbling. She tries to open herself up to Thomas's emotions, but again, there's nothing there.

Suddenly, the remaining light seeps out of the memory. Thomas and Ginger fade into the darkness. Even the fiery reddish tint of her hair disappears.

Tipsy can tell the memory isn't supposed to end this way, but she cannot find Thomas. There is no intoxicated prostitute. No Unity Alley or blueish moon. Only Tipsy in a silent, frightening black void. She reaches for the ivy-covered walls, but she meets nothing but whatever passes for air in these visions. She turns to run back into the moonlight, and wakes up.

Chapter 5

F or a second, she thought she'd actually smacked into an ivy-covered wall in Unity Alley, but natural daylight reassured her. She'd slumped over into one of Jillian's planters, face first into some petunias. She opened her phone's camera to check the damage. Scratches near her chin and right eye, but makeup would cover them.

The piazza wobbled as she sat up. She gripped the end of the joggling board and took a brief inventory of her vital systems. No nausea, so she stood. Her head throbbed, but like a popsicle headache, when she squinched her eyes, the pain dissipated. Nagging thirst proved to be the worst of her supernatural hangover.

She went inside, poured herself a glass of water, and returned to the porch with the idea of waiting on Jillian. She felt smug satisfaction. Not only had she avoided regurgitation, she'd secured two memories in as many days. Her clandestine creeping had indeed proved more effective than her past candid cajoling. After thirty minutes, Jillian was a no-show, and Thomas didn't reappear. Given today's progress with both herons and ghosts, Tipsy decided to head home and take some Tylenol. Give it time to kick in before she met Scott, and ward off a deferred headache.

She thought about the latest memory as she drove up Rutledge Avenue toward the Crosstown and the beginning of Interstate 26. Still no emotions from Thomas. She wasn't sure exactly what had happened on Chalmers Street, but it wasn't a simple chat between the boss and his hired help.

A different kind of hired help, said Granna.

He was jealous and she was stumbling drunk…in the pitch dark, down an empty alley. Not a recipe for a peaceful interaction.

You can't be sure. Maybe he's naturally cool, calm, and collected.

That kind of detachment doesn't mesh with what I've seen of his gregariously enthusiastic personality.

Better a talkative, happy, relaxed ghost than a sullen, angry, explosive one.

Patience was center stage in the first memory, and Thomas's lady friend mentioned her. She must *be relevant. I wonder why she goes by Patty, when her real name is so pretty.* She frowned. Patience. *Why does that sound familiar?*

Doesn't ring any bells for me. Hopefully you'll learn more about her in the next memory. Maybe you should go back this evening rather than having dinner with Dr. Brandt.

I need time to recover between memories. I'm just getting back into the swing of it.

The more you practice, the sooner you'll be swinging from the rafters.

Tipsy let Granna's comments lie with the clothes strewn across her bedroom in her search for the perfect outfit. She settled on a short periwinkle dress with fluttery sleeves, then fixed up her face and hair, and drove toward Sullivan's Island. Her jitters were jitterier with every block. As she crossed the intersection where Coleman Boulevard turned into Ben Sawyer Boulevard, her shuffling music library chose a somewhat obscure song by folk rocker Jason Isbell.

Palmetto rose in the sidewalk mud…curly white stem and a big green bud…

By the time she reached the Ben Sawyer Bridge, anxiety had shortened her breath. She opened the window, even though the wind would muss up her hair. The smell of pluff mud soothed her. The Intracoastal Waterway was an aquatic interstate, teaming with boats. Mr. Isbell's soulful voice singing about the beaches of Sullivan's Island— *where the big boats roll in*—synced with the scenery. With every verse of the song, she closed in on a rendezvous that frightened her even as it drew her in. As if Scottie Brandt was beaming her up to the deck of the *USS Enterprise*. Thoroughly scrambling her molecules.

Tipsy was meeting her ex-in-law for dinner. *Really* meeting him, Granna and Lindsey's words of wisdom be damned.

I'll follow my own free will...

The song encouraged her. That she *had*, and that she *would*. She'd weighed everyone's advice, and what she knew of Scott so far, and made the decision to get to know him better.

She kept driving to Sullivan's Island. She allowed herself to be sucked into Scott Brandt's gravity.

———+)(+———

Tipsy found a parking spot a block down Middle Street, across from The Obstinate Daughter, a restaurant known for its whimsical name and delicious, eclectic food. The OD took its handle from a Revolutionary War era political cartoon that likened the South Carolina colonists to rebellious teenagers. It proved an apt moniker, as the place had been stubbornly popular for years.

Scott had suggested they arrive as soon as the doors opened for dinner. She balanced speed walking for punctuality's sake with remaining sweat-free for her deodorant's sake. She found a gap between an orange Clemson-themed golfcart and a Range Rover and jaywalked her butt across the street. She passed the outdoor diners and clipped up the stairs to the main restaurant on the second floor. The hostess greeted her like a musketeer guarding the personal chambers of the Sun King.

"Reservation, ma'am?"

"No, I'm meeting someone—" Scott's blue eyes met hers across the restaurant. He waved, and her stomach went flippity-floppity again. "There he is, at the bar."

The hostess lowered her figurative lance and let Tipsy pass.

Scott stood and put a hand on her back before helping her scoot her barstool into place. She took in the rustic grayish wide-planked wood walls, dainty blue and white curtains and tilework, and thick nautical ropes and quirky natural fiber light fixtures strung from the vaulted ceiling—like a spa, inside a church, inside the Mayflower.

"I gave the hostess my name," said Scott, "but I doubt we'll get a table. You okay eating at the bar?"

"Sure." She ordered a Bud Lite and Scott ordered a Guinness.

"We match," he said. He wore khakis and a pale blue button down. "Your dress and my shirt. Even the walls in this place."

She smiled. "A soothing palette. I wear a lot of this color."

"So do I."

"It brings out your eyes," she said, and immediately grimaced. "Oh, lord. I must sound like a salesgirl at The Gap."

"No, you don't. This color brings out your eyes, too. They remind me of thunderclouds. That's a compliment. Thunderstorms are beautiful and powerful."

"Thank you. Interesting comparison, since I'm finally starting to feel powerful again."

"You gave birth to three kids. *That's* a superpower."

"In a way, yes. But nothing like how I felt before I got married, when the whole world was my Sistine Chapel. Things are getting better the past couple years. Especially since I'm cranking out the paintings again." She couldn't mention her supernatural accomplishments, arguably the stronger source of her burgeoning confidence. "I've learned more about myself in the past two years than I did in the decade before it."

"I agree. Sounds so cliché, but growth is painful. I think about the roots breaking through the sidewalk when I walk downtown. There's a metaphor for the last couple years in there somewhere. Still, I wouldn't trade the lessons to avoid the agony. Maybe that sounds…hyperbolic."

"Not to me, it doesn't. How do you define your personal agony?"

"There's the obvious. Missing the kids. Fighting with Kate."

"Y'all fight a lot?"

"Not when we were married. Our marriage was more T.S. Eliot. *This is the way the world ends—*"

"*—not with a bang, with a whimper.*"

He nodded. "We mostly ignored each other, but when she got mad, watch out. She regularly threatened me with divorce, but when *I* pulled the plug, she lost it."

"Ayers was the same. I always felt like a failure because he was so unhappy, then I wanted out, and he suddenly claimed to be heartbroken."

"Kate never claimed to be heartbroken. She was enraged. Nonplussed. She couldn't fathom I'd actually leave her." He shook his head. "I shouldn't talk negatively about her—"

"It's okay. Ayers has already told me she's a *my-way-or-the-highway* gal. And she can maintain the silent treatment for days."

He chuckled. "Can't believe he told you something like that."

"That's Ayers. One day he hates me, the next day I'm his therapist."

"Kate and I didn't fight a lot because—"

"You wanted to keep the peace."

Now a grin. "Exactly."

"Same with us. I crept around like I lived in an emotional minefield."

"Oh, boy. Now the tension between them makes sense. They spent years with spouses who tolerated their behavior—"

"I can't speak for you, but I prefer *enabled*. I understand how I contributed to our family ship sinking like the *Hunley* hitting the bottom of the Charleston Harbor."

"I did the same thing. It was easier to focus on work and the kids and let her temper run the show. So now they're together. Doesn't sound like the makings of a peaceful relationship."

"No. But it might work for Ayers. He thrives off high emotion. He did say she's pretty controlling, though. Wants to know what he's doing at all times. Jealous, too."

"Truer words have never been spoken."

"Not sure how *that* will go over with Ayers."

The server returned, and they ordered another round of drinks. The conversation raced by in a spoken version of their texts from the previous night. By the time the bartender politely harassed them about a food order, Tipsy understood Scott's marriage better than she ever understood

Will's. As if sensing her thoughts, Scott said, "Is it bad to talk about our marriages? I don't want to be some guy who always talks about the past."

"I don't think so. Helps to avoid making mistake after mistake. My friend Pamella said people either repeat the same patterns or overcorrect."

"What did you do?"

"I dated a guy for about a year. Will. I met him through mutual friends and we got in pretty tight with our kids, so there were multiple levels of complications. But it just wasn't right. He was a partial overcorrection. Time revealed that Will and Ayers are polar opposites, yet cut from the same cloth."

"Dichotomously dysfunctional."

"An oxymoron—heavy on the *moron*. On my end, for not reading the signs before I leaped on that emotional hamster wheel."

"Don't be so hard on yourself. Maybe it's something about people with *W* names."

"You have a Wendy? Winona? A Winifred?"

"Ha. Whitney was my oxymoron of choice."

Perhaps a reference to the Hellraising Highlighter. She posed her follow-up question casually. "What happened there?"

"We went to the same high school. She was a hairdresser back in Johnson City. Never married, no kids. Big partier.

Kind of a wild child, you know?"

"I've been single in Mount Pleasant for several years. I'm familiar with over-thirty wild children."

"She reached out to me over social media when a buddy told her I was getting divorced. For me it was a weekend thing. I went up there to escape when I didn't have the kids. Then she got a job in Mount Pleasant and moved here without consulting me."

"Yikes. *That* sounds complicated."

"Yeah. It was." He took a sip of his beer and picked up the menu. "I'm thinking about the grouper. You had the farro? It's great."

"That's one of my favorites."

"Want to split one?"

"Sure." Tipsy wasn't quite ready to change the subject. She wondered how Kate and Whitney were oxymoronically similar yet different. Sedate versus wild? Mutually controlling, temperamental, and grudge-holding?

"So you eventually ended it with Whitney?" she asked tentatively, after they ordered their meals.

He nodded. "I finally sent a text ending it. She didn't seem to care much."

"A relationship that ends via text is probably not meant to be."

"Yeah." He finished his beer, and then took a sip of water.

"I'm sorry. I'm being nosy—"

"No. Not at all. I don't know how much to say about this kind of stuff. I don't want you to think I'm bashing all the women in my life. Especially not the mother of my children."

"I understand, but you're reiterating what Ayers already told me about Kate. I don't feel like I'm bashing Ayers anymore. I spent years defending him, and now I'm being honest about who he is. That leads me to how we ended up here—how will their relationship affect the kids? I was happy when Ayers started dating Kate. She seemed like a strong female role model and a good mom."

"She is those things. I believe she genuinely likes your kids."

"I think Ayers feels the same way about yours. Last summer, Little Ayers mentioned he heard them arguing. Otherwise, my kids haven't said anything about tension over there beyond their usual complaints about their dad's moodiness."

"Tristan mentioned their fighting a few times. One morning Chloe overheard Kate on the phone with her mother, complaining about Ayers being an asshole."

Tipsy leaned back as the bartender placed a steaming gourmet pizza in front of her. "Ugh. I haven't heard any of that, but if Big Ayers is willing to talk to me, I'll keep you in the loop."

"Thanks. I want them to work it out. If she's happy—"

"She won't give you so much grief."

"That's like the fifth time you've finished my sentences tonight. You sure you're not the shrink?"

"You're the one who psychoanalyzes everyone, remember? How am I doing so far?"

"Can't diagnose you with anything...yet."

Tipsy laughed. "Tell me about your work."

"It's low tide. How about we finish eating and take this convo down to the beach?"

After dinner, they walked down the street to the long boardwalk beach entry at Station 21. Butterflies swarmed the yellow and white flowers in the thickets on either side of the boardwalk. Scott put his hands on Tipsy's waist and gently moved her aside when they passed wet dogs and exuberant kids swinging sandy boogie boards. A few seagulls circled overhead. They shrieked like children embarrassed by a display of parental affection.

Tipsy and Scott left their shoes in the sand when they reached the boardwalk's end. Scott meticulously tucked his socks into his loafers and lined up both pairs of shoes like a professional cobbler displaying his wares. He rolled up each pants leg exactly three times. Tipsy twisted her hair into a side braid.

"Which way?" he asked.

Tipsy pointed south, toward the clunky black and white lighthouse. An uninspired midcentury architect had driven it into the dunes like an inelegant Excalibur. "That way. Toward the sunset."

"Seems a little soon to walk off into the sunset." He took her hand. "But maybe not."

Soft, creamy sand hardened into compact gray as they splashed through a tide pool and approached the flat, quiet ocean. Footprints lingered with precise definition in the hardpack. Dog prints, human prints, bird prints. Sandpipers played tag with gentle waves and a rigid airborne pelican infantry soared past. Tipsy and Scott stepped over the jellyfish blobs that beached themselves this time of year like rejects from Granna's gelatin recipes.

Tipsy listened, enthralled, as he spoke passionately about his profession. True to their Sir Mix-a-Lot inspired joke the day she met him, Scott loved the human brain, and he could not lie. He was board certified in neurology and psychiatry, so he'd studied that mysterious organic computer's effect on physical capabilities and behavioral patterns. "I'm more on the psychiatry side these days, but neurology is helpful in diagnoses and comorbidities."

"What made you lean toward psychiatry?"

"We volunteered at the local homeless shelter during medical school. So many of those people are mentally ill, and it's frightening how vulnerable they are. Working in the hospital, I can help the weakest of the weak. The most forgotten. It's a good feeling at the end of the day."

"It's rare to have such a meaningful career."

"Yours is equally meaningful."

"You think?"

"Tipsy, your artwork is amazing. I'm a doctor because I'm disciplined and I studied—"

"You're also brilliant, from what I know so far."

"Thank you, but you're the one in a million talent. Your work speaks to people. You've left your mark on the world." He gently bumped his hip against hers. "I admire you."

"Right back at you."

They walked in comfortable silence for a while, until he broke it. "This is the best night I've had in two years."

"Me too."

"You don't have to say that."

She stopped in her tracks. "I am *absolutely* not just saying that."

He pulled her closer. "Driving out here tonight, I wasn't sure if I was supposed to call this a date."

"I will if you will."

He kissed her, and the wind sighed. If Tipsy had joined Henry and Jane in the afterlife at that moment, at least she could say she'd experienced a fairytale kiss.

Chapter 6

After the girls' Saturday morning volleyball clinic, Tipsy returned to the psych ward to visit Sophie. A recent shower had pinkened her skin and she'd slicked her hair back in a wet bun. She wore a black hoodie and pink plaid pajama pants, and sipped from a green Yeti tumbler emblazoned with *KAPPA ZETA*.

"I was a KZ, too," said Tipsy, "at the University of South Carolina."

"Cool." Sophie flashed a KZ hand sign. Her twisted fingers were supposed to form a *K* and a *Z*, but despite her advanced fine motor skills, Tipsy had never gotten the hang of it.

"It's kind of silly and full of drama," said Sophie, "but it's fun."

"That sums up sorority life. At least you get cool merch out of it, like that tumbler."

"Mom harasses me about drinking enough water," she said. "She wants me to drink at least two of these a day."

"It's because she's worried. If you're throwing up, you need to stay hydrated."

"I haven't been as nauseated in the hospital as I was at home."

"Good. My Granna still harasses me about hydration from the afterlife. When I was your age, she'd ask me, *Tipsy, is your pee clear?*"

"Oh my *God*. I would literally die if my mom asked me that."

Hmph. You took my advice to heart, said Granna. *You have the most hydrated kids in Mount Pleasant.*

Tipsy threw Granna a bone. "I'm on the hydration bandwagon myself. If my kids complain about any aches or pains, I make them drink a glass of water."

I feel vindicated, said Granna.

The overlapping chats with Sophie and Granna sparked an idea. During Granna's lifetime, Tipsy and Granna could communicate without words. She'd interacted with one other living clairvoyant—an older African American woman who regularly walked up and down Rifle Range Road. Tipsy referred to her as the Walking Lady, and she spoke up once in Tipsy's mind as she mused to herself in a traffic jam.

Hey Sophie, she said in her head. *Yo! Can you hear me? Helllllllooooo!*

Sophie had no reaction. She checked her phone and then fiddled with the end of her braid. *She's not on my wavelength, Granna.*

As we've learned, these things are different for everyone.

A slightly disappointed Tipsy pointed at the cup. "Have you talked to any of your college friends?"

"Not really. They texted me when I first left school, but they gave up when I didn't answer much. They probably think I'm insane."

"Have you ever told *any* of your friends about your talent?"

"Are you kidding? No way." She opened her phone again and started flipping through Instagram. Tipsy waited for her to speak, but she didn't, so Tipsy went on.

"I met Thomas."

"Huh." A pause in the scrolling, but nothing else.

"He seems pretty with it for a ghost. Friendly. Happy to talk to me. I can see how you became friends with him. Is he always like that?"

"Yeah. He's…cool. Nice. Understanding. Totally different from the immature frat bros at school."

"Don't be too hard on those boys. Thomas has had over a century to grow up."

She hugged her knees. "What did you tell Mom about him?"

"Not much. I wanted to think about it. Get some feedback from you."

"Do you have to tell her we're friends? She'll freak out."

"I'm not going to lie to her. She's right to be worried, Sophie, after what happened."

She took a long, irritable slurp from her straw.

"You and your mom aren't close right now—"

"Wow. What a brilliant observation."

"—but she says y'all used to be pretty tight. What happened?"

"I realized she's toxic. Hang around her for a while, you'll agree with me."

Tipsy searched for commonality beyond ghosts and KZ. "I'm not close to my mother, either."

"Is she a shallow, snobby bitch?"

This young lady is pretty rude, said Granna. *The psych ward isn't an excuse to be a jackass.*

"Whoa. That's harsh," said Tipsy. "As for my mom, she's as shallow as a mud puddle, but she's not in a position to be snobby."

"Mom always claims she's *so worried* about me, but she's more disappointed in me."

Tipsy tried to hide her distaste for Sophie's disrespect and downright nastiness toward her mother. Jillian's overzealous concern for her daughter's well-being put her leagues ahead of Denise McNair Denning, who exposed Tipsy to her father's alcoholism throughout her childhood, abandoned her when she was fourteen, and only got in touch with Tipsy when she wanted money. "Why is she disappointed by you?"

"I'm *crazy*, of course, and I'm not like her, or my sisters. They're all, like, *hardcore*. Doctors and lawyers and executives."

"You have no interest in any of that?"

"None. *Nooo* thanks."

"What were you studying in college?"

"I hadn't decided yet. I like art. But I'm not into drawing, like you."

"There are plenty of ways to be artistic. What do you like?"

"Flowers."

"Growing them?"

"I mean, yeah. That's one reason I love BeeBee's house. I wanted to bring the gardens back to life, but Mom called it a waste of time until she finished the pool and the rest of the landscaping. So I stuck to the planters and flower boxes on the piazza. Has Mom been taking care of them?"

"She must be keeping those flowers hydrated, too, because the porch looked amazing to me." Tipsy pictured the glorious, colorful annuals fighting for space on the first floor piazza. "Girl, you got one hell of a green thumb."

"Thanks. I like growing flowers, but I also like *arranging* them. When Mom drags me to events with her—benefits and openings and stuff—the flowers are my favorite part. My Pinterest board is all flowers. I follow floral designers on Instagram. I *love* wedding bouquets—" She squirmed. "I sound like a weirdo."

"Not at all. Floral design is an artform, and a career. Have you told your mom?"

"She *knows* I love flowers. When we moved to Charleston, I was, like, *obsessed*."

"A lot of flowers around here, and a lot of weddings."

"I told her that. She doesn't care how I feel. I have a trust fund. My own money." She glared. "Eventually I'm going to do what I want to do."

Good lord. She's not only rude, she's spoiled.

My own mama would have given her a swift kick on her rear end, said Granna.

"Maybe she's surprised by the idea," said Tipsy.

"I don't want to talk about her anymore. I want to get out of here and go *home*! When can I *leave*?"

"Your mom is understandably worried about you interacting with Thomas. She thought about y'all staying in a hotel—"

"No. No. *No!*"

A nurse peeked into the room. "Everything okay in here?"

"We're just fine," said Tipsy, with a friendly wave, and the nurse disappeared.

Sophie pressed her fingers into her eyes. "I'm sorry. I'm low-key going crazy in here. What if...what if I stay in the backhouse? That's what we call the old servants' quarters. Near the pool. Thomas can walk outside on the piazzas, and go a little way into the yard, but no farther."

"Hmmm. That makes sense. There are limits to every haunting, and that property is huge. You promise you'll stay in there?"

"Yeah. There's a guest room in there, and a big bathroom, and even a kitchen. I'll have everything I need."

"A more convenient arrangement than a hotel."

"You'll talk to my mom? And Thomas? So he knows what's happening."

"Yes. She'll probably want to talk to Dr. Brandt, so you may be here a couple more days."

"Dr. Brandt is the hot dad, right?"

Tipsy smiled despite her annoyance with Sophie's overall irascibility. "Yes. That's him. He'll be in Monday morning."

"But will you go to Legare Street *today* and talk to Mom and Thomas?"

Tipsy nodded. Not unlike her mother, when Sophie said *jump*, she expected Tipsy to go all Van Halen on the situation.

Tipsy said her goodbyes and left the room as the nurse entered to check Sophie's vitals. *What do you think, Granna?*

About your love life?

No! About Sophie. Aside from her delightful disposition.

She claims she's going crazy in here, but crazy is what got her here in the first place. You think she'll keep her promise to stay in the backhouse? Such an obstinate and spoiled child might tell y'all to go to hell once she breaks out of here.

I don't know. But she can't stay in a hotel for months. Things are going well, but I can't predict how long it will take to understand Thomas's death. We're stuck with her for a while.

And her battle ax mama.

Tipsy entered the elevator and pressed the lobby button. *Jillian is a battle ax, but I would have given anything to have a mother go to war for me like that.*

I wish I'd raised one for you. I'll never understand what went wrong with your mama.

It's okay, Granna. Your relationship with Mama was complicated. My relationship with her—if you can call it that—is just as confusing. At least we had each other.

As sometimes happened when Tipsy was deep in thought, a memory came back to her. Not a *normal* memory. She looked back at her own life the way she looked into a ghost's past. She always thought of them as her movie memories. As she watched the elevator buttons descend, she found herself back in Martinville. In a strange way, it comforted her to remember that even then, she hadn't understood her mother.

◆✕◆

The Martinville Town Park is Tipsy's version of Disney World. A happy place, made happier by the little details. The squeak of the swing as Mama pushes her. The way her stomach drops and lifts with the swing's momentum. Granna on the bench behind them, exchanging friendly gossip with Mrs. Berger from church. Tipsy is only five, and the day seems about perfect to her so far.

Granna, Mama, and Tipsy just left church. Mama usually doesn't go to church. She either sleeps late or she goes to her job at the Texaco station. Daddy never goes. He always sleeps late, because his work is something he does at night, although Tipsy isn't sure where his work is. Mama says he's "going to the bar" so maybe it's a place where they make candy bars. That would be fun, but Daddy doesn't bring home candy bars. Sometimes Tipsy looks in the brown bags he's always carrying, but they have bottles inside, not chocolate.

When Tipsy was real little, her PopPop went to church with her and Granna. He's sick now with the cancer, *which is worse than a cold or an earache or even a throw up bug, so he stays home for some* peace-and-quiet *on Sunday mornings.*

Granna wears nice black pants and a blue shirt with her hair pinned up on her head. Her earrings are plastic jewels and they clip on her ears. Tipsy tried them once and they hurt so bad she snatched them off, but Granna doesn't mind them. Her mama, Denise, looks pretty in a green dress that makes her eyes look bright. She just got her hair done, so it's real blonde. She's even wearing pink lipstick.

Tipsy is wearing her yellow Easter dress with the flowers sewn on the collar, even though Easter already happened. It's her nicest dress, and it was Mama's when she was little, so Tipsy likes to wear it every week. The dress's scalloped edges float around her like a bird's feathers. Her black saddle shoes and her white lacy socks woosh over the playground mulch as she swings.

It's a perfect day, what with having donuts at church with Mama and Granna and the three of them looking all fancy. During the service, she saw a strange little boy sitting by himself in one of the first pews. He gave her a big gap-toothed smile. She grinned back and wrinkled her nose at him, and then they both stuck out their tongues, until Mama bopped her on the head with her church program.

Mrs. Berger goes walking on down the street, and now there's no one at the park except Tipsy, Granna, Mama, and one other family having a picnic under a big oak tree. Tipsy gets bored on the swing, so she says, "Ready to get down, Mama."

Mama grabs the swing chain and it whips Tipsy around. It's a little scary but also fun and she laughs. Mama laughs, too, and says, "Hang tight, baby monkey!"

Tipsy jumps down and Mama joins Granna on the bench. They smoke cigarettes. Tipsy wishes they wouldn't because those things stink, but they never listen to her when she's whiny, so she runs to the slide. As she slows down, and the sound of her own pounding feet grinding on the mulch quiets, she hears something else.

Someone crying.

At first, she doesn't see anyone. Then the crying gets louder. As loud as a baby screaming, but it doesn't sound like a baby. It's not squeaky enough. It sounds more like Mama, when she gets mad and yells at Daddy.

Tipsy spins in a slow circle under the slide. Her eyes settle on a female form sitting on the merry-go-round. That circular, spinning thing scares her when the big kids push it too fast and she can't get off.

It's a woman who looks younger than Mama, but not too much. She wears a long gray dress with an apron and brown boots. Her dress has a high collar and long sleeves. Her brown curly hair is mostly in a bun, but escaped pieces stick up around her head like a lion's mane. She has a stub nose and a square chin.

She's not talking to anyone Tipsy can see, so maybe she's talking to her own self. "If I don't find the pig, we'll all starve. They probably 'et it up themselves already. Damn Yankee soldiers. Where is that damn pig? Damn pig! Daaaamn piiiiig!"

She walks toward Tipsy, who peeks at her from behind the slide's support poles.

"Here, pig! Here, pig-pig-pig! Here, piiiiiig! Goddamnit!"

Her use of the lord's name in vain scares Tipsy enough to send her shooting out from under the slide. She runs to her mother and Granna on the bench. Straight into their cloud of smoke, no matter the stink. Granna drops her cigarette and steps on it as Tipsy squeezes into the space between them. "Mama, Granna—the lady. The lady is so mad—"

"What lady?" Mama holds her cigarette away from Tipsy. Tipsy wishes she'd snuff it out.

"The lady in the long dress over there who lost her pig—"

Mama laughs. "Girl, what are you talking about?"

"The lady, Mama!" Tipsy jabs a finger toward the slide, but to her surprise, the lady is gone. "Oh. She's not there. But she was—"

"Don't be silly. It's just us. Ain't we lucky to have the park all to ourselves?"

"But Mama, I saw a lady—"

"Shhh, sugar," says Granna. "I bet you did."

"Mama," says Tipsy's mama, who also calls Granna mama. It's funny to think how all mamas have their own mamas. "Don't encourage her. Sometimes I wonder if she knows what's real and what's not."

"She does," says Granna. "Let her be."

"She thinks there's a woman and a pig over there—"

"No," says Tipsy. "She doesn't have a pig. That's why she's mad. She wants the pig but the soldiers took it."

"You see?" says Mama to Granna, in that way grownups sometimes talk about children as if they can't hear. "She actually thinks someone is there."

"Denise, she's fine."

"Easy for you to say. Your child isn't showing signs of being crazy. I'm going to talk to Dr. Henderson. He said she just has a wild imagination, but this is too much."

"You let me handle it. I know how to manage what's going on with Tipsy."

"This is the eighties. We let a doctor handle it. Not some backwoods, up mountain voodoo."

Granna laughs. "Miss High and Mighty. Who's paying those bills when you take Tipsy to the doctor?"

"There you go, making me feel guilty. Randy is looking for a new job. Bo Scruggs might take him on at Scruggs Plumbing—"

"Let's see how long he lasts before the drink gets him fired."

Tipsy hates when they argue, especially when she causes it. "There wasn't a lady," she says. "I made it up."

Granna leans toward her. "Tipsy, it's okay if you saw something—"

"Mama, stop!" Denise stands in a huff. "It's hard enough for me and Randy, with everyone in town judging us. You're gonna make us the couple who got pregnant before we got married, and have a crazy kid, to boot!"

Granna stands, too, and puts her hands on her hips. "Denise McNair—"

"It's Denning. I'm a grown, married woman."

"Then act like it! This ain't about you. It's about your daughter, who feels scared."

"Take her side then! Like always!"

"Will you listen to yourself? I'm not taking sides. I'm trying to teach you how to be a mother."

"You know everything, right? Forget this. I'll be in the car. Y'all have fun." She stomps toward Granna's car, which is burgundy and silver and is called a Datsun. When Granna switches the gear while she's driving, Tipsy can see the road go by underneath them through a hole in the leather around the shifter-thingy.

Tipsy watches her mama go, but only until Granna spins her around and looks into her face. She sits on the bench and holds Tipsy's arms. She stares at Tipsy with intense gray eyes.

"Tipsy, listen to me. Was the pig lady different from regular people? Like me and PopPop, or your mama and daddy, or those people over there, having a picnic?"

"No."

"Think hard now. Picture her in your head."

Tipsy scrunches her eyes shut. "Okay. She's…she was…kind of fuzzy."

"Anything else?"

"She had very white skin. A little…shiny. Like the blue water in the swimming pool at the YMCA."

"Have you seen other people like her?"

"A boy at church. He sits in the front row when it's not crowded. He's bigger than me."

"Does he wear short pants and suspenders?"

"Spenders?"

"Straps like this—" Granna makes a line up her chest and over her shoulder. "That hold up his pants?"

"Yes."

"With blonde hair and a brown cap."

Tipsy nods. "Yes. At first, he didn't see me. But then he saw my eyes and I saw his eyes, and he smiled at me."

"I should have noticed, but I get caught up with my own business at church. The business of praying, and the business of gossiping. Shame on me."

Tipsy isn't sure what to say, so she digs her feet into the mulch. A fat ant crawls across her sock. She almost squishes him, but that would be mean, so she lets him crawl over her shiny black shoe like it's a mountain.

Granna exhales. "I agree you have a wild imagination. That's a good thing. But that boy, and the woman you saw today—they're not imaginary."

"I know. I see them, even if they're fuzzy. I hear them, too."

"I'll explain more to you about the fuzzy people as you get older. But for now, when you see them, only tell me, okay? Not Mama. Not Daddy. Not the kids at Sunday School."

"Yes, ma'am."

Granna hugs Tipsy. *"I knew this might be your fate, but I hoped it would pass you by. But if it is, and I gave it to you through my own kinship lines, I'll make sure you can handle it."*

"Okay," says Tipsy, even though she has no idea what Granna is talking about. Granna pulls away from her, and wipes at her cheeks, even though Tipsy isn't crying. Granna's mouth isn't moving, but all the sudden, she can hear Granna talking.

Sweet girl. You got a lifetime of seeing spirits ahead of you.

What's spirits, Granna?

Granna's eyes widen. Goodness. You heard that?

Yup. I did.

Well, looks like we got something else in common, too. This will be our secret, too. Okay?

Tipsy smiles. Yes. Our 'especial secret.

Let's get back to PopPop. Make some blueberry pancakes to tempt him.

I bet he'll eat those up! *PopPop isn't hungry anymore, so Granna always makes his favorite stuff hoping he'll eat it.* With bacon and sausage, too?

Sure. No man can resist bacon and sausage. And let's talk to your mama. Help her out of her grumpy mood. *"Okay?" she says aloud.*

"Okay. I'll pick a flower for her." Tipsy runs to the edge of the playground and picks a few buttercups.

"Now those will brighten anybody's mood," says Granna.

As Tipsy walks to the car, she hears the crying woman again. Granna hears it, too, because she looks in the same direction. Granna takes her by the shoulders. "Don't look at the fuzzy people, sugar. It's better that way."

"Okay, Granna," says Tipsy, because she always listens to Granna. It's easy to listen to her, because she always listens right back.

＊✕＊

Tipsy arrived to an open iron gate at the Bonneau house. As she drove onto the property, Jillian's Mercedes disappeared into the carriage house garage like a badger into a burrow. Tipsy parked inside the gate and waited on the piazza until Jillian huffed across the yard. She had her phone in one hand and a Diet Coke in the other. She'd slung two overflowing reusable grocery bags over her left shoulder, and her Louis-Chanel over her right. She finished reading something, then dug around in her purse.

Her keys emerged from her satchel as she climbed the stairs, but she dropped them. The grocery bags and her purse slid off her shoulders as she stooped to retrieve the keys. "Shitballs!" she yelled.

"Jillian?"

Jillian yelped and dropped her errand running accoutrements. The groceries stayed in their bags, but the contents of her Louis-Chanel spilled on the piazza's white wooden planks.

"Sorry," said Tipsy. "Didn't mean to scare you."

"It's okay. It really is." Jillian knelt and scooped up her wallet, receipts, lipsticks, pens, and spare change.

Tipsy crouched to help, but Jillian waved both hands, then squeezed her nose. "I got it. I do. *Really.* I'm okay…" Her shoulders shook, and her skinny butt slammed on the porch. Her head hung between her knees.

"Uh…Jillian? Can I get you anything?"

Jillian swiped at her face. "I'm fine. I'm *just fine.*"

Pamella used to reiterate her exceptionally *fine* status whenever Tipsy caught her in the throes of a wine bender. "It's okay if you're *not* fine."

Another chuffing sob escaped Jillian. Tipsy picked up her keys and unlocked the door. She retrieved a box of tissues from the powder room, then returned to the front porch and handed the box to Jillian. She covered her nostrils with a few tissues. Once she had a grip on her nose, she seemed to get a grip in general.

"How embarrassing," she said, but she didn't stand, so Tipsy sat beside her.

"The human race needs to declare a moratorium on being embarrassed by tears. If I checked one of my daughters into the psych ward, I'd boohoo with the best of them."

"Crying won't help her."

"It's good for her to see how much you care."

"It's obvious nothing else matters to me. That's why I'm paying you a hundred grand so she can come home."

"I think we may have a solution." Tipsy explained the idea of Sophie staying in the backhouse, and Thomas's limited mobility. "At my house, the ghosts have free rein in the yard. But this house alone has a bigger footprint than my whole property."

"If that's the best option we have." Jillian got to her feet. "I'll freshen up the bed in the backhouse. Bring some of her clothes out there."

"Can I help?" Tipsy wanted to get home and make more progress on her commission, but she also needed to earn her pay.

"What time is it?"

Tipsy looked at her phone. "Almost two."

"You like Jimmy Buffet?"

"Not really. But he's right about it always being five o'clock somewhere."

For the first time, Jillian laughed. "Want to raid the bar and join me?"

"Uh, sure. Why not?"

"I'll have a bourbon on the rocks."

Tipsy walked into the kitchen. She selected a Bud 55 from the drink fridge. She often drank that watery beverage on boat days because of the low alcohol content. Shelby's husband Brian, who brewed IPAs in his garage, said she might as well sip fruit punch from her kids' juice boxes. Perfect for an unplanned sympathy drink with her boss.

She turned to the liquor shelves. Not a Wild Turkey or a Jim Beam to be seen. She ran her fingers over the ornate bottles. Old Fitzgerald. Michtner's. Jefferson's Presidential Select. She chose the one with the most interesting name. Pappy Van Winkle's Family Reserve, Twenty-three Years Old.

She found a koozie and a cocktail napkin and returned to Jillian with the drinks. Jillian sat at a table beside the pool. She'd written *Stuff For Sophie* across the top of her notebook. She read aloud and counted on her fingers. "*Bedding. Pillows. Towels. Shampoo, soap, etc.* I remember whenever Catherine went…away… she always wanted her own shampoo. To take the smell with her. That reminds me; I need to find some photos of Catherine for you."

Tipsy sat beside her. "Great, but I'd like to learn more about who she was, not just what she looked like. The more I know, the truer to life the painting will be."

"My goodness. I haven't thought about *who she was* in a long time. But I'll give it a shot." She set the pen beside her notepad. "She was my best friend when we were little. More talkative than me, and always making up stories and plays. So many imaginary friends. I didn't notice her strangeness, or other children avoiding her. After her kindergarten year—or maybe first grade—my mother kept her home from school. Told me she was sick, but no one understood the extent of her sickness. By the time we were ten, she couldn't be in public."

"If she had so many imaginary friends, maybe she *was* like me, and Sophie."

"Sophie's issues pale in comparison to whatever was going on with Catherine. It would take an army of ghosts to explain all the voices she heard. Even the house was too loud for her. Too big and echoey."

"The place is huge. I bet voices—imaginary or real—carry up that crazy staircase."

"Voices weren't her only problem. She was paranoid, too. She believed the brick walls around the house were shrinking, so she used Daddy's measuring tapes to prove the walls were closing in. She saw secret messages in magazine advertisements and on license plates. She'd spend hours in the greenhouse, talking to the flowers. Once she tried to commiserate with the rose bushes when Mama cut them back."

"How does one commiserate with flowers?"

"Chopping off your own fingers will do it." Jillian tapped her pen against her notepad. "Thankfully, Daddy grabbed the pruning shears before she did too much damage."

"Wow. *Okay.* Even if she was a clairvoyant, she was definitely schizophrenic, too."

Jillian nodded. "It broke my mother's heart. Daddy too, I suppose, but he was old school. He couldn't handle it, so he hid in the study with his booze. As a parent, I understand why she did it, but back then, I resented how Mama doted on Catherine. Seemed like they punished me for being normal. Making good grades and not causing trouble. Easy to ignore me. But even my mother had her limits. She first sent Catherine *away* when she was about twelve, and we had peace for a while, but Mama's constant crying annoyed Daddy. He started going to the Yacht Club on East Bay Street for his drinks. At least when Catherine was home, Mama tried to be positive and Daddy didn't run away every night. They brought her back, and we got on a family roller coaster. Catherine would break down and my parents would send her away. Mama would get depressed, and they'd bring her back. From Legare Street to the state hospital in Columbia, over and over, until she passed away when I was seventeen."

"What happened?"

"An accident." Jillian watched the shimmering pool as if staring into a crystal ball. "She was hit by a car."

Tipsy waited for her to offer more, but she didn't. It didn't seem appropriate to press her, so Tipsy commiserated instead. "How awful. Even if you weren't close to her."

"She was still my little sister. She loved puppies and teddy bears and gardening. The gardens were neglected when we moved into this house. Not as bad as they are now, but in need of some serious TLC. Catherine spent the whole year pruning and transplanting old plants and planting new ones. The hydrangeas and azaleas. Roses and daffodils. She was a lovely girl. Much prettier than me. Mama resented nature for wasting all that beauty on Catherine, while I was a sane, plain Jane."

"You're not plain—"

"Tell that to Betsy Rose Porcher, Second Runner-up, Miss South Carolina 1955. Anyway, my sister wasn't a bad person, but she was trapped inside the wreckage of her own mind. Her passing brought us no peace. I ran away to California and stayed away. Daddy passed away the year after I got married. Mama lingered in this house, going crazy long before she had Alzheimer's." She pointed at the greenhouse. "She made me *swear* I wouldn't tear down that mouse-infested tetanus factory, because Catherine loved it. Now Sophie wants to rebuild it for her own flowers."

"Sophie told me she loves flowers. Even if Catherine wasn't a clairvoyant, they have other things in common." She backpedaled. "Not schizophrenia, thank goodness."

"Catherine's symptoms started unusually early. With Sophie, Dr. Brandt told me there's plenty of time for that dragon to start spewing fire. Anyway, thanks for your help, but you can leave. I'm sure you have things to do on a pretty Saturday afternoon."

"I thought I'd look for Thomas—"

"I need some quiet today."

"I don't have anything planned for the rest of the day, and my schedule can be intense. I'll stay out of your way—"

"Not today. Talking about Catherine…makes me…never mind." She cleared her throat, as if to cough up her emotions and spit them out. "Did Sophie bring up the florist stuff to you? Despite what she probably told you, I'm not *totally* opposed to it, but I want her to finish college first. She's got to prove she can manage her life."

"Maybe pursuing her passion will stabilize her. She's lucky. Few artistic people have her kind of financial safety net." Although Tipsy's own safety net was non-existent, her words seemed inappropriate. "Sorry. Y'all's finances are none of my business."

"It's fine. You're…dismissed."

Jillian expected Tipsy to get rid of Thomas, like, yesterday, and then prevented her from doing her job. Tipsy started to explain that conundrum, but Jillian leaned over her notebook and started scribbling.

As she walked to her car, Tipsy considered the Porcher-Yates women she'd met and heard about so far. Betsy Porcher lost one daughter to mental illness and a driver's slow reflexes. She spent decades cloistered in her house with no one but Thomas Bonneau, a ghost she couldn't see, while estranged from her remaining daughter and her family. Catherine Porcher's brain never allowed her to truly live, and she died a brutal death on top of it. Jillian Porcher Yates, the ignored child, still mourning her sister, while worrying her daughter might end up just like her. Sophie Yates herself, so young and already full of resentment, the newest iteration of all that hurt.

These ladies are as intergenerationally discombobulated as we are, Granna.

True, replied Granna. *You've waded through some screwy families since you started messing around with these ghosts.*

Remember Ivy's mother? What a piece of work. Never met Henry's mother, but he's said they didn't get along…

Tipsy stopped. Granna's presence rattled between her ears, as if forward momentum had flung her into Tipsy's forehead.

Whoa, Nelly! What is it?

Hold on, Granna. I just remembered…

She spun around and ran back to the house. She called out to Jillian. "I left my….uh…sunglasses!" Jillian responded with an absentminded wave. A minute later, Tipsy stood in front of the study's fireplace.

Great balls of fire, said Granna. *It's her. Patty.*

Yes. I wonder if… Tipsy gently removed the photo from the frame and turned it over. She read the spidery writing on the back. "Patience Mary *Lewiston.*"

No! Isn't that—

"Henry's mother."

———✕———

Beyond a brief factual history and the occasional snide comment, Henry didn't talk much about his family. Tipsy knew his parents could not tolerate their odd little boy, so at age ten, they shipped him off to boarding school. Henry had no great love for his father, or his only brother, Edward, but he saved his most bitter enmity for his mother. She wasn't sure how to tell him she'd spied on the teenaged Patience, so she waited for him on her front porch with the framed photo in her hand.

"Something on your mind?" he asked, as he materialized beside her on the joggling board. "Perhaps romantic ruminations on Dr. Brandt?"

"Yes, something is on my mind, but nothing romantic. The opposite, in fact."

"Intriguing. Out with it. You'll tell me eventually." He smiled. "You've come to rely on me."

He unintentionally gave her a means to broach the topic. With John and Ivy's mystery, she'd needed Henry's information. Now he might provide insight into Thomas Bonneau.

"Okay…remember Patty, the young woman from Thomas's memory?"

"You believe she's important."

"Right. We've already considered a romantic connection. They're different social classes, but look at John and Ivy."

"What do you know of her background?"

Tipsy swallowed. "She grew up on Edisto Island—"

"Interesting. My mother was born out that way."

"—and their fathers were friends. Her parents died, and Thomas took her in. I know her full name, and I found *this* portrait."

Henry leaned toward the photo. His brow wrinkled. "That's—but it can't be."

"It is. Henry, this is difficult but—"

"Maybe I'm mistaken."

"No. She said her real first name during the first memory. It struck me as familiar, but I couldn't place it. Then I remembered I read the name in your obituary." She turned the photo around. "You just said her family came from Edisto. It's her. Your mother."

"No."

"Yes." Tipsy tapped the handwritten name. "Patience Mary Lewiston, who became Patience Lewiston Mott."

Henry's eyes rolled back in his head. The color bled out of him, starting with his fiery hair. Red leaked down his face, and his freckles melted. Reddish brown stained his white shirt, as if she'd stabbed him in the heart, and his tan trousers dripped on his shiny shoes like wet sand.

Tipsy had never seen a ghost's fading turn into such alarming liquification. "Henry, be careful—"

He wobbled on the joggling board, then he tipped backward. Rather than banging into the wall, he fell right through it. In a ghostly version of a faint, his slushy form vanished.

Tipsy wanted to take advantage of Henry's—yet again—fortuitous proximity to the players in her mystery, but he didn't reappear that evening. She sensed him hovering somewhere in the shadows, nursing his Freudian angst, so she let him be. If he wanted to talk, he could have sought her out in the parlor, where she spent the rest of the day attending to her persnickety herons. Their skinny black head feathers created arched eyebrows over their beady eyes. They scowled through her four-hour painting session, clearly unimpressed with her efforts to cover their nakedness with plumage.

The next morning, Scott and Tipsy kept their original coffee date. They sat at Vintage Coffee on Coleman Boulevard for hours, talking about everything under the sun, moon, and stars. She would have stayed there all day, hopped up on caffeine and amazing conversation, but she had to make the Great Sunday Grocery Run in preparation for the kids' evening return.

She wandered the familiar aisles of Harris Teeter. As her arm instinctively reached out for fruit and milk and snacks and a couple rotisserie chickens, she relived their conversations and pondered. What *exactly* had she been doing with men all these years? What manner of male persons had dominated her conversational time and space?

To cut herself some slack, she hadn't known men like Scott existed. Granna's husband, her PopPop, had died when she was five. Her own drunken, absentee father—*negative, Ghostrider, haha.* Her daddy's father drank himself to death. She had no brothers or uncles. She turned her analysis to those XY chromosome carriers to whom she was not related by blood.

Of course, she'd had pleasant talks with Ayers, despite his volatile personality. He dominated the conversation, but in the early days, Tipsy was too in awe of him to care. As their relationship stretched on and he continued to *ramble* on, she casually tuned him out. She turned to St. Dave, the morally deficient hypocrite she'd briefly dated before Will, who put her off churchy men forever. Admittedly, she'd been rebounding harder than a poorly shot basketball, and they'd spent most of their time making out. Will was easy to talk to, especially in the beginning, when they were getting to know each other and the problems inherent to their relationship still churned below the surface. They'd spent pleasant evenings chatting on her porch. But something about Scott was different.

He's not just telling stories or giving his opinion, or asking after my experiences and worldview. He's thinking about the why and the how, and what they mean for future whens. He's naturally introspective, Granna. He's capable of growing.

Tipsy almost heard Granna's sigh. *I can't argue with you, Tipsy. So far, the man seems like Prince Charming crossed with Doctor McDreamy. He's winning me over. But he's still Kate's ex, and I hate the idea of more conflict for you. Or the kids.*

I know. I haven't made up my mind about how far I want this to go.

Strangely, Granna's tentative approval of Scott unnerved Tipsy more than her hesitation. If Granna didn't point out the potential complications, Tipsy must identify them. So far, none of her worries originated with Scott himself. Every red flag hung from the rafters of Ayers and Kate's fancy new house.

Scott had kissed her in the coffee shop's parking lot and said he'd *talk to her soon*. In another interesting development, she felt no anxiety about it. When she started seeing Dave, she'd agonized over the time between his text messages. With Will, it had taken weeks to lose a sense of unease if she didn't hear from him by dinner time. He always turned up in her text messages eventually, sometimes as she got ready for bed, but better late than never. Based on her experience with Saint Dave, and Shelby's horror stories of men who went radio silent for days, she'd thought of Will as slow, but steady.

For whatever reason, she wasn't worried about when she'd hear from Scott, and his definition of the word *soon* suited her just fine. Within an hour, he sent her a link to a documentary about the flawed American healthcare system.

SCOTT: SINCE YOU SEEMED INTERESTED, BUT DON'T FEEL LIKE YOU HAVE TO WATCH IT. THIS STUFF DOESN'T NECESSARILY INTEREST EVERYONE ELSE LIKE IT INTERESTS ME, OR WE'D HAVE BETTER MENTAL HEALTH FUNDING, HAHA.

Tipsy replied with a happy affirmative, asked him a question about his opinion, and received a thoughtful, witty answer.

Ayers and Kate aside, the more she interacted with Scott, there seemed less to worry about. It was early days—the New Year's Day of the relationship—but she'd never had a dating interaction start so smoothly. Maybe it was *too* smooth.

Maybe she was missing something.

Or maybe she was being paranoid, and needed to get a grip.

By the time she put her groceries in her car, her feelings were nonsensically jumbled, a laundry pile of emotions she must sort into lights and darks. She was standing on a magic carpet and wasn't sure how to keep it on the ground. She wasn't quite ready to fly, but the carpet might take off at any moment and dump her on her ass.

She slammed the Tahoe's back hatch and steered her buggy across the parking lot. About ten feet from the cart return, she gave it a push and let go. The cart rattled across the pavement and slid obediently between the metal railings.

Flying carpets and unhinged shopping carts. She simultaneously tried to hold on tight and let go. Two seemingly contrarian concepts, but Tipsy wished she didn't have to choose between them.

Chapter 7

B y request, Tipsy made Breakfast for Dinner when the kids got home. They plowed through their eggs and bacon before retreating to their rooms for the rest of the evening. Three straight days of boating with Ayers, Kate, and Kate's children had wiped them out, and they didn't even have the energy to bicker. Tipsy's caffeine binge wore off, and the workweek loomed before her, replete with grumpy herons, long hours at the GQB, and Jillian Porcher's expectations. Henry remained reclusive, so she made no progress on questioning him about Patience Mary.

All members of her household were tired and crabby, so everyone called it an early night. Before she fell asleep, she answered a text from Pamella, who wanted the scoop on her ghost-busting referral.

TIPSY: SORRY I'VE BEEN MIA, SO BUSY! I FEEL LIKE IT'S TOO COMPLICATED TO TEXT!

PAMMY: THEN LET'S GET TOGETHER! HOW ABOUT A SMOOTHIE DATE DOWNTOWN TOMORROW? I'LL BE AT C OF C ALL MORNING!

Pammy had adopted the College of Charleston into her expansive charitable repertoire. She was a Friend of the Library, a member of the Randolph Hall Preservation Society, and proud supporter of C of C's perennially strong basketball program. Soon she'd be sitting pretty on the Board of Directors.

Tipsy agreed to meet for a pre-work chat. She parked at a garage on Wentworth Street near C of C's fraternity row. She walked down Glebe Street, past the Mount Zion AME Church, the College president's elegant brick home, and the Charleston single houses that housed academic departments. She was early for her catch up with Pammy, so when she crossed George Street, she detoured around the greenspace of the Cistern yard in front of Randolph Hall. She lifted her feet to avoid tripping on College Way's famously uneven bricks and marveled at the seamless mix of old and new. More historic homes converted into academic buildings. A state-of-the-art library. Overhanging oak limbs draped with the requisite Spanish moss, perfectly manicured landscaping, and wrought iron benches. Lush flower baskets and motivational banners hung from old-fashioned gas lantern lamp posts. Hand-painted sheets dangling from piazzas and stucco walls announced club meetings and Greek life events. Spring semester wrapped up a couple weeks ago, so only a few backpack-bedecked summer students strolled the bricks or relaxed on the benches.

As he sometimes did, Henry abruptly appeared at her side. She removed her phone from her purse and put it to her ear so they could speak naturally.

"Lovely morning for a stroll around campus," he said.

"Sometimes I wonder why I didn't go to C of C. Their art programs are very well-regarded, and it's so beautiful." Tipsy gestured around her. "If eighteen-year-old me had walked through this campus, I'd have fallen in love with this place instead of Ayers Lee Collins, IV. You grew up close by, right?"

"Yes. On Bull Street. The neighborhood is called Harleston Village. My parents' house is down the road."

"I'd like to see it. We can continue this pleasant stroll after I meet Pammy."

"No, thank you."

Given his curt refusal, she circled the conversational wagons. "What was the College like back then?"

"A small institution with a few hundred students. Only Randolph Hall and Towell Library inside the walls surrounding the Cistern yard. These streets were open to traffic. My brother and I sometimes played catch by the Cistern. I was a terrible baseball player, and Edward not much better. Still, my father expected us to pursue such manly activities."

"You've never returned to your family's house, in all these years?"

"Before I entered your life, I rarely came downtown. Too many memories." Henry paused at another cross-campus path known as Green Way. He faced west, toward the corner of Coming and Bull Street. His own personal yellow brick road. "I have no idea what happened to my parents, or my brother." He looked down at her with weary eyes. "Tipsy, I know very little about my mother's life. When I told you she grew up on Edisto, I revealed the last of the pithy information I have."

"I'm sorry to push you, like I did with John Huger, but—"

"John was different. I was being stubborn and prideful."

"You know Patience appeared in Thomas's first memory. I saw another memory on Friday, before I went to dinner with Scott." She told him the story of the strange Unity Alley vision. "...and then it ended all the sudden. Weird enough on its own, but the woman with Thomas—the prostitute—she mentioned Patience, too. She *must* be relevant, and if you and Thomas make the connection, you can get him talking about her."

"You believe this Thomas Bonneau, who frequented whorehouses, was involved with my mother?" He grimaced like a baby with a spoonful of pureed spinach before his lips. "So many levels of distasteful."

"Y'all weren't close, but she's still your mother. You can be a Debbie Downer—"

"Who?"

"Like, a Negative Nancy."

"I'm a *man*, Tipsy."

"A Pessimistic Peter?"

"Ah, I take your meaning now. You're right, but as it relates to my mother, I'm not being melodramatic. I promise." He stopped. "When do you have to meet Pamella?"

She checked her phone. "I still have about twenty minutes."

"Would you care to take a gander into my brain? Get a heaping dose of Patty-Patience?"

"Hmmm. Okay. I *do* have some time to kill."

A fountain bubbled and splashed in the overlapping shadows of Randolph Hall and a few towering oak trees. She sat on an iron bench, outside the fountain's spray. Henry sat beside her.

Tipsy donned her sunglasses, so no one would notice her brief bought of unconsciousness. After the frightening darkness of Thomas's night time stroll down Chalmers Street, she hoped Henry's memory took place in the daylight hours. She gripped the railing with one hand and the bench seat with the other. She squeezed until her knuckles went white and willed herself to stay upright. "Hit me, Henry."

"No need for violence." He put a hand on her shoulder.

⸺◆✕◆⸺

When Tipsy wakes up in Henry's memory, it's definitely daytime. She shades her eyes against the sunlight, and recognizes a brick and clapboard house. The Old Cannon, Jane's family plantation on the Wando River. It must be spring, given the jade green grass and the deciduous magnolias' fat pink blossoms. She inhales the earthy smell of a recent rain. Under the magnolias, rows of white chairs await a wedding ceremony, or perhaps a church service.

Several large sweetgrass baskets are laid out on a white tablecloth atop a round table. Four people stand around the table, a co-ed version of King Arthur's retinue. Henry's red hair glows like polished copper. To Tipsy's delight, Jane stands beside him in a white calf-length dress with a lavender sash and a matching lavender bonnet. Her dark hair is wrapped in a chignon at the nape of her neck. She chatters as she points at the house, the chairs, and the baskets.

Tipsy approaches to get a better look at the man and woman who accompany her favorite couple. The man appears about Henry's age, but he's shorter. Henry has dark blue, storm-tossed eyes, while this man's eyes match the pale blue sky. His lighter hair skews toward strawberry blonde, but he has the same high cheekbones, full lips, and freckles. It must be Henry's brother, Edward Mott. The siblings' unusual handsomeness makes the observer scrutinize their faces to identify exactly what is so appealing.

The woman is older, although it's hard to tell her age. She's rather stout, with a full bosom, and ashy graying hair. When Tipsy squints, she sees remnants of Patty Lewiston's blandly pretty features in her small, straight nose and dark blue eyes. Other than Henry's eye color and Edward's light hair, the Mott boys don't take after their mother.

"Should we leave these in the basket, or place them on the chairs?" Jane holds up a woven sweetgrass cross.

"I suggest placing the baskets at the end of each row. Our visitors can take one if so inclined—"

"Ridiculous, Henry. Of course everyone will be so inclined. It's Easter service." Patience picks up one of the crosses. "Will Reverend James approve of them?"

Good ol' Proctor James, *thinks Tipsy, in reference to the minister of St. Philip's Church—a man who had proved much more complicated than she expected.*

"It is 1917. *The modern age," continues Patience. "They're rather... quaint. The colored help made them. He may find such countrified favors to be tacky. Jane, what does your mother say? She's always so stylish."*

Henry's mouth sets in a thin line. He turns toward the river, but Jane touches his arm. "Miss Patience," Jane says, "Reverend James is coming all the way out here after Sunday morning service at St. Philip's. If he didn't love the country, and all its quaintness, he wouldn't make the trip."

Edward Mott enters the conversation. "What about those?" Palmetto roses peek over the edge of another basket.

"Oh, yes," says Jane. "The roses. I asked Jenny and Tess to make them for me. Why hand out Easter lilies that will wilt? We can bunch these together and our guests can take them home with their crosses."

Patience frowns. "No lilies on Easter?"

"There are no florists around here, Mother," says Henry.

"He's right, and ours haven't bloomed yet," adds Jane. "Easter is so early this year."

"They're rather pretty. I like them." Edward smiles fondly at Jane. "Leave it to Janie to personally tailor the Easter service."

"Thank you, Ed. Mama also likes the idea," says Jane.

"She does? Then of course!"

"Theresa Robinette approves, and now it's the height of fashion," mutters Henry.

"What, Henry?" asks Patience.

"Nothing."

"Speak up! Your mumbling is so unbecoming. You're a grown man, and you stammer like the gloomy five-year-old you once were. When the guests arrive, you speak clearly. They'll think I raised you with a rag in your mouth."

"Heaven forbid." Edward winks at his brother, but Henry is unamused.

"Henry, darling," says Jane. "Will you retrieve another basket of roses from Jenny?"

"Yes, dear." He takes a few steps toward the house.

"Thank you. Last I saw her, she was down by the barn with a pile of sweetgrass."

Henry stops. "The barn. Near the old slave cabins? Ah…I don't fancy going down there. My hay fever."

"Oh. My word, I forgot. Then maybe—"

"Good heavens, Henry!" says Patience. "Your wife asked you to do her a small favor. Go get the roses."

"I…If I could…"

"Mush mouth! Jane, I don't know how you tolerate him. I tried with him. I swear I did, but he was always an odd child. Although, I don't need to remind you, since you've known each other your entire lives."

"I remember. Henry was quiet and—"

"I hope it ends with him and your children take after you."

"Goodness, Miss Patience—"

"When y'all have children, you'll understand. There's only so much you can make of some of them."

"Maybe Edward can go—"

Patience won't let Jane complete a sentence. "You asked Henry. But apparently the man who lives to stick his nose into dusty books can't manage a skinny minute among the hay bales."

"Mother—I simply can't."

"Stop making excuses. Just go on, now."

As is par for the course in Henry's memories—everyone's memories, save Thomas Bonneau—Tipsy feels his powerful emotions. Discomfort, apprehension, even fear. Henry doesn't want to go near the barn, but not because of his hay fever. No matter how many ghosts he's seen, from Charleston to Montreal to the castles of Europe, nothing repels him like the Old Cannon's slave cabins, and the men, women, and children who haunt that hallowed, terrible space. There are too many faces, and he cannot avoid eye contact. He can't shut out their voices when they question him in their old timey Gullah dialect and sing mournful tunes of loved ones lost.

"No. I won't."

"Henry, are you alright?" Jane touches Henry's cheek. *"You're pale."*

He turns away from her. *"I'm fine, Jane. But I have better things to do than decorate for a party."*

"Like what, Henry Mott?" asks his mother. *"And don't snap at your wife. Jane, he doesn't mean to be an ass. I'm sorry you must put up with him."*

"There's no problem, Miss Patience. I'm more worried than annoyed."

Edward steps in. *"Mother, I'll get the baskets. Why don't you come with me? You can ask Miss Theresa about the crosses."*

"Good idea. I'm sure she and I will be of the same opinion. We're so alike."

They walk away, and Jane tentatively takes Henry's hand. *"Dearest, something is wrong. Please don't deny it."*

"You won't understand."

"I can't understand, if you don't tell me."

For the hundredth time, Henry considers telling Jane about the ghosts. In the end, he can't do it. He told his mother once, when he was small. She whupped his behind and told him if he ever said such ridiculous things again, the next whupping would go through his pants.

"I'm sorry if I snapped at you. It's...my mother."

"It's always her. I wish you could shut out her jabbering."

"One might easier shut out the sun. You close your eyes, but it still burns a hole in your eyelids."

"Perhaps we shouldn't have invited your parents to the Old Cannon for Easter."

"If she felt snubbed, it would have been worse when we returned to town."

She slides her arms around his waist. He stiffens, and then relaxes into her embrace.

"I'm so blessed with my own parents. I'll never understand how a mother or father can be cruel to their own child."

He squeezes her. "She's far less cruel since I married you. She loves you."

"Henry. You know Patience better than that. She loves my family name and our social connections. She doesn't give a hoot about me personally."

"More hoots than she's given me."

"That breaks my heart." She tilts her head back to look into his face. Given Tipsy's own height, she's never had the pleasure of staring so far up at a man.

"I don't want you associating me with heartbreak." Henry says, and kisses her. "I want to bring you only happiness. Although I know I can be difficult. Forgive me."

"That's your mother talking."

He chuckles. "The difficult part is very much me talking, as is the apology."

She rests a hand on his cheek. "I married you because I love you. Difficulties and all."

"I love you, Janie."

Tipsy's eyes water as she watches them. If this memory is 1917, everything changed over the next six years. She longs to fully understand what went wrong. But at least the memory has helped her understand one thing. She'll never again question Henry's contempt for his mother.

<hr />

Tipsy swiped at tears under her sunglasses. "You always get me with those tender moments between you and Jane."

"I have to make up for the version of us you witnessed in our house."

"I figured you'd show me a memory from your childhood."

"Children are automatically sympathetic. I wanted to incite unbiased empathy."

"She was that way all the time?"

"Constantly."

"You're right. She's awful. But I still believe she has some role to play in the saga of Thomas Bonneau. If Thomas will talk to you about her—"

"I will consider talking to him. Is that sufficient?"

"It will have to do."

Henry disappeared with a flourishing bow, and Tipsy walked through the passageway under Randolph Hall to the Cistern yard. As she opened the door on the other side, she saw Pamella's dark hair and spindly form atop the old reservoir that gave the yard its name. The Cistern hadn't contained water in decades. Instead, the filled-in trough had become a sort of oversized stucco planter. Grass grew on either side of the brick path across it.

Under the oaks, students chased frisbees, tossed footballs, or lounged in the grass on blankets. Pammy watched the goings on from her perch, a two-armed, animated Venus de Milo, decked out in the latest summer couture. She saw Tipsy and waved frantically. "Heeeeey! What's up, lady!" she yelled. The beading on her floral skirt jiggled enthusiastically. Curious students looked up at Pammy, an interloper from the world of parents who had invaded their unsupervised serenity.

She bounded down the Cistern's stairs and dragged Tipsy to a bench in the shade beside Porter's Lodge. The picturesque structure served as a grand, formal entryway to campus and separated the Cistern yard from George Street. A wholly unique building, Porter's Lodge was built into the stucco wall, with three arched porticos on the first level, and a second floor chamber that once served as the groundskeeper's residence. Before she sat, Tipsy snapped an artsy photo and sent it to Scott.

Pamella handed Tipsy a tumbler with a straw. "Packed with greens, lady," she said. "Made it myself this morning."

"Thanks, Pammy." Given that she'd just returned from Henry's memory, Tipsy sipped tentatively. Pamella made some weird concoctions in her blender, and her tender tummy might rebel. Fortunately, she tasted mostly kiwi and apple juice. Just enough kale to make it officially healthy. Blessedly palatable.

"You like it!" Tipsy sputtered reassurance, but Pammy waved a dismissive hand in her face. "You don't fool me. My treats usually make you gag. Did you find the ghost who is traumatizing Sophie?"

Tipsy told her the latest from Legare Street. "So now I'm on a mission to get memory number three out of him."

"Daddy and I went to a few garden parties at that house. Weird to imagine a mysterious guest we couldn't see."

"Ironically, his lack of mystery creates more mystery. The other ghosts I've hobnobbed with lately have ranged from aloofly uncooperative to actively enraged. Thomas is like someone you'd chat with at a country club bar. Aside from his old fashioned clothes, he's oddly reasonable and friendly. Almost...*normal.*"

"That should make things easier, right?"

"I hope so. But he's so chill and content, I'm afraid if I ask to see into his memories and help him move on, he'll *stop* being communicative."

"Why would a ghost stick around if he didn't have to?"

Tipsy thought of Proctor James. "Fear, mostly. Even if they don't remember exactly how they died, they sense something wasn't right about it. Some don't *want* to know what happened. Or they're afraid of hell or the devil. Whatever eternal damnation they believed in during their lives."

Pammy shivered "When you put it that way, I don't blame them for lingering."

Tipsy's phone dinged. She swiped over Scott's reply to the photo.

SCOTT: COOL! THAT'S C OF C, RIGHT? I'M STILL LEARNING THE LOCAL LANDMARKS.

TIPSY: YUP. I'M MEETING MY FRIEND PAMELLA FOR A CATCH UP. SHE'S A REAL CHARACTER. YOU'D HAVE A BLAST ANALYZING HER.

SCOTT: INTERESTING. TELL ME ABOUT HER.

TIPSY: SHE'S TOO COMPLICATED FOR TEXT! She paused, then sent another message. MAYBE WE CAN TALK ON THE PHONE TONIGHT?

"Who you texting, lady?" asked Pamella.

"You're going to think it's weird. Possibly inappropriate."

"Then it's a man."

"Yes. It's Scott Brandt."

"You mean your ex-husband's current wife's ex-husband?

"Ugh. It sounds so *complicated* when you say it like that."

"Whoo-hoo! As Mount Pleasant Turns."

"I *know* how weird it is—"

"Why is it so weird?"

"Because of what you just said. He's my *ex-in-law*. Lindsey thinks it's a terrible idea. Granna says—"

"Your grandmother in your head?"

"Yes. Granna wasn't on board at first, but now she's coming around. She understands why I like him so much."

"Why *do* you like him so much?"

Out it came. "He's amazing so far. We've only hung out a couple times. But the way we talk about everything—I've never had someone hit me like this. Like a...rogue wave. He's so smart. And he's funny. Not *sarcastic* funny, like so many guys. Where you can't tell if they're truly joking or subtly insulting you. He's witty."

"Sarcasm is the passive aggressiveness of the male sex, for sure."

"He's also thoughtful, and sensitive, and openminded. I've never been with that kind of man."

"From my observation, you *have* chosen old school men in the past."

"He doesn't even hunt. But none of that makes him any less...*manly*. He, like, sweats testosterone."

"Tipsy, you just described the perfect guy."

"Good lord. You're right. How can *anyone* be so perfect?"

"I assume Ayers is not a fan of his new wife's sensitive, witty, non-hunting ex."

"Correct. Ayers fancies himself an alpha male. Someone who is better educated, better looking, and doesn't work for his father is a threat on a level he can't articulate. He flat out told my kids he hates Scott."

"Another example of his great parenting."

"That's the biggest problem. Lindsey and Granna think Ayers will go apeshit if he finds out I'm spending time with Scott. They're probably right. Ayers and I have been getting along. He's even been confiding in me about problems he's having with Kate."

"They're already having problems?" Pamella winced. "Not a good sign. But the *weirdest* thing going on here is Ayers confiding in *you*."

"But if it helps us get along, and helps him manage his own issues, I don't see how I can avoid it. It's better for the kids if he's in a good emotional place. By seeing Scott, I'm risking all that—"

"You said you've never met a man like Scott. You're not taking a chance for a casual *swipe right*. You think there's real potential."

"Yes. But it's also freaking me out. It came out of nowhere. I went from casually running into him to making out with him in the span of three days."

"Sometimes love hits hard when it's right."

"I don't want to dive into it without weighing all the pros and cons. What if I'm just lonely, and he's not as great as I think he is? What if I'm missing red flags? He didn't want to talk about his ex-girlfriend. The Hellraising Highlighter."

Pammy laughed. "The who-raising what-lighter?"

"Some chick he dated post-divorce! I wonder what happened there?"

"Maybe he doesn't want to talk about his *ex-girlfriend* because he's focused on you becoming his *current* girlfriend."

"Why does he want to date *me*, anyway? I'm *his* ex-in-law. It's crazy, right? Maybe *he's* crazy."

"Tipsy. He probably wants to be with you because you're smart, talented, kind, beautiful, and a great mom. You're also sane and you don't need to join me in AA, unlike a lot of single people in this town."

"Thank you, but—what if I'm getting in over my head?"

"You're overthinking! Your *head* is doing overtime!"

"But *why* does he have to be Kate's ex—"

"Whoa, whoa, whoa. Take a deep breath. He *is* Kate's ex, whether you like it or not. Y'all *met* because he's Kate's ex. If you were kind of *meh* about him…I'd say it's not worth the risk. But I know you. You put your kids first. You're a cautious person. Maybe too cautious, given how you're picking the poor man apart."

"You're right. Maybe I'm driving myself nuts for nothing. He's the shrink, right? How mentally unstable can he be?"

"That's no *guarantee* of mental stability. There are plenty of crooked lawyers and overweight heart surgeons. The real problem here—you've got a touch of relationship PTSD. Your past is haunting you." Pamella poked Tipsy's arm. "I can see it, and I'm no clairvoyant."

"I guess." Tipsy felt like crying. "I *really* like him, Pammy."

"Let yourself like him. If this guy hit you like a wave, you owe it to yourself to grab your surfboard."

"Should I tell Ayers?"

"Not at this point. Let this time be for you and Scott."

Tipsy's phone dinged again. SCOTT: I'D LOVE TO TALK TONIGHT.

"What did he say?" asked Pamella.

Tipsy held up her phone. Pamella smiled as she read. "A man who *wants to talk*. So talk to him, lady."

Chapter 8

"T his place is great. It's like your own apartment," said Tipsy, as she admired the guest quarters in the Bonneau House's remodeled backhouse beside the pool. The space consisted of a bedroom, a full bath, and a great room complete with a pool table and a huge TV, a kitchenette, and a fully-stocked bar.

Tipsy and Sophie sat on stools at the bar like unlikely friends about to partake in wine and gossip. Sophie wore a C of C sweatshirt and she'd draped a chenille blanket over her thin shoulders. Her KZ Yeti sat beside her. She'd been home for two nights. Shelby was finally replacing the wonky HVAC system at the GQB, so she'd closed the gallery. Tipsy had dropped the kids at school and descended upon the Bonneau House to check in with its enigmatic inhabitants, living and dead.

Sophie's lodgings did not impress her as they did Tipsy. "It's cool enough. Could use some artwork." She pointed at the exposed brick walls. "You got anything lying around?"

"Not really. My work is either commissioned, or for sale at the gallery. At the moment I'm short on stock. Two gallery paintings sold recently. I need to refill my exhibit walls, but I'm finishing a commission piece, and your mom asked me to paint a portrait of her sister. I gotta fit that in, too, while working at the GQB—"

"And being my supernatural therapist. You can't make much money *working* at the gallery, so why are you doing it?"

"Not a ton. But it's a steady paycheck." A paycheck that would be leaner than usual, given two recent days off. But she planned to use the time to paint this afternoon, and—

Sophie interrupted Tipsy's ruminations with the annoying logic everyone from Shelby to Granna to Big freakin' Ayers had been laying on her. "Wouldn't you eventually make *more* money from selling more of your own paintings?"

"Yes. But it's not so simple…" She trailed off. Hard to explain her tenuous financial situation to a trust fund baby. "Enough about me. How are you feeling?"

"The headaches are back. I feel queasy again, too. Not all the time. But nothing tastes good. Mom brought a salad out here last night. Smelling it made me want to puke."

"Shoot. How do you feel, emotions-wise?"

"Same, I guess. I don't want to talk—"

"You don't want to talk about it." Tipsy interjected before Sophie shut down, or got pissed off. "So let's change the subject. I have a surprise for you. Nothing too crazy. Your mom doesn't want you getting worked up."

She pointed across the room. "So I can be an emotional *brick wall*, like her?"

Tipsy ignored the jab at Jillian. "How about some *proof* you and I share this talent?"

"How can you *prove* that?"

"Can I get y'all a drink, ladies?" Henry stood behind the bar, the most retro of hipster bartenders.

"Holy crap. You're…pale, and you just appeared…you're…a ghost!" Sophie turned to Tipsy. "Is he the guy who haunts *your* house?"

"Indeed, I am," said Henry. "I *also* shared your strange ability during my life. It allows me brief changes in scenery in death. My name is Henry Mott, Miss Sophie. Always at Tipsy's service, now at yours." Henry snapped his fingers, and the drink fridge opened. A Coke can floated toward the bar. "I would ask if you wanted something stronger, but I've learned in this day and age, young people aren't allowed to partake. That's better than *no one* being allowed to partake."

"Coke is great, thanks." Sophie took it from midair. "Did you live in the Prohibition days?"

He nodded. "Born in 1894. Died in 1923. A brief, but glorious life."

"That sucks."

"Ah, Tipsy often uses that phrase. Sometimes her children use it—"

"I don't *like* them to use it. I prefer stinks."

"Sucks, stinks; tomay-to, to-mahto," said Henry. "Tipsy told me you've been alone with our abilities for most of your life. My family didn't believe me, either."

Sophie shook her head. "It's the same for *everyone* like us. Not you, Tipsy. You had your grandmother. But for the rest of us, even our own *families* don't believe us."

"You can't blame people," said Tipsy, "for not believing in something they've been taught to *disbelieve* their whole lives."

"Hmph. I *guess*. So what happened to you?" Sophie asked Henry. "You don't look old enough to be dead. Although, all the ghosts I've seen lately are youngish. You." She squirmed in her chair. "And uh…Thomas."

"Early and violent deaths often lead to hauntings," said Tipsy.

"My life was on an upward trajectory once I stopped talking to shadows in public. Married a beautiful woman whom I adored. No fairytale ending, but that's more attributable to my overall temperament than my supernatural abilities."

"You must have gotten divorced," said Sophie.

"Divorce wasn't an option in my day. In fact, we had an abnormally long marriage, since it didn't end with death do us part."

"Y'all haunt the house, together?"

"Uh…yes," said Henry, and Tipsy subtly nodded. She'd prohibited any talk about ghosts *moving on*.

"Did y'all die violently?"

"Yes. For a hundred years, give or take, she fancied I killed her and then myself." Sophie's eyes widened and Henry rushed on. "But I didn't. We…learned the truth. Many years later. So while our deaths were both early and violent, there are no hard feelings anymore."

"That's good. At least y'all aren't lonely. If you love someone, it wouldn't be *so* bad to be ghosts together, as long as it's a nice place. You never get old. Never have to be sick. No breaking up or cheating. Maybe that's what the stories mean by happily ever after."

A clairvoyant romanticizing a haunting, after observing dozens of miserable, insane ghosts, didn't set well with Tipsy. The thought of being a ghost had always terrified her. She'd spoken to Ivy about the idea, and Ivy agreed. "I believe happy endings come from searching for contentment in life, not an unending state post-death," she said.

"I agree with Tipsy," said Henry. "Jane and I loved each other very much, but it proved difficult to maintain our love when we were trapped together."

"But that's because she thought you killed her. You said you're happy now."

"I wouldn't describe the current state of our union as happy, and for years, it was a kind of hell on earth. Even together, we were far apart. A lonely century."

"I initially thought Henry and Jane's situation wasn't so bad. *Couple's haunting*. But believe me, forced company for all eternity is hard on any human relationship."

Sophie watched the bubbles in her Coke, then set it on the bar. "It's nice meeting you, but I'm tired. I don't feel good. I'm going to watch TV, then take a nap."

"Henry has to go anyway. He can't stay away from the house for long. I'll go inside and chat with your mom."

Sophie's face darkened. "God knows I wouldn't want to be trapped with *her* for a century."

They said their goodbyes and Sophie took her blanket to the couch. She wrapped it tighter around herself, grabbed the remote, and flipped on the television to reruns of *Gilmore Girls*.

"What do you think of her?" whispered Tipsy, as she closed the door behind them on the backhouse stoop.

"She seems a sad, moody young woman. Perhaps a wee bit… ungrateful."

"Yeah. She doesn't appreciate what she's got. Not only this big house and the money. Jillian isn't the warmest, fuzziest mother, but she adores her children. She has a tight relationship with her other two daughters, who also adore their little sister. They've had some hard times, but she's got a loving family. She had college and her friends. I know she's in a mental health crisis, but her nasty attitude still turns me off." Henry opened his mouth, but Tipsy said, "*Turned off* means, like, repulsed."

"I agree with your appraisal. Their strained relations seem trivial in light of my family, or yours."

"Jillian is no absentee dingbat Denise, nor overbearingly critical Patience. She'd do anything to protect Sophie. Probably kill Thomas herself if he wasn't already dead," said Tipsy. "Sophie certainly put a positive spin on you and Jane's situation."

"A young person's tragic romantic whims. I overflowed with such notions in my youth." He stretched. "On to our next task, shall we? I won't be gone long. Just a dip back to Bennett Street to recover."

"Okay. I'll touch base with Jillian, then find Thomas and keep him occupied till you return. I'm really interested in your insight about him, too. Remember, no talking to him about *moving on*. Keeping my plan on the DL is working so far."

"Understood."

"Are you willing to discuss your mother with him?" Henry had agreed to visit the Bonneau House, but he remained stubbornly vague about Patience Mary Lewiston Mott.

"Ta-ta, Tipsy." He disappeared, so Tipsy walked across the yard to the Bonneau House. As the house loomed over her like a smothering auntie offering an unwelcome embrace, she envied Henry's ability to dip out of any distressing situation. He sidestepped discomfort like a professional dodgeball player. Even if she couldn't literally vanish, she longed for some element of her life to be magically free of complications. Her challenges tended to stick to her like old lollipops on a wool sweater.

The familiar urge to *do something* seized her. To take control of something—anything, really. To make progress *and* guide the narrative. Even Sophie Rose Yates, a trust fund baby with no life experience, had aptly assessed Tipsy's professional life. She'd never reach her full income potential spending so much time working at the GQB, but she needed her bi-weekly paychecks to make ends meet. Unlike Sophie, she had no net underneath her while she walked the tightrope between regular employment and her artistic endeavors. She'd *always* wanted to be a full-time artist. After college, she'd been on her way to making a decent living from her paintings. But back then, she had few expenses or responsibilities. Truth be told, she'd had Ayers—or Ayers's family business and the security it provided them—as a buoy when financial seas got rough.

Now she was wholly on her own. But if she sought true financial independence, she must remove herself from the GQB's payroll. Once she earned the cushion of Jillian's payment, she had to sit down, manipulate her budget, and make a firm plan. For the first time since her brief post-college creative nirvana, she would focus solely on her own work.

Notwithstanding Ayers's potential nuclear meltdown, her unexpected budding romance with Scott was the one surprisingly easy element in her life, but she was no moody adolescent. She couldn't afford to lose herself in romantic notions. She was a thirty-six-year-old woman with three children.

Thoughts of her kids forced her to acknowledge her anxiety about *all things Ayers*. First and foremost, the explosive fission when he inevitably learned about Tipsy and Scott, but what about the additional chemical fallout if Ayers divorced Kate after less than a year of marriage? Would Tipsy and Scott's radioactive relationship render Planet Kayers uninhabitable?

Tipsy slowly walked up the five steps to the piazza, but her heart beat in her ears as if she'd stopped too quickly after a sprint. She sat on the top stair and rested her forehead on her hands. Anxiety hopped around her midsection like the little green lizards skittering across the wooden planks. Her eyes closed, as if to disappear into self-imposed darkness.

It's all right, sugar. Remember what you've learned in the past year or so. Sometimes you have to ride things out and see how they unfold.

Yes, but no one else is going to solve this mystery if I don't.

So talk to Thomas, but get a hold of yourself first. You don't want to plain old faint out here before you supernaturally faint inside.

Okay. I can do this. All of it. Just not at once.

Her pulse slowed and she opened her eyes to the sun's harsh, glaring reality. She noticed movement by the greenhouse through her squint. Sophie Rose, squeezing past the rickety door.

What the heck is she doing? Tipsy asked Granna. *I thought she was watching Gilmore Girls. Or was it Gossip Girl? Maybe The Golden Girls.*

I loved that show! Dorothy was my favorite. No, Blanche, since she was a southerner—

Don't get all Pamella ADD on me. Tipsy frowned. *That place is about to cave in, and it's the perfect home for copperheads and wasps. I should get her out of there.*

It might take a while to find Thomas, said Granna. *Henry will be back soon, and he can't stay too long.*

True. I'll text her. She sent a quick text. I DON'T THINK IT'S A GOOD IDEA TO HANG OUT IN THE GREENHOUSE. IT'S DANGEROUS. COME OUT, OKAY?

Tipsy walked up the stairs. As she put her hand on the doorknob, she looked over her shoulder, but she didn't see movement through the greenhouse's remaining opaque glass panels. Sophie wanted to refurbish the gardens. Perhaps she was retrieving some gardening tools. A positive sign, if she felt well enough to dabble in the dirt.

Tipsy had her own supernatural dabbling to do, so she went inside to get her hands dirty.

Tipsy found Jillian at the kitchen table with her nose in a book called *When Mothers and Daughters Clash: How to Communicate When Your "Little Girl" Seems Impossible.* She peeked over Jillian's shoulder and made small talk, but Mrs. Yates was engrossed by Chapter 6 (*Is She Crazy, Or Am I?*). Tipsy went in search of the dead man of the house.

So far, she'd seen Thomas on the front porch and in the study, but he wasn't hovering around either location. She perused the first, second, and third floors and their respective piazzas, but found no Byron-esque spirit gazing through a window or hobnobbing with the flowers. She stood on the third floor landing and peered up the stairwell. Elaborate wooden railings with carved newels and rounded balusters connected the staircases of floors one through three, but the fourth floor railings were plain spindles. Some had cracked and a few were missing. She didn't see much reason for Thomas to frequent the fourth floor, but she'd run out of places to look.

The AC units had little luck pumping cold air up there, and the heat increased as she ascended the stairs. She broke a sweat when she reached the landing. "Thomas! You up here?"

She planned to haul ass back into the blessed coolness if he didn't appear, but he materialized beside the attic door. "*Hello*, my friend," he said, with his friendly smile. She wondered if he'd been waiting there, listening to her huff up the stairs like a hooptie with a broken muffler.

"Hey. Wanted to tell you Sophie is home. She's resting in the backhouse."

"That's nice. Being home should raise her *spirits*." He laughed. "Do you see the joke?"

"Hilarious. I know another ghost who loves death-related puns," said Tipsy, in reference to Proctor James.

Blue light bathed the dim landing, as if someone had switched on an electric Hannukah menorah. Thomas slid across the floor like he had magnets in his shoes. He huddled against the attic door. "Go...away! Go, go, go—"

"Hey! Thomas! It's okay—"

Henry pushed his discombobulated hair from his face as the blue light faded. "Sorry to surprise you, Mr. Bonneau. Tipsy, did you warn him of my imminent arrival?"

"Didn't get a chance. I wasn't expecting you to arrive like a K-Mart blue light special."

Thomas straightened out of his protective hunch. He exhaled a few times, like Tipsy pulling herself out of her front porch panic attack. His expression had elements of surprise, confusion, and relief. He scratched his neck, and then pointed at Henry. "Who—what—"

"Henry Mott is *who*. *M-o-t-t*, with no final *e*. As for the *what*, I'm merely a ghost, like you. All good, lad. I'm visiting, not taking up residence."

To give credit to the stubborn South Carolina heat, Tipsy still sweated in the presence of two ghosts, but their collective chill lowered the temperature from toaster oven to tolerable. Thomas shook out his dark hair. Henry's mop always snapped back to its usual state of dishevelment, but Thomas's tresses fell over his forehead in cooperative waves. "Welcome, I suppose?"

"I haunt Tipsy's house across the Cooper, in Mount Pleasant. Since I was a seer like Tipsy during my life, it allows me some limited mobility in death—"

"Yes, yes. I see, now! I'm merely surprised, as I wasn't expecting *my kind* of company." Thomas reached into his overcoat for a good scratch, and then smiled. "Now that I've recovered my wits, I'm tickled to have a fellow spirit visit my home. This is *truly* exciting. I have so many questions!"

"Ask away."

"Pray, *when* are you from? And where?"

"I was born in 1894."

"He grew up on Bull Street," said Tipsy. "His father was—"

"I was born in '63, so I could have *been* your father," said Thomas. "Yet you appear older than me. Meaning no offense. You're quite well preserved."

Henry chuckled. "I was only twenty-nine when I died. A rare perk of our state. No worries about wrinkles or balding or bad knees."

"Perhaps we know the same families, but I don't recall any *Motts*. The Family *M-o-t-t-e*, yes. I attended church with a passel of them. But no Family *M-o-t-t*."

"Unlike your esteemed family, we're no refined French bloodline. Just common English stock. My father was about your age, but he grew up on the peninsula's northern neck. Born of modest means. He built up his own empire in dry goods."

"I admire a bootstraps kind of story. Wanted to be my own man and raise race horses, but my father thought it a frivolous endeavor."

"I went to the races in Saratoga once," said Henry.

"Was it glorious?"

"Entertaining, certainly. But when you've seen Westminster Abbey, a racetrack full of shouting, drunk gamblers can't compete."

"I would have placed some winning wagers on those fancy ponies. Regrets, regrets!" Thomas shrugged. "Life was still good. Death isn't bad, either. I'm chatting with you two lovely people! I'm beside myself, hosting a fellow *ghost*! A world traveler, at that! I adore my home, but I'd love to take a turn around the block. What other fascinating talents are you harboring?"

A lot of chitchat when y'all should be getting to the point, said Granna. *Before somebody disappears.*

This convo is a stubborn mule. I'll have to use spurs and take the reins.

"Henry, maybe you and Thomas know people in common. For example...*Pa*..." Tipsy twirled her fingers, as if to roll Patience's name off Henry's tongue herself.

"Pierre Robinette?" asked Henry, in reference to Jane's father.

"I remember *Pierre*," said Thomas. "He was a few years younger than me. I sometimes saw him playing ball in Whitehall Gardens with his friend R.J. Huger."

"Pierre was my father-in-law," said Henry. "And R.J. fathered a close friend."

"You knew those young hooligans as grown men!"

Come, on, Henry, Tipsy said in her mind.

I'm getting there. I swear it!

"This is fun!" Thomas scratched his chin. "Let me think. Did you know—"

The topic isn't going to get any easier. No time like the present! You got this!

You're even pushier than my wife, said Henry, and then aloud, "My mother's name was Patience Lewiston."

A shadow settled over Thomas's features and dulled the twinkle in his eyes. His skin darkened from pearly white to slate gray. "Did you say *Patience Lewiston?*"

"Yes. Lewiston was her maiden name."

Thomas scratched his neck, and the storm lifted. His face lightened to its usual shade of deathly pale, and his lips once more bloomed rosy red. "Fancy that. I *also* knew Patience. I called her Patty."

"Tipsy told me."

"Did she?" asked Thomas.

"I—uh…I saw the photo of Patience on the shelf. There's a similar photo in our house. I noticed the resemblance, so I borrowed it. Thought Henry might be happy to see his mother's face."

"I was not happy, if you're wondering. My mother and I did not get along. How did you know her?"

Thomas replied with a summary of things Tipsy already knew—their father's friendship, the deathbed request that Thomas employ her, and her management of the house.

"Did you enjoy her company?" asked Henry.

"I hate to speak ill of someone's mother."

"Don't truss up the pig on my account."

"At first, she was a great help around the house. But I ultimately found her to be a simple, senseless girl. Mostly concerned with climbing the social ladder." Thomas studied Henry like one of the fine horses he never had the chance to raise. "You appear a well-bred fellow. Tall. Well proportioned. Something noble about your face. She must have found a gentleman husband in your father."

"Father was never enough of a gentleman for Mother, despite her own humble roots. She rose higher than she had a right to hope for, but nothing satisfied her. What of your parents? Tipsy said they died when you were young. Your mother at your own birth."

"Yes. I brought on the greatest tragedy of my own life, and my father's life, as he liked to remind me."

"What happened to your father?" asked Tipsy. "Did he fall ill?"

"He *fell*, but without the ill part. One of our boarders found him after a tumble down the stairs. He probably tripped, although another physician said his heart may have given out. He was quite stout toward the end. Sounded like a tired steam engine walking these stairs in the summer."

"That could do it. I about passed out walking up here today myself."

Hairline, scratch. Wrist, scratch. Thigh, scratch. "His gluttony was a blessing. He always lamented my inheritance of the slight stature of the Barres. I wasn't smart or hardworking enough for him, or even sufficiently tall and burly, but at least my comparably lithe physique allowed me to outmaneuver him when he became too slow to catch me. Fewer beatings."

"Even if he saved a lot of lives during the Civil War," said Tipsy, "he sounds like a real jerk."

Thomas waved a dismissive hand. "As they say, we all have our cross to bear. I believe the war…depleted my father. I once overheard him tell Reverend Dupre he wanted to *end it all himself.*"

"Suicide?"

"Yes. Better he fell down the stairs than take the coward's way out."

A ghost had once again offended Tipsy's modern sensibilities. "Hold on. If someone is *truly depressed*—"

"Ah, Tipsy," said Henry. "Don't climb on your twenty-first-century high horse. For good or ill, that's how it was. Given your opinion, I assume *you* didn't kill yourself?"

"I doubt it," said Thomas. "According to the reverend, such persons boil in the Inferno's dismal seventh circle. I don't like the idea of hell, much less the darkest depths of it. But enough of that bleak talk. Tell me of your wife. Young Pierre's daughter. Did you have children?"

"We never had the chance. It's a rather bleak story in itself. It ends in murder."

"As much as I prefer to think only good thoughts, you've intrigued me."

Henry explained the circumstances of his haunting. Thomas listened intently and only scratched a few times.

"Now *that* is a heartbreaking yarn," he said, as Henry finished. "But you must have reconciled when y'all learned the truth, so not without a happy ending."

"I suppose we did reconcile, but we're not together any longer since Jane moved on."

Hush up, Henry! thought Tipsy. "What Henry means…uh—"

"You mean she's *no longer haunting* your house?"

Oh, damn. It slipped. Henry tried to back track. "Ah, well—"

"Y'all," said Tipsy. "We got distracted. We were talking about Patience—"

"Did *Tipsy* send your Jane on?"

"That's complicated…and boring! I'll tell you about it next time I visit. So you didn't get along with Henry's mom? So interesting. Tell us more!"

"Nothing more to tell. But I'm very interested to hear how your wife moved on—"

Henry's edges started to run, as if he were sweating himself into oblivion. Nowhere near as bad as his front porch fainting spell on Bennett Street, but he was showing the strain of consecutive trips. "I'm afraid I'm running out of time—"

"You do look worn out. So does Tipsy, which I assume to be an effect of the heat I can't feel." Thomas pointed at the dormer windows. "Too bad we can't let in some fresh air. A soft breeze would blow right through Henry and me, even if Tipsy is too solid for such soothing."

Henry eyed the window. "No reason we can't open it."

"Alas, those windows have been sealed for years."

"Nothing but a little paint. How about a parlor trick?" Henry raised his hand. The seams along the closed window cracked as if he'd run a razor along them. With a turn of a lock and a puff of dust, the window opened.

"Wonderful!" Thomas placed both hands on the sill and leaned forward. Tipsy peered around him at the neighboring mansions and their grounds, a canopy of oak trees, and the steeple of the Catholic cathedral. Children's laughter rang out in the pauses between the growls of gas leaf blowers. A tour guide shouted historical tidbits over his carriage horse's clopping hooves. Tipsy peered through the branches for her equine buddy, Creamsicle, but the horse was black.

"It sounds so busy!" said Thomas, as a lifted pickup truck rumbled down Legare Street.

Henry motioned to Tipsy. "Tipsy, I must go, but you *come closer* and take in the view."

"I'd love to have a good look. Thomas, do you mind if I—" She edged closer and braced one hand against the scuffed wall.

Thomas stepped away from the window in two backward strides. "I'm getting a little tired myself, what with all this talking. Lovely to meet you, Henry. Come back anytime."

Tipsy mimicked Thomas's backward momentum with her own forward steps, as if they were practicing a waltz. "Wait, Thomas. Did you see the…um…the pool? I bet you've never seen it, since you can't go in the yard. Come look—"

"I don't swim," he said.

"Oh, well. It's…pretty." A couple feet closer, and she'd fake rolling an ankle, or an aggressive sneeze. Some sudden motion to incite contact between her flailing limbs and his still ones.

"Another time, perhaps," said Thomas. He pivoted and strolled through the closed attic door.

◆———◆✕◆———◆

Henry also left—*poof, see you boys later.* Tipsy heard the shower running in Jillian's room as she descended into the house's cool lower reaches. She poked around the study, but Thomas did not reappear. She examined the framed photo of Thomas's mother, renowned local beauty Agnes Barre. Had she been able to observe her husband and her son from the next life? Did she know Rene beat on Thomas, and blamed him for her death? She thought of Dr. Legbone's silvery eyes in the portrait she'd seen in Thomas's memory, and imagined Agnes wouldn't recognize his cold stare and the hard set of his mouth. Perhaps a kind young doctor left for a supposedly noble war, only for the agonizing blood and guts reality of it to ruin him.

Tipsy was a rarity throughout human history—a mother whose son would not likely die on a battlefield. Millions upon millions of men had perished in wars. Ax fodder, sword fodder, cannon fodder, machine gun fodder, mustard gas fodder, bomb fodder. Gangrene and dysentery fodder. Men knew no other way, and wars begat wars. Some justified, like the routing of that odious German fellow, as Thomas had called him. Some terribly unjust, like Rene Bonneau's hopelessly Lost Cause. What of the destroyed men who survived? Their festering rage, or quiet sadness? Their trauma coexisted with their families like an unwelcome house guest.

Tipsy felt intense compassion for Thomas, even if he seemed happy with his afterlife existence. She regretted questioning his good humor. Good for him, if he'd managed to remain positive through the many trials of his existence.

"Thomas? You here?" she whispered, but she got no reply, so she walked onto the first floor piazza. She smiled when she saw him sitting on the top step. He stared across the yard, at the backhouse, or the greenhouse. Maybe the pool he'd never swim in.

"You look like you got a lot on your mind," she said, as she sat beside him.

He disappeared and reappeared on the bottom step. "Your friend is an interesting fellow. Thank you for bringing him to chat with me."

"When we learned you might know his mother, he... uh...felt compelled to come. I'm sorry about *your* mother. It must have been traumatic to grow up without her, especially given your father's PTSD."

"P...T..."

"S.D. *Post-traumatic Stress Disorder*. It means...he kept suffering from all the bad things he saw during the war long after it ended. So you also suffered. Maybe your mother would have suffered, too, if she'd lived. Nowadays we understand men who live through wars often abuse their families—"

"That's all too theoretical for me. I survived my father's wrath. As for whether my mother would have survived, she didn't even survive childbirth."

"Lots of women didn't—"

"As they say, y'all *are* the weaker sex."

His comment, and his condescending tone, chipped away at the empathy that had incited her philosophical chattiness. "*Men* say that. If *y'all* had to go through childbirth, *no one* would use that phrase."

"No need to get huffy over a figure of speech."

"I'm not huffy—"

"A rose by any other name would still smell as sweet." He stood and pointed at the bedraggled tea roses. "Catherine's mother tried to maintain her roses after she passed, but Betsy Rose had thorns instead of a green thumb. Sophie told me she'll make these gardens bloom again. I hope she does. It will make my porch time all the more pleasant."

"When did she say that?"

"I don't recall exactly when. Don't worry. I haven't spoken with her since she came home. If she stays in the backhouse, I *can't* speak with her."

Tipsy walked down the stairs toward him. Once again, Thomas disappeared. This time, he reappeared on the porch behind her.

Tipsy's compassion and comradery folded in the face of his sexist comments and his evasiveness. None of the ghosts she'd interacted with over the past two years had showed any awareness of her time-hopping abilities until she revealed them. Still, the abrupt ending of Thomas's last memory, his interest in Jane moving on, and his attempts to put space between himself and Tipsy indicated he knew *something*. "You alright?"

"Yes. Why?" He gave his head a good scratch. His hair stuck up for a moment, before obligingly reorienting itself.

"You seem…distracted."

"I'm well. As fine as a frog hair split three ways. Are you leaving us soon? What entertaining engagements do you have this afternoon?"

"Nothing too exciting. Got my own house to run, including yard work, and I—" She remembered Sophie disappearing into the greenhouse. "Speaking of yardwork, have you seen Sophie? I saw her going into the greenhouse."

"Ah, no. Why would anyone go into that moldy old hut?"

"I don't know, but she did. I'm afraid it's dangerous in there—"

"There's nothing in there. Nothing at all."

"But you said you can't go on that side of the property."

"I can't. I'm merely…imagining. Sophie told me, and—"

"I'll check it out for myself, thanks." Tipsy started across the yard.

"Tipsy!" said Thomas. "Don't go in there. Don't!"

He spoke with none of his usual jocularity, nor today's moody distraction. His agitation made Tipsy pick up the pace. Thomas followed her a few more feet into the yard, but then stopped. He strode along an invisible line, like an anxious football coach facing a fourth down.

He clearly preferred she *not* enter the greenhouse. All the more reason to see what was up in that moldy old hut.

Tipsy scuttled along the greenhouse wall. Upon cursory inspection through broken panes and foggy glass, the building contained nothing alarming. A hodgepodge of cracked pots, dead plants, dusty shelves and tables, broken gardening tools, and a moldy office chair. Contractors had dumped concrete from the old driveway in one corner and rotting wooden floorboards in another.

Tipsy tugged the storm door until it stuck in the grass. She sucked in her gut and squeezed inside. "Sophie? You in here?"

A protective mama mourning dove *coo-cooed* somewhere in the roof's nooks and crannies. Gently moving air eked a few jingles from ancient windchimes, and goosebumps popped up on Tipsy's bare arms.

I'm not complaining, Granna, but it's a little too chilly.

You think there's another ghost in here?

If there is, neither Sophie nor Thomas wants me to know. They both claimed he's a solo haunting. I can't think of a reasonable justification for hiding another ghost. Thomas plucked my sympathy chords today, but that tune sounds flat right now. Tipsy scowled. *Even if he had a hard life and he's as pleasant as Mister Rogers, I don't trust him as far as I can drop kick him with a broken leg—what's that humming sound?*

It wasn't the doves' monotone coos, or windchimes a'tinkling, or the buzzing of lost mosquitos.

"Who's there? Sophie?"

A cloyingly sweet smell overwhelmed the scent of rotting vegetation. She thought of the Walmart flower-fairy doll she had as a child. Generic Strawberry Shortcake couldn't decide on one flowery scent, so she'd doused her neon pink hair in all of them.

The humming originated under a crooked rectangular card table covered in small black pots. Tipsy knelt and crept toward the sound on her hands and knees. "Hello?"

Something moved in the darkness, and the humming started again. She caught a few words. Something about someone being here and then gone.

What the heck? The intense floral aroma made her gorge rise.

The voice called out to someone named Mary. Then a giggle, and the tune changed. "Can you come a little closer? How about now?"

"Hel-*loooo*?"

Bright blue eyes appeared in the gloom. "Hi...*Sharona!*"

Tipsy fell backwards on her butt. She spun around and scrambled into a crouch, a ninja in jean shorts. A thin female form stood at the opposite end of the greenhouse, near the discarded cement. She wore white terrycloth shorts, rainbow knee socks with no shoes, and a white tank top.

Her long, tangled auburn hair hung into her eyes like rotting seaweed. "Do you...want to come little closer...now?"

"Hello? Hey!" Tipsy held up both hands. "I'm sorry if I scared you—"

"*My-yi-yi... Whooooop-dee-do!*" Like shifting continental plates, the cement blocks behind the girl creaked and ground against one another. A rusty shovel tipped over and shattered a clay pot.

"No need to throw stuff around. Let's talk, alright?" The girl's arms fell to her sides, but she kept muttering. With her mop of auburn hair, Tipsy had no trouble guessing her identity. *Hair color is the one thing Betsy Porcher's wannabe artist friend got right.*

Catherine Rose, replied Granna.

"How about I introduce myself—" Two windows exploded over Tipsy's head. She covered her face, but flying bits of glass stung her arms. "Hey! *Stop it!*"

One blue eye appeared from behind the ghost's hair. "Are you...*real?*"

"I'm as real as the Velveteen Rabbit."

"*When you're real, shabbiness doesn't matter.*" A crooked smile chased itself over her face.

"Do you like that story? I always loved when the Skin Horse says—"

"So! Sharona! It's just a matter of time, you know." Another window burst. Catherine bounced on her toes and her hair flipped and flopped. She was the creepy girl from *The Ring* crossed with a headbanging AC/DC fan.

Not AC/DC, said Granna. *A pair of lips on her shirt.*

Tipsy seized the opportunity to make a connection. "You like the Rolling Stones? My Granna *loved* Mick Jag—"

"I'm *so* pleased to meet you! I hope you can guess my name."

"Catherine Rose Porcher, right?"

A windchime detached from the ceiling and sailed through an empty windowpane with a strangled *clinkety-clink*. The frantic beating of wings, and two doves followed.

Follow that bird and get out of here, Tipsy, said Granna. *You can always come back!*

I gotta try, Granna! "Shhhh! Catherine, please. It's frightening, but—"

"*Tipsy!* What are you doing in here?" Sophie stood just inside the greenhouse door.

"Is it Sophie-Soph?" Catherine peered through the parted curtains of her hair. "And who is *she?*"

"That's Tipsy, Aunt Catherine. I know her. She's a…friend."

"Good lord, Sophie," said Tipsy, with a frustrated laugh. "We're friends, right. Yet you failed to mention you also know your *dead aunt.* I've been obsessing over Thomas Bonneau, while your damn aunt was chillin' up in the greenhouse. To top it off, you and Thomas lied to me! Y'all claimed he's a solo haunting."

"He *is* a solo haunting. Catherine died *somewhere else.* She isn't stuck here like Thomas. She can *move around,* like your friend Henry—"

Tipsy was having none of Sophie's psychic-splaining. "You don't need to enlighten me about traveling ghosts, missy. What you need to do is tell me which of these ghosts is responsible for you losing your shit. Your own personal Dorian Gray, or this deceased version of *Girl, Interrupted?*"

"Stop yelling!" said Catherine, but these Porcher-Yates women were slam-dancing on Tipsy's last nerve.

"*Miss Porcher,*" barked Tipsy, in the kind of voice she reserved for breaking up fisticuffs among her children. "I'm discussing something important with your niece, who has been lying to me *and* your sister—"

"My sister?"

"Don't bring up Mom. She doesn't like—"

"Ooh! Jilly! That snake in the grass! I'd like to give her what for! A piece of my mind! My twenty-five cents on the dollar!" Catherine levitated, and her wild hair blew around her head like an ill-fitting halo. Glass *pop-pop-pop-popped* as rows of mason jars shattered.

Back in the day when she first started cooking, Tipsy had accidentally poured cold water into a hot glass baking pan. The pan had exploded with a comparable staccato cracking. With glass embedded in their porkchops, Tipsy and Ayers had ordered pizza. A shard of flying glass to the face, and her eyesight might meet a similar fate. A seemingly paralyzed Sophie stared at her floating, deceased auntie. Her big hazel eyes were equally vulnerable.

"Sophie! Watch out!"

Tipsy darted across the greenhouse and embraced the frozen Sophie. Windows disintegrated above their heads. Tipsy pulled Sophie close and buried her own face in the girl's hair.

The breeze stopped. When Tipsy raised her head, she smelled dirt. Maybe some bird poo. Catherine Porcher was gone, and she'd taken the scent of cheap perfume with her. A brave dove flew through an open window pane. Like any good mother, she sought to confirm the safety of her children. The dove cooed comfort from the rafters, but Tipsy felt no reassurance.

Within the span of fifteen minutes, she'd doubled her paranormal workload.

Tipsy stepped away from Sophie and looked down at her own arms. A thin line of blood ran from her wrist to her elbow. Something tickled her neck, and she swiped another bloody scratch. She ran her hands over her face, but thankfully, no more blood appeared on her hands.

Sophie backed away from her. "Wow. That was *crazy*, right? You're... uh, bleeding—"

"What in the *hell*, Sophie!" Tipsy swiped her bleeding arm with her shirt.

"We should get you a band-aid—"

"Band-aid my behind! I *asked* you if there were any other ghosts in the house. You looked me in the face and said *noooo.*"

"I only found her in the greenhouse recently—"

"You said she died somewhere else. Jillian told me she was hit by a car, but she didn't say where."

"Up by Colonial Lake."

Tipsy pictured the tree-lined, rectangular body of water less than half a mile from the Bonneau House, bordered by Broad Street, Ashley Avenue, Rutledge Avenue, and Beaufain Street. Walkers and joggers made good use of the wide promenade encircling the lake. As children, Henry and his brother had paddled around it in canoes, back when locals simply referred to it as The Pond.

"So Catherine *was* a clairvoyant." She laughed again. "A *schizophrenic* clairvoyant. Now that's a new one."

"Yes," said Sophie. "She's like us—"

Tipsy paced the dirt greenhouse floor. "So she died by Colonial Lake, but her clairvoyance allows her to visit the house. But I've never seen her *inside* the house—"

"When she visits, she stays in the greenhouse for the most part. She doesn't *like* the house."

"Right. Jillian also told me Catherine's voices were worse in the house."

"Yes. Louder, and echoey," said Sophie. "But there's also the issue of…"

"What? How many issues can we have here?"

"Catherine and Thomas don't get along."

"Why not?"

"I'm not sure. She's never really explained it. She can't explain much of anything. But she does not like him *at all.*"

Tipsy's head might be the next thing to explode in that greenhouse. Her frazzled brain sought the order of a timeline. "When did you start talking to Thomas?"

"I first noticed him on the porch when we visited BeeBee. I avoided him. He didn't even realize I saw him. But BeeBee's death made me *so sad.* I thought about my father. I wanted to talk to *someone* who understands what it feels like to be dead. I waited for him in the study and I introduced myself."

"In January, right? And you met Catherine—"

"Before spring break. I wanted to plant a new rose bush in BeeBee's memory. I came into the greenhouse to find some trowels, and she was here."

"Then a few weeks later, you're in a mental hospital. Neither ghost is good for you." Tipsy made for the door. "Your mom will freak out when she finds out Catherine is here—"

"Please don't tell her! She'll probably move us out that day."

"Sophie, this secretiveness is not healthy, and Catherine is dangerous. Look at all this broken glass."

"You upset her by busting up in here. She doesn't do that stuff all the time. She quiets down when I talk to her calmly, but she doesn't let me get close to her, or say much beyond singing some weird old songs. Except when she talks about—uh…never mind."

"No, ma'am. No *never minds* allowed. What does she talk about?"

"I told you. She doesn't like Thomas. And she doesn't like…Mom. But Thomas is really nice to me—"

"You believe what this crazy woman says about your *own mother*, but not about Thomas?"

Sophie ignored Tipsy's question. "All I know is Mom will make us leave if she realizes Catherine is here. It's already annoying being stuck in the backhouse—"

Cry me a river of alligator tears! said Granna.

"—but who knows where Mom will take me? Maybe back to California."

"Would that be so awful?"

Sophie crossed her arms over her chest. Tipsy recognized a standoff when she saw one. "I didn't ask for you to be involved in this. That's my mom's idea. I'm sure she's paying you to be my clairvoyance counselor, or *whatever*, and you want your money."

"I admit she's paying me, and I do want the money. *Need* it. But I'm also looking at a nineteen-year-old girl with major problems, including depression, anxiety, and two possibly dangerous ghosts. I'm trying to do the right thing, too, and you won't let me help you."

"You and Mom want me to stay in the backhouse, away from Thomas. I've been cooperating, but I only agree to *keep* staying away from him if *you* don't tell Mom about Catherine. Mom can't watch me all the time. I might just end up *back inside*, having a little chat with Tom."

Tipsy considered her steely eyes. Even if she didn't realize it, Sophie was her mother's daughter.

"For now, I won't tell her," said Tipsy. "But for your safety, I want you to stay away from Thomas *and* Catherine. If I find out you're talking to either of them, Jillian will be in the know. Your butt will be in a hotel faster than you can say Belmond Charleston Place."

"Okay, fine." Tipsy's stare finally caught up with Sophie, and she shuffled her feet. "I'm sorry you got hurt. There's a first aid kit in my apartment. You should get some band-aids, for real."

"I'll live. But I'm not leaving you in here, so please lead the way to the band-aids."

Sophie soundlessly turned and left the greenhouse. Tipsy followed her to the backhouse's bathroom. She examined her reflection in the mirror as Sophie retrieved a box of band-aids from under the sink. She gingerly pulled a chunk of glass out of her hair.

Still have two functional eyes, Granna.

You got lucky.

Agreed, and not only with my eyeballs. I unintentionally identified a second problematic phantom, who may have useful information about the first one. Catherine may be even crazier than your average ghost, and maybe she's the one who put Sophie over the edge. Still, I can't ignore the fact that she doesn't like Thomas. She's a clairvoyant, and she lived in this house with him. She'll have some insight into him, if we can get it out of her.

I hoped his pleasant demeanor was as straightforward as a marching army, but your instincts about him may be right.

We agree it was a productive, if dangerous, encounter. Tipsy unwrapped a band-aid and covered the cut on her arm. *While there's still a hell of a lot to figure out, at least now I fully understand what I'm dealing with.*

Hopefully. In this business, there's always another ghost waiting to be found.

Chapter 9

Tipsy resisted the urge to immediately discuss Catherine Porcher with Henry, and forced herself to spend the afternoon painting before picking up the kids from their school's aftercare. Henry was still recovering from his consecutive downtown trips and didn't make an appearance, so she got in several productive hours on the front porch. To her satisfaction, she'd painted her way down to the heron's knobby knees. Only their lower legs and feet remained unfinished, as if both birds wore white knee socks. Once modestly covered with purply-gray plumage, their dissatisfied expressions seemed to soften into wise avian benevolence.

She tidied her supplies, changed her paint splattered clothes, retrieved the kids, and whisked them through the Chick-fil-A drive through. "How about y'all watch a movie while you eat dinner?" she said, as they piled through the front door and into the kitchen.

"You serious, Mom?" asked Little Ayers. "Chick-fil-A in front of a movie?"

"Are you feeling alright?" chimed in Mary Pratt.

"Yes, goofballs. I have some…work stuff to take care of. But I demand silence in return for this fun evening. No fighting about the movie or anything else." She handed the Chick-fil-A bag to Little Ayers, and divvied up the drinks and napkins between the girls.

"Okay, Mamacita," said O-Liv. "Unless something craaaazy happens, we'll leave you alone."

"Like what kind of crazy? The roof blowing off?" said Mary Pratt. "Or a psycho murderer climbing in the window?"

"Ugh, stop, M.P.," said O-Liv. "That stuff scares me."

"Don't worry," said Little Ayers, as they disappeared into the little den off the kitchen. "No one is getting murdered in our house in boring ol' Mount Pleasant."

"Can we watch *High School Musical*?" asked M.P.

"Again? Barf."

"Ayers, we *can't fight*," said O-Liv.

Tipsy cringed as she shut the door behind them. If they knew about Henry and Jane's unfortunate demise, Little A's speech might lose its comforting effect.

She made a loop of the first floor, but she didn't find Henry, so she returned to the kitchen. "Henry, come out. Talking about your mother might have been uncomfortable, but after you left, things got *even weirder*."

He appeared at the table. "I can never resist your weirdness."

"I'll get to that, but first, what did you think of Thomas?"

"He's very pleasant. Smart, polite, inquisitive. Enjoys a good laugh. You were right about his congeniality."

"It doesn't strike you as strange that he's so happy?"

"If he's found a way to be at peace with this state, I admire him."

"That line of thinking crossed my mind, too, but something about him sticks in my craw." She sat beside him at the table. "Maybe your mother admired him, too. I still wonder about a romantic connection between them. Was your mother married before your father?"

"I don't believe so. She was close to thirty when my brother was born. I came along two years later. I got the impression she lost a baby or two before us, but she never gave details."

"You sound so casual, like she lost a couple pet cats."

"Most people lost *at least* one child. Your generation takes healthy children for granted. But if she married anyone else, she never spoke of it. Besides, Thomas didn't like her."

"Maybe he liked her at one point. Even loved her. Let's think…Say they got hitched and then he died. She never told your father, or you and Edward, because—" Tipsy's eyes widened. "*She* killed him! Maybe they had an affair and she got pregnant and—"

"Tipsy, I understand we must explore all scenarios, but that one verges on asinine."

"Why? Like I told Ivy, I've learned anyone—"

"Can kill anyone. I know, but my mother may have been catty and mean, but she was no murderer. She was too concerned with appearances. She wouldn't get an invitation to Theresa Robinette's bridge club with *murder* following her."

"I can't rule it out. You never know what someone will do in the heat of the moment."

Henry shrugged. "I can't make you rule it out. As for Thomas's jovial contentment, by my estimation, he had a cheerful character in life, and he somehow maintained it in death. He's not *wholly* innocent. I don't approve of his shenanigans with the…scarlet woman. But he was young, and in those days, people were less tolerant about most things, but more inclined to look the other way about others. I doubt the man with one hundred and forty years to consider the moral implications of such behavior would condone it now."

"You drank his…" Henry probably wouldn't know Kool-Aid, so Tipsy improvised. "…sugary…lemonade. One meeting with him, and he's some great guy. Maybe you like him because he *doesn't* like your mother."

"That's quite unfair, and insulting. I'm not so shallow. I like him because he's—"

"I don't want to argue. The fact is, Patience wouldn't be in these memories if she wasn't relevant to Thomas's death. He employed her around the time he died." She leaned toward him. "Henry, we may need to take things a step further. A *whole bunch* of steps, down Bull Street."

"Are you suggesting we look for my *mother's ghost?*"

Tipsy nodded. "She's probably not there. But if she is, we can ask her directly about Thomas."

"I *do not* fancy talking to some crazy old crone with the remnants of my mother's face."

"Please, Henry. I'll go with you. If Patience does happen to be there, maybe y'all can reconcile—"

Henry raised one hand. She blinked, as if he'd exhaled into her face. The gust of his supernatural agitation lifted her hair.

"Once again, I will consider it," he said. "Now on to other topics, please. You promised me something *even weirder*."

She told him about Thomas's evasiveness, and how he'd insisted she shouldn't enter the greenhouse. She finished with the *piece de resistance*: Catherine Porcher's intermittent presence on the property. "According to Sophie, she stays in the greenhouse. She doesn't like the main house in general, but she also doesn't like Thomas. She must have a reason."

"Catherine does not sound like a reliable source of information," said Henry. "But if she dislikes him, the feeling must be mutual. I can't see any other reason Thomas would want you to stay out of the greenhouse."

"Right. I wonder what happened between them? Does she know something he doesn't want *us* to know?"

"Again, you must consider the source of anything she claims to know. Perhaps Thomas is a superfluous spirit and Sophie Rose's real problem lies with Catherine. Catherine is wholly insane. Such a person cannot by her very nature be a positive influence on a young woman with her own hysterical tendencies. Besides, Catherine is the one who has dangerous powers."

"It's possible I've been chasing the wrong ghost. But I still think Thomas—"

"Is a fine, lovely man. Wonderful! We agree he's harmless, so no need to look for my mother."

Before Tipsy responded, Henry vanished. "*Argh*," she said.

As she emptied the trash, she bemoaned the unfairness of it all. How could she win an argument with someone who so definitively ended every conversation? Such a talent would have come in damn handy during her marriage.

———◆✕◆———

Tipsy is twenty-three, and she and Ayers just returned from their honeymoon in the Bahamas. They're staying with his parents on Sullivan's Island for a week. She's counting the days until they move into their new apartment on Society Street.

Of course, she loves her new family. Ayers's sister Mimi has become a dear friend. She was two years ahead of Tipsy at Carolina, and her sorority, Tri-Gamma, mixed with KZ. Mimi and Mr. Tripp always make Tipsy feel welcome, but Miss May Penny is the alpha-gamecock in the Collins' family's roost. Even after five years, Tipsy isn't sure what to make of her. She's always very nice, but Tipsy senses something chilly under her compliments, like a cold current swooshing around her legs in a warm creek. After four days in her house, Tipsy is ready for her own space.

Miss May Penny and Mr. Tripp—no…plain May Penny and Tripp. They're related now, so she has to drop the honorifics. May Penny and Tripp set up the guest suite and its adjoining bathroom for Tipsy and Ayers. It's decorated prettier than their honeymoon suite at Sandals, with an even better view. They're married, and it's perfectly fine for them to sleep in the same bed, but May Penny seems to be judging Tipsy for sleeping with her own husband. When Ayers tries to get frisky, she claims a headache. The idea of having sex in her in-laws' house—even legitimate, married sex—is a real mood killer.

After a long day on the boat, and a wonderfully hot washdown in the outdoor shower, Tipsy feels as relaxed as she can be in May Penny's luxurious domain. Tipsy and Ayers sit on the balcony off their bedroom, overlooking the Intracoastal Waterway and the marsh, and talk about their plans for the apartment. That conversation leads to some friendly gossip about their friends.

"Can you believe Shelby is already engaged again?" asks Ayers.

"I don't think she'll follow through with it." Tipsy props her feet on the little table between their chairs. Ayers pulls one of them into his lap and runs his hands over her calf. It feels good, and she's glad she shaved her legs that morning. "Her parents will freak out. They're still mad about all the money they lost on the last wedding."

"*So wild how she called it off two weeks before. Did she give back all the wedding gifts?*"

"*The unmonogrammed stuff. Mrs. Patterson was so embarrassed. But better two weeks of notice than Shelby pulling a runaway bride and fleeing down the aisle with her Vera Wang veil trailing in her wake.*"

He laughs. "*Yeah. Weddings are crazy. Ours was really fun, but it felt like it was more about my parents than us.*"

Tipsy had tentatively expressed the same sentiment during the planning, much to Ayers's annoyance, but he usually came around to her point of view if she waited long enough.

"*I agree,*" *she said,* "*but it was a beautiful day and a great party.*"

"*I can't wait to get the video from the videographer. The dancing. The toasts and speeches. Clifton's best man speech cracked me up. Too many fraternity house stories for Mama's liking, but the laughs were worth it.*"

"*Hmmm.*"

Ayers shakes her foot. "*You're not still pissed about my speech, are you?*"

"*I never said I was pissed. My feelings were hurt.*"

"*I'd had a few drinks. I wasn't thinking about anything but who I needed to thank.*"

The list of people he thanked was long and effusively delivered, and included his parents, his parents' friends, his dad's business associates, his mother's church friends and his dad's golf buddies, his fraternity brothers, his other college and high school friends, his cousins and aunts and uncles, and at the last second, his sister Mimi and her own brand new husband. The one person he didn't mention: Tipsy herself.

She'd sat there listening to him, with her dramatically upswept hair, in the gown she'd scrounged for months to buy from David's Bridal. No Vera Wang, but she loved it, with its trendy, tightly cinched dropped waist and billowy ballgown skirt. She had no family in attendance, but Ayers's jovial shout out to their college friends seemed to include Shelby and the rest of her sorority sisters. It was Tipsy herself who received zero recognition. She had no one to speak up for her—congratulate her—tell her she looked beautiful and she was valued.

"We don't need to go over this again, Ayers."

"You brought it up."

"What? No, I didn't."

"Yes, you did. With your hmmmmm when I mentioned the speeches. I can tell you're pissed—"

"I told you. I was hurt. There's a big difference."

"It slipped my mind, okay?"

She hates fighting with Ayers, but as he yammers on, her irritation grows. Somehow, any reference to his blushing bride—who would, God willing, be the mother of his children—had slipped his mind. Like he forgot to get eggs at the grocery store.

"It was my wedding, too. It would have been nice to be mentioned by someone. You said everything was about your parents, but it was more about you than anyone else. It's like you were the bride, not me."

"Really, Tipsy? That's the pettiest damn thing I've ever heard. Our life is all about your princess fantasies?"

"No! Please, let's forget this. We've already had this conversation at least twice."

"Because you're not seeing it the right way!"

"How is there a right or wrong way to see it? It's how I feel."

"You shouldn't feel that way. You know I love you. It was a lot of pressure to stand up there and talk in front of everyone—"

"You love being the center of attention!"

"—and worry I'd forget someone."

His logic is beyond her comprehension. That's the whole point. He had forgotten someone. His new wife.

"You're always so sensitive about everything. Damn." He stands. "I'm going downstairs to see what Mama's making for dinner and get a beer."

He disappears into the house. She watches puttering boats crisscross the Intracoastal. As the minutes tick by, she starts questioning herself. Is she too sensitive? About this issue, and others? His parents paid for the wedding, even though they just footed the bill for Mimi's six months ago. Tripp hadn't planned on two big weddings, as he only had one daughter, *but they made it as nice as Mimi's. Maybe Ayers felt bad for putting them out. And he must have been super nervous, standing there in front of nearly four hundred people.*

Her own feelings try to stake themselves out, but she rips them up. She's being a prima donna. Expecting the whole day to be about her, when Ayers is equally important. Doesn't she consider herself a modern woman, all about equality?

Her position is pretty selfish. Unreasonable. Immature. Soon guilt overrides hurt and irritation.

She stands to find her husband and apologize, but he's standing in the doorway. "I brought you a beer," he says. He hands her a Corona with a lime. She doesn't much like Corona, but it's the thought that counts.

This is Ayers's way of making peace. He breaks the silence first. Brings her something. Sometimes she wishes he'd just say he's sorry, but it's still sweet.

She sips the beer and murmurs thanks. He starts to turn around, but she takes his arm. "I'm not mad about the speech, baby," she says. "Seriously. It's a silly thing to be upset about."

"True," he says, as if she's shared some great revelation.

"Let's forget it, okay?" She squeezes his bicep.

He grabs her around her waist and pulls her close. "I'll forget it if you forget about that dress. Why don't you just forget it on the floor, right now?"

She laughs. "I'm gonna spill beer on your Mama's carpet and there will be hell to pay."

He sets her beer on the dresser. He kisses her, and she does forget it, for a while. She doesn't know that for years to come, whenever anyone speaks of conjugal unions and their associated pomp and circumstance, she'll think about Ayers's speech. About being forgotten at her own wedding. But she'll just as quickly remind herself her feelings were wrong, and he'd been right. Such a silly thing to be upset about.

——◆✕◆——

Tipsy navigated her Tahoe through the last day of school carpool craziness like a border collie darting between a bunch of frantic sheep. She squeezed into a spot by the curb and hit the unlock button. "Happy LDOS, buddies!" she said, as the kids piled out of the car. "Love y'all!"

"Love you too, Mama-Mia," said Olivia Grace. "Peace out, second grade!"

"Love you, Mom—Emily! *Emily*, wait for me!" Mary Pratt slammed the door, but Little Ayers was still exiting the car.

"M.P.!" he yelled, as the door banged off his backpack.

"Mary Pratt!" said Tipsy. "You about squashed your brother!"

"Sorry!" M.P. raced after her friend.

"You okay, A?" asked Tipsy.

"Yeah. Why is M.P. always in such a darn hurry?"

"Now that's a mystery, isn't it?" said Olivia Grace.

Tipsy laughed. "I'll see y'all this afternoon."

Little Ayers and O-Liv joined the line of excited kids walking into the school building. Tipsy looked for M.P., but the social butterfly had already fluttered inside.

She is a mystery, Tipsy said to Granna. *She's got more of her daddy in her than the other two. The good parts, thank goodness.*

We all got good to pass on, even Big Ayers, said Granna. *Speaking of mysteries, when will you have time to go back to the Bonneau House?*

Not sure. I'm at the GQB the next few days.

Hmm. I won't begrudge any mama time with her new baby, but hopefully Shelby decides to come back to work soon.

I know, but if it's quiet at work, I'll work on sketches for new paintings. Besides, with Catherine on the scene and Thomas actively avoiding me, a few days of forced, off-site strategizing might be just what Dr. Legbone ordered.

Tipsy eased on the brakes at a stoplight. She looked in the rearview mirror at the brown paper-wrapped rectangle of the heron painting. It was finally ready for delivery, and she didn't want to jostle it. She checked her phone, and as usual, she smiled at a text from Scott. HEY. I'M GOING IN TO THE HOSPITAL A LITTLE LATE. YOU STILL DROPPING OFF THE HERONS IN I'ON?

TIPSY: HOW CONVENIENT. YES, I AM ☺

SCOTT: YOU HAVE TIME TO STOP BY FOR A FEW MINUTES?

TIPSY: YUP.

SCOTT: YAY ☺

He sent her his address. She opened the window and let the wind whip her hair across her cheeks and into her eyes. A typical Charleston early summer day, with minimal humidity, brilliantly blue skies, and fluffy white clouds like towering, airborne Persian cats and Angora bunnies. The Tahoe's worn leather seats felt warm under her butt. Her phone's shuffling landed on one of her favorite Pearl Jam songs, and she blasted it. Like Eddie Vedder, she was very much alive.

She dropped off the herons with her client's nanny, along with strict instructions to forbid the family's children from touching it. Several minutes later, she arrived at Scott's house, a sage green nouveau Charleston single with a matching detached garage and a short driveway. A sprawling oak tree spread its limbs over the small, tidy front yard and across the narrow street. The swing hanging from its sturdiest limb moved with the breeze, as if the tree was waving at her. She parked and walked up the steps. A quick visual sweep of the front porch: a shiny joggling board, two rocking chairs, two matching potted palms, a eucalyptus leaf wreath, and an iron welcome mat engraved with a swirly B. She raised her hand to knock, but he opened the door.

He had on jeans and a tee-shirt and he was barefoot. "Come on in."

She walked inside and he shut the door behind her. "Your house is so cute," she said.

"It's a work in progress, but I'm pretty excited about it. The first place I've bought on my own. Decorated on my own. You know how it is."

She nodded, although she had no personal experience with such satisfaction. Ayers had dominated their home purchases and interior decorating, complete with his contrarian drab, IKEA-inspired aesthetic. Her current house wasn't legally hers, but at least she had her own space. She envied Scott, who could slap any shade of paint on his walls. Hot pink, electric blue, pea green. If he had space and inspiration, he could set up the master bedroom in the kitchen. It was all up to him.

He spent ten minutes showing her around the cozy four-bedroom house. Tipsy noted a fastidious neatness. She almost saw her reflection in the hardwood floors. Not a bit of clutter. No evidence of kids' sports equipment, nor a piece of junk mail. Not one errant shoe or abandoned sock on the staircase, waiting to be taken upstairs to someone's room. The jackets on the hooks outside the laundry room were arranged by season and color, dark and heavy to light-hued and lightweight. They ended in the kitchen, where the island and countertops were equally pristine. No tangle of random electronic chargers or water cups clustered beside the sink. A Swiffer leaned against the pantry door like a soldier awaiting its next orders.

"Do you have a live-in maid? This place is spotless."

"No maid. Only me."

"Not to be cliché, but that's kind of unusual for a man. At least the men I know."

"I have a touch of OCD." He opened a drawer. Cooking implements were lined up by function and size; hand towels perfectly folded in color-coordinated stacks. "Maybe more than a touch."

She laughed. "Very *Sleeping with the Enemy*."

"You should see my pantry. It may or may not be alphabetized." He pointed at the Swiffer-sentry. "I tend to Swiffer when stressed. Hope that doesn't scare you off."

"Not scary. Attractive! And a tad intimidating. I consider myself neat, but I could not keep up with *this*."

"You may want to reserve judgment. You haven't seen my neuroses in full effect yet."

"I can't wait." She leaned against the island and pointed out the trees through the window. "You have some great trees on your lot."

"I do," he said, with a smile.

"What, silly?"

He held out his arms. "Can I just—"

"Do you have to ask?" She rested her head on his shoulder. He squeezed, just tight enough, and tension drained out of him. "You okay?" she whispered.

"Yeah. Totally. Some work stress. I can be a little…tightly wound. But hugging you…makes it feel better."

She looked up at him. "I'm *so* glad."

He kissed her and that was it. She's seen his bedroom on her tour, and she saw it again. This time, from the bed's perspective.

———◆✕◆———

It was a damn good thing the Bonneau House was not on her agenda. A cruise ship dumped off several thousand tourists in downtown Charleston, but she didn't mind that approximately half of them wandered into the GQB. She had no time to draw, as they asked her umpteen mundane yet time-consuming questions. They purchased no art, but their queries solicited autopilot answers. Blessedly little need to concentrate, as brain fog would have hindered both her mystery solving and her artistic inspiration.

To be clear, her muddled state was no *dreary* brain fog. Far from it. More like an electrically charged, smoky fireworks display.

Tipsy had never hopped in the sack with someone like she swan-dived into Scott's neatly made bed. She'd only been on a few dates with him, but the whole interaction felt as healthy and natural as the Whole Food's produce section. She hadn't taken it *all the way*, as Granna would have said, but she'd taken it a hell of a lot farther than she'd expected.

As the clock had reminded them of their daily responsibilities, he'd pulled her onto his chest and ran his fingers over her back. When she could delay no more, she rose to get herself together. He hovered over her and helped her track down strewn pieces of clothing. He even retrieved his comb and made a sweetly comical attempt to brush her hair. As she left, he stood in the doorway in his jeans, bare-chested and a little shivery. This time, he asked if *she* was okay. She gave him an unequivocal *yes*, and he assured her they'd talk soon. Within an hour, she received a text from him.

Amazing. I'm really happy, Tipsy.

I'm really happy too, Scott.

I'm at work. Then taking the kids to dinner later. I'll call you tonight when I get home.

KK. ☺

It felt *good*. It felt *right*. But for some inexplicable reason, tears once again pricked her eyes.

How can I be so happy and so scared, Granna?

I think Pamella is right. You're reliving a lot of old, unpleasant feelings.

I just want to enjoy this. It's what I've wanted since I decided to leave Ayers. Although, I don't know if my hopes were ever this high.

High hopes come with a fear of a far fall. I'm sorry if I made it worse with my grumbling.

Your concerns are legitimate. I'm still worried about Ayers's reaction.

Me too. But I love seeing you happy when you're with this man, and y'all can forget about Ayers for a while.

Thank you, Granna. I hope it's not too good to be true.

That evening, the primary source of Tipsy's worry showed up on her doorstep as she helped the girls clean out their backpacks. They stood around the kitchen table, sorting through notebooks, topless markers, art projects, and old assignments. With a bang on the door and the creak of it opening, Big Ayers's voice echoed through the foyer. "Anybody home?"

"Daddy!" O-Liv dropped her cracked pencil case and ran down the hallway. M.P. followed her.

Little Ayers walked inside with his lacrosse stick as Big Ayers hugged the girls and listened to their chatter about the last day of school.

"How was practice?" Tipsy asked her son.

"Good, but I'm so tired, and my coach is making me play goalie this weekend. Ugh." He clumped toward the stairs.

"Go up and take a shower. I'm making tacos for dinner."

"Yay, taco night!" said M.P. in a singsong voice.

"Tacos, tacos!" O-Liv joined her.

"Blah, Mom," said Little A. "I'm sick of tacos. Can't we order pizza?"

"We just had Chick-fil-A. Not tonight, buddy."

"But—"

"Hush up, A," said Big Ayers. "Your mother is making a nice dinner. You eat it. This isn't a restaurant."

"Sorry, Mom. I'm annoyed about being goalie."

"It's all right, buddy."

The girls drifted back to the kitchen. They happily argued about whether tacos should have beans on them or not.

"Thanks for backing me up," Tipsy said to Ayers.

"No problem. These evening practices are hard. But other than playing goalie once in a while, he likes lacrosse. Funny game. We didn't have a lacrosse team at Pinegrounds in my day."

"No lax at Martinville High School, either."

"Now it's all the rage. All the Yankees moving to town." He sniffed. "Everything good with you?"

"Yeah. Thanks for asking." She sensed he wanted her to ask him the same thing, so she said, "How about you?"

He waved her outside and she followed him into the front yard. "Remember what we talked about the other day?" he asked.

"About you and Kate fighting?"

"Yeah. It's…it's constant. I'm losing it."

"What happened?"

"She accused me of flirting with the woman who came over to measure the windows for drapes. I was *nice* to her. Offered her some water. She went to USC, so we talked about Columbia. After she left, Kate got mad, saying I talked to her too much and was inappropriate. She made me feel like a creep. The woman was only like twenty-five. Pretty girl, but come on. I'm not that kind of guy."

"No. You've never been the type to go after younger women."

That's Will's problem, said Granna.

Haha, but true.

164

"Then last night she demanded to go through my phone because she thinks I'm texting the damn blinds girl. I was so pissed."

"What did you do?"

"Told her to back the hell off. Stop accusing me of being a cheater and a goddamn cradle robber."

"That's one way to deal with it. Did y'all work it out?"

"I don't even know. We haven't spoken all day. It's funny, but I *almost*...nah."

"What?"

"I almost feel sorry for her ex. The doctor guy." Ayers snorted. "Mr. GQ with his perfect hair and freakin' suit every day."

"Uh. Yeah. I've met him. He probably wears a suit for work—"

"Whatever. It's not *natural* for a man to be so put together, and he's a dickhead from everything Kate's told me. Still, he must have had the patience of a nun with a whisky buzz to deal with this bullshit for so long."

"Ayers, this does not sound good. Y'all just got married. You can't be ready to throw in the towel yet."

"Calm *down*, Tipsy. Damn. I didn't say I'm throwing any towels anywhere. Don't get all—what the hell?"

A white Lexus pulled into Tipsy's driveway. She caught a glimpse of blonde hair and a flash of mirrored sunglasses. Kate got out of the car in head-to-toe Lululemon. "Hey!" she said. "You're still here. Hey, Tipsy."

"Hey, Kate." Tipsy had always gone out of her way to be nice to Kate. She wanted to have a good relationship with someone who spent a lot of time with her kids, and she had nothing against the woman. She genuinely wished Kate and Ayers the best, and for a while at least, marriage had made him chill out. "How's it going?"

"Oh, *you know*. Running errands."

"Where are Tristan and Chloe?" asked Ayers.

Tipsy knew the answer to that question, since Scott had told her, but her face stayed as blank as the twins' leftover wide-ruled composition paper.

"Scott is taking them to dinner," said Kate. "*Shocker.* He actually wants to spend extra time with them."

"So…what are you doing here?" asked Ayers.

"Stopped by to tell you I'm heading to Pilates. Since the studio is around the corner."

She's checking up on him, said Granna. *Making sure he was really at Little A's practice, and not getting measured for window treatments in the back seat of his truck.*

Tipsy bit her lip to keep from laughing.

"Huh. Okay. Thanks for letting me know," said Ayers. "I'll see you at home."

She smiled. "Yup, sure!"

Ayers turned to Tipsy with a hint of desperation in his eyes. "I'm going fishing tomorrow. Might not be home in time to take A to practice."

"All good. I'll get him there."

"Fishing, again! If it's not the fish, it's the deer or the ducks or the turkeys," said Kate. "I don't know how you put up with it, Tipsy! Haha!"

"Haha, right."

"I do hope Ayers will teach Tristan to hunt. A man should learn, right? My ex grew up in the sticks in Tennessee and has never shot a gun in his life." She rolled her eyes.

"Wow. Crazy," said Tipsy, who already knew that bit of information, too.

Kate stood beside her car, as if waiting for Ayers to get into his.

"See you, Tipsy," said Ayers. "Thanks for getting A to practice."

"Sure," said Tipsy.

Once Ayers was in his truck, safely out of the reach of window treatment girls and ex-wives, Kate disappeared into her own car. Henry materialized beside Tipsy as Ayers and Kate drove away.

"Big Ayers has his own problems," said Henry. "Amusing, how he loves to insist upon you *calming down*, when he's the one who is *worked up*." He smiled. "Did I say that right?"

"Yes. Well said. Granna thinks men fall back on that defense when they can't control their own emotions. Easier to dismiss a woman's feelings, or make up new feelings for her, than address your own issues."

Henry scowled. Tipsy knew he was sorting through his own memories for examples of such reprehensible behavior. She saved him from his self-flagellation. "Anyway, that was bizarre. Good lord. There is *so much* going on right now. Add Kate showing up at my house to stalk Ayers to the list of things I have to process."

"I've done some processing myself."

"About your mom?" asked Tipsy. "Are you ready to see if we can find her?"

He nodded. "Yes. But no need to search for her."

"But Henry, if she's there, it's the only way to—"

"No *if's*, Tipsy. She's there. I already found her."

Chapter 10

T he next morning, Tipsy dropped the kids at her former sister-in-law Mimi's place to hang with their cousins and kids from Mimi's neighborhood for a first day of summer pool party. Mimi thrived on the chaos of children running in and out of her house. She'd made homemade popsicles and baked cupcakes; restocked her pool noodles and planned arts and crafts activities. She even hung a *School's Out* banner on her front porch and tied sunshine-shaped mylar balloons to her mailbox. God bless such mothers, as for all her personal artsy creativity, Tipsy had long ago accepted she'd never achieve such Instagram-friendly maternal perfection.

Mimi welcomed Tipsy's brood a few hours early so Tipsy could get to work. Tipsy raced downtown to squeeze in a palaver with Henry's dead mother before she had to open the gallery for business. She met him at his family's former home, the largest building on the rather cramped Bull Street block between Smith Street and Rutledge Avenue. The rundown white clapboard house with faded black shutters direly needed a pressure washing. Vines crept around the foundation, leaving mildewy green snail trails. Rather than the usual long, slim profile with piazzas along one side, the house sat horizontally on its large lot. Double decker piazzas faced the street, and a brick staircase with iron railings swooped toward the sidewalk.

"Wow," said Tipsy. "This place is huge. A good living to be made in dry goods, huh?"

Henry shrugged. "Bull Street isn't Legare Street. The address always irked my mother. My father bought this house when I was about four years old. I don't remember anyplace but *this* place."

"What was your father's first name again?"

"Frederick."

"Is it still a private home?"

"From what I can tell the main floors are occupied by an older couple. The lower level—under the piazza, where the servants lived in the old days—seems to be a flat. A few young men live there. Lads from the College, I believe. They drink a sizable amount of beer." He pointed out a few kegs lined up on the cement patio under the piazza, beside empty planters, cracked garden hoses, and an ancient weed-eater.

A squeak, and Tipsy looked down. A fat orange cat twisted around her legs. She stooped to pet him.

"How did you find your mother?"

"I wandered the house for a while. Took in the changes. I found her on the second floor piazza. Her favorite place to sew. She looked at me and said my name." He chewed on the inside of his cheek.

"What did *you* say?"

"Nothing. It was as if she'd sewn my lips shut. I returned to Bennett Street."

"Henry. *Come on.*"

"You know how well I handle sensitive situations!"

"You handle them pretty well."

"When they're not related to me, yes. I can be a wonderful—what do you call it? Councilman?"

"Counselor."

"But my own problems are another matter."

"Regardless, you can't vanish on me now." She smiled down at the cat and sat on the warm sidewalk. "Garfield here gives me a good excuse to sit a while, and I'll try to do most of the talking, but *you* have to call out to her."

"If you insist." He faced the staircase with resigned determination. "Patience? Mrs. Mott? Patience Mott?"

"Try Patty," Tipsy whispered as she stroked the cat.

"Patty? Patty Lewiston?"

Still nothing.

He sighed. "Mother?"

A stocky woman appeared in the middle of the staircase. Tipsy shifted to get a look at her.

This version of Patience Lewiston Mott was maybe fifteen years older—and at least fifteen pounds heavier—than the Patience of Henry's unpleasant memory at the Old Cannon. She had short, bobbed gray hair and wore a brown calico print dress with a lacy white collar, finished off with a string of pearls. Her dress stopped midcalf, above tan low-heeled shoes.

The cat hissed at her and crawled into Tipsy's lap. Its tail puffed up like a feather duster.

"Henry," said Patience, in a quivery voice. She squinted through wire-rim spectacles. "It *is* you, isn't it?"

"Yes, Mother. It's me."

"Saints and angels. At last, one of my sons came for me." She held out her arms, but Henry stepped back. "No embrace for your mother after all these years?" she asked.

"Er…we can't embrace in this state. We'd pass through one another… like…a sneeze into a high wind."

"It must be you, with that kind of strange poetry. Are you…like *me*?"

Tipsy sensed a snarky retort on the tip of Henry's tongue, like hot pepper flakes he wanted to spit out, so she intervened. "Yes. He's a ghost. You're *both* ghosts."

"No matter," said Patience. "Living, dead, or something in the middle, your presence is a relief."

"It surprises me to hear you say so," said Henry.

"Why?" Patience's haughty irritability finally revealed a resemblance to her son. "You're my *child*."

"Your *child* who you believed to be the perpetrator of a murder-suicide."

"Oh, *nonono*. No one wanted to discuss *that business* when it happened. I surely don't want to discuss it now."

"Don't you care that I didn't—"

"Are you here to take me home? Did your father send you?"

"*No,* Mother. Father didn't send me. I'm here because…I need to ask you some questions. We do. This is my friend Tipsy Collins."

"Hi, Mrs. Mott. Nice to meet you."

Patience looked down her nose at Tipsy. "This *today woman* is your friend?"

"Today woman?" asked Henry.

"Yes. You and me are *yesterday* people. She's a today person. Eventually, she'll become a yesterday person once enough todays have become tomorrows." Her quirky observation and her wobbly smiled hinted at a typical level of ghostly kookiness. "Here, puddy-tat."

The cat growled and spit at her again.

Patience's lip trembled. "Kitty doesn't like me. No matter what I do. He hates me!"

"Pay no mind to the cat, Mother. Like I said, we have questions for you."

"Easy for you to say. You don't have to exist with such a hateful feline! And poo-poo on your questions. You must be here help me go *home.* Your loved ones are *supposed* to lead you home."

To be safe, Tipsy opted for her *I'm-on-the-phone-not-talking-to-a-ghost* ruse. She removed her phone from her purse and put it to her ear. "We may be able to help you—"

"You're in my father's house," said Henry. "You *are* home."

"Mrs. Mott, if you help us by answering our questions, we may be able to help you move on to the…the…" As always, Tipsy wasn't sure how to explain something she couldn't describe herself. "The next realm."

Patience looked up and down the sidewalk, as if God had set up heaven somewhere along Bull Street. "Which way is it?"

"Still figuring that out myself. As is Henry."

"Interesting how the Lord chose Henry to lead me home. Quite an important responsibility for one with his temperament."

Henry laughed. "You assume my ghostly existence serves merely to ferry you across the river Styx? To serve as your own personal Charon?"

"Who? We had no one in our employ by that name. Ernest Brown was our man. You remember Old Ern, don't you?" She smiled at Tipsy. "Ern was quite loyal. Cheap, too."

"Argh, Mother. You remain as *insufferable* as ever!"

"You see?" Patience spoke to Tipsy in a conspiratorial whisper. "An unexpected heavenly welcome wagon, given Henry's surly disposition. But who am I to question the Lord's plan?"

Before Henry could scream, Tipsy asked, "Did you know any *Bonneaus*, Mrs. Mott?"

"Pardon—*who* did you say?"

"Specifically Thomas. *Thomas Bonneau.*"

Patience froze, as if she'd paused to rummage through thoughts she hadn't entertained in decades. She was fishing around in a drawer of old clothes for a specific, threadbare shirt. She found it, shook out the wrinkles, and noted the stains.

This time, her smile was shrewd. Even a tad suspicious. "Why, *yes.* I did know him. Why on earth would y'all ask about Thomas?"

"What was your relation to him, Mother?"

"None. He wasn't blood kin. All my relations on my mother's side were from—"

"For the love of God. Just answer the damn question!"

"Henry, hush," said Tipsy. "Let me."

Henry turned away from them, but he kept muttering about *dotty old bats* and *daffy old biddies.*

"It sounds as if you'd like to move on from this house," said Tipsy. "See your husband again. Your other son."

"I'd *like* to see the son in front of me, if he'd stop being cross with me for one skinny minute."

"If you help *us*, I believe we can help *you*. But first we need to talk about Thomas Bonneau. He was an old family friend, right?"

She nodded. "Although I didn't know him until near womanhood. I worked at his family's boarding house on Legare Street when I first came to Charleston."

"You probably don't know this, but Thomas haunts that house."

"My *word*. Who knew so many souls ended up like this?"

"*I knew*," said Henry. "If you'd ever listened to me—"

"He appears to be about twenty years old," said Tipsy. "Do you know how he died?"

"I believe it was an accident. Or perhaps…a sudden illness? I don't recall the particulars."

"Okay. Damn." Tipsy hoped Patience would reveal *exactly* how Thomas died. Tipsy would thus regale him with the tale of his own demise, and he'd stroll into the afterlife.

"Let's cut to the chase," said Henry. "Did you have a husband before Father? A lover? Maybe Thomas Bonneau?"

"Henry Whitestone Mott. I am *your mother* and a lady. How *dare* you speak to me that way."

"Spare me your vanity, and your modesty. This isn't 1920. I tiptoed around you enough when we were alive—"

"You never tiptoed. You've always had a heavy foot. Your own wife recognized your difficult nature."

"Don't you talk about Jane. You never cared about anything but her last name."

"That's not true! Jane was the daughter I never had."

"Thank God you didn't have a daughter. Some poor, sensitive girl for you to simultaneously smother and ignore. Someone you didn't care about, even as you forced her to be the center of your world."

"What? My children *were* the center of my world. Are. *Have always been*. Since Edward emerged into the world through *my pains*, and you not long after."

Someone of Patience Mott's generation would never understand Henry's impromptu family therapy session. Things were going downhill like a sled on icy snow. "Wait, y'all," said Tipsy. "How about we—"

"You see?" Henry said to Tipsy. "It's about *her* pains. Nothing about *my* pain. She doesn't care that I'm here. She only wants someone to move her on."

"Why are you so hostile?" asked Patience.

"Because you were a *terrible mother*. Don't pretend like you don't remember." He stepped toward her. "I'll move on straight to hell myself before I help you go anywhere."

"He doesn't mean that, Patience, he doesn't—"

"You. Haven't. Changed. *One bit*." Patience disappeared. A curt end to the argument. Like mother, like son.

A day at Mimi's left the kids appropriately waterlogged, with red, goggle-lined eyes, but even a long day soaking up sun, eating homemade baked goods, and ingesting chlorinated water couldn't dull their *school's out* energy. She set them loose on the neighborhood while she made, served, and cleaned up dinner, then joined them to watch *High School Musical 2*. All good cusp-of-summer fun, until her own eyes started twitching from vicarious exhaustion and she had to throw down the bedtime hammer.

Post-showering, Tipsy stood behind Olivia Grace in the girls' skinny, midcentury bathroom, with its matching salmon pink bathtub, sink, toilet, and tilework. She inhaled the smell of bubblegum shampoo as she brushed O-Liv's hair. O-Liv closed her eyes when Tipsy ran the brush over her head, like the orange cat from Henry's old house getting a good scratch. Mary Pratt sat on the closed toilet and dabbed sparkly pink polish on her toenails. She chattered about their classmates' latest intrigue.

"Emily didn't invite Ella to her sleepover," said M.P.

"Aw. Is Ella upset?"

"Yeah. But Ella didn't invite Cadence to *her* sleepover, and Cadence and Emily are best friends. Cadence told Emily to tell Ella she can't come."

"It hurts to be left out. I remember feeling that way sometimes."

"We'll invite everyone to our birthday sleepover," said M.P.

"D-R-A-M-M-A," said Olivia Grace.

"One *M*, buddy," said Tipsy.

"No drama," said M.P. "I want to invite everyone, so everyone has to invite us."

"Is that the best reason?" asked Tipsy.

"Also because of what you said, Mom. I don't want to hurt anyone's feelings. Or cause any fights."

"I hate fighting," said O-Liv. "Why can't the whole world say, *let's all never fight again*, and everyone stop it?"

"Tell that to Dad and Kate," said M.P.

"Someone should." O-Liv leaned into the brush.

Tipsy tread carefully. "Your dad and Kate having some disagreements?"

"Yeah. They think we don't know, but we do," said M.P. "They go into their bedroom and close the door."

"But Daddy has a hard time being quiet."

"They should yell and get it over with. It's worse when they scoot around each other not saying anything. It makes everyone else like…" M.P. grimaced, stood, and crept around the bathroom on her sparkly toes.

"That's called walking on eggshells," said Tipsy, as she divided O-Liv's hair into three sections and started braiding.

"You have to tiptoe so you don't break the eggs," said O-Liv.

Tipsy nodded, but her heart sank. She'd divorced Ayers so her kids would not have to tiptoe. She wanted them to dance and spin and stomp freely.

"It must be stressful living with that kind of tension." Tipsy was in quite the co-parenting bind. Allow girls to vent, rock. Discuss adult matters with them, hard place. "How do…ah…Chloe and Tristan feel about it?"

"The same as us," said M.P. "But once Tristan and Ayers got into their own fight. Tristan said Dad was mean to Kate, and men are supposed to be nice to women."

Tipsy twisted a hair tie around the end of O-Liv's braid. "That's generally good advice. Most men are bigger and stronger than most women, so men must keep their hands to themselves, but women don't have the right to be mean and nasty to men. Did Tristan and Ayers work it out?"

"Yeah. We did." Little Ayers appeared in the doorframe. "I told him Kate started it by going through Dad's phone without asking him. Tristan would be mad if anyone did that to him."

Tipsy sat on the edge of the tub. "I hope Dad and Kate are getting used to living together, and having some growing pains. Y'all know what that means?"

"Like when you get taller all the sudden and your legs hurt," said Ayers.

"Right. Your body can't keep up with all the changes, so the hurt is its way of calling out for help. But your legs have to grow to the length they're supposed to be. Dad and Kate have to adjust to the size of their new lives, too. Big new house. Big family. Two big personalities under the same roof."

"I never thought of a personality as being big," said Ayers. "But it makes sense with Dad."

"Like I said, he's *loud*," said O-Liv.

"A big personality isn't a bad thing in itself," said Tipsy. "Just be big in positive ways. But if y'all have concerns, I can address it with Dad. Or you can talk to me and let it all out."

"Okay, Mom. Thanks," said Ayers.

"Please remember, it's not your responsibility to fix anything, and it's not your fault if they can't get along. Not y'all's fault, or Chloe and Tristan's fault, either. They're adults and they have to figure out how to handle their disagreements in a healthy way."

"Yes, ma'am," said O-Liv.

"I hope they don't fight on our trip with Gigi and BopBop," said Ayers. "That might ruin the whole time."

"I wish Chloe and Tristan could come but Kate stays home," added M.P.

Tipsy's former in-laws, May Penny and Tripp Collins, were taking their grown children and their families on a ten-day Disney Cruise for Tripp's sixty-fifth birthday.

"I don't want to listen to Daddy and Kate yappin' at each other," M.P. went on. "Blah, blah, blah."

"No complaining," said Tipsy. "It's really nice of Gigi and BopBop to take everyone, and there are bound to be a few arguments on any family trip. Try to focus on the positive."

"Okaaaayyyy." M.P. folded her hands under her chin and closed her eyes. "Good vibes. Good vibes. *Good vibes only.*"

O-Liv giggled and Ayers shook his head. "M.P., you're so dramatic," he said. "If y'all are finally done and there's some hot water, I'm gonna take a shower."

"Good, 'cause you *staaaaaank.*" M.P. held her nose and gagged. "Your lacrosse helmet makes me want to puke."

"Your *face* makes me want to puke," said Ayers, and he threw a sweaty sock at her.

M.P. shrieked and chased him out of the bathroom.

"Y'all!" yelled Tipsy. "Time to chill out!"

"Good luck with that, Mama," said O-Liv. Tipsy laughed and patted her knee. O-Liv sat on her lap. Tipsy hugged her and stroked her bubblegum-scented hair.

"Does M.P. have a bigger personality than me?" she asked.

Tipsy kissed her cheek. "You have a wonderful personality. So does she. You're both big in your own ways."

"Like she's an elephant and I'm a giraffe."

"So what is your brother?"

"Ummm. A moose? I saw one on YouTube, and they're *so* huge. Huger than you think they are."

"I was thinking walrus, but moose works."

Mary Pratt screamed for backup. "O-Liv! *Heeelllppppp!* Ayers stuck his sock in my mouth!"

"You better go to her defense," said Tipsy.

"I'm always having to save her from something," said O-Liv. "This time it's socks. Next time it will be underwear."

Tipsy smiled as she scampered out of the bathroom, and then she picked up her phone. Her kids had confirmed the problems at *Maison du Kayers*, so she texted Scott. KIDS TALKED TO ME TONIGHT ABOUT ISSUES AT AK'S. UGH. THEY'RE GETTING READY FOR BED NOW, BUT I'D LOVE TO TALK ABOUT IT. SO HARD TO KNOW WHAT TO SAY. I'M A LITTLE WORRIED ABOUT THE INAUGURAL NATIONAL LAMPOONS BLENDED FAMILY VACATION.

She stood and ran the brush through her own hair. The line between her eyebrows deepened with each stroke as she mulled over how to deal with Ayers and Kate. At what point did she step in? Would her involvement make things better, or worse? Hard to tell, given Ayers's recent solicitation of her opinion. She rubbed her forehead. Leave it to Ayers to add years to her face, even if she no longer looked at his every day.

Her phone dinged. SCOTT: UGH IS RIGHT AND I AGREE. I'LL CALL YOU TONIGHT TO DISCUSS. IT'S A RELIEF KNOWING WE CAN TALK ABOUT THESE ISSUES.

TIPSY: AGREED. ☺

She indeed felt better as she set the phone on the back of the toilet. Scott had a mutual interest in the children's welfare and they shared a working knowledge of Kate and Ayers. But she'd also started understanding how his mind worked. He wouldn't try to force his own opinions on the situation, even as he sought creative ways to deal with it. Level-headed, yet innovative thinking.

She leaned over the sink and splashed water on her face. When she straightened, she yelped at the sight of Henry over her shoulder.

"Sorry for the abrupt entrance, but we can speak freely in here while the children are distracted. Since you've taken to talking with Dr. Brandt once they're asleep." He mimed firing an arrow at her. "Another supernatural force has joined me in this house. I've seen Cupid floating around your bedroom."

"Haha." She closed the door. "Thanks for pissing off your mom today."

"Tipsy, I simply cannot stand that woman. It's no good for me to go to her."

"*Au contraire*. It would *benefit* you to make peace with her."

"I came to peace with the person she is a hundred years ago."

"But we need to talk to her again."

"Why? She doesn't have details about Thomas's death."

"People lie, Henry. If we have a source of contemporaneous information, we have to take advantage of it." He opened his mouth, but she held up a hand. "Enough arguing. We're as bad as my kids. I'll go to her myself. You don't have to be involved."

"I don't want *you* to be involved with her."

Tipsy's eyes narrowed. "You think I'll see *her* death, and help her move on."

Henry didn't contradict her.

"Good lord. She's not a very nice person, from what I've seen. But she's a ghost, like any other. You hate her so much you want her to be trapped in limbo, forever?"

Once again, nothing.

"That's BS. I'll go by myself—"

"No."

"You can't stop me."

His stormy eyes darkened and his mouth set in a stubborn line. "No. But I can tell you this. If you help her, I'm finished with you."

"What? You're kidding. Stop it."

"I am *not*." The edges of his face smeared, and the individual strands of his hair blended into an angry red globule. "I meant what I said today. I will race headlong into hell myself before I rejoice in that woman's freedom, or even condone it!"

"Henry. Don't be ridiculous—"

He spun around, locked his arms at his sides, and marched through the shower wall.

✦⟡✦

Once the dust cleared from Henry's temper tantrum and Little A's attempt to suffocate Mary Pratt with his socks, Tipsy called Scott, but M.P.'s mood went south and she had trouble falling asleep. She entered Tipsy's room several times, complaining of stomach aches and monsters in her closet, until Tipsy got off the phone. As she scratched M.P.'s back, Scott texted an enticing idea. He suggested they meet in person the next day to continue the convo, so Tipsy recruited the rare weekday evening babysitter.

After another long day at the GQB, she picked up the kids from Aunt Mimi's Pool Day II, freshened up, welcomed the sitter, ordered pizza, and drove downtown again. She met Scott at the Hotel Bennett on Upper King Street, downtown Charleston's mecca for all things trendy: ethnic restaurants, boutiques, pulsating nightclubs, retro cocktail lounges, and gourmet ice cream shops.

When Tipsy first visited Charleston with Big Ayers, most of the buildings on King above Calhoun Street were boarded up. Storied dive bars—seemingly eternal watering holes like A.C.'s and The Silver Dollar—breathed new life into those tired blocks. In the twenty years since the first thirsty college students meandered north in search of cheap beer, Upper King had exploded.

On the weekends, it was a mini-Mardi Gras, peopled by roving packs of C of C students, Citadel cadets, giddy tourists, and local professionals out on the town. Long lines stretched down the sidewalks in front of the most popular bars and clubs. The golf bros and bachelorette parties alone could support the economy of the entire neighborhood. The city shut down King Street to vehicle traffic to prevent revelers from getting run over by SUVs, limos, and pedi-cabs.

It was a relatively sedate Tuesday evening, so Tipsy pulled up in front of the Hotel Bennett, handed her keys to the valet, and walked into the cavernous lobby. She passed a winding staircase and a massive, ornate floral arrangement, then hopped an elevator to the rooftop bar overlooking Marion Square. She squeezed through the chic post-workday crowd, and found Scott on a sofa on the terrace, waiting for her with a

Bud Light. With the blue sky behind him, his navy suit, and his aviator sunglasses, he looked like a Southern 007 waiting for a helicopter to sweep him off on another mission impossible.

He smiled and removed his sunglasses when he saw her, then stood and eased a few people out of her path. He kissed her, and whispered in her ear. "Hey, you."

"Hey, yourself."

As they sat, he pointed at her strappy, low-cut black top. "I love that—what is it? A shirt? A half of a shirt?"

"The proper term is a *top*." She pointed down at her flare-leg jeans and bedazzled, high-heeled sandals (inherited from Pamella, naturally). "Fun tops are the glue that holds the female wardrobe together."

"I don't know much about the female wardrobe except what I like. That top is *definitely* fun."

"Thanks, silly. How was your day?"

They caught up for a while about the everyday goings on at psychiatric hospitals and art galleries before getting into the topic of the hour—the tension at *Maison du Kayers*.

"I'm not sure what to do about it," said Tipsy. "At what point do I intervene in his parenting? I struggled with that even when we were married."

"You have to choose your battles when you live under the same roof with the other parent. It's no different when you're divorced."

"I can't micromanage what happens at his house."

"Or on the Griswold Family Disney Cruise, either."

"I still worry, whether at home or at sea. Sometimes lines have to be drawn, and sometimes disagreements are just part of family dynamics."

"At least Ayers talks to you so you have some sense of what's happening. I only get eleven- and nine-year-old versions from Tristan and Chloe."

"Yeah, but I'm only getting Ayers's side of the story."

"His side lines up with what I know of Kate. Your version of him, too, right?"

She nodded. "With you and Ayers describing Kate the same way, and my long experience with him, it's not hard to imagine the dynamic over there."

"Between us, we have an unusual amount of insight. You know, I was really attracted to you the first time we met. Like I've said, I wasn't in a place to get into a healthy relationship, but I also hesitated because of the connection with them. I wondered if it would be too close for comfort."

"Me too. I got some negative feedback about the idea. Don't go there—it will be weird."

"That will probably be the initial consensus, but it's actually convenient. Think about it. Only two families involved. Kids are only dealing with one other set of kids and parents. We can keep each other in the loop."

She smiled at his comfortingly rational observation. "When you put it that way, it does make sense. But I still worry about Ayers freaking out. We've been getting along, and my friend Lindsey is convinced he'll explode like lightning striking a dynamite factory when he finds out."

"Do you think he will?"

"Hey—Tipsy!"

She looked up at the sound of her name. A grinning man stood in the crowd above them. He was attractive in a slick way, with curly, gelled blonde hair and teeth so white he looked like he drank bleach through a straw. Brad Humphries, a colleague of Ayers.

Tipsy's stomach turned. Brad wouldn't be so smiley if he knew Mimi had confided in Tipsy about their mutually adulterous affair. Mimi swore her to secrecy, so her disdain couldn't be too obvious. "Hey, Brad."

"I haven't seen you in forever. Heard you moved to the Old Village. Mimi Lathrop mentioned it. I *think* she told me... at the...ah... ColSouth Christmas party. Her husband's family place, right?"

Tipsy wanted to punch him for having the nerve to mention Mimi, after he seduced her and then unceremoniously dumped her when she called him out about it. "Yup. *Jimmy's* mother's house."

A youngish blonde woman elbowed through the crowd toward him. "Hey!" said Brad, as he slid a hand over her back. "Kelly, this is Tipsy Collins. Ayers's *ex-wife*. Kelly is a new sales associate at ColSouth. We're having drinks to review this quarter's numbers."

"Nice to meet you." Given the cozy placement of Brad's hand, Tipsy guessed he'd migrated his extramarital activities to younger, unmarried, child-free territory.

"Nice to meet you, too, Tipsy! Your kids are so cute." Her eyes swept appreciatively over Scott. "Hi there."

Tipsy had no choice but to make introductions. "Brad...Kelly. This is Scott."

"Scott Brandt. Nice to meet you." Scott half stood to shake Brad's hand.

Tipsy noted a flicker of recognition in Brad's eyes. "Scott. Nice to meet you, too."

"Y'all have a nice night." Tipsy gave them a closed mouth smile. When Scott's butt returned to the sofa, she turned her back on them.

"I sense that was an uncomfortable interaction," he said quietly.

She dropped her own voice. "You could say that."

He brushed her hair off her shoulder and put an arm around her. Tipsy leaned into him, even as out of the corner of her eye, she noticed Brad whispering to Kelly.

"I don't like him," she said, as Brad and Kelly tossed back Fireball shots. "If we remove ourselves, hopefully he'll get hammered and forget he saw us."

"From the looks of it, he's on his way. How about a venue change? Someplace quieter?"

Tipsy considered the nearby establishments. Hall's Chophouse was possibly the biggest scene in town. Besides, Upper King's uneven sidewalks were perpetually slick from spilled beer. A safety hazard in her Pamella-style footwear. "What about Camellia's downstairs?"

"The pink palace? Home of all things Cosmo and mimosa?"

"It's the most beautiful, girliest bar in town."

"From the looks of your man Brad, the testosterone will drain out of his body if he steps foot in there." He smiled. "However, I am secure in my masculinity."

She squeezed his hand. "You're the best."

"I try," he said, as they stood.

Three minutes later, they sidled up to the lobby's elaborate pink marble champagne bar, where well-dressed ladies huddled up in pink leather chairs around midcentury marble-topped tables. Hand painted camellia blossoms on silver foil backgrounds adorned recessed porticos between carved white pillars. An oval-shaped crystal lighting conglomeration—too large to be called a chandelier—dominated the otherwise petal-pink ceiling.

Tipsy pointed at one of the few couples in the bar. They were drinking champagne and sharing a platter of tiny cakes. A birthday gift bag sat on the table beside her. "What a nice guy, treating his lady to a birthday…" She picked a random drink from the extensive beverage list. "…Don't Kale My Vibes."

Scott looked at the menu. "I prefer the…Dragonfruit Slayer."

"So manly! You and that dude are taking one for the team."

"Eh, it's not so bad, but I do feel like I'm squeezed between a few of Chloe's Squishmallows."

Tipsy laughed at his reference to the popular plush toys. "Oh, lord. My girls love those things too. They are pretty darn cute."

"What are you thinking? Kale cocktail? A simple Cosmo?"

"No way. I have to drive. I'm a lightweight."

"How about a glass of bubbly? We have a lot to celebrate. A midweek night out." He squeezed her knee. "And just…finding each other in general."

Tipsy's heart swelled. She nodded and squeezed his knee right back. They ordered their champagne and relegated Ayers and Kate to the backburner. Like a gentle river, their conversation meandered easily around rocky topics like first memories and the joy and terror of having children of their own. General music taste led to an intensely personal review of favorite song lyrics. They cracked up over embarrassing tales from the darkest depths of middle school. Tipsy's story about sneezing Coke out of her nose at her church's youth group bowling outing somehow made them both question the meaning of life. She listened raptly and offered her own thoughtful anecdotes and opinions, until the free-flowing dialogue hit uncomfortably choppy currents.

"Since we both grew up going to church," said Scott, "do you believe in heaven and hell?"

"Umm. Jeez." Tipsy couldn't begin describing her version of the afterlife. "Let me think."

"Sorry. Is that too personal?"

"No. Not at all. I love all this personal talk. But it's a complicated question for me."

"It's okay if you're not one to dwell on that stuff."

Good lord. If only you knew.

You're not going to tell him, are you? asked Granna, after staying quiet all night. *He's growing on me, but that* does *seem too personal.*

No. I don't want to scare him off. He'll think I'm as crazy as his most insane patient. Besides, I told Will, and look how that ended up.

"You okay? We can change the subject."

"It's good. Really. I have…a lot of thoughts. The simple answer is, no. I don't believe in the heaven and hell I learned about in church."

"Neither do I. I can't imagine anything is so black and white. Good, bad. Eternal bliss, or eternal damnation."

"I think there's something out there that leads us to peace, but it's beyond our understanding. Maybe hell…or damnation…is different for different people. It isn't so much about how *good* or *bad* you were in life, and more about what life handed you."

He stared into her eyes. "Your philosophical nature turns me on."

"Stop it, silly," she said, with an anxious giggle. "You asked me a serious question so I gave you a…serious…yet incomplete answer."

"I *am* serious." He leaned in and kissed her. "I'm *so damn* serious. Serious like…Old Father McGrady leading the Stations of the Cross on Good Friday."

She laughed again. "I'm not sure what that means, but it sounds intense."

"Catholic imagery usually is." He looked at his phone. "You have to get back to the kids."

"I do. Hopefully they're asleep, but with M.P.'s tween angst, who knows."

"No problem. We'll get you out of here. But I thought—maybe—I mean, if it's too soon—"

She smiled. "What?"

"The kids are all leaving on Friday. We'll both be kid free for over a week. I thought maybe you'd like to…spend some time at my place. If you're comfortable with that. If not, it's totally—"

"Yes. I'd love that."

"Oh. Great. I can make dinner for us Friday evening. And you're welcome to stay…as long as you'd like. Or we can go to your house—"

She touched his cheek. "*Scott.* I'd love to spend time at your house."

"Okay. Whew." He grinned. "I feel like I just asked you to the middle school dance."

"I would have said yes to that, too."

"You might think differently once you see my middle school yearbook. My dorkiness was unparalleled."

"If you saw mine, you might not have asked. Gawky toothpick with rabbit teeth comes to mind."

"I doubt it. I can't imagine you being anything but beautiful and elegant." He motioned to the bartender for the check. "But now that I spit out my eloquent invitation, let's get you home."

They stood, and Scott rested his hand on the small of her back as he pushed her stool under the bar. She followed him toward the exit. He took her hand when they reached the door.

She smiled down at her own shoes, certain everyone was admiring her, on the arm of such a gorgeous, obviously considerate man. Brad Humphries—should he prove intelligent and sober enough to add one and one together and remember two—might bring down Ayers's wrath. Even that worry couldn't dull her happiness. She felt *wonderfully right*. Exactly where she needed to be.

She lifted her chin, and indeed caught a few eyes. Male eyes, female eyes. Young and old eyes. Some onlookers glanced away as soon as her eyeballs met theirs, but she smiled and said hello to those who lingered. As they passed the staircase and the enviable floral arrangement, she met an especially bleary gaze. Or, stare. *Leer.*

Brad stood beside the door with his latest fling. Tipsy had already forgotten her name. Unfortunately, despite his intoxication and the distraction of what's-her-name's perky cleavage, Brad didn't look forgetful. He appeared uncomfortably aware.

Tipsy was too hopped up on one glass of champagne and new love to care. To hell with Brad Humphries, and to hell with Ayers Lee Collins, IV. She waved to Brad and breezed through the door on Scott's arm.

Chapter 11

B y Friday morning, Tipsy's kids were more excited about the Disney cruise than they were worried about Ayers and Kate's fighting. Tristan and Chloe waited for them on Kayers's front porch, and when Tipsy parked, Mary Pratt once again plowed over her siblings to escape the car. A miracle she didn't fall on her face as she alternated skipping, spinning, and cartwheeling across the yard.

Little Ayers dragged the suitcases across the back of the Tahoe and clopped them on the driveway.

"Be careful, A," said Tipsy. "If your suitcase explodes, the whole cul-de-sac will get a view of your underwear."

O-Liv clung to Tipsy. "I wish you were coming, Mama."

"That would be so fun, honey, but y'all will have the best time. I'll paint a lot and have some peace and quiet, so I'm fine."

"Sounds kind of boring."

"When you're a mom, sometimes boring is actually exciting. I know *you're* excited. Go jump around like your goofy sister!"

"Okay. Have fun being boring! Love you." She kissed Tipsy and ran to the house as the front door opened. Kate, dressed in white shorts and a red Mickey Mouse tee-shirt, waved to Tipsy and called the kids inside. Tipsy dragged the suitcases to the bottom of the porch stairs, called M.P. and Little Ayers for hugs and kisses, and left before Big Ayers emerged and complained about something.

Shelby's lovably domineering mother, Elizabeth Patterson, was conducting one of her personal quarterly financial and inventory reviews, so Shelby gave Tipsy another day off. She fretfully recalculated her shrinking bi-weekly paycheck as she drove downtown to the Bonneau

House. She had eight hours until her first home-cooked meal at Scott's house. She planned to stay as busy as a cheap plaid suit. No GQB meant a full day to paint, but she hadn't been back to Legare Street in days. She'd try to wrangle a memory out of Thomas, and even take a stab at communicating with Catherine. Make progress toward her big payout, with time leftover to start some sketches. She'd crush her productivity expectations, while making the time pass faster.

She sauntered into the Bonneau House, full of clairvoyant bravado and ready to slay the space-time continuum, but she found the house eerily quiet. Jillian had taken Sophie to a therapy appointment. Tipsy walked the house from top to bottom and lingered on all three piazzas, but she didn't see Thomas. A turn about the greenhouse proved just as fruitlessly ghost-free. No Catherine, either.

She wasn't surprised about Catherine, as she came and went from the property, but Thomas's reclusiveness worried her. Each time she entered a room, she amiably called to him, but the hitherto gregarious ghost failed to appear.

I've got two sketchy dead people who dislike one another, and Sophie's been interacting with them both, said Tipsy, as she walked from the greenhouse to the main house. *True peace in this house will require getting rid of both of them, Granna. No doubt about it—another multifaceted, dual-era mystery.*

Thomas was right about one thing. It's all starting to sound very official.

Maybe I'll write a how-to book someday. Like Beetlejuice's Handbook for the Recently Deceased. *I'll call it* Exorcisms for Dummies.

I suppose there has to be a method to this madness.

Especially since Catherine Porcher takes the madness factor to heretofore unseen levels. Tipsy walked into the kitchen for a glass of water. *Speaking of Catherine...*

Jillian had left some old pictures of Catherine on the kitchen table, so Tipsy retrieved her sketch pad from her truck and settled in to draw for a while. Even in life, the blue-eyed, auburn-haired young woman in the photos was fair and thin, although not as cadaverously pallid or painfully skinny as her ghost. She wore her long, straight hair in two braids, or held back with a wide headband.

Jillian made her own bell-bottomed appearance in several shots. Aside from her Farrah Fawcett hair, she favored the healthier, curvier version of Sophie in the framed photos in her daughter's room. Jillian grinned and mugged for the camera, but Catherine's smile was as forced and one-dimensional as a gulp of flat ginger ale. She stared at the camera as if someone stood behind the photographer, waiting to eat her.

Only one photo portrayed a natural expression. In it, a teenaged Catherine straddled a bicycle. The bike was too tall for her, so she gripped the handlebars and stood on tiptoe to keep her balance. She'd tucked her hair behind her ears, and reddish wisps framed her face. She smiled at someone beyond the camera.

Tipsy eyed the photo's background. A tall brick and stucco wall topped with iron spikes, and a row of low hedges. The Bonneau House's garden. Aside from Catherine's carefree smile, the bike basket was her favorite element of the scene. Catherine had filled it with long-stemmed white and red roses. If Catherine didn't keep the bike upright, her flowers would spill on the grass. Tipsy imagined her laughing up at her mother or her sister on the third floor piazza.

Bingo, Granna. This is the version of Catherine I'm going to paint.

Tipsy set about working on face studies of Catherine. By the time her bladder asked her to take a break, two hours had passed, so she packed up to go home. She felt good about her drawings, but it had been a ghostbusting fail. Jillian and Sophie still weren't home, so she had no opportunity to determine if Sophie was keeping her promise to avoid the house's spiritual interlopers. She sent Scott a text. No breakthroughs with Sophie today, but I succeeded in avoiding Big Ayers when I dropped off the kids.

Scott: Small victories! I'll hit the grocery store on the way home. Salmon sound good to you?

Tipsy: Delish!

Scott: Can't wait to see you. Come over any time after 6.

She spent a few more hours on her front porch, working on drawings for Catherine's portrait. She envisioned a zoomed in perspective, so the flower basket appeared to be tipping over into the viewer's lap. In the photo, Catherine appeared to be wearing striped pajamas. In other shots, she wore cut off shorts and tank tops and had bare feet, so Tipsy changed her outfit. She added the Rolling Stones logo from Catherine's death day ensemble. She sensed this painting would come together much faster than her recent battle of wills with the needy herons.

A freshly showered and sun-dressed Tipsy arrived at Scott's house at 6:03pm, with a bottle of prosecco, her Granna's homemade brownies, and an overnight bag. After his delicious home-cooked meal (salmon, brussels sprouts, and roasted potatoes), they retreated to his backyard firepit with her Tupperware of brownies, where they talked and laughed until Tipsy figured his neighbors had their ears to their windows to discern the source of such merriment. The fire burned low around midnight, and they went inside. He took her hand and led her through the house, but he paused at the foot of the stairs.

"I have to ask...you good with..." He pointed up the staircase.

"I brought an overnight bag like you suggested, didn't I?"

"Yeah, but I mean...you know. Us. Upstairs." He grimaced. "Dammit. I'm so awkward about this stuff. I'm not used to talking openly about—"

"*Yes.* I'm good with it. I can't wait, honestly."

"Wow. Okay. Then let's not waste any time." He kissed her, and then looked into her eyes. "I told myself I'm going to be completely open with you. For some reason, it feels comfortable. More comfortable than it's ever felt. If we're doing this, I want to make sure you understand I'm *all in.*"

"I believe you." She took a deep breath, because she didn't want to make love to him for the first time with tears on her cheeks, even if they were happy ones. "I'm all in, too."

She followed him upstairs.

———◆✕◆———

Saturday morning, Tipsy and Scott went for a run together, and then she returned home to shower. She resumed her quest for supernatural productivity, but upon arrival, she once again found the Bonneau House as still and silent as a muggy day on a deserted island. She texted Jillian, who replied that she and Sophie were running errands. To Tipsy's increasing frustration, still no Thomas.

Time to make him come out? asked Granna.

Ugh. I'd really rather not. Not yet, after only two successful glimpses into his memory. Forcing him to come out will be rough on me, from a headache and pukey-ness perspective, and it might make this whole endeavor antagonistic. I might get one new memory, and then months of fighting both him and my own body to get more.

It's already antagonistic, since he's avoiding you.

He must know something's up. He was distant the last time I saw him, and now he's hiding. Maybe he'll talk to Henry if I send him back here.

Aren't you and Henry in a tiff?

Yeah. But it will pass. It's just a Henry-hissy.

She'd witnessed Henry's temper, but she'd never been on the receiving end of it, and she didn't know how long he'd hold a grudge. Being on the outs with him unhinged her, like last summer when she and Shelby got into a heavyweight bestie brawl. She scowled her annoyance as she peeked into the greenhouse. Still a Catherine-free zone.

Catherine was a lunatic. Henry's mother was an asshole. Jillian, a tyrant in yoga pants. Sophie, an entitled pain in the butt. Without explanation, Thomas Bonneau had gone from overbearingly social to altogether reclusive. So far, everyone involved in this mystery was unpleasant.

She was getting nowhere, so she drove back to Mt. P. She stopped by her own gloomily quiet abode. Her kids were slipping down waterslides and eating Mickey Mouse pancakes. Henry was somewhere in the house, sulking about his mommy issues. She suddenly needed to talk to Scott—

even if she couldn't give him *all* the specifics—and feel like everything would fall into place, like they had naturally come together.

For the time being, she set aside the quirks and whims of dead people. She had a wonderful, living, breathing man waiting on her. She gathered her drawing supplies, repacked her overnight bag, and hightailed it to Scott's house.

That night, Tipsy and Scott walked to I'On's Irish pub for beers and burgers. They worked off their heavy dinner with a stroll through the neighborhood's treelined thoroughfares. Retro southern mansions loomed over the Venetian-style canals connecting the community's two signature lakes, and passing cars and golfcarts performed a carefully choreographed dance on the skinny streets. Neighbors of all ages and family dynamics congregated on manicured green spaces. Canine companions abounded, from Great Danes to yorkies. Tipsy noted oodles of Doodles in various colors and sizes. Several of those curly-haired, drooling pooches jumped on her as they passed. She mentioned their hyperactive, hypoallergenic prevalence to Scott.

"An astute observation," said Scott. "Doodle-dogs have replaced labs and golden retrievers as I'On's bougie dog of choice."

A frazzled teenaged boy chased a galumphing black and white puppy down the sidewalk. The kid yelled for Charlie to heel, but the animal cheerfully ignored him. "They're *all* named Charlie," said Scott. "I sense a conspiracy."

Tipsy and Scott held hands and said hello to passersby. Early-rising bats swooped through the tree limbs and powerlines, and a lone white egret stalked fish along the edge of East Lake. The gauzy sunset thickened to a comforting nighttime blanket. Tipsy once again cast anxiety aside like a determined child waiting in line for the Tilt-a-Whirl. When they got back to his house, she stood behind him with her arms around his waist as he unlocked the front door. They tumbled over the threshold and straight up the stairs in a flurry of wandering hands and cascading clothing.

She was so…ahem…*out of practice*, another passionate night left her a little sore the next morning. They ate a light breakfast, and then Scott had some work to do. "The emails never stop," he said, with a tense scowl. "Hundreds of them. The bane of my existence."

He emptied the dishwasher, straightened a few slightly off center cereal boxes in the pantry, and got in a good anxiety-busting Swiffer of the kitchen before opening his laptop. Tipsy stood behind him and rubbed his shoulders, and as she'd started to notice, he relaxed under her touch. She brought him a cup of coffee and a banana to sustain him. Once he was calmly typing away, she drove downtown to the Bonneau House to attend to her own responsibilities. She hoped her third visit in as many days would be the charm.

She parked inside the gate and walked toward the backhouse in search of Sophie. The adolescent grump in question sat on the stoop, beside two woven baskets. Tipsy thought of Jane, Henry, Patience, and Edward organizing sweetgrass fronds on Easter Sunday in 1917.

Tipsy stopped in front of her. "Hey. You good?" she asked, like Big Ayers breaking the silence after an argument.

"Hey. Yeah. Good enough."

"What are you doing?"

"Making bouquets." One basket contained real long-stemmed roses—red, pink, yellow, and a peachy-orange. Palmetto roses in the other one. A row of mason jars behind her contained clusters of vibrant living flowers interspersed with the neutral palmetto roses.

"I love the contrasting colors," said Tipsy. "Looks like you're making a bunch."

"Mom's friend is hosting a last minute bridal shower. Since Mom wants me to *do something*, she asked if I had any ideas for flower arrangements."

"It's good she's showing interest in *your* interests. You suggested the palmetto roses?"

"Yeah. It's a small party. Each guest can take home a bouquet. It will look pretty in her house for a while, and then she can keep the palmetto roses."

"Ah," said Tipsy, as she thought of Jane's replacement of Easter lilies with palmetto roses. "I had a friend who was similarly inspired."

"Did you talk to Mom about my flowers? She's suddenly more enthusiastic."

"Eh, maybe it came up."

"Then thanks."

"No problem. When a third party says, *hey, maybe your daughter is on to something with this flower thing*, it suddenly makes more sense."

"I was kind of a jerk about it. Like, *demanding* she give me money to start the business. Sometimes I can be a little...extra."

"From what I've seen of your mom, you come by that trait honestly. Maybe that's why y'all haven't been getting along."

"We're both pushy assholes?"

"Haha. That could be part of it, but you're growing up. You've got more opinions."

"I know she loves me. And I've always thought she's a badass. So tough and smart. But lately, it's like I'm learning about a whole new side of her. Maybe she's not who I thought she was."

"Another part of growing up. You see your parents as real people, with strengths and weaknesses." Tipsy leaned back on her hands. "That brings me to the elephant on the stoop."

Sophie selected flowers and deftly twisted them together. She pulled and tugged until the bouquet of eight real roses and eight palmetto roses formed a perfectly round nosegay. She wrapped a clear band around the base, and then tied ribbons around the mason jars. She attached a handwritten tag (*Congrats, Brynn!*). "What do you mean?"

"Sophie, sugar, don't play coy with me. Your aunt. Haunting the greenhouse. Pray tell, what has Catherine been saying about Jillian?"

"I told you. Catherine doesn't make much sense at all. But I think Mom had something to do with her death."

195

"How? I haven't talked to Jillian about the details, but I can't see her driving around the block to Colonial Lake and running over her sister."

"I don't know for sure. I've caught bits and pieces from Catherine. It sounds like BeeBee went into the greenhouse and talked to herself, so Catherine overheard her. Catherine knows she was hit by a car. BeeBee said it was Mom's fault. Like, she caused her own sister's death."

"I see." Tipsy took a moment. If Catherine had truly died via automobile impact, *and* she knew it, *and* she was still around, that indicated one of two scenarios. Either she had the incomplete story, or she chose to stick around the land of the living. Tipsy vehemently hoped for Option Number One, as she didn't relish the idea of two ghosts planted on the property like stubborn, invasive weeds. "I think you should give your mom the benefit of the doubt over third-hand information you got from a crazy ghost and a senile old lady. Have you asked Jillian about it?"

"No. If I ask her, she'll want to know why. I told you I'm not down with her knowing Catherine is here." She retrieved another palmetto rose from the basket. "Mom barely talks about Catherine. When she does, it's just complaining about the stress of living with her. She probably feels the same way about me."

"No way, Sophie. She adores—"

"She tells everyone how tough she had to be in her career. *Take no shit from anyone.* Blah, blah, blah. Maybe she got tired of taking shit from her sister, and…" She shrugged and picked up her scissors. "Took her out. It would explain why she wasn't close to BeeBee, if BeeBee knew she'd done something awful."

"I can see the logic in everything you're saying, and I've heard about some crazy deaths from my ghost friends. Still, I can't believe Jillian would be so heartless."

"I wouldn't have believed it either, but maybe it's like you said. Maybe I'm seeing her as a real person. I'm not sure what she's capable of." She held up a living rose and snipped the stem in half. "How strong she is, or how weak."

Tipsy wasn't going to convince Sophie Rose of her mother's innocence, so she sunk into silence. Could Jillian have contributed to her childlike sister's violent demise? Her pondering turned philosophical as Sophie sorted flowers beside her. If she had, would it be considered a show of cold brute strength, or innate selfish weakness? Perhaps both. Maybe sometimes, strength and weakness are one in the same.

Tipsy left her musings and Sophie on the stoop and went in search of Jillian. She found the lady of the house in the foyer. "You're *finally* back," said Jillian.

Her reaction struck Tipsy as unnecessarily cantankerous, but Tipsy's defensive reaction may have been influenced by Sophie's nefarious insinuations. "I've come by the house the past two days. I just haven't—"

"How's Sophie's project coming along?"

"She seems enthralled by it, and those bouquets are lovely. A very creative use of mixed-media."

"If you give it the thumbs up, I trust you. I'm still not sure about this *florist business* thing—"

"*Floral artisan* has a nice ring to it. If she's getting paid, it's a business."

"One personal friend paying her does not a business make. But I'm impressed with her product, and happy to see her interested in something unrelated to death."

"Has she said anything about Thomas? Or…ghosts in general?"

"Nothing. I've tried to talk to her about it, but she clams up. You've spoken with this Thomas…person…a few times now. Does he strike you as dangerous?"

"He can't physically hurt her, but he might be…*emotionally* dangerous. Like, manipulative. Or deceitful. Generally toxic. You know how some people seem too nice?"

"Yes. People who seem too good to be true often are."

"Exactly. For the most part, he's oddly…affable, for a ghost. But something about his good humor rubs me the wrong way. Sophie thinks he's the nicest guy ever. My friend Henry met him. Henry is the ghost who—"

"You're bringing other ghosts around here?"

Tipsy explained Henry's limited mobility.

"Thank goodness," said Jillian. "One ghost is more than enough."

That's what you think, Mrs. Yates, said Granna.

If I can't figure out this mess, I'll have to tell her about Catherine, whether Sophie likes it or not.

"Henry hasn't interacted with Thomas as much as I have, but he genuinely likes him."

"All fine and dandy, but between another ghost who lived through the Jim Crow era and my unstable daughter, I'm more concerned with *your* opinion. If you think Thomas is manipulating her, he has to go."

"I'm working on it. I haven't seen him in a couple days. Initially, he chatted me up as soon as I walked in the door. The past week, he's MIA. I might have to *make* him come out."

"How do you do that?"

"It's like…I think about moving my fingers, and they move. But I can't explain how I'm moving them. Everything related to my supernatural talent is difficult to explain. I'm still learning myself."

Jillian's stern expression melted like springtime snow on a sunny morning. "I *feel* for y'all. You and Sophie. Anyone who has these abilities. It must be *so hard*, especially when no one believes you."

Her show of genuine empathy relieved Tipsy. "You believe her now. She'll appreciate it eventually."

"In the meantime, I'll reap what I sowed, and she'll keep on resenting me."

Tipsy thought of her conversation with Sophie—how she'd acknowledged Jillian's bad-assery and their mutual assertiveness. "Jillian, there's a lot of love there. Have you tried talking to her about—"

"I have to run." Jillian retrieved her Louis-Chanel from the old-fashioned coat rack by the front door. "Consultation at a kitchen design showroom."

As she put a hand on the doorknob, Tipsy's mouth opened of its own accord. "Hey, Jillian. Wait."

Jillian's wrist paused mid-twist. "Yes?"

"Are you sure Catherine never said anything about ghosts?"

"*Schizophrenia* was Catherine's problem. She had a terrible, legitimate mental illness."

"Right, but…" Tipsy trailed off. Either Jillian didn't know about her late sister's clairvoyance, or she had no interest in telling the truth.

"Even if she was like Sophie, I don't see how it matters. One issue among many."

"How did she end up getting hit by a car?"

"She had one of her spells and ran out of the house in the middle of the night when I was away at summer camp in North Carolina. She died in the middle of Broad Street, by Colonial Lake."

"You weren't in town when she died?" asked Tipsy.

"No. My parents didn't even tell me she'd passed away until I got home. By the time I knew anything about it, she was already a couple weeks buried, poor soul." She turned the doorknob, and squeezed past the cracked door.

"Wow. So sad—"

"Tell me when you find Thomas."

"By the way, I have a final sketch for the portrait. Do you want to review it before I start painting?"

"No, no. Surprise me!"

"Okay. I'm going to look for Thomas before I—"

The door cut off Tipsy's words with a *snick-click*.

"—leave." She turned toward the staircase. "*Alrighty* then. Goodbye to you, too, Mrs. Yates. Even the living are disappearing on me."

As promised, she spent an hour wandering the house from top to bottom. Each time she entered a room, she called to Thomas, but he didn't appear. No Catherine in the greenhouse, either. Another ghostbusting bust. Nothing to be done but go home and start the painting phase of Catherine's portrait.

Once again, she got to pondering as she crossed the lawn. She looked forward to informing Sophie that her mother couldn't have been involved in Catherine's death, as she was ensconced at sleepaway camp in another state. Next steps, figuring out Catherine's comprehensive death scenario, and enticing Thomas out of his hidey hole.

Her initial quick procurement of two memories had encouraged her, but in retrospect, neither vision strongly indicated any specific conclusion. The next memory might show her his death, or it might require multiple memory hops over a prolonged effort. As she'd told Granna, repeatedly strongarming him out of hiding would lead to headaches, nausea, and exhaustion. The last thing she wanted, given her many obligations…and her reinvigorated love life.

She looked at her phone as she approached the Tahoe.

SCOTT: HELLO, BEAUTIFUL. AT THE RISK OF SOUNDING LIKE A CREEPER, I KIND OF MISS YOU ALREADY. WANT TO GET A DRINK WHEN YOU'RE FINISHED WITH WORK?

Oh, lord, Granna, he's so sweet. Tipsy sensed Granna opening her mouth, so she beat her to it. *I know, work comes first—*

The two aren't mutually exclusive. Why not invite him over while you paint? He can have a beer and watch sports on TV or something.

You think he'll want to do something so…domestic?

No way to know but to ask.

So Tipsy asked him. His typing bubble lit up right away and she waited for his reply.

SCOTT: I'D LOVE TO COME OVER. SIT ON THE SIDELINES WHILE THE ARTISTIC GENIUS DOES HER THING!

TIPSY: HAHA, SILLY. BUT IF YOU DON'T MIND, THAT WOULD BE GREAT. MY STRESS LEVEL WILL GO DOWN IF I CAN MAKE SOME PROGRESS ON JILLIAN'S SISTER'S PORTRAIT.

SCOTT: HOW ABOUT I PICK UP THAI FOOD FOR DINNER? I'LL STICK WITH THE HISTORY CHANNEL OVER ESPN THOUGH. NOTHING MUCH ON BUT GOLF THIS TIME

OF YEAR AND I'VE BEEN WATCHING A DOCUMENTARY ABOUT VIKINGS. GETTING SOME INSPIRATION FOR MY BEARD.

TIPSY: THAI FOOD + AVERSION TO GOLF + VIKINGS = YOU ARE THE PERFECT MAN

SCOTT: THAT'S A LOT TO LIVE UP TO, BUT I'LL DO MY BEST.

TIPSY: BTW, I KIND OF MISS YOU, TOO.

SCOTT: ☺ SEE YOU SOON.

Eeeek, Granna. I cannot even. I'm so happy! Even as she thought it, her insides seized up, her eyes stung, and a whale of a lump surfaced in the back of her throat. She was an umbrella, unexpectedly turned inside out by a high wind. *I have to get off this fear-joy seesaw. I have this perfect guy who seems to really like me and—*

No one is perfect, Tipsy. Be careful how much pressure you put on him. And yourself.

Tipsy got into her truck and slammed the door. She yelped when her thighs touched hot leather. She grabbed an old painting rag and shoved it under her butt.

Therein lies the problem, said Granna. *Your ass has already been burned. More than once.*

I'm in the emotional hot seat.

You are, but so is he. Y'all have both been on a long, strange trip, and you both have baggage. You got to give both of y'all a break, or this suitcase will explode as sure as Little Ayers strewing his underpants all over Kayers's driveway.

I'll try Granna. I swear I will. She gripped the steering wheel and made herself start trying right that second. *Tonight, I'm going to enjoy painting. Plus a glass of nice wine, some pad Thai, and Scott's company.*

That's my girl. Good thing your guy is bringing all that to you.

So he's my guy now? You must like him.

I guess he is, sugar. And I guess I do.

→⇥✕⇤←

Scott pulled into Tipsy's driveway as she laid out jars of paint, brushes, and her palette on her front porch. He walked up the steps with a bottle of red wine and a brown paper bag. He wore shorts, flip-flops, and a Nirvana tee-shirt.

"Hey, beautiful," he said.

"Hey, handsome." The scent of ginger wafted from the bag. "That smells good."

"You smell good." He kissed her, then brushed her hair away from her neck. He touched one of the healing scratches from her run-in with Catherine. "How are those cuts doing?"

"Getting better."

She shivered when he ran his finger over her throat. "Stay out of the greenhouse, okay? I keep picturing Audrey Two from *Little Shop of Horrors.*"

"I'll try." Despite feeling a twinge of guilt for leaving out the details, she said, "Sophie spends a lot of time in the greenhouse, but there are sharp objects in there."

"Darlin'…you have to be careful."

The endearment induced a pleasant squirm out of her. "I'm fine. I didn't think you'd notice, but you are a doctor."

"Doctor notwithstanding, I noticed because I care. About your hurts. Big ones and little ones."

"You sweet man. I should have covered it with makeup. I don't want you to worry about silly things."

"Don't ever cover anything up with me, Tipsy, literally or figuratively. I want all your *things*. Big. Little. Silly. Serious. All of it."

No one had ever said such a thing to her before, and she couldn't respond. Instead, she swiped at a tear.

"Hey, hey, hey. If that was too much—"

"No. Good lord. Not too much. But sometimes *this*…you…us. It's…just…so perfect. It's *terrifying*."

"I understand. I feel the same way." He hugged her. "And I promise I am *not perfect*. Stick around long enough and you'll see."

She buried her face in his chest. "Thank you. I'm sorry I'm being ridiculous."

"Don't apologize, okay? We got a lot of food to eat. And you have some painting to do, right?"

"Yes." She pointed at the palette. "I've been mixing paints."

"I brought a book, so I can sit out here with you, if you want company. I'll try not to distract you with my annoying questions about your artistic process."

"Company sounds lovely. I don't think any man has ever genuinely asked me about my process, so it won't be annoying. I'll just have to figure out how to explain it."

"We have eight more nights until the kids get back. You have plenty of time to explain. That is, if you don't get sick of having your boyfriend around."

She kissed his nose. "I will *absolutely* not get sick of having my boyfriend around."

"I'll put the food inside. Bring you a glass of wine—if that won't infringe on the process?"

"A sip or two won't hurt at this stage."

"You got it."

Boyfriend always seemed like a silly term to me, said Granna as Scott walked into the house. *Seems even sillier now.*

Don't start raining on my parade again. I'm already creating my own deluge with all my damn worrying.

Let me be clear, sugar. It's silly because Scott Brandt is no boy. That's a man.

Chapter 12

For Tipsy, the Collins Family's Inaugural Waterborne Walley World Adventure proved both fabulously productive and irritatingly stagnant. On the moribund front, she made a whole lot of *zero* progress on her mystery. Daily stops at the Bonneau House resulted in no new ghostly interactions. Even Jillian and Sophie avoided her. Sophie grumped around in the backhouse, while Jillian suddenly had umpteen errands to run. Tipsy sensed she didn't want to talk about her sister, but she sent daily texts pressing for updates. Unfortunately, Tipsy had none. If not for Charleston's lack of competing professional ghost-hunters, Jillian might have already yanked her hundred-k.

Speaking of yanking, I've got to get my supernatural hands on Thomas soon, Granna.

What about Catherine?

I've never tried to retrieve a clairvoyant ghost from her natural haunting space. I don't know if it's possible. Then again, I didn't know any of this was possible two years ago.

On a more positive note, oppressive heat made the tourists stick to the bars and breweries, and an unusual quiet settled over the GQB. Tipsy had free time at work and no kids to feed and chauffeur, and as had been the case in the past, supernatural inspiration made for quick artistic work. She finished the garden, the driveway, and the textured wall, and moved on to Catherine's oversized bicycle. Next, she'd work on the overflowing bike basket. Each flower would have its own thorns and leaves, and be unique in shape and color. No simple reds, pinks, whites, or yellows. They'd be ivory and cream, crimson and cherry, bubblegum and coral. Even the bright melon-y shade she'd admired in

Sophie's bouquets. She'd paint them in varying states of bloom—from tight baby buds, to floral senior citizens shedding petals like old men losing hair.

Scott cheered her on from the sidelines every evening. He bought an easel, placed a tarp underneath it, and declared his air-conditioned sunroom to be Tipsy's new studio. They went out to dinner together, cooked meals together, worked out together. On Friday evening, they had an impromptu old school hip-hop party for two in his kitchen. He served as DJ while she bounced and swerved in her exuberant white girl way. Beyoncé and Jay-Z would have laughed their asses off.

On Saturday, they spent the day at the beach on Sullivan's, then met Pammy and Doug for dinner at Home Team Barbeque in their bathing suits. During a trip to the little girls' room, Pammy couldn't contain herself any longer.

"Tipsy! He's a dream!" she said, as Tipsy entered a bathroom stall. "A legit fantasy in a baseball cap and a pair of swimming trunks!" Pammy's voice floated over the metal door. "How far have you taken this fantasy? *Bow-chicka-bow-bow.*"

Tipsy almost fell into the toilet. "Good lord, Pammy! I'm not trying to broadcast my—" She peeked through the crack in the stall door and whispered. "—*sex life* to any random person whose bladder has hit capacity." She flushed, exited the stall, and started washing her hands.

"Everyone in this place is drunk on sunshine, pulled pork nachos, and frozen Painkillers. No one remembers what they hear in this bathroom. Spill it!"

"We've spent every night together since the kids left—"

"Ooooh! You *went there.*"

"I will neither confirm nor deny your suspicions." Tipsy grabbed some paper towels. "But let's just say…the fantasy is *real.*"

Pamella squealed and dragged her out of the bathroom.

Her enthusiasm heartened Tipsy, as did Shelby's equally boisterous texts. Lindsey remained on the fence, but Shelby promised to browbeat some positivity into her. Tipsy missed the kids, of course, and the

Bonneau House and its dilemmas stuck with her like sandspurs on wool socks.

Still, it was the best ten days of…well…the last ten years.

By Sunday, Tipsy was torn between happiness and foreboding. She couldn't wait to see her kids, but she'd trade missing them for missing Scott. She already relished the comfort of falling asleep beside him, the dessert spoon to his ladle. Each morning, she threw her own arms over his broad shoulders. She dozed with her cheek against his back, lulled by his strong, steady heartbeat.

She woke before the sun on their last morning together. He rolled in her direction and sleepily pulled her close, but to her dismay, dismal anxiety crept up on her. Tipsy buried her face in his chest and inhaled the smell of last night's leftover cologne. She hid in the crook of his arm, as if something much more frightening than a ghost might pounce on her.

The unsettled feeling stayed with her during their omelet breakfast, and while she gathered her belongings. He'd emptied drawers in his dresser and bathroom, so she stored a few things—some pajamas and a Gamecocks sweatshirt, extra bottles of shampoo and conditioner and a razor. She considered telling him about her feelings, but he seemed so content and relaxed. She didn't want to come off like a needy weirdo, so she smiled and kissed him. Only when she got into her Tahoe did she allow herself to tear up.

I'm acting like I'm never going to see him again.

You're learning to trust him, sugar. Trust him, and trust life that's pulled the rug out from under you a bunch of times.

She went to Target for groceries and household supplies, but the place was like Interstate 526 at rush hour—crowded, backed up, and full of irritable people. She chided herself for not arriving early enough to beat the after church crowd, as there's no more peaceful place than the Mount Pleasant Target early on a Sunday morning. Scott texted his commiseration as she waited in line. He also said he already missed her, which somewhat soothed her nerves. When she got home, she unpacked the Target bags and got to work on Catherine's portrait. Each sweep of her arm and tiny brush stroke increased her confidence. *This is gonna be good, Granna.*

Her work consumed her, and she didn't notice Ayers pulling into her driveway. She looked up when his truck doors slammed, and checked her phone. Yesterday, he'd advised her of a five o'clock drop off, but it was just past three.

The children clutched souvenirs: plush toys, mouse ears, glow sticks, and princess crowns. Tipsy spritzed water over her canvas and swiped her hands over her paint-covered shorts. She clipped down the steps to meet them in the yard.

They were coming in hot, so she sat in the grass. Olivia Grace got to her first. "Mama-Mia!" she yelled, and threw herself into Tipsy's lap. Tipsy flopped backwards as Mary Pratt landed on her sister.

"Oof! Y'all, watch my back!" She tickled them and rolled over. "I'm old, remember?"

"Not too old for these earrings we bought you!" said M.P., as she whipped a gift bag out of her sparkly *PRINCESS LIFE* fanny pack. She opened a jewelry box and removed a pair of sterling silver princess crown earrings, bejeweled with tiny garnets.

"They were supposed to be a surprise, M.P.!" said O-Liv.

"They *are*! Aren't you surprised, Mom?"

"Yes, I am! I love them!" She examined the earrings. "My birthstone! So thoughtful."

"Dad got them on his credit card, but they're from us," said Little Ayers. "He said it's lucky you were born in January, not April."

"Like me and O-Liv," said M.P., who loved to remind everyone about the twins' glamourous birthstone. "Diamonds are a princess's best friend."

"Thanks so much, buddies." She looked up at Ayers and smiled. "Thanks. Super cute."

"Huh." Ayers walked to the back of the truck. Little A's suitcase hit the driveway with an ominous thud.

"Be careful, Dad! Jeez! My Switch is in there." Ayers protected his portable Nintendo game player like a treasured heirloom.

"Watch your tone," said Big Ayers. "Don't be bossing me around."

"I *missed* y'all a ton!" Tipsy said, in a typical deflection of Big Ayers's anger.

"Sorry we didn't call you much, Mama," said O-Liv. "Phones didn't work good on the cruise boat."

"All good. Y'all were busy."

Big Ayers snickered. "Mama was *busy*, too."

"As always," said Tipsy, even as her Ayers radar blipped faster.

"*Huh*," he said, again. He leaned against his truck.

Usually, she counted on Big Ayers to carry stuff to the front porch, but he stood amidst the suitcases and backpacks like the Bonneau family's obelisk looming over the Huguenot cemetery's smaller gravestones.

"Go inside, buddies," Tipsy said to the kids. "I'll get the suitcases up to the house, but y'all grab your backpacks."

"*Daddyyyyy*," said M.P. "I'm *sooo* tired. Can't you just—"

"Inside, Mary Pratt," said Big Ayers.

While Little Ayers and O-Liv rarely talked back to their father, M.P. had no such qualms. "But my backpack is heavy—"

"Girl, you heard me. I'm not your personal valet service."

"Ouch," said Little A.

"*You* mind your business, Ayers Lee," said Big Ayers. "You got a mouth on you today. I'm about sick of all y'all's whining."

"We were *not* whiny! You always help with the bags when we go back and forth from your house or mom's house—"

"M.P., come on," said O-Liv, ever the diplomat. "Let's go inside. Let's watch some Disney."

M.P. was having none of it. "Y'all are the ones who got *divorced* and live in two houses so we have to drag all our stuff around town! So *y'all* can get it!"

She stomped toward the house. Big Ayers's face reddened. "Mary Pratt Collins! Get back here!"

"No!" she yelled, and kept on going.

"Let her be, Ayers," said Tipsy. "She's tired. She's had a long week. I'll talk to her."

"We've all had a *long week,* haven't we?"

The blips on her radar flatlined into an unending, consecutive wail. "You got something on your mind? No. Wait. O-Liv, I like your idea to watch some TV and chill out. Y'all go inside. *Now.*"

Little Ayers and O-Liv scampered out of the line of their father's fire. The front door closed behind them.

Tipsy eyed Ayers across the cracked concrete walkway leading to the porch stairs. She was a rabbit standing off against a grizzly bear, but she forced herself to hold her ground. Instinct told her to follow her children into the house, but she chose fight, not flight. "What's the problem, Ayers?"

"You know *exactly* what the problem is."

"No, I don't. Last I heard from you, you sent me a picture of the kids with Goofy, and bunch of smiley face emojis. Now you're being rude to them, and me, and dumping their stuff in my yard."

"*Your* yard? Whose yard *is this*, Tipsy?"

"It's technically Jimmy's yard. But it's been mine for over two years."

"Jimmy. Right. My *brother-in-law*. My *family*. You always gotta be up in my shit, even when we're divorced."

"We share children. I'm up in your shit. You're up in mine."

"Yeah. I thought we'd reached a place where maybe, *just maybe*, we might consider each other friends. But guess what?" He stepped closer. "Got a text from *Brad Humphries* this morning."

Oh, hell. Here it comes, Granna.

"Great. I ran into Brad the other night. He looked pretty friendly with your new sales associate—"

"You're gonna get all *high and mighty* and judge Brad? When he saw you cuddled up with *Scott Brandt*?" His face reddened to crimson. Soon steam would shoot out of his ears. Tipsy had Disney on the brain. The animated anger emotion from *Inside Out* popped into her head. Rage, incarnate.

"I'm not denying it—"

"What the *hell*, Tipsy? You out of your goddamn mind? What the actual fu—"

"Stop yelling! The kids will hear you!"

"I don't give a damn who hears me! Are you whoring around with Kate's ex-husband?"

Tipsy would not have been more shocked if Mr. Anger's fire plume had blasted from the top of his head. "I'm not *whoring around* with anyone. Scott and I are seeing each other—"

"Oh, *hell no*. You've got to be shitting me."

Tipsy opened her mouth to reply, but Old Faithful Ayers had predictably exploded. "All the men in this town, and you pick that *toxic douchebag*? I thought Will what's-his-face was bad, but this—what have you been telling him about me? Or Kate? You *asshole*! You're a spy!"

"Ayers. We need to *talk* about this, not scream—"

"That bastard is the absolute *worst!* He's a master manipulator!" Ayers's eyes narrowed, as if he were about to reveal a nasty secret. He crept closer, until he stood in a morning rain shower's leftover puddle. "Why do you think he wants to be with you, huh?"

"Maybe because he likes me?"

"He's *using* you! Because he *hates* me! And Kate! He's just trying to get information about *us*! Then he'll *dump you* on your ass! He dumped his last chick on her ass. Sucked her in with his Mr. Nice Guy George Clooney *bullshit* and then tossed her!"

"I don't know anything about that—"

"Because he hasn't told you, right? You don't wonder why?"

"Ayers, stop! Just *stop* it!"

"No. No. *No.* I'm *not* having this. When Jimmy finds out what you're doing to me, he'll kick you out! Then where will you go? Where will the kids go?"

"You've lost your mind. Leave before I call the cops."

"You will *not* have him around my kids. Over my *dead body*." He stomped with each exclamation. Brownish puddle-water dripped down his calves and soaked his socks. "I'll call my *lawyer*. I'll call the *police*. I'll call my *parents*—"

"You're insane! Get out of my yard!"

"Don't you tell me what to do, you two-faced, lying, sneaky—" He closed the space between them, and for the first time in almost twenty years, it crossed her mind that Ayers might use his clenched fists. He'd always huffed and puffed, but he was a leaky dragon. She'd never imagined the son of May Penny and Tripp Collins would have the nerve to raise his hands to any woman.

"*Back off,* Ayers!" she yelled. "Get the hell out of here and cool down."

He ripped off his Mickey Mouse baseball hat and his remaining hair stood up in sweaty little spikes. "I swear to *God,* if you keep this up, I'll—"

Cold air whipped around them, strong enough to lift Tipsy's heavy ponytail and slap her in the face with it. Henry's tall, rangy form materialized before her, like Wyatt Earp stepping into the Okay Corral. Ayers sucked in harsh breath, as if he'd turned a corner on a windy winter day in New York City.

Henry raised both hands with palms out and fingers splayed. The puddle around Ayers's feet creaked and went shiny. Henry pointed toward the road. Ayers slid backward, as if the walkway had turned into a hockey rink and Henry was an invisible Zamboni driver. Ayers's feet slipped out from under him. He went down on his ass, hard.

"Go *inside,* Tipsy," said Henry.

Like her two less rebellious children, she didn't offer a challenge to that command. She ran inside and locked the door behind her.

Tipsy tried to talk to her kids about their father's behavior during dinner, but they alternated between chatting about their trip and exhaustedly staring into space. Fortunately, the den's proximity to the rear of the house had prevented them from hearing the worst of it, but she still wanted to address his snippiness with them. Finally, Little Ayers broke it down in his uncannily mature way. "That's just Dad. We're used to it. It rolls off us like oily water off a mallard's back."

"You sound like BopBop. Everything is about a duck with that man, bless his heart," said M.P.

Tipsy smiled. "Now *you* sound like GiGi."

"Ayers is right, Mom. Dad made me mad out there, but I don't even remember what we argued about."

"He said you were a whiny jerk for not carrying your own stuff. You told him to take a flying leap." O-Liv flapped her arms. "Like a quacker taking off when BopBop sneezes in the duck blind."

"Sounds about right." M.P. stood and took her plate to the sink. "I'm getting in the bath."

"Don't use all the hot water," said Tipsy.

"Yeah," said O-Liv. "Stink-er-oo Ayers needs to shower."

"Ayers, why *are* you so stinky, anyway?"

"Because I'm a *dude*, M.P."

"Okay, y'all. *Okay*. Just *please* remember there are better ways to handle disagreements."

They disappeared upstairs to wash off their residual pixie dust, and Tipsy tidied up dinner. Big Ayers barraged her with angry text messages as she cleaned. She read the first few (I CAN'T BELIEVE YOU'RE DOING THIS 2 ME AFTER EVERYTHING I'VE DONE FOR U...IF I FIND OUT YOU'VE BEEN TALKING TO BRANDT ABOUT ME I'LL NEVER FORGIVE U... U R PITIFUL CAN'T U FIND YOUR OWN MAN????), and then moved on to the messages that should have reassured her, but were now intrinsically tied to her angst.

SCOTT: HEY. YOU OKAY? KATE KNOWS ABOUT US. SHE LOST HER MIND. LEFT ME THREE VOICEMAILS CALLING ME EVERY NAME IN THE BOOK AND THREATENING EVERYTHING UNDER THE SUN. I DIDN'T ANSWER, SO SHE SENT ME ABOUT A

HUNDRED TEXTS IN THE PAST HOUR. I ASSUME YOU'RE GETTING THE SAME THING FROM AYERS.

TIPSY: HE WENT OFF ON ME, TOO.

SCOTT: WE FIGURED THIS WAS COMING. TIME TO BATTEN DOWN THE HATCHES AND RIDE OUT THE STORM.

TIPSY: I GUESS SO.

SCOTT: YOU DIDN'T ANSWER MY QUESTION YET ☺ ARE YOU ALRIGHT? CAN I DO ANYTHING TO HELP?

Ayers's name popped up again at the top of her phone. And again. And *again*.

She typed a reply to Scott. I'LL BE OKAY. IT'S JUST A LOT.

SCOTT: WE GOT THIS, TOGETHER. I'M BLOCKING KATE FOR THE REST OF THE EVENING. MAYBE YOU SHOULD BLOCK AYERS, TOO.

TIPSY: GOOD IDEA.

SCOTT: CALL ME WHEN THE KIDS ARE ASLEEP. I MISS YOU. I WISH I COULD HUG YOU.

TIPSY: OKAY. She hesitated, as if Ayers might see into her phone. I WISH YOU COULD HUG ME, TOO.

"Are you alright?"

She looked up from the screen. Henry sat at the kitchen table.

"You're the second person to ask me that question tonight."

"Quite a performance from the elder Ayers this afternoon."

"Thank you for your help."

"You're welcome. I try to help when I can."

"I know you do. Nice move, icing down the driveway. Mysterious, but not as outlandish as the time you levitated his truck."

"The least I could do. I acknowledge I've been...challenging...of late." He rested his elbows on the table. "It's as if exposure to my mother incited me to prove her point."

"What point?"

"That I am, as you might say, a huge pain in the ass."

"Henry, parent child relationships are complicated in any century. My kids have already figured out their father is a particularly complicated guy."

"Be that as it may, I'm sorry for my behavior. I hope you know how much I value our friendship. I wouldn't have stayed angry forever."

"I hope not, since forever is a real option for you. But it's all good. Friends argue sometimes."

"I planned to put aside my squeamishness about Patience and offer my services again, but if Catherine Porcher is the real problem, then perhaps the point is moot."

"Don't get all *moot* on me yet. I still sense there are connections between all these ghosts. Thomas. Your mom. Catherine." She looked at her phone again. Eleven texts from Ayers. "I'm going to bed. I'm exhausted."

"A little advice," said Henry, gently. "Don't read Ayers's texters. Is there any way to prevent him from sending them?"

"I can block him. Like, put up a technological wall."

"You should take advantage of your modern masonry."

"Scott said that, too."

"You've told me Dr. Brandt is an intelligent man."

"He is," said Tipsy.

Henry disappeared, and Tipsy trudged upstairs. The kids had voluntarily put themselves to bed. M.P. was asleep, worn out by her own theatrics. O-Liv had her nose in a Harry Potter book, and Little Ayers was messing around on his phone.

"Hey, buddy. Set a timer for fifteen minutes and then lights out," she said.

"Okay, Mom. Are you friends with Tristan and Chloe's dad?"

She leaned on the door frame. "I know him. Why?"

"Dad sent me a text saying he doesn't want me talking to him if he comes to our house because he's not a good person."

Tipsy gagged on her anger, like a cat choking on a hairball. "Really," she croaked out.

"Y'all must be friends, or else why would he come over here?"

"We are friends. He's a very nice person."

"Dad does *not* like him."

"Don't worry about that, A. He's not coming over here… anytime soon."

She said goodnight and retreated to her room. After she washed her face, she donned a frumpy old nightgown she'd purchased during her pregnancy with Little Ayers. The collar had disconnected from the rest of it. An ancient stain on one sleeve refused to disappear, even though she'd washed it hundreds of times. She should pitch it, but the soft, familiar threadbare cotton comforted her, as if she wore a beloved baby blanket.

She picked up her phone and read a text from Scott. HEY. I CAN TALK WHENEVER YOU CAN.

She rubbed her eyes. The rhythm of her heart gave her clear marching orders to call him. She'd sob out her fear and anxiety, and he'd tell her everything would be okay. *We got this, together.* Exactly what she wanted—no, needed—to hear.

Instead, she reread some of Ayers's messages.

AYERS: HE'S USING U AND YOU'RE TOO CLUELESS TO REALIZE IT

AYERS: KEEP THAT BASTARD AWAY FROM MY KIDS

AYERS: MAYBE U SHOULD TALK TO KATE ABOUT WHY THEY'RE DIVORCED

She bit her lip as she typed a response. IT IS HIGHLY INAPPROPRIATE TO TEXT OUR SON ABOUT ADULT MATTERS SUCH AS WHO I MAY OR MAY NOT BE FRIENDS WITH. PLEASE REFRAIN FROM DOING SO IN THE FUTURE.

AYERS: DON'T U DARE TELL ME WHAT TO SAY TO MY OWN CHILDREN

TIPSY: I AM NOT HAVING THIS CONVERSATION. STOP TEXTING ME BEFORE I BLOCK YOU.

AYERS: GO AHEAD AND BLOCK ME. I'M NOT WASTING TIME ON STUPID TEXT MESSAGES ABOUT THIS ANYMORE. U WILL REGRET THIS.

Tipsy scrolled through her recent calls until she found Scott's number, but at the last second, she opened the text window instead. She typed a short message. HEY. CAN WE PLEASE TALK TOMORROW? I'M SO TIRED.

SCOTT: YES, OF COURSE. GET SOME REST AND KNOW I'M THINKING ABOUT YOU AND WISHING WE WERE BIG SPOON-LITTLE SPOON.

She'd been playing an emotional game of hide-and-seek since Ayers pulled into her driveway, and Scott's sweet words were *it*. The tears hiding behind her eyelids fled down her cheeks like her chin was home base. They plopped on her phone's screen. She wiped them away, and then typed a reply. THANK YOU FOR BEING SO SWEET. I HOPE KATE GIVES YOU SOME PEACE TONIGHT. I'LL BE THINKING ABOUT YOU, TOO.

Tipsy lay on her side with one hand under her cheek. She relived Ayers's vicious threats and his personal attacks…and his insistence that Scott wasn't what he seemed.

Why do you think he's with you, anyway?

Tipsy herself had asked Pamella that question. Ayers provided a horrible, painful, mortifying answer. Scott didn't care about Tipsy or enjoy her company. He wanted revenge on—and information about—Kate and Ayers. She curled into a ball, as if to protect herself from an emotional gut punch.

And what about Ayers *already* dragging Little A into it? Indescribably toxic behavior. She couldn't put her kids in psychological harm's way. Especially for a man she didn't know very well. A man who may be using her. A Dr. McDreamy, George Clooney look-a-like who might dump her on her ass, as he'd apparently done to the Hellraising Highlighter.

A million counterattacks and denials of Ayers's over-the-top accusations and complaints tried to rein in her dread. Far from being subdued, the panic bucked and reared, an unbroken horse with a burr under its saddle. When she closed her eyes, she saw Ayers's texts, their cruel messages flashing like grammatically incorrect highway billboards.

I should block him. But she didn't. She wanted a warning if he threatened to show up on her doorstep, but she also felt guilty for dismissing Granna and Lindsey's advice. Guilt for bringing this mess on herself. Even guilt for betraying Ayers after he confided in her.

Tiffany Lynn, said Granna. *I love you more than anything in my life or my death, but if you allow yourself to feel guilty for betraying Ayers, I might come back as a ghost myself and knock some sense into you with one of Catherine Porcher's flowerpots.*

I can't talk right now, Granna. It's too much. I need to sleep.

Close your eyes, then, but I got one more opinion to share. I don't know nothing about y'all's fancy phones, but I wholeheartedly agree you need to cinderblock that fool.

Tipsy still couldn't do it. As she lay there, aching for Scott's reassuring presence on the other side of her bed, another thought crossed her mind.

She was destined to only get comfort from old nightgowns.

Chapter 13

The next day, Tipsy dropped the disgruntled kids off at May Penny and Tripp's on Sullivan's Island. The annual summer camp shuffle hadn't started yet, and Tipsy had to work at the GQB. As her fearsome threesome ascended the stairs in their bathing suits, her former mother-in-law, May Penny, stepped onto the front porch in a pink and lavender Lily Pulitzer beach coverup. Giant tortoiseshell sunglasses perched atop her signature smooth blonde bob.

"Hey, y'all," said May Penny.

The kids replied in an exhausted, unenthusiastic chorus. "Hey, Gigi."

"Thanks for your help," said Tipsy. "Between the cruise and keeping them this week, you and Tripp are Super-Gigi and Bat-BopBop."

"No problem. They're probably sick of us, but we never get sick of them."

"They're still wiped out. Feel free to take advantage of Disney Plus. A fairytale marathon to commemorate the trip."

"Good idea." May Penny looked down at her appraisingly. "You doin' alright?"

Tipsy forced a smile. "Everyone keeps asking me that."

"You're a little puffy under the eyes."

"I didn't sleep great last night, but I'm fine." She backed toward her truck. "Gotta get downtown. Thanks again."

"Hmm." Inexplicably, May Penny flipped her shades to her nose as she retreated into the dim house.

As was often the case, May Penny's words and actions befuddled Tipsy. *Does May Penny know Ayers has called up the troops, Granna?*

She covered her poker face with her shades. Hard to tell.

Ugh. May Penny and I have been getting along. I rely on her help. But she's Ayers's mother. She'll side with him.

She drove down Meeting Street, turned on Cumberland, parked in the garage, and walked toward the GQB. A few tourists peered through the windows. She'd have less time to work on Catherine's portrait in a busy gallery, but maybe her sunflowers would find a home today.

A sale would be awesome, but that's my last painting. I'll be Old Mother Hubbard. Bare cupboards, and nothing to tempt any puppies.

Sugar, when Shelby starts coming back in, you gotta start easing out. You've put in your time in this place.

I can't seriously contemplate quitting until I solve this mystery and get the payout that comes with it.

The tourists lingered around the door, resplendent in Ohio State regalia. When she unlocked the door, they spilled into the air conditioning. They were fresh off a ghost tour, and Tipsy smiled and nodded as they told ridiculous tales of impossible hauntings.

The Buckeyes insisted Tipsy accompany them throughout the exhibit rooms like a museum curator. For two hours, she discussed the paintings and their creators. They were impressed by Tipsy's sunflower painting, but when they learned the price, they quickly moved on to the next piece. By the time her new Midwestern friends cleared out, the noon hour was upon her.

She set up her easel, brushes, and paint jars, and then took measure of the canvas. She'd start with red and pink roses, as the colors made for easy paint mixtures. She unscrewed the top from a jar of white acrylic paint, and then perused the other bottles for a nice shade of red.

The doorbell clanged and a dark-haired woman entered the gallery. She wore skintight black jeans, a black tank top, and zebra print platform mules. She removed her black sunglasses and stuck them in her handbag. Black Chinese calligraphy was tattooed on her forearm, below a multicolored mermaid on her bicep.

She was what Tipsy thought of as an Instagram Vampire—the opposite of a Charleston Dress Code Blonde. Such women eschewed basic blonde, but rather than embracing their God-given hair colors, they doubled down in the opposite direction. Truly black hair should be left to persons naturally blessed with such tresses; for the most part, those of Asian, African, or Native American descent. This woman's inky hair, and her matching aggressively black eyebrows, did nothing for her very Caucasian complexion.

Her pretty dark eyes were lined in darker eyeliner, and thick lip gloss coated her collagen enhanced lips. Like the best of the Charleston Dress Code Blondes, she had a noticeable boob job. Her bombshell sexiness would surely draw a man's eye, but Tipsy found her more intimidating than appealing.

She chided herself for her superficial assessment. The woman did not fit the GQB's typical browser profile, but she might be a serious collector. Even an artist herself. She had a New York look about her.

"Morning," said Tipsy. "Can I help you?"

The woman half smiled and shook her head.

"Okay. Feel free to look around."

Tipsy returned to her palette as the woman wandered into the next exhibit room. She mixed puddles of color in graduated shades of pink, like a Home Depot paint sample card. Fuchsia to the softest pastels. *Blush to bashful,* she thought. Like Shelby from *Steel Magnolias,* pink was temporarily her signature color.

The intricate mixing process required concentration, and she didn't look up until the gallery phone rang. She recognized a spam number and ignored it. As she twisted her neck from left to right to work out the kinks, she realized the dark-haired woman hadn't appeared again.

Tipsy walked into the main exhibition room, where her sunflowers, propped on a windowfront easel, flirted with passersby on Queen Street. The visitor typed on her phone in the corner. Tipsy glanced at the ornamental clock on the wall behind her. She'd been in the exhibit room for thirty minutes. Odd, even for the most dedicated art critic.

"Hey, again," said Tipsy. "You have any questions?"

A broader smile revealed large, blindingly white, cosmetically enhanced teeth. "Yeah. I do, actually. Are you Tipsy?"

"Uh. Yes. Did you come in to see my work?"

"Not exactly. But I did come to see...you." She looked Tipsy up and down. "I should have introduced myself. Whitney Morrison."

Something about those W names...

Tipsy wanted to reply, but nothing came out. As sure as Little Ayers putting too much TP in the toilet, surprise had blocked her up.

"I'm *Scott's ex*," said Whitney.

Tipsy got a hold of herself. "As far as I know, his ex's name is Kate."

"That's his ex-wife. I'm his ex-*girlfriend*."

"Most adults only use the term *my ex* to refer to former spouses."

Whitney sputtered, and emitted a series of barking fake chuckles. Tipsy hadn't meant to sound snarky, but once it was out, she embraced the snark. After all, this random woman had showed up, uninvited, and lurked in her place of employment for half an hour.

Whitney retorted with her own snideness. "Scott was the love of my life. I was the love of *his life*. That makes up for the lack of a marriage certificate."

"Really." That didn't sound like the relationship Scott described to Tipsy.

"Let me start over." Whitney's marshmallow teeth reappeared. "It might seem odd for me to come here—"

"It *does*. Very odd."

"—but I'm here to *help* you. Kate told me you're seeing Scott—"

"You're friends with Kate?"

"I wasn't. When Scott and I were dating, we *hated* each other. Like all girlfriends and ex-wives hate each other."

"I don't hate Kate, and she's married to *my* ex-husband."

"Oh, my *Goooood*, I *heard*. So *weird*—" She waved fingers tipped with talon-like burgundy nails. Her metal bracelets clinked. "I'm not even getting into that—"

"Good. Since it's none of your business."

"I'm here about *Scott*. Kate reached out to let me know Scott had moved on to *you*. Everything makes sense now that I've talked to her. We both realized *Scott* is the problem. Not *me*, and not *her*."

"I don't know what you want me to say—"

"We're trying to *warn* you. Kate's husband is so *pissed* at you. She didn't want to cause more problems by talking to you herself. So I said I'd do it."

"You could have texted me."

"In person conversations are so much better."

Uh, huh, said Granna. *She came to check you out, like Kate wheeling up in your driveway to stalk Ayers.*

"Look, I don't have a problem with you," said Tipsy. "But I'm *not* talking about Scott with you. It's not appropriate—"

"Is he the most perfect man you've ever met?"

"Uh—"

"I bet he's so sweet to you, right? Like you've never had anyone be so *nice* to you?"

"I would hope he'd be nice to me. We're dating."

"Don't you think he's too nice sometimes?" Whitney and Ayers were part of the same conspiracy. Same squinty eyes. Same knowing leer.

"I don't *know*. He's really nice."

"*And* he's a doctor. *And* he's got his perfect house where he lives with his perfect kids. *And* he's always perfectly dressed and perfectly buff and…it's not *natural*." Once again, she sounded eerily like Ayers. She dropped her voice to a whisper. "He might be gay."

Tipsy thought of her past few weeks with Scott and blushed. "I doubt *that*."

"Me and Kate think so. You better watch out. You want to be one of those clueless women whose man turns out to be gay?"

"No. Of *course not*. But I don't think—"

"He broke my heart. I *loved* him. I don't have kids—kids are *not* my thing—but I *loved* his kids. And then one day, bam! He breaks up with me out of the blue. Never even got to say goodbye to them."

"You knew Tristan and Chloe?"

"*Yes.* I *just told* you. We were the loves of each other's lives. He wanted me to move here from Tennessee. So I did, and then he abandoned me. Luckily, I have my *own friends* in Charleston. They all sided with me. They didn't really like him. Have you been to a party with him? He's so awkward."

"He told me he's kind of shy, and he's not into the party scene. Maybe he didn't want to be there."

"Oh, *poor Scott.* Whatever. It's all manipulation. You should break it off with him, right away. Before you get hurt."

"I'm not—I—"

"If you don't listen to me, you *seriously* have a problem. But some women aren't strong enough to see the truth."

"I don't—If I—" Tipsy had never had more trouble stringing words together.

Tipsy, you don't owe this woman nothing.

Granna was right. Who the hell was this chick, to appear out of nowhere and demand Tipsy acquiesce to her opinions?

"Whitney," she said. "I...appreciate your concern, and Kate's, too. But you haven't named one thing Scott actually did *wrong.* You say he's too perfect and he dumped you. I don't see how that means he's a *terrible person.*"

"Everything he says and does is a lie. He's not this super *nice guy* who loves you. He's a *master manipulator.*"

Tipsy laughed, as Whitney once again parroted Ayers's front yard tirade. All these descriptive phrases had to be coming from the same source. "Kate must love that phrase. My ex-husband said the same thing, and Ayers isn't one for multisyllable words."

"Then maybe you should listen to *him,* too."

"If you knew Ayers, you wouldn't advise that."

"Fine. Suit yourself. I'm trying to be *nice* here." She wiped her spidery lashes and her mascara smeared. "That's probably why Scott targeted me. Because I'm a good person. I *always* put other people first." She retrieved some tissues from her purse, dabbed her tears, and blew her nose.

It was possibly the most bizarre conversation of Tipsy's life, and given her marriage to Ayers and her frequent interactions with dead people, she was accustomed to unusual tête-à-têtes. She was at a complete loss. Whitney may be the *good person* she claimed to be, or she may be, to quote Ayers quoting Kate, a master manipulator. To further confuse things, her Instagram Vampire hair and her black makeup running down her face were so pitiful, Tipsy felt sorry for her.

Tipsy, such a nice person wouldn't have been fired after a drunken brawl with a customer. You should be watching out, not feeling bad for her.

Either way, I gotta get her out of here, Granna. Help!

The front bell *ding-donged*, as if an angel had heard Tipsy's plea, reached down from heaven, and rung it. Shelby walked into the gallery with little Charlotte in a Baby Bjorn. "Hey, Tips?" she called out.

"Over here," Tipsy replied. She turned to Whitney. "That's my boss. I have to talk with her about... stuff."

"I did what I said I'd do. Now you have to figure it out." She flounced past Tipsy.

"Hi! Thanks for...stopping in..." Shelby's smile froze as Whitney strutted out the door. "Damn. Is Elvira collecting art these days? Who *was* that?" She bounced the sleeping baby. "Power walking with this munchkin, so I stopped in to catch up on your *passionate love affair*. With my wonderfully boring life, I'm finally living vicariously through you!"

Tipsy opened her mouth, but she produced nothing but an onslaught of noisy tears. Shelby grabbed her arm. "Whoa! Sister, what the hell?"

"Oh, Shelby. I don't know *who* she is. I don't know who *Scott* is. And I don't know *what* to do."

— ·)(· —

Tipsy, are you sure you want to do this?

How the tables have turned, Granna. A few weeks ago, you told me to avoid Scott like a medieval serf shunning a plague-infested rat.

If we're making disease comparisons, you're being as rash as the chicken pox, and Shelby agrees with me.

I appreciate y'all's advice, but I've made up my mind.

Tipsy waited for Scott on a bench at the Pitt Street Bridge, a popular green space in the Old Village. The long, skinny spit of land led to the remnants of the bridge that once crossed the Intracoastal Waterway between Mount Pleasant and Sullivan's Island. In front of her, the Old Village's waterfront mansions, Fort Sumter, the harbor, and the endless ocean beyond it. Over her shoulder, acres of marsh stretched past Clarice Andrews's swanky neighborhood, Toler's Cove, and its yacht-stocked private marina. The tide was high, but she still smelled hidden pluff mud and oyster shells.

Everyone around her seemed happy and content. Couples strolled hand in hand. Chatting mothers pushed strollers while their toddlers sipped from juice boxes and munched Pirate's Booty. Multiple Doodle-dogs romped, woofed, and drooled. A couple days ago, she would have sent Scott a photo of the Doodles, with an accompanying goofy comment about the canine conspiracy. Instead, she turned her attention to a plot of marshfront land, once owned by Ivy's tyrannical father, Bubba More. A rambling ranch-style house had replaced the More family's shack. If Tipsy dug in that damp dirt, she might find Ivy's old buttons or sewing needles.

Despite Tipsy's attempts to focus on the scenery and her own melancholia, Granna would not be silenced.

I changed my tune about Scott because I saw how good he is to you and how happy you are with him. Now you're letting Ayers's temper tantrum and that Whitney person's hairbrained opinions rule the day. What happened to the woman who was determined to see this out?

I made a mistake. It's too complicated, Tipsy replied, as the slowly retreating tide revealed the tallest spiky oyster beds.

You had no reason to pursue it when you didn't know him, and you pursued it anyway. Now you know him, and he seems wonderful, and you're dropping him.

Maybe Whitney is right. Maybe he's too wonderful.

So you're saying you wouldn't ditch him if he started acting like an asshole?

"Hey."

Scott settled on the bench beside her. He wore suit pants and a white button down shirt, but he'd removed his jacket and tie. She thought he might kiss her, but he didn't.

"Hi," she said. "Thanks for meeting me here."

"This is neutral ground. You're going to tell me something I don't want to hear."

"Whitney came to the GQB."

Scott looked like Tipsy had told him Jesus Christ himself stopped in and bought one of her paintings. "Whitney? As in Whitney Morrison?"

She nodded. "Your *ex*, as she calls herself."

"*Kate* is my ex. Whitney is a woman I dated for a while."

"Apparently, Whitney places a lot more stock in the relationship than you did." Tipsy told him everything Whitney had said. She finished with the *piece de resistance*. "She said you were the love of her life and she was the love of yours."

He chuckled. "But she *also* thinks I'm gay."

"Uh, yeah. I guess."

"Do you think that?"

"Given the past few weeks, I don't see how I could reach that conclusion. It's been pretty amazing."

"I agree. It's been—" He shook his head. "Wait. I don't want to get distracted, and nothing will distract me faster than *that* topic. I can't believe I have to go into detail about…that aspect of my past…with you. I don't exactly want to hear about your other intimate relationships."

"I'd rather not hear the gory details of yours, but this particular detail showed up at my job."

"Kate and I were like roommates for years. Work and kids kept me so busy, I figured, *this is how marriage is.* So that part of our life was nonexistent. And as for Whitney…I don't *know.* She was just…*there.* Someone to hang out with. It worked for a while because it *wasn't* passionate and intense. For either of us."

"That does *not* sound like the relationship she talked about. She even said she was close to your kids—"

He guffawed. "What? She met them a few times in passing, but I promise you, she had no interest in my kids."

Despite his transparency and reassuring answers, Tipsy's anxiety increased as she rambled on. "She said you *wanted* her to move here. That y'all were, like, *soulmates,* and you were so good to her, and it was a perfect relationship—"

"Stop." He rubbed his eyes again. "I'll give her the benefit of the doubt. Maybe to *her* it seemed perfect. She told me she'd had a bunch of abusive relationships. I *was* good to her. I treated her well and I tried to help her when she needed me. Maybe she *interpreted* that as me wanting her to move here."

"When I saw her, I couldn't believe you dated her. She seemed so…*ugh.* I can't explain it without sounding like a catty, shallow, judgmental jerk."

"Jesus Christmas, Tipsy. You're always so hard on yourself."

"I'm not just talking about how she looks. She seemed so…tragic. For some reason, I felt sorry for her."

"I guess I did, too. But I *swear* to you, she *always* had one foot out the door. She disappeared for weeks at a time. I got the impression she'd bail on me if someone cooler or richer came along. She was always unhappy with me. But after Kate, I was used to that kind of behavior."

"So you were with her because her dysfunction felt normal?"

"Maybe. Why were you with that guy Will?"

"Like I said at the OD, Will was a combination of repeating old patterns and overcompensating in the opposite direction. Probably the *most* dysfunctional thing someone can do."

"Can't you see I did the same thing? Kate is professional and successful, and kind of prim and proper. Whitney is a wild child who lives to party. But deep down, they're so similar. It's not surprising they've buddied up now."

"But can't *you* see how I should at least consider what they're saying?"

"No! *No,* I can't."

"I've made terrible relationship decisions. I've ignored red flags. What if I'm ignoring them right now? You and Ayers have the same complaints about Kate, so I take it as gospel. Now Kate and Whitney have the same complaints about you."

"Seriously, Tipsy?" The hurt in his eyes about broke her heart. "What flaws are they *actually* revealing? That I'm too nice? They probably thought I was a pushover, but they eventually learned I can only be pushed so far."

"Why didn't you explain all this to me? Why do I have to drag it out of you? It feels like you're hiding something."

His face reddened, as if anger had seeped into his hurt. "I've never been more honest and open in my life. But figuring this stuff out is *embarrassing.* Have *you* got it all figured out?"

"Obviously not. I'm listening to myself, and I sound like a crazy person."

His voice softened. "You are *not* crazy. We've both spent time working on ourselves, and we both want to do things differently this time. For me, that means dating someone totally different. You."

"How do you know I'm different? We don't know each other *that* well yet."

"I *feel* different with you. You make me feel good about myself. That in itself is new to me."

"I find that hard to believe. You're smart and handsome and a successful doctor—"

"So I can't have problems? I have them. Guess what, world! I have issues!" He yelled out over the marsh and a big brown Doodle-dog woofed at them. "I didn't want to get too much into my past yet, because we already have to talk about Ayers and Kate. I wanted to focus on us and the future, but since we're jumping in, I might as well go head first."

"You don't have to—"

But he'd tossed the dice, and he was on a roll. "My dad who died? He was a drunk. He beat up my mom. He used to scream at me, too. Smack me around. Nothing I did made him happy."

"Oh, lord. I'm sorry." She bit her lip, but a few tears snuck over her eyelids.

"I was *glad* when he died. How messed up is that? A four-year-old, happy his father died. I don't know how I understood what death really meant, but I was relieved when Mom told me he'd never come home."

"I can imagine you as a little boy. An old soul, like my Ayers." She tried to take his hand, but he pulled away and raked his fingers through his hair.

"After he died, it was just me and Mom for so long. She was *so strong*, but I always felt like…I had to *fix her life*. Take on her problems. So what do I do? I go into psychiatry, where my whole job revolves around helping people fix themselves. Then I married Kate, who made me feel like I was the source of her problems, so I had to be the solution, too. And *Whitney*… Everyone says their old girlfriends are crazy, but that woman's problems go so deep, I can't even get into them."

"I know exactly how you feel. My dad is an alcoholic, too, remember?"

"I thought we'd eventually bond over that, like we've connected about everything else. But I couldn't get into it all yet. I'm a shrink, but cobblers have broken shoes and what not. I'm finally acknowledging my own issues. My choices. My relationships. Even my perfectionism. My OCD. You've seen my damn house."

"*Sleeping with the Enemy*."

"Exactly," he said. "I'm *not* keeping anything from you. I *don't want* to keep anything from you. Do you want me to tell Whitney to stay away from you?"

"It might provoke her."

"Maybe it will. Damnit, I wish I never got involved with her."

"So she was *not* the love of your life?"

"*No.* And I promise you, I was not the love of hers. She didn't care when we broke up. Now that I've moved on, it sounds like she's seeing it through rose-colored glasses." This time, he took both her hands and squeezed. "I don't know how to say this without sounding like one of my own patients on a manic bender. Maybe…*you're* the love of my life."

"See, there you go! Saying stuff like that! It's like something out of a dream! *You, this, us.* It's too perfect for me to trust it!"

"I am *not* perfect, Tipsy. I don't *want* to be perfect. Please don't put that pressure on me."

"I'm sorry—"

"And don't tell me you're sorry! I've never met someone who apologizes as much as you."

"I can't do this. There's still the issue of Ayers and Kate. Ayers is already putting my kids in the middle by texting Little A weird stuff about you. I'm sure Kate is doing the same with your kids. They'll hate me—"

"They will not. I will not let her control the narrative anymore. With my kids, or you."

"But it's so complicated!"

"Yeah, it is! It's complicated! But they won't stay mad forever—"

"You've already told me she can hold a grudge like no one else—"

He released her hands and laughed, and it was bitter. "You're going to argue with me no matter what I say, aren't you?"

"I *can't,* Scott. I can't do this to my kids. I can't risk Ayers attacking me again. I can't—"

"Why don't you admit this has more to do with *you*—your trust issues and your fear of Ayers—than it does with me?"

"That's not fair. We both knew how bad it would be when they found out—"

"If I wasn't prepared to deal with it, I wouldn't have gotten involved. You're not the only one who is afraid of being hurt."

"I'm so *sorry,*" she whispered.

"So that's it? You're ending it?"

She nodded. If she opened her mouth, she'd tell him *no, no, no, I'm not ending it, of course not, I'm not crazy.*

"Okay. Wow. I'm leaving. I need to process this."

"Scott, please. I'm sorry—"

"Stop. *Saying.* That." He stood, shoved his hands in his pockets, and stalked down the gravel path. A plastic bag blew past him. He grabbed it, and stuffed it into a trashcan.

Tipsy gasped as she watched him go, like a fish caught in a fast retreating tide. She'd unintentionally beached herself. *What just happened, Granna?*

Give it some time, sugar. For you both to catch your breath.

———✦✕✦———

When Tipsy got home after picking up the kids from May Penny's house, she sent Big Ayers one terse text message. I BROKE IT OFF. DO NOT TEXT ME UNLESS IT'S ABOUT THE KIDS OR I WILL BLOCK YOU, AND YOU CAN REACH ME THROUGH MIMI OR YOUR MOTHER.

He sent a monosyllabic reply, a sprung arrow to her fast pitch. GOOD.

She expected some relief after making a decision, but she felt exponentially worse. She hated herself for letting Ayers control her life, but whenever she thought of Little A's questions, she couldn't fathom how to be involved with Scott without dragging her children into toxic parental conflict that would scar them for life. She tried to convince herself she was doing the right things—paying attention to red flags and putting her kids first. None of those internal conversations soothed her. She'd dated Will for a year, and Scott for only a few weeks, but her heart was just as broken.

Tipsy shared the news she'd broken it off with those closest to her, and received predictable feedback. Henry expressed tragically romantic disappointment, and joined her in moping around the house in resigned melancholy. Pamella and Shelby both enthusiastically poo-pooed her decision and demanded she call Scott immediately to reignite the fire. Only Lindsey agreed she'd done the right thing, although she must have sensed Tipsy's abject sadness. Their conversations revolved around commiseration, not vindication.

She focused on the kids and the portrait of Catherine. The weather matched her dreary mood, but rain kept the tourists off the streets, so she got in painting time at the GQB. Thankfully, Whitney a/k/a The Hellraising Highlighter a/k/a Instagram Elvira did not make another appearance.

All the while, she fended off increasingly frustrated texts from Jillian, who demanded she up the ante at the Bonneau House. Tipsy hated to fib, but she claimed a sick kid. Money or no money, her heart needed a few days before she returned to that house and its toxic occupants, living and dead.

Scott reached out once, on Wednesday evening as she got into bed in her *COUGAR MOM* tee-shirt.

SCOTT: I APOLOGIZE IF THIS TEXT IS INTRUSIVE. I WANTED TO MAKE SURE YOU'RE OKAY. I HOPE AYERS BACKED OFF.

TIPSY: HI. IT'S NOT INTRUSIVE. AND YES, HE'S BACKED OFF. HOW ABOUT KATE?

SCOTT: YEAH. SHE HAS, TOO.

Either Ayers had told Kate that Tipsy had ended it, or Scott had told her himself.

TIPSY: I'M SORRY AGAIN. FOR EVERYTHING.

SCOTT: YOU DIDN'T ANSWER ME. ABOUT WHETHER YOU'RE OKAY.

TIPSY: I'M SAD. THAT'S THE TRUTH. BUT OTHERWISE I'M OKAY.

SCOTT: I'M SAD TOO. GOODNIGHT, TIPSY.

TIPSY: GOODNIGHT, SCOTT.

She retreated into the covers until only her nose poked from under the comforter. An old defense against her childhood fear of thunder and the occasional bear that wandered onto Granna's property. The benign phobias of a little girl with no reason to worry about supernatural monsters. She couldn't hide from her heartbreak, so she cried herself to sleep.

On Thursday, she dropped the kids with May Penny, but she didn't get out of the car, lest May Penny notice her increasingly swollen eyes. She looked at herself in the mirror on the sun visor. Her faced had puffed up, as if she'd had an allergic reaction to life. As Granna used to say about everyone from Tipsy's hungover daddy to her colleagues at the Piggly Wiggly bakery during pie season, she looked rode hard and put away wet.

Gotta get it together, she said to herself.

She expected Granna to chime in with sage advice. Pontificate on prioritizing the practical over the romantic. Remind Tipsy of her genetically inherited toughness. Life goes on, yada-yada-yada. Granna didn't say anything, so Tipsy gave herself a pep talk. She walked into the GQB with grim artistic determination. By the time she closed up shop, she'd finished the last of the roses in Catherine's bike basket. She tidied the gallery, but as she stood over the slop sink to clean herself up, her phone dinged in her pocket. She removed it and swiped over a text from Sophie.

SOPHIE: CATHERINE IS HERE IF YOU WANT TO TRY TO TALK TO HER.

Tipsy considered her options as she scrubbed paint from her hands and forearms and dried off with a couple old dishtowels. She splatted the dishtowels in a pile beside the sink. Her heart remained balled up somewhere in her stomach, like that clammy, damp clump of rags.

I barely have the energy to deal with Sophie, let alone Catherine, but my internal monologue has been a motivational soliloquy all day long.

Granna finally spoke up. *Yada-yada-yada, sugar.*

Tipsy sent May Penny a text asking to pick up the kids at 6:30pm, and her former nemesis congenially agreed. May Penny's promise to order take out from Home Team Barbeque erased any remaining guilt, since Tipsy planned on serving her culinary masterpiece, Breakfast for Dinner. She left her car in the garage and biked to the Bonneau House with her skirt tied up to prevent it from catching in the spokes. As she approached the gate, she stopped and swung one leg over the seat. She yelped when her bare ankle hit the pedal. The bike bounced over a tree root and crashed on the sidewalk.

She pushed the bike upright, examined her bleeding ankle, and hobbled through the gate. Jillian stood in the driveway with her hands on her hips. "Look who crashed the party."

"Sorry I've been MIA, but my whole life is a bit of a bike wreck these days."

Tipsy's last exorcism client would have invited her to sit on the piazza for a commiseration chat, but Jillian was not Pamella. She spoke over her shoulder as she walked toward the house. "My career forced me to compartmentalize. I highly recommend it."

Tipsy followed her. "I'm trying."

"I'm dealing with Mama's estate today. If it's helpful for me to clear out while you look for Thomas, I'll work beside the pool."

"Look for Thomas, right. Will do. But I'll check in with Sophie first...and...get a band-aid from her bathroom."

"I have band-aids in here." She walked up the piazza steps into the house.

Tipsy paused on the stairs. Sophie peeked through one of the backhouse's windows. Their eyes met, and Sophie pointed at the greenhouse. Tipsy held up one finger in the universal symbol for *hold on*.

She met Jillian and her band-aids in the foyer. As she squatted to attend to her ankle, Jillian talked to the top of her head. "This is *your* area of expertise, but I feel like we're losing steam here."

"We're not. It's going well. We're making progress."

"How? You haven't seen Thomas in over a week."

"I've been making other...connections. With other ghosts. Remember the old photo of the blonde woman on the mantel in the study? White dress, parasol?"

"Vaguely."

"I borrowed it. To show my friend Henry, and he knows her. She's a ghost. I've talked to her to get information about the Bonneaus."

"Interesting. Do you have any yet?"

"Nothing we can definitively use. But I'm working on it—"

"Should I find another exorcist? Do y'all have LinkedIn profiles?" Hysteria tinged her laughter. "I'm trying to keep it together, but I'm afraid he's found some way to see Sophie. I found her talking to herself in the greenhouse this morning. She started screaming at me about how I don't care about her and what she wants. I said, *I'm supporting your floral business, aren't I?* But she kept yelling about how I'm selfish and I don't care about her. Absurd! How could she possibly think that?" She grabbed her nose, but the tears came anyway. "It must have something to do with Thomas. He's poisoning her against me for some reason! Do you think he's trying to seduce her or something? Would a dead man do that?"

"I can't say for certain what Thomas's intentions are…but she wasn't talking to him out there."

"Then who? Is she turning into my sister? Does she have schizophrenia?"

Tipsy froze in a moment of indecision. If she told Jillian about Catherine, Jillian would want to remove Sophie from the house. Sophie would pitch a fit and dig in her heels. A contest of wills among two blonde, female gladiators. At best, Sophie would have no reason to stay away from the ghosts. She'd be right back under their physically and emotionally toxic influence. Worst case scenario, she'd immediately meltdown like Chernobyl and end up right back in the psych ward.

At the same time, Tipsy's performance so far clearly underwhelmed Jillian, and she'd withheld a significant piece of information. Besides, she hadn't made any progress by sitting on her hands. She weighed prudence against proactivity, and chose action.

"Jillian. I'm going to tell you something, but you have to promise not to freak out."

"It's *my job* to freak out when my daughter is in danger!"

"There's another ghost on the property."

"And you *just* figured this out?"

"Not a full-time ghost. It's someone who died somewhere else, and visits here from time to time. She can travel, like my friend Henry, because she was a clairvoyant herself in life."

Jillian's eyes widened. "Hell's bells. A clairvoyant *herself*. Who died somewhere else."

"Yes. She goes to the greenhouse—"

"Because it was her *favorite spot*."

"Sounds like you understand. I'm talking about—"

"Catherine." She bolted out the front door.

⬥⚹⬥

Jillian had about two decades on Tipsy, but in her maternal panic, she would have challenged the Kenyan marathoners who wallop the Cooper River Bridge Run competition every year. Tipsy's longer stride didn't make up for Jillian's adrenaline. Her short legs were a cartoonish, spinning blur carrying her across the Bonneau House's lawn. Her yank about tore the greenhouse door of its hinges. Quite a feat, as the door had withstood Hurricane Hugo, and Jillian weighed about a buck o' five.

"Sophie!" Jillian yelled, as she vaulted into the greenhouse. "Get out of here right now!"

Tipsy eased past the rusty door. She caught Sophie, in her green and purple KZ sweatshirt, scolding her mother. "...the hell, Mom? You do *not* need to be in here."

Behind Sophie, the ghost of a teenaged Catherine Porcher stared at her living sister—now woman of almost sixty—with twitching eyes. Jillian didn't see her, so she couldn't read her expression, or the tension in her limbs. She would not note Catherine's hair standing on end.

"Are you going to follow me every damn place I go?" asked Sophie.

Jillian looked around with wide eyes, as if straining to see in the dark. "Where is she?" She turned to Tipsy. "Do *you* see her? Cathy? Catherine?"

"You *told* her!" Sophie glared at Tipsy. "This will make everything worse!"

She might be right, but those beans had already bubbled over.

Jillian grabbed Tipsy's arm. "Where is my sister? *Where is she?*"

"Good lord, both of y'all take it down a notch!" Tipsy felt like the axis of a spinning Ferris wheel. She pointed at Catherine. "She's there, Jillian."

"It's Jilly-Jilly." Catherine glided toward them. "My favorite sister. Haha! Just kidding. *Sike!*"

"Catherine, *stop*," said Tipsy. "*Hold on.* Y'all haven't seen each other in years—"

"I *still* can't see her!" said Jillian. "How is this fair? She can see me, and I can't see her?"

"Fairness is irrelevant, but she's *right there.*"

"Everyone is so loud. So very *loud!*" Catherine put her hands over her ears. "It feels close enough to look me *right* in my eyes, Miss Sharona." She started warbling that old song by The Knack, like an out-of-tune, punk rock parrot.

"What's she saying? Someone *tell* me!"

"She's singing," said Tipsy. "She… likes *My Sharona.*"

Catherine scratched her nails down her face. "*Jilly-Jilly-Jill…*gimme some time… Jillian…"

"It *is* her. She loved that song. It was popular the summer she died—"

"Of course it's her!" said Sophie. "Jesus, Mom!"

"Watch your condescending tone, Sophie Rose. Not to mention your swearing!"

Tipsy's patience was a bottle of aerosol hairspray. With a fizzle, it ran out. "Y'all, *hush up!* This is a complicated situation involving a mentally unstable, potentially violent ghost. Y'all aren't listening to me or each other. You're like female versions of my *ex-husband!*"

Jillian and Sophie hadn't heard much about Big Ayers, but any female person knows *that* can't be a positive comparison. They shut up, and Catherine's singing dropped to a low hum. She wrapped her arms around herself and rocked. Her face disappeared into the thunderheads of her electrically charged hair.

"*Thank you,*" said Tipsy. "Listen, Jillian…Catherine looks…agitated. Sophie and I can both see it."

Sophie nodded and stepped back.

"Catherine can move physical objects. *Violently* move them. Unless y'all want to be skewered with a gardening trowel, *stop arguing.*"

They both stayed quiet, but Tipsy did not trust their ability to remain thus for long, so she addressed the ghost. "Catherine. I'd like to talk to you about—"

"Shhhh. This is my quiet place," said Catherine. "Where I escape the voices. Outside, someone is always screaming at me."

"Who screams at you?" asked Tipsy.

"The same people as always. Although, sometimes a *new* someone just...butts in. The new ones are *so pushy.*"

"The voices in her head," said Sophie.

To Jillian's credit, she spoke softly. "When we were kids, she called the voices her *backup singers.*"

"My backup singers are quieter in this greenhouse," said Catherine. "The greenhouse keeps heat inside, and it keeps voices *outside.*"

Tipsy wanted to get her comfortable with talking. "Your home haunting is by the lake, right? I bet it gets busy—and loud— around there."

Catherine twirled her finger, and the windchime above her head tinkled gently. Tipsy cautiously pressed her line of questioning. "How did you learn to travel?"

"Many days and nights passed beside the lake. Season after season. Then one day, *Daddy* spoke up for the first time. Right there in my head. He told me to imagine myself at home. To think about the smell of my flowers and the taste of Mama's pecan pie. The sound of my windchimes. Even how the backup singers used to echo through that big ol' house. He said I had to feel it all, the good and the bad."

"And to *believe* you could make it back here," said Tipsy. Henry's traveling lessons had included similar instructions for Ivy.

"Yes. And then *here I was*, but all the flowers were dead. I looked out the windows. Overgrown yard. Broken fountain. I didn't see Daddy or

Jillian anywhere. Mama was an old woman. Whenever she sat outside, she held a little box in her hands and stared at it."

Tipsy whispered to Jillian in an attempt to keep her abreast of the conversation she didn't hear. Jillian nodded. "I made my mother get a cell phone about two years ago."

"Sometimes Mama came into the greenhouse. She talked to me, and I thought maybe she saw me. But no. She was talking to her own self. About all the sad things in her life. A sad song in this greenhouse. Like Barry Manilow. Or…Aerosmith!" Catherine made twitching, deranged eye contact with Tipsy.

Tipsy's brain couldn't wrap itself around *that* musical combination, but she nodded agreeably, as if Barry and Stephen Tyler made as much sense as Lennon and McCartney.

Catherine closed her eyes. A cloud of rainbow light swirled from her striped socks, up her legs, and over her midsection. As it crept toward her face, everything else about her went blurry. She had limited time in the greenhouse, and Tipsy had so many questions for her. She blurted out an important one.

"Catherine, why do you dislike Thomas Bonneau?"

Catherine inhaled the woozy rainbow like Tipsy's Dyson sucking up cobwebs and chip crumbs. Her lines resharpened. "Thomas Bonneau is evil."

"Why is he evil?"

At the word *evil*, Jillian lost her resolve to listen quietly. "I have an *evil ghost* in my house?"

"Jillian, *shhhh*." Tipsy spoke calmly to Catherine. "Can you explain why he's evil?"

Catherine's eyes lost focus again. "He…just *is*. I saw…something."

"Thomas is *not* evil, Mom," said Sophie. "What did you see, Aunt Catherine? How did you see it?"

"It was…bad."

"But how?" asked Sophie, as she approached Catherine. "How do you know?"

Catherine matched Sophie's forward progress with her own in the opposite direction. She never let Sophie get within six feet of her. "I looked," said Catherine. "I opened my eyes and *looked* and I *saw*."

"Okaaaaay," said Tipsy. "So you say he's evil—"

"Damnit!" said Jillian. "Y'all are throwing around the word *evil* like we're playing hot potato. Someone better explain this devilry to me, stat."

Sophie turned to Tipsy. "It's probably just *the voices* telling her bad things about Thomas."

"I can't hear her, Soph, but if she says this guy is evil, we should listen to her."

"Give me a break, Mom. You never listened to her even when she was alive. Never wanted to spend time with her, or help her. You were embarrassed by her!"

"She was!" said Catherine, as her personal rainbow once again threatened to consume her. "Mama said Jilly hated my guts."

"Sophie, sweets," said Jillian. "You don't understand what you're talking about."

"Yes, I do." Sophie's chin jutted in her mother's direction. "It's your fault Aunt Catherine got hit by a car!"

"Is Catherine saying that?" Jillian's eyes flitted between Sophie and Tipsy.

"She told me you *killed her*, Mom," said Sophie.

"Hold on," said Tipsy. "Not exactly—"

"But I wasn't even here—" Jillian facepalmed. "This is asinine. How can I defend myself when I can't hear what's being said?"

Catherine whispered to herself, about forty-thousand men and women who died every day. As she had when Tipsy first found her, she beseeched someone named Mary. Her hair slowly lifted, as if she were sitting on an electric chair with faulty wiring.

"Y'all," said Tipsy, as Catherine's eyes rolled. "Uh…Catherine has to return to the lake and rest. Maybe we can come back—"

The windchimes clinked with the sound of tiny rattling sabers. Clay pots jittered on the wooden shelves. A metal rake levitated behind

Catherine's head. Jillian watched, agog. She soundlessly pointed at the rake.

For the first time, Sophie seemed to grasp the gravity—or lack thereof—of the situation. "Aunt Catherine," she said, "I'm sorry. You like the quiet and here I am yellin' like…like…that guy from Led Zeppelin."

"Zeppelin is overrated." The rake vibrated like a plucked guitar string. Catherine's arm swung in an air guitar circle and the rake flew across the greenhouse. Whether purposeful or not, it made a straight line toward Jillian.

Tipsy had dealt with this kind of thing before. Instinct took over. She inexplicably reached out with her own power. She grabbed the rake with her mind, like the Wicked Witch of the West plucking a broomstick out of a tornado. Vibrations shot up her arm, as if she'd struck her funny bone. The rake changed course and hit a shelf.

Catherine squealed. Behind her, three pots rose into the air.

"Sophie!" Jillian darted across the greenhouse and grabbed her daughter's arm. She swung her around so her own body blocked the pots. Sophie protested as Jillian shoved her toward the exit.

Tipsy remembered Ivy More throwing her across Pamella's backyard with her supernatural strength. She'd never done anything similar, but as with many of her supernatural shenanigans, the situation necessitated action and she knew what to do.

She *shoved*.

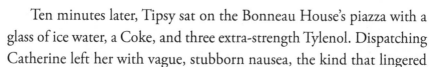

Ten minutes later, Tipsy sat on the Bonneau House's piazza with a glass of ice water, a Coke, and three extra-strength Tylenol. Dispatching Catherine left her with vague, stubborn nausea, the kind that lingered after an aggressive roller coaster ride. The inside of her head felt like a Led Zeppelin stadium performance.

"Can I get you anything else?" asked Jillian, with uncharacteristic meekness.

"Maybe some crackers?" added an equally cowed Sophie Rose.

Tipsy looked from mother to daughter as Robert Plant wailed inside her skull. *I'm dangling at the end of my rope with these people, Granna.*

Go ahead and let go before you rub your hands raw, sugar.

"There's only one thing y'all can do for me, and that's get your collective shit together."

"*Well,*" said Jillian, but she didn't elaborate beyond one ambiguous syllable. Sophie Rose's hands squirmed in her lap like submissive puppies.

"I've dealt with some demanding people in my life," said Tipsy. "I've already mentioned my ex-husband, and as the saying goes, he got it from his mama. May Penny Collins chews up nails and spits 'em out, all without smudging her lipstick. Over the past two years, I've managed multiple stubborn, arrogant, belligerent ghosts. That said, y'all still qualify as the biggest pains in my frequently chapped ass."

Sophie scooted closer to Jillian on the wicker sofa, as if to hide in her mother's shadow, but Tipsy kept her spotlight firmly focused on them. "Y'all have my sympathy. You lost a husband and a father. Sophie has suffered through this ghost business alone, which forced Jillian to face… *unique*…parenting challenges. And let's not forget the family history of severe mental illness."

Jillian's hand on the sofa crept toward Sophie's.

"Despite all that," said Tipsy, "I envy y'all. Not because of the material stuff—although I wouldn't turn down a hedge fund-trust fund—but because you have each other, and Sophie's sisters. A fierce girl tribe to love and support each other. When I was growing up, it was only me and my Granna. My mother was useless, and I didn't have any sisters or aunts or cousins." She turned to Sophie. "What did you say to me the other day?"

"Uh…about what?"

"You and your mom."

"We're both pushy assholes?"

Jillian's gasp was an attempt to cover a laugh, not a reprimand. Sophie bit her own lip, but the corners of her mouth twitched.

"Exactly," said Tipsy. "You can't hear each other because you're both so sure you're right. You're determined to die on that hill—"

"Mountain," said Jillian. "With us Porcher-Yates women, it's more than a hill."

"Bossy Mountain." The smile finally broke free of Sophie's lip chewing.

Jillian laughed, and wiped her eyes. "I prefer Mount Opinionated."

Tipsy couldn't help but relax at their banter. "Look y'all, *bossy* isn't an insult to me. My daughters are bossy in their own ways, and I want them to keep it up from the playground to the boardroom or the courtroom or the operating room. But you two are like a football team, tackling its own players."

"I understand what you mean," said Jillian. She looked at Sophie. "I've been screaming at you, sweets, about how much I care. Trying to convince you, when I should have been listening to what you need."

"I know you care, Mom. I do. But you don't understand this ghost business. It's not your fault—you *can't* understand unless you live through it, like Tipsy, or Aunt Catherine." Sophie's eyes watered. "I feel so bad for her. And...I'm only a few floors below her level of crazy. I hope someone would help me if I got like...that."

"You won't," said Jillian, fiercely, as if she'd dismiss any misfiring neurons in her daughter's head the same way she'd handled underperforming employees. "You will *not*."

"Jillian," said Tipsy. "I don't know if you understood exactly what happened in the greenhouse, but—"

"Catherine clearly believes I had something to do with her death. My mother must have thought the same thing."

"But you didn't. I didn't get a chance to explain the situation to Sophie yet. How you weren't even *in town* when she died."

Sophie's brow wrinkled. "You weren't?"

"No," said Jillian. She explained how she'd been away at camp, and didn't know about her sister's death until she got home. "The last year before she died—after we moved into this house—she went downhill like a runaway Mack truck. Only the gardens and the greenhouse made her happy. She barely ate anything. Nothing she said made sense, and everything we said made her angry. My parents sent her *away* at least twice."

"No wonder, if she was cohabitating with a ghost for the first time," said Tipsy. "A ghost she disliked, to boot. Supernatural angst is *exhausting*."

"Preach," said Sophie. She turned to her mother. "If you weren't even here, obviously you didn't have anything to do with Catherine's death. Either BeeBee was confused, or whatever she said confused Catherine. Maybe both."

"Your grandmother had so much loss in her life," said Tipsy. "Perhaps she needed somewhere to place at least some of the blame."

"I shouldn't have listened to what Catherine said about you, Mom. I was just so mad about everything else."

"Don't you worry about it, sweets." Jillian put an arm around Sophie and squeezed.

"Maybe we can figure out a way for Jillian to communicate with her and explain everything," said Tipsy. "Then we can help her move on. Truly be at peace."

Sophie sat up. "What do you mean?"

It was time to enlighten Sophie, at least about the basics. "I have ways of...*helping* ghosts," said Tipsy. "Helping them escape hauntings."

"*Seriously?* How?"

"It's complicated. Let's just say, it has something to do with understanding a death. Like, *complete* understanding."

Sophie looked about ready to jump out of her flip-flops. "But *how*, if someone died a long time ago?"

Tipsy doubted this sweet, cooperative version of Sophie would stick around once Tipsy actively tried to expel her buddy Thomas. Besides, she didn't want Sophie trying any paranormal tomfoolery on her own, especially not with Catherine. The girl might get her own self blown to high heaven. "I'll explain the details soon."

"*Come on.* Aren't you here to help me understand all this stuff? How can you *not* explain something so important?"

"Yes, but…"

Thankfully, Jillian jumped in. "But now she can help Aunt Catherine *and* you. Right, Tipsy?"

"Right," said Tipsy. "I'll have the best chance of helping her if we keep things super quiet around here. Can y'all, like, do a staycation somewhere?"

Sophie flopped backwards on the wicker sofa. "Ugh. I figured this would happen."

"Not forever. Just till I sort out…this…Catherine stuff."

"If it will help Aunt Catherine be at peace," said Sophie, "I guess a temporary scenery change wouldn't be so bad. It feels like I've been stuck in the backhouse forever. Hopefully being away from the ghosts for a while will help me feel better."

"I've wanted to spend time on Kiawah. We can stay at The Sanctuary."

"'Kay. The Sanctuary is fine."

"It's supposed to be pretty nice," added Jillian.

Tipsy let their milquetoast enthusiasm about the famous five-star hotel slide. "It's supposed to be great."

Jillian stood. "We need to pack up, Soph. I'll call the hotel on the way out there."

"You should confirm they have rooms available," said Tipsy. "It's high season—"

"The concierge will figure it out," said Jillian, from atop Bossy Mountain.

Sophie said goodbye and went into the house to gather extra clothes from her bedroom. Jillian joined Tipsy at the railing. She watched the greenhouse. "I remembered you don't want Sophie to know about your commission to *decommission* Thomas. Sorry I busted into the conversation. I have a penchant for interruption."

"No need to apologize. Sophie was having her own conversation bulldog moment. I was at a loss for words, so thanks for backing me up."

"You think she really...*likes* him?"

"Seems like it. You heard her defending him to Catherine. Now I've got to get going. Got to pick up my kids."

"Thanks for your insight," said Jillian. "I bet you're a good mama."

"You are, too."

"Now you have two ghosts to exorcise. More than you bargained for."

"Yeah. But it's all part of the job, as my grandmother says." No need to mention her grandmother was dead, and said such things in her head. Best to keep easing Jillian into it.

Chapter 14

O ver the next few days Tipsy balanced parenting, the GQB, Catherine's portrait, and visits to the empty (relatively speaking) Bonneau House. Once again, she was torn between forcing ghosts into her presence and waiting for them to appear. If she got Thomas's chatty ass voluntarily talking again, maybe he'd offer more information about Catherine. As for Catherine herself, Tipsy still wasn't sure how to pull a traveling clairvoyant ghost from her home haunting. She stood in the greenhouse and contorted her brain, but her mental yoga had no effect. In other situations, she had somehow known what to do, but always under the pressure of danger to herself or someone else.

If she's present, then I'm potentially in danger, but if she's already here, then I don't need to call her.

Ain't that a chicken and egg, said Granna. *You gonna try to find her at the lake?*

It's a big, busy, public area, but if she doesn't make an appearance soon, I'll have no choice.

The mornings were agony, as her dreaming mind still fancied she'd wake up and see Scott's dark hair on the pillow beside her. Nights were equally bad. She longed for the simultaneous comfort and stimulation of their evening conversations. For the most part, however, her hectic schedule forced heartbreak to the backburner during the work-and-kids hours. She averaged only one teary potty break in the GQB's tiny bathroom per day. Jillian would be proud of her compartmentalization, but as the weekend loomed, she found herself *dreading* Saturday. Dreading it like an amputation appointment with Dr. Legbone.

The kids were getting older, and they often had their own weekend plans. Tipsy served as a mere taxi service. The girls were invited to an overnight birthday party, complete with a daytrip to Family Kingdom in Myrtle Beach. Little Ayers planned a day of tubing on his friend's family's boat. He was already angling to spend the night. In a week, all three children were heading to their first sleepaway camp experience. Ayers and Mimi had attended Falling Creek Camp and Camp Greystone, respectively; two single-sex, woodsy, rustic bastions of a youthful southern gentility tucked into the North Carolina mountains. Ayers insisted on sharing the experience with their kids. Despite his inherent cheapness, he even offered to pay for their sessions. Kate had signed up Tristan and Chloe for the same weeks, and the Collins and Brandt kids were counting down the days until their high end wilderness adventures. Tipsy had perused the camps' websites. The lists of activities and traditions, and the sheer beauty of both places, made her want to check in herself for a few weeks. As always, she was incredibly grateful for her children's good fortune. They led far more exciting lives than she did.

This weekend would be good practice for her upcoming camp-induced loneliness. Tipsy would drop them off at their friends' houses, and then face Saturday on her own. She reminded herself that she'd come to enjoy the solitude. When she finished her painting sessions, she'd binge watch whatever caught her interest on Netflix. She could eat half a box of Cheez-its for dinner if the urge struck her. Still, the idea of a solo Saturday made her stomach hollow out like a leaky wooden canoe.

No denying the reason for her change of heart. Last weekend, Tipsy and Scott were climbing the celestial ladder past cloud nine. Extra painting time, *Game of Thrones*, and a fresh box of Cheez-its could not compete with such euphoria.

Friday evening brought unexpected salvation via the bestie group chat. Lindsey and Shelby had nursery fever, so they recruited the Grandma Squad for afternoon baby minding. Like Tipsy's kids, Lindsey's older daughter had her own social life. So, with all six of their collective children accounted for, the ladies planned a Saturday Mom's Day Off Boat Day Fun Fest on P.D. and Lindsey's boat.

After Tipsy dropped the kids off for their own weekend fun, she swung by the Bonneau House to ease the guilt of taking some personal time. For once, she hoped Catherine wouldn't show up. A disturbing supernatural vision and its accompanying nausea would sink her boat day. She peeled wheels out of there after only thirty minutes of whispering Catherine's name in the greenhouse. Back over the Ravenel Bridge she went. She dumped her Tahoe at her house and walked the few blocks to the marina on Shem Creek where P.D. kept his boat in a dry stack.

The dockhands had deposited the boat in the water with a gassed-up tank and iced-down coolers. Tipsy sat on the bench seat in front of the console as P.D. steered through bustling Shem Creek. A perfect day, hot but not yet humid. Despite the beautiful weather, the eternally irritable seagulls complained under a splatter of fat clouds. Silent pelicans perched on dock pilings and regally looked down their long bills at their garrulous feathered cousins. P.D. had to avoid other boats, kayaks, and a group of precariously wobbly upright paddleboarders. Definitely out-of-towners. Only tourists would risk navigating Shem Creek on those floating shoehorns.

Lindsey sat in the captain's chair beside P.D., while Shelby and Brian took the seat along the bow. Over the past year, Tipsy had accepted her fifth-wheel status, but as Brian put an arm around Shelby, her thoughts turned to Scott. She longed for his company, and his shared perspective.

Tipsy grew up in the Appalachian foothills. The endless, immobile granite waves of the Blue Ridge would always stir something in her mountain soul. Her ancestors had clung to those craggy faces like landlocked barnacles. In childhood, her roots grew tough in sparse, rocky soil. As a grown woman, however, they had relaxed, expanded, and dug deep into the Lowcountry's rich pluff mud. Saltwater had replaced spring water in her veins.

She wanted to share her brackish passion with Scott, a fellow mountaineer and relative newcomer to the Lowcountry. He'd understand why she loved it all, from the hugeness of the horizon-to-horizon sky, to the chirp of waves against an anchored boat hull. That sound always reminded her of a chorus of hungry baby birds. If the marsh hadn't already besotted him, she wanted to watch him fall in love.

She fondly observed Shelby and Brian whispering through Shelby's flowing hair as the boat picked up speed across the harbor. Brian, a northern transplant, preferred brewing beer in his garage and flipping burgers on his grill to sipping whiskey from a flask and hunting his dinner. He'd appreciate some male company who didn't live to tell deer and fish stories. She imagined Scott's easygoing banter with her friends. He wasn't a center of attention kind of guy, but after Ayers, Tipsy certainly didn't mind. On the occasions they'd chatted with other people at bars and restaurants during their fairytale week, Tipsy found Scott to be friendly, funny, and curious about others.

Scott and I both acknowledged our dweebish adolescence, but Whitney's assessment of him as a weird, anti-social adult seems off the mark.

Remember what I used to say about peaking in seventh grade. No harm in being a late bloomer. Tipsy sensed Granna's derisive sniff. *I'd say Whitney was as full of it as a neglected Port-o-John.*

Tipsy didn't answer. If she allowed herself to compare Whitney to an overflowing mobile potty, her resolve to watch for red flags would tumble to half-mast.

They entered the Intracoastal Waterway between Sullivan's Island and Mount Pleasant. A long no wake zone meant slow going and good chatting, so Lindsey asked Brian to switch places. The girls caught up as the boat followed the churned up water behind a dozen other vessels. Tipsy glanced in the direction of Clarice Andrews's house in Toler's Cove. He'd finally spruced the place up with a new coat of bright yellow paint. She hadn't spoken to him in months, and planned to keep it that way. Clarice and last summer's Windjammer humiliation were permanently linked. If they passed his giant boat pulling out of the Toler's marina, she'd put a towel over her head.

They reached Breach Inlet, the fiercely fluctuating channel dividing Sullivan's Island from the Isle of Palms. A sharp right, and P.D. entered the deep, narrow trench between the beach and the sandbar that magically appeared off Sullivan's for several hours each day during the tide's low swing. Swimmers crossed the narrow space between the beach and the perpetually crowded sandbar, but given the currents and the boat traffic, Tipsy had sternly forbade her kids from doing so.

P.D. found a space between a Jon boat of shaggy-haired teenaged boys and a smallish yacht with five 350-horsepower engines. The sandbar attracted all ages, from families to floating frat parties to Charleston Peter Pan guys and their surgically enhanced Tinkerbells. Wet dogs of all shapes and sizes—including the insidious doodles—raced around on the sand. Dads set up beach chairs, stripy sunshades, and even portable grills. As always, multiple speaker systems arguably blasted out conflicting musical tastes, from pop country to house music to the driving guitar riffs of Led Zeppelin's *Immigrant Song.*

"*Ah-ah-ah-aaaaah.*" Tipsy sang along under her breath. *Catherine's not a big LZ fan, but this jam must be part of her rockin' 70s repertoire, Granna.*

She strikes me as more a Stairway to Heaven *kind of gal. Even if she hasn't found hers yet.*

"Y'all, come on," said Shelby, from halfway down the ladder. "I'm sweatin' like a pimp in church."

Lindsey followed her. She held a red solo cup of prosecco and OJ, otherwise known as a redneck mimosa. "Isn't that supposed to be a whore in church?"

"Let a man take responsibility for some of the sinnin'." Shelby dipped her shoulders under the water and shivered. "Tips, can you get me a beer?"

"Y'all both doing the pump and dump?" asked Tipsy, as she handed over the beverage in question.

"Yup. Thank the lord for bottles, breast pumps, and the occasional beer."

Tipsy joined Shelby and Lindsey in the water. A passing boat, weighed down with impossibly attractive college students, purred past them. The driver scoped out potential anchoring spots while his buddies downed shots. Scantily clad girls shook their rear ends until their cheeks about vibrated out of their thong bikini bottoms.

"I remember when I could shake my butt like that," said Lindsey. "All wiggle, no jiggle."

"Ah, don't we all," said Tipsy. "But I wouldn't trade the wisdom of old age for the hotness of youth."

"Easy for you to say." Shelby glowered down at her straining bikini. "You've had years to work off the baby bulge and your boobs aren't the size of your head."

"You have gotten pretty wise, Tipsy," said Lindsey. "I predicted you'd get sucked into drama with Scott Brandt, but you resisted."

"Yeah. I guess I did."

Shelby squeezed her arm. "Nothing is carved in stone, sister."

"You thinking about going back to him? No *way*, Tips."

"No. It's done. But it's…really hard."

"How hard can it be? You didn't date him for long." So much for the simple compassion of Lindsey's recent text messages. After months of pregnancy and nursing and one redneck mimosa, she intended to offer Tipsy her unfiltered opinion.

"She spent like ten days with him, and *nights*, too," said Shelby.

"Do *what* now?"

Tipsy had shared more detail with Shelby than Lindsey. "I…uh. Spent most of the kids' trip with him."

"Oh, hell. No wonder Ayers is freaking out."

"I told Ayers I ended it. He's backed off."

"For now. But you better watch out, and don't even *think* about going there again."

"I said I'm not," said Tipsy. "Jeez."

"I don't mean to sound harsh, but you have to be careful. You've been through some shit—"

"So have you, and so have I. We waded through it and came out clean," said Shelby, "although poo is currently a major theme in my life." She laughed and inhaled. "Give me the smell of boat fuel over poopy diapers any day."

"I'm telling y'all, the Scott thing is too bizarre."

"There are bizarre-er things in this world than dating your ex-in-law," said Tipsy, her irritation growing. "We're consenting adults. I acknowledge we weren't together long, but I've *never* felt like I did with him. It's actually *very* hard, so please stop riding me."

"Honey, I'm sorry. I'm trying to look out for you, but maybe I'm overdo—" Lindsey took a step toward Tipsy, and then abruptly sank out of sight.

"Whoops!" Shelby fished around and dragged Lindsey to the surface. Lindsey sputtered and coughed and clutched her sunglasses.

"Damnit! Too short—stepped in a hole—" Her wide straw hat drooped and her mascara ran down her face. Seawater filled her solo cup. "My mimosa! P.D.!"

Tipsy and Shelby pushed her toward the ladder. They didn't let themselves laugh until she was safely on the boat. "Salt goes with margaritas, not mimosas," said Tipsy.

"That's what she gets for her unsolicited advice." Shelby touched Tipsy's arm again. "You're keeping a stiff upper lip like you always do, but I know how much you liked Scott. I still think you should tell Big Ayers, Kate, and the Hellraising Highlighter to suck it."

"Thanks, sister. I'm gonna take a walk down the sandbar."

"You want company?"

She smiled and shook her head. Shelby and Brian had earned some couple time, and as Tipsy kept reminding herself, she was used to being alone.

→•✕•←

Tipsy was in no mood for small talk as she walked in the direction of the Isle of Palms. Her baseball cap and sunglasses did her a solid by hiding her face from any nosy people-watchers. Two unleashed doodles and a Jack Russell Terrier accosted her, and a little boy of about four ran up to her and threw his arms around her legs. She gently removed his clutching hands. "Wrong mama," she said with a smile. He looked up at her, bewildered, until his mother swooped in and saved him from this stranger with his mommy's legs.

As she walked, she felt a little better. She was moving, everyone around her felt happy, and it was too beautiful to lose herself in melancholy. As she started to declare victory over her angst and about face to return to her friends, a voice called out her name. A *male* voice. A *familiar male* voice.

"Hey, Tipsy!" She turned, and to her horror, Will Garrison was jogging toward her.

"Will?"

"Uh, yeah. Remember me?"

"Of course. But I…haven't talked to you in…" Tipsy tried to remember the last time she'd seen Will. She'd pulled up beside him and his kids at a gas station last fall, and simply waved, pumped gas, and moved on. She ran into him and Julia at Harris Teeter about four months ago. Once again, she'd waved and beat it out of their presence. Her friends regularly hung out with Will, but they respected Tipsy's desire to avoid him, in person or in conversation. "…a long time."

"I thought about texting to see if your girls want to get together with mine, but it seemed… not the time."

Tipsy's daughters were so caught up in their own social lives, they rarely asked about Will's girls anymore. They seemed over it, and Tipsy had no desire to pick at that scab. "Yeah. We're pretty busy."

"You out here with P.D. and Lindsey?"

"And Shelby and Brian. They have grandmas on baby duty."

"It's good to see you. I couldn't see your face, hiding under that hat…but I recognized that white bikini."

The thought of Will staring at her as she walked down the sandbar kind of grossed her out. "Where's Julia?" she asked.

"She works most Saturdays, so I'm on my own a good bit. I'm here with Glen and some other people." He pointed at a boat and Tipsy recognized Glen, the womanizing creep who broke Shelby's heart two summers ago. A mishmash of vaguely familiar Mount Pleasant party people surrounded him. They were in their thirties and forties, with few responsibilities, seemingly endless free time, and iron livers. The diehards of Shem Creek.

"Between fishing, hunting, and doing this kind of thing," she said, "Julia's work schedule works out well for you."

"Always gotta get a dig in, don't you?"

"I'm being straight up. That sounds like an ideal arrangement."

"How's it going with you? You dating anyone?"

"Great, and nope. Why?"

"That's not what I heard."

"What are you hinting at, Will?"

"Just asking. Don't get all *worked up.*"

The next man who insisted Tipsy *calm down* or *chill out* might get one of Catherine's rakes upside his head. "I am absolutely not *worked up.*"

"I heard you were dating Ayers's new wife's ex-husband."

Shelby and Lindsey would never tell Will her personal business, and Brian wasn't gossipy, but she wouldn't put it past P.D. He and Will had been friends for years, and they were middle-aged, male, Mount Pleasant Gossip Girls. Always twittering on about somebody else's problems. "And where, *pray tell*, did you hear that? Let me guess. P.D."

"No. Ayers told me. He shot me a text."

"Ayers Collins, *my* ex-husband, texted you about my personal business?"

"It's his personal business, too. You're shacking up with his wife's ex."

"I was *not* just *shacking up.* I don't appreciate you and Ayers talking about me."

"It was only a few texts. I agree with him about the weirdness. I can't imagine dating Michelle's new man's ex-wife. Or if she dated my girl's ex who I didn't like, I'd be pissed."

"Since I'm the only one of your former girlfriends who is old enough to have been married, that's not likely."

"Give me a break. Julia is almost twenty-eight."

"And you've got a decade on her. Cradle robbing is in the eye of the beholder."

"We're talking about *you*, not *me*. It didn't seem like you to make such a bad decision, so I was curious."

"I'm not going to stand here and listen to you and Ayers—two people with a history of making questionable decisions—judge my life." She corrected herself. "Wait. I can't say that about *you*. You made a great decision, dumping me and getting together with Julia. She's perfect for you. Y'all will live happily ever after."

"Whoa, Tipsy. I never said I'm living happily ever after with Julia. I don't know what I'll do, long term."

She laughed. "Right. Good ol' Will, can't ever hem him in."

"I thought we could be friends, after all this time. I always wanted us to stay friends. But you're still pissed at me."

"No, I'm not. But you're reminding me why I was pissed at you in the first place." She turned to walk away.

"I came over here to check on you, Tipsy. To make sure you're okay. I'm just being a nice guy."

"Sure. Thank you for mansplaining my life to me." As she spun around, a cackling from Glen's boat caught her attention. Such loud, braying laughter was fun and natural from some people, like her ghostly friend Jane, but sounded like an attention-seeking foghorn from others.

A woman in a tiny string bikini stood on Glen's boat seat with a beer in each hand. She stumbled, and Glen, ever the gentleman, caught her. Her sunglasses fell off. It was Whitney.

"Good. Lord. *Above*." Tipsy stepped around Will. Whitney was clearly somewhere between sauced up and stone drunk. Tipsy needed to get back to P.D.'s boat before Whitney recognized her.

"Tipsy—" said Will.

She put a finger to her lips. "Do not yell my name. Don't you *dare*."

"What's wrong with you?" He looked around. "You see a ghost around here?"

She couldn't believe she'd told Will her lifelong secret. It seemed so stupid now. "No! Would you be quiet?"

"Yeah, but…you seem agitated."

"You going to run to Ayers and tell him I'm crazy? I'm surprised you haven't told him about my secret."

"I told you I wouldn't tell anyone. I haven't."

Regrets aside, Tipsy had made herself vulnerable by telling Will about the ghosts. At least he'd done her the courtesy of not telling anyone. If she blasted him now, he might get pissed enough to tell Ayers, who would use it as an excuse to ask the Family Court to order a psych eval. "Thank you for not telling anyone about the ghosts. I appreciate it. I'm not…mad at you. I wish you the best. But please don't talk to Ayers about me. Please."

"Okay. If he contacts me again, I won't. I'm sorry I ran over here out of the blue. But…it was *weird* hearing you'd moved on, and things have been *weird* with Julia, and…I'm repeating myself. Weird, weird, weird. I need one of those dictionaries with different words in them. The one that sounds like a dinosaur."

All dictionaries have different words in them, but she knew what he meant. "A thesaurus."

"Yeah. You know I'm not good at talking."

She sighed. There was a time—albeit a brief time right after they broke up—when she would have loved to know she'd been on Will's mind. Now, she had absolutely no interest in whatever Will might be trying to say, with help from a thesaurus or a brontosaurus. "Will. Don't go there, okay? I don't know if Julia is right for you, but you and me are *wrong* for each other. We always were."

"Damn. That was blunt."

"It's reality."

"So you must be into this Scott guy. Even if you say you're not."

"I've been over you and me for a long time. Way before Scott. But since I met Scott…I…understand what I want. Now I *have* to go, okay?"

"Yeah. Good to see you."

She didn't do the nice thing and agree it had been good to see him, too. "Bye, Will."

She power walked toward P.D.'s boat. Thank God for small favors, White Claws, and Jell-O shots; she didn't hear Whitney yelling after her, too. Between Lindsey's overbearing opinions, Will's insertion into her personal life, and a glimpse of the Hellraising Highlighter, she would have been better off at home with her Cheez-its.

Tipsy hid on the boat for the rest of the afternoon. Given her pasty skin tone, she relished the sun, but she wished P.D. would pull anchor and head home early. Unsurprisingly, P.D. wanted to take advantage of every second of baby-free time. He would milk it, so to say, until Lindsey's nursing schedule demanded they return to his infant namesake. He moved the boat several times as the sandbar disappeared below the waves. Finally, Lindsey and her increasingly achy chestworks snapped. She pointed at Breach Inlet's famously roiling currents, where whitecaps churned over the recently submerged sandbar. "Let's *go*, P.D. Before we get swept out to sea and orphan our child."

"Give me a break, baby," said P.D. "This ain't no kayak."

Brian diplomatically stepped in. "We got to get back, dude. Shelby misses the bambino, and so do I."

"Y'all sure? We got a couple hours of daylight. We could hit Shem Creek."

The worst idea Tipsy had heard in years, as Will, Glen, the Hellraising Highlighter, and the rest of Mount Pleasant's finest were surely motoring toward the Creek. "Nah, let's head back," said Tipsy. "I may have to pick up my kids." The girls were in Myrtle and Little A had confirmed his sleepover, but she wasn't above fibbing if it got her back to the peace of her sofa.

"Okay. Y'all are a bunch of party pooperin' people," muttered P.D.

Lindsey already sat up front, wrapped in a towel, and she missed that comment. Tipsy yanked a sweatshirt over her head, flipped her baseball cap backward so it didn't blow off, and joined Lindsey on the bow. The boat floated over the restless water with the gentle rise and fall of a carousel horse. She thought of the old-fashioned metal spring doorstops in Granna's house. As a small child, she used to lay on the carpet, pull on those things, and release them. The wind vibrating past her ears sounded oddly similar; *whacka-whacka-whacka.*

A pelican appeared in her field of vision like a time-traveling visitor from a prehistoric age. It flew along beside them with its wings skimming the surface. She wondered how something could simultaneously be so clunky and graceful; so inappropriately aerodynamic. The bird's one visible blue-green eye seemed to stare in all directions—the sky above, the water below, and Tipsy herself. Her mental camera clicked, and she added the bird to her queue of painting ideas. On a whim, she whipped out her phone and snapped a real picture. While she never had luck with such shots, this one was surprisingly good. Near *National Geographic* quality. Maybe because she hadn't thought about it too much.

I think about everything too much, Granna.

It's a blessing and a curse, sugar.

She studied the picture. Before she thought herself out of it, she sent it to Scott. She included a text. THOUGHT YOU'D APPRECIATE THIS.

She put her phone away until they reached the no wake zone near the mouth of the Intracoastal. The boat slowed to a waterborne crawl as they passed other vessels jockeying around the public boat ramp. She flipped her hat around to shade her eyes and read his reply.

SCOTT: I DO. THAT'S WHAT FREEDOM LOOKS LIKE.

TIPSY: MY THOUGHTS EXACTLY.

SCOTT: YOU GOING TO PAINT IT?

TIPSY: HOW'D YOU KNOW?

SCOTT: LATELY I'M LOOKING AT THINGS DIFFERENTLY. CAN'T DRAW TO SAVE MY LIFE, BUT I SEE PAINTINGS IN EVERYTHING.

Tipsy's eyes stung. THAT MAKES ME HAPPY.

SCOTT: GOOD. I WANT THAT. HAVE A NICE EVENING, TIPSY.

TIPSY: YOU TOO.

She wondered what he was doing that night. She wondered why she wasn't doing it with him, whatever it was. She wondered, for the thousandth time, if she was making a huge mistake.

But before I broke it off with him, I wondered if I was making a huge mistake in the opposite direction.

There's no way to be certain which way is the mistake, sugar. You traded one kind of hurt and frustration for another. Last summer we talked about choosing between two negatives. Well, it's not always that way. Sometimes you're choosing between potential joy and potential misery.

But I don't know which is which.

And that's the conundrum.

Chapter 15

ipsy got up with the sun the morning after her ill-fated boat day. The girls were not due home until late afternoon, and she didn't have to pick up Little Ayers until lunchtime. She drove downtown and set up her easel in the greenhouse. She decided to entice Catherine with a portrait of herself.

"So, Catherine," she said out loud. "I got this painting you might like. You know the subject very well." She waved her brush with a flourish. "An interesting young woman. Reddish hair. Blue eyes. Bit of a wild look about her. The subject is… you! Catherine Rose Porcher, come on down! I'd love to hear your opinion!"

That ghost has requested silence on multiple occasions, and you're yakkin' away like a standup comedian whose jokes keep bombing.

Tipsy chuckled. *Catherine might not want to give me her opinions, but I can count on yours, Granna.*

She accepted her comedic routine had flopped. She shushed up and returned to her easel. The remaining windchimes tinkled overhead and her paintbrush *swish-scritched* on the canvas. She lost herself in details and forgot her surroundings. She could have been painting in her living room, or the GQB. On the beach, or in the Harris Teeter parking lot. As sometimes happened during such artistic immersion, her breathing slowed to uncomfortable shallowness. She sucked in some much needed oxygen, but when she exhaled, she saw her breath. Goosebumps appeared on her bare arms.

Unless a tiny ice age had descended upon the greenhouse, Catherine must be close. Tipsy rinsed her brushes and spritzed water on her canvas. A warbling voice rose above the buzz of the backhouse's AC unit.

"A little closer now…just a *little* closer now…"

Tipsy turned toward the greenhouse's flimsy metal door, where colors swirled as if Tipsy had stirred them out of the muggy air with her paintbrush. Catherine took shape: reddish hair, white tank top and shorts, the blue splotches of her eyes. The colorful cloud spiraled toward the ground and striated into the multicolored stripes of her rainbow knees socks. Her features and limbs sharpened. Tipsy inhaled her all-encompassing floral scent, like a scratch-n-sniff sticker.

Catherine squinted at the painting. "So, Sharonaaaaa. My friend, my pal, my buddy. You got time for me today?"

That song predated the Tipsy Era by a few years, but she remembered her parents singing its nonsensical lyrics in her father's beat-up Ford pickup truck. She listened to it over the past few days to reacquaint herself.

Tipsy hummed its quirky tune under her breath.

"Are you *making fun* of me?" Catherine disappeared and reappeared on the other side of the easel. She crossed her arms over her chest and tapped one socked foot. She had only a passing resemblance to Sophie, but she shared her teenage attitude.

"Just singing along to one of my old fave's."

"The girl in that picture looks like *me*."

"It is you. Jillian asked me to paint your portrait. To replace the one in the dining room."

"*Ewwww.* Those paintings were gross to the max. Jilly and I cried when Mama hung them up." She held up one finger, like Marc Antony giving his funeral speech in Shakespeare's ode to Julius Caesar. "Mary! Come! One last night of sadness—"

Tipsy had figured out the identity of Catherine's mysterious *Mary*, too. She switched her humming to the tune of Blue Oyster Cult's catchily morbid 70's rock opera classic, *Don't Fear the Reaper*. "It's was clear Mary can't go on, right? Poor thing."

Catherine stared into Tipsy's face as if her next words were a test. "SOS! SOS! Sending out an SOS—"

"You got a bottled up message to deliver?"

"No." She turned away, but she kept humming that old Police song. Tipsy set her brushes on the table. "If you do, I'd love to hear it."

Catherine whirled around. She didn't sing this time. Just a simple sentence, yet it meant no sense outside the context of the appropriate song. "I rode all the way through the desert on a horse…" She tilted her head and pursed her lips. "Don't know his name. Maybe he didn't have one!"

Tipsy couldn't recall the words to that one. "Uh…."

"Skata-moosh, skata-moosh, do *you* hear the voices?"

"I don't think so. Not the same voices you hear—"

"When I was young, everyone told me the voices were not real. But they also told me *ghosts* were not real. But here I am, space cadet. So why can't the voices be real, too?"

"I'm not here to tell you what's real and what's not."

"They're very important. They're *my* backup singers," she said, with her nose in the air, as if daring Tipsy to deny the backup singers' existence. "We stay out here. In the greenhouse. Me, and them."

"Sophie told me you don't go in the house much. That it's—"

"It's loud in there. It echoes. I don't much like it. Never did."

"But you go inside sometimes, right?"

"Yes. Maybe. I do. Yes. *Mi-yi-yi…* SOS! SOS! S…O…S!"

Ugh, Granna. I've never tried to communicate with a ghost who is this far gone.

She was already crazy when she entered ghost-hood. Your other ghosts were post-death dotty. There's a difference.

It's like compounding insanity interest. I wish I could ask Scott how to talk to her.

"I went inside the house yesterday," said Catherine. "When it was dark. It was night. Night when I died by the lake. The lake is dark. I went in. Then I came out. Went back to the lake."

Tipsy plucked important tidbits from that disorganized information. "Why did you go inside yesterday?"

"When? Yesterday. Why? Because."

Tipsy felt like she was communicating with Siri over a bad wi-fi connection, but at least Catherine was talking. "Did you…happen to see Thomas Bonneau last night?"

"Ohhh, he's bad. So, so bad. He's *the worst*. He should have gone to the loony bin. Not me. My mother sent me there when I went bananas. That *place*. Loud, messy place. It was the worst, too."

"I'm sure it was awful, but why is Thomas the worst? Why should he have gone to the…the…loony bin?" It felt wrong to use such a pejorative with someone who had been committed, but Catherine used it herself.

"Don't send me there again, Mama. Mary… *is* afraid of the reaper…"

"Catherine. Can you try to focus for minute? On Thomas? You don't like him—"

"No. No. No. I don't like him. Told him last night. Stay away from him. Her. Sophie. Us. Boom! I told him."

"What exactly is your problem with him?"

"I saw it. I *saw*. Saw *it*. SOS."

Tipsy, you're going to overwhelm her. She's either going to blow something up or disappear.

You're probably right, Granna, but what else am I supposed to do?

"Are your lips moving?" Catherine crept closer. "You're *talking* to someone. Jeepers creepers, you *do* hear voices!"

"I hear one voice. My grandmother in my head. She passed away. But she was a clairvoyant, and we were very close. So somehow, we can still communicate. Even though she's in heaven, or wherever it is."

"You're crazy! Craaaaaazy! Talking to your dead grandmother in heaven? That's nuts! Wacky! Cuckoo for cocoa puffs!"

"Maybe, but at least I've never been sent to the loony bin."

"You're *so mean*."

"Sorry—that didn't come out right." Tipsy instinctively held out one hand.

"Don't touch me, *Sharona*!" Catherine tried to swat Tipsy's hand away, but instead, her fingers—topped with ragged nails she must have chewed to nubs before she died—passed through Tipsy's arm.

◆─✳─◆

Tipsy opens her eyes and she's looking over someone's shoulder into a 1970s version of the Bonneau House's library-family room. Greenish carpet covers the beautiful wide-paneled wood floors Tipsy knows. The place reminds her of the old Sears catalogs in Granna's basement: orange and green draperies, a brown and orange plaid sofa, a papasan chair. The television is inside a clunky wooden console on the floor.

She's standing in the foyer, beside the staircase. Behind her, in the dining room, the old portrait of Catherine stares at her with slightly crossed eyes.

Like Granna holding a menu away from her face, Tipsy steps back so she can focus. The person standing in front of her has long, straight, reddish hair in need of a good brushing. Tipsy walks around Catherine to get a look at her face. Dark circles weigh down her blue eyes. She's holding a cream-colored cocker spaniel. The dog whines and licks her thin wrist.

"Hush, Stevie," she whispers.

She's wearing navy blue pajamas, but the buttons are not lined up correctly. One side of the collar is jacked up toward her ear. The rest of it hangs almost to her knees like a misplaced coattail.

The dog whimpers again. "Stevie Nicks, hush yourself," said Catherine. "The echoes are so loud today. I'm trying to hear what they're saying about me, but I don't want them to see me—"

The four-footed Stevie Nicks squirms and Catherine releases her. The dog runs into the family room. Catherine grips the ornate crown moldings and peeks around the doorway. Unlike Tipsy's recent visions from Thomas's head, Catherine's emotions are there, but they're scattered, conflicting, inconsistent. Tipsy pictures them as a cloud of swarming noseeums. Tiny flies that bite hard and retreat before they can be properly swatted. She gets hints of curiosity, jealousy, anxiety, frustration, confusion, and paranoia. It's enough to make Tipsy feel nuts, even in noseeum-sized doses.

Tipsy doesn't have to hide, so she steps into the room and stands beside the bookshelf. Another teenager is arguing with a rail thin woman with a bouffant hairdo.

The new young woman is Jillian. The drawn face Tipsy knows hides under glowing cheeks and pretty dimples. She wears a yellow peasant top and a pair of tight bellbottom jeans. Sparkly blue eyeshadow and frosted pink lipstick complete her stylish ensemble.

Young Jillian is enviably curvy, nothing like the marathon warrior of Tipsy's when. As for the older woman, Tipsy guesses her sharp features are the result of a cruel 1970s fad diet. Something involving grapefruit and wheat germ. Few women purposefully broke a sweat in the days before jazzercise and Jane Fonda. Certainly not wealthy South of Broad ladies who draped pearls over their turtleneck sweaters and wore panty hose and high heels in their own homes.

"You look too busty, Jill," says the woman, who must be Jillian's mother, Betsy Rose "BeeBee" Porcher. "You're not wearing that top out of this house."

Stevie Nicks snuffles and scratches at Jillian's leg and she reaches down to pet the dog's head. "Stop trying to change the subject, Mama."

"When you dress like you belong up on Spruill Avenue, I'll say something."

"Niiiiice. Now I look like a North Charleston hooker."

"Don't use such language with me, missy. If you want to go out on Friday evening, you'll cool your jets."

"That's why I'm trying to talk to you, if you'll listen to me for five seconds! I can't have friends here—"

"Who says you can't have friends here?"

"You know I can't! You never have friends over to play cards when she's here. Daddy doesn't invite any of the men from the yacht club for cigars. We don't do anything but creep around, so she doesn't explode like some psycho jack-in-the-box!"

"Jillian Rose! How dare you speak of your own sister so cruelly, and swear, too!"

"I will swear the roof off this house if you don't do something about her, Mama!"

Tipsy looks at Catherine, who watches from around the corner. She chews her nails.

"We both know she's getting worse again," says Jillian. "She's complaining about echoes and backup dancers."

"She always talks about those things."

"Not every day! Besides, last week she told me there's a damn ghost in this house!"

Tipsy has a real answer to her question about whether Catherine ever confessed her clairvoyance to her sister. Jillian can't hear Tipsy's blasting, exasperated sigh, but Betsy is equally flummoxed and perfectly capable of demanding clarification. She frowns. "A ghost? Like…someone dead…in my house?"

"Yes. She told me there are ghosts around us all the time, and when she looks at them, she can see right into their heads."

"Did you tell her she's having one of her spells?"

Jillian rolls her eyes. "No. I asked her if the ghost will go trick-or-treating with me on Halloween."

"I cannot believe your smart mouth—"

"Yes! I always tell her that! But she's getting worse and worse. She barely comes out of the greenhouse. She's probably out there right now, singing My Sharona with her new dead friend! Please, send her to the hospital. I just want to have a normal life. I want to have Debbie or Amanda over to study. Joe Albertson asked me if I'll go to the movies with him—"

"Joey Albertson? Marion and Paulette's son? They're such a nice family. Joey is so handsome. He wants to take you to the movies?"

"Weeping Jesus. Don't act so surprised."

"If you swear and wear that shirt you won't last long with Joey. Boys don't want girls who dress cheap and talk cheaper." She puts both hands on her bony hips. "As for your sister, I can't send her off whenever you get upset by her."

"When Roger Simmons came to pick me up for the baseball game last month, she ran into the foyer in her pajamas, screaming about how the backup singers won't sing Aerosmith!"

Catherine starts muttering behind Tipsy. "I'll dream until my dreams come true…Hush. Shhhhh."

In the library, the canine Stevie Nicks cocks her ears in Catherine's direction.

"The incident with Roger was unfortunate, but—"

"We have a crazy girl in this house. A real, true One Flew Over the Cuckoo's Nest *situation. So why isn't she tucked away with Nurse Ratched? Why do y'all keep bringing her home?"*

"She's my child, Jillian. Maybe when you have your own children, you'll understand."

"When I have my own children, I'll listen to them and care about how they feel!"

Betsy laughs. "It's easy to say what you will and won't do with your children before you have them. You can't understand what it's like."

"It's you who doesn't understand. Everything is about Catherine. Our whole family revolves around her like she's the sun. But she's too damn hot."

"She's your sister. You only care about yourself."

"I've never been allowed to care about anything but Catherine! I'm only asking to have a normal summer. A normal senior year."

In the foyer, Catherine sways on her feet. "My-yi-yi-whoop-de-dooo…"

Stevie Nicks whines in Catherine's direction.

"When does your sister get a normal summer? Never," says Betsy. "No, Jillian. I'm not sending her away. Besides, you're leaving for camp in a couple weeks. Lucky you, with your fun, normal *summer. Flittering away in the woods with your camp friends while your sister suffers."*

"Maybe if the doctors kept her there long enough to make her better, none of us would suffer. Instead, she's getting…so bad. Like this ghost business. She's never talked about ghosts before."

"I bet she heard you talking on the phone with Amanda about one of those sick movies y'all see at the theater. The Exorcist. *Or* The Omen. *One of those devilish films."*

"No. She really believes it."

"She always believes these things. But ghosts…that's new. I should mention it to her doctors. I'll put in a call. But I'm still disappointed in you. You have no compassion for your sister."

*Catherine puts her hands on the sides of her head and squeezes.
"Shhhhhh. Please. Shh. Shh. Shh. My…whooooooo…."*

*Stevie Nicks darts across the room and into the foyer. Jillian watches
the dog scamper up to her sister. The girls' eyes meet, and Jillian's narrow.
"I have plenty of compassion for her," said Jillian. "In fact, I wish she was
dead. Then we'd all get some peace, her included."*

*Catherine gasps and retreats behind the doorframe. Jillian stomps past
Tipsy, through the foyer, toward the kitchen. Betsy follows her. "Jillian Rose!
How dare you say that!"*

*The sound of their arguing fades as Tipsy walks into the foyer. She looks
up the staircase at Catherine, huddled on the first landing beside Stevie
Nicks. A few tears track down her face and drip off the end of her nose. She
squeezes the dog, who snuffles her hair and licks her cheeks.*

"That was quite a row."

*Thomas stands on the next flight of stairs. He gingerly descends toward
Catherine. "Are you hurt, Cathy?"*

"She told Mama about the ghosts," says Catherine, as Stevie Nicks growls.

"Yes, she did. Quite a betrayal."

*"Mama is going to call the doctor." Catherine's heartbeat quickens.
Her feelings abruptly splatter Tipsy, as if she brought down the emotional
flyswatter and downed the noseeums with one smack. The overriding message
rings loud and clear.*

*"They'll come take me away again from Mama Daddy, Stevie Nicks.
Away from stupid Jillian who doesn't believe me but I don't want to leave
her anyway nonono I won't go I won't I won't—"*

*"Dear girl, you're shaking," says Thomas. "Perhaps you should go to your
room? I can meet you there. We can talk about all this. Like we used to talk."*

*She looks up at him. "No! I never want to speak to you again. Stay
away from me! Stay away from Mama Daddy Jilly Stevie Nicks! Get out of
our house! Get out!" She starts singing Blue Oyster Cult. She tells Mary she
mustn't be afraid. Asks to take her hand.*

*"Catherine, honey, listen here. I understand how you feel. My own
family—"*

"Get out, Thomas! Out, out, out!" She bangs her head rhythmically against the wall behind her.

Catherine's thoughts and feelings scatter throughout Tipsy's head like confetti tossed into a high wind. The backup singers start a chorus. It's The Knack mixed with The Police mixed with ABBA. Add a dash of the Bee Gees to make it even more confusing. Tipsy wonders how Catherine functions at all amidst that cacophony.

Stevie Nicks stands sentry between Catherine and the ghost, bristling. She barks, and barks, and barks.

Catherine claps her hands over her ears. "Stop it. Staaaaap. Stop!"

"You should go to bed, Catherine—"

"The greenhouse!" yells Catherine.

She races down the stairs with Stevie Nicks hot on her heels and flings open the front door. She launches onto the piazza and Betsy calls after her. "Cathy? What's going on?"

Tipsy starts to follow her, but she remembers Thomas. She turns around, but he's gone. Up the staircase, or into the study, or to the place ghosts hide where even Tipsy can't see them. Regardless, Tipsy can't follow him, because she's waking up.

—◆✖◆—

Once the kids were in bed, Tipsy settled herself on the sofa in the family room in her *COUGAR MOM* shirt and a pair of fuzzy socks. She turned on CNN, where multiple pundits yelled over one another about gun control. If one of her kids woke up and came looking for her, the political racket would serve as cover for her conversation with Henry.

"You around, Mott?" she asked, as she sipped green tea.

Henry appeared on the other side of the sofa and crossed one leg over the other. He laced his hands over his knee, like a professor about to deliver a favorite lecture. "I thought you'd never ask. I wondered if you hadn't forgiven me for my freak up."

"Freak out. You know I forgive you. You might be a moody, gloomy dude, but you're also one of my dearest friends. Dear friends fight sometimes."

Henry bit the inside of his hollowed-out cheeks, creating the impression of a skull on the verge of tears. "So touching."

"Besides, I need someone who understands ghostbusting. Pamella thinks it's an easy-peasy hobby that makes extra money. Like I have an Etsy shop."

"I have no idea—"

"Forget it. Let me give you the latest lowdown on the Bonneau House showdown." For the next thirty minutes, she entertained Henry with her supernatural mystery. She finished with Catherine's memory of the overheard argument between Jillian and Betsy. "So what do you think?"

"Did this memory seem close to Catherine's death?"

"Yeah. They mentioned summer camp and Jillian's senior year of high school, so the age works out. Plus Catherine sang a song that was popular when she died—*My Sharona*—"

"*My-yi-yi-yi-whooo?*"

"How the hell do you know *My Sharona?*"

"Old Miss Callie's radio. It played non-stop when Jimmy and his sisters were young. Predictably, Jane found it very amusing and it put me in a foul mood. And you're sure Catherine heard everything Jillian said?"

"Yes. Jillian was super upset. She even said they'd all be better off if Catherine was dead."

Henry winced. "I thoroughly embarrassed my brother Edward, but even he never threw down *that* gauntlet."

"Jillian had been festering for a long time. She felt like Betsy refused to hear her." Tipsy thought of Jillian and Sophie. "That dynamic still runs in the family. Anyway, Betsy mentioned Jillian leaving for camp soon, so Catherine's death must be impending." She set her mug on the end table. "What do you think of Thomas's appearance toward the end of the memory?"

"It doesn't tell us much. He tried to offer comfort to no avail, and Catherine lost herself in hysterics."

"Hysterical, no doubt. But she must have *some* reason to be so anti-Thomas."

"You experienced a significant level of confusion and paranoia in her emotional inventory. Perhaps she misunderstood something he said or did and latched on to it."

"Maybe. I can't get any straight answers out of her, but I can't tell if she's purposely ignoring my questions, or her scattered thinking is moving the cursor on the conversation. The whole *evil* thing feels a bit extreme, but I feel somewhat vindicated she doesn't like him."

"You're so accustomed to ghosts being difficult, you're finding problems with Thomas. I found him so pleasant. Have you considered that *he* might have reasons to be *anti-Catherine*? As has been established by a lot of flying glass, she's far more dangerous than he is. Do you remember how afraid he was when I appeared in his house? It was as if he…expected a threat. Someone unpleasant."

Tipsy recalled Thomas cowering away from Henry's blue light. "I supposed that's possible, although I don't know how one ghost could harm another. Since you like him so much, why don't you visit him without me? Get a better read on him."

"Certainly. If you want me to speak with him I—"

Tipsy's phone dinged and she looked down.

"—will. And now you're distracted."

"Sorry. It's Mimi."

MIMI: CAN YOU MEET ME FOR LUNCH TOMORROW? HAVE SOME UPDATES ON YOUR HOUSE FROM JIMMY.

TIPSY: SURE. She had to work at the GQB, but she'd beg Shelby to come in for a couple hours. If Mimi had house news, Tipsy needed to hear it.

MIMI: GREAT. THE CO-OP AT 11:30AM?

TIPSY: THAT WORKS! SEE YOU THERE.

"Mimi wants to meet for lunch to talk about the house. I hope Jimmy isn't raising the rent. I've been managing the payments, but I can't pay more." She stood. "I wonder what Mimi knows about the Ayers situation. I don't want to hear someone else say I made the right choice by breaking it off with Scott. Although, given how much I miss him, maybe I need to hear it."

"Tipsy, if you need so much convincing, perhaps you should reconsider." He looked up at her with maddeningly reasonable dark blue eyes. "I still don't understand how the man's seemingly excellent character is a problem."

"What have I been saying all this time about Thomas? He's too nice to be true. How can I take that approach with one new...person...and not with another?"

"You're comparing Thomas's superficial charm to something between you and Dr. Brandt that seems quite intimate. Just a few weeks ago, you complained about everything in your life being difficult. How did you put it? You're always kicking, screaming—"

"—and clawing. I remember."

"You wanted things to *fall into place*. Doesn't Dr. Brandt meet your criteria?"

"I know, but there are so many variables—"

"You seem to have what you sought, and you can't tolerate it." He scowled. "Such behavior is more reminiscent of me than you. I'm the one who is arguably addicted to melancholy, as you like to remind me."

"You're making some valid points, but—"

"Enough buts, Tipsy. You've *made* the situation overly complicated, *and* overly simplistic. I understand you're afraid of heartbreak—"

"Do you though? You spent your life married to the woman you loved."

"In the end, she broke my heart, no matter how it deserved to be broken." He also got to his feet. While she didn't have to crane her neck like Jane, Tipsy still looked up at him. He gazed down at her with his chin nearly touching his chest. If Tipsy's father had been a decent, caring man, or ever offered his only child any meaningful insight, maybe she would have been reminded of him.

"I hope you heed this, my friend," said Henry, in his oddly hypnotic, sonorous voice. "All great love—or any meaningful endeavor, really—comes replete with the danger of tragedy. There can be no beauty without potential ugliness. No flower would ever bloom if ruled by the threat of excessive rain…or excessive sunlight."

He didn't disappear this time. He stepped around her and ambled up the stairs. His footfalls were soft, as if Jane slept soundly in their bedroom above. As if he might join her, and heal his perpetually broken heart.

Chapter 16

Tipsy waited for Mimi at the Co-op, a Sullivan's Island cafe known for creative sandwiches and myriad frosé flavors. Despite Tipsy's general disdain for Lily Pulitzer chic, she approved of the Co-op's décor, which relied heavily on hot pink flamingos. Industrial-sized blenders churned out the restaurant's signature pastel beverage, and a huge neon *FROSÉ* sign hung on a floor to ceiling Astroturf tapestry. The Co-op exemplified Sullivan's Island—whimsical yet sophisticated, down home yet current.

She got her food and a seat at the alfresco bar between the shop proper and the parking spots along Middle Street. She tried to wait for Mimi before eating, but she'd already worked out, showered, and ran a few hectic errands. Her caprese sandwich's crispy grilled bread and perfectly oozy cheese would not be ignored.

"Hey, Tips! Got room for two more?"

Tipsy swallowed and wiped her mouth as Mimi parked her mother's golf cart. To Tipsy's surprise, the mother in question sat shotgun beside her.

She stood and gave Mimi and May Penny cheek kisses. May Penny wore a pair of crisp white shorts, Jack Rogers sandals, a white linen blouse embroidered with tiny yellow flowers, and a wide-brimmed straw hat. She'd somehow traversed the windy half mile from her house without losing the hat or mussing up her blonde bob. As always, huge sunglasses hid half her face. White circles today; coastal grandma chic meets Audrey Hepburn.

Of late, Mimi preferred Golden Goose tennis shoes over Mr. Rogers's high-end flip-flops. She'd paired her pricy kicks with a striped prairie goddess maxi dress. Classic Ray-Ban aviators perched atop her shoulder length blonde hair.

Aside from May Penny's sandals, which were far too basic for her taste, Pamella would approve of their get ups. May Penny and Mimi were a fashion dynasty unto themselves.

Mimi got in line to order food for both of them. Tipsy started to slide down a seat, but May Penny snuck around her.

"I'll sit here. Let Mimi sit on the end."

"Uh, sure." If they planned to surround her, it couldn't be good.

Tipsy and May Penny made small talk until Mimi brought their lunch and two fat globes of frosé. As soon as May Penny started nibbling her salad like a high-fashion guinea pig, Tipsy's curiosity won out.

"I'm happy to see y'all, but this feels like an ambush." She tapped Mimi's arm. "If Jimmy needs me to move out, please tell me."

"Nah. Jimmy and his siblings are suing each other…and his mother's estate," said Mimi, in her breezy, asthmatically-influenced voice. "The house will be tied up in litigation for at least a year…probably two."

"The judge appointed Jimmy as executor of the estate during the litigation," said May Penny. "He can choose the tenant and set the rent."

"What a relief. Please tell Jimmy I'm so grateful. It's been two years. He can get a lot more in rent."

"Tripp and I want you to stay in that house as long as possible."

May Penny and Tripp's collective wants held the Collins family solar system together. If Jimmy knew their preference, Tipsy wasn't moving anywhere. "Thank you. I appreciate *that*, too."

May Penny sipped her frosé. "Little A and the girls have had enough change. Especially with Big Ayers getting remarried out of the blue and moving out of y'all's old house."

While Tipsy had talked to Mimi about the shotgun nature of Ayers's wedding to Kate, May Penny had never mentioned it. "I agree it's best for the kids to stay put at Miss Callie's."

"A diplomatic response," said May Penny, with a small smile. "But we're not only here to reassure you about your living situation. We hope you can give us some insight into what's happening with Ayers."

"Oh, jeez. I don't know if that's appropriate—"

"We were all shocked when Ayers decided to remarry so quickly. I told him it wasn't a good idea. There was no rush, but he can be bullheaded. He was hell bent on it, so Tripp and I focused on the positive. Kate seemed nice, and she's professional, and has her own children. *Oh, yes.* It could have been much worse. Louann Coltrane's son left his wife and three children, married a twenty-six-year-old yoga instructor who refused to sign a pre-nup, had two more kids, and was divorced again in four years. Now he's paying alimony to two ex-wives and child support for five kids. At least Kate brought things to the table—"

"—and left other things off it," said Mimi. "We also hoped she'd be a stabilizing influence on him...like you were. Ayers might talk like a general, but he needs a drill sergeant to give the real orders."

"I thought the same things," said Tipsy. "Plus, no matter what happened between us, I want him to be happy. He was my first love and he's the father of my kids."

"You're an angel to say that, given how he's treated you," said Mimi. "On the cruise, we noticed things seemed...tense...with Ayers and Kate."

"No yelling, but they weren't talking much, either," said May Penny. "Certainly not laughing or holding hands or gazing into each other's eyes—"

"May Penny, you remember we're talking about Ayers, right?" Tipsy's own borderline sassiness surprised her.

"My son is no romantic, but they're still newlyweds. We watched the kids for Mimi and Jimmy while they had a nice adult dinner. Made the same offer to Ayers and Kate, but they weren't interested."

"Kate kept complaining about him," added Mimi. "How she managed all five kids, and he was...drinking too much."

"To the contrary," said May Penny, "she lay beside the pool most of the time with a cocktail and read *People* magazines. She got two massages and a pedicure. *Ayers* was the one managing the children, including hers."

"She even complained about his loud chewing," said Mimi. "If you can hear someone chewing at a cattle call breakfast buffet…with hundreds of kids screaming about Cinderella and Buzz Lightyear, you're listening too hard."

"On the last day, I asked him how things were going," said May Penny. "He admitted they were struggling. He said you were helping him sort through it."

"That's a bit of an exaggeration," said Tipsy.

"But he *has* talked to you?" asked May Penny.

"Confided in me, yes."

"God bless you," said Mimi. "See, Mama? Tipsy is a saint."

"I do appreciate you talking to him, Tipsy. He won't come to me. He knows I'll worry."

More than likely, Ayers wouldn't go to his mother because she'd remind him of the idiocy of marrying someone he barely knew.

"I thought he might go to *you*, Mimi," said Tipsy.

"We've talked some. Once we get into any detail, he loses his temper and storms off. Do you think he'll get divorced again?"

"Hmmm." Tipsy considered the question. "Not right away. He's too proud. He'd have to admit he made a mistake. And it would be embarrassing."

"Your divorce humiliated him," said May Penny. "Especially since *you* left *him*. No offense, honey, but no one saw that coming on your wedding day."

A few years ago, Tipsy would have taken *much* offense, but she was in a different place, with herself and with May Penny. "So if it gets bad," said Tipsy. "He might leave her first to save face?"

"I worry about it. They haven't been married long and she makes her own money. His trust is protected—but you know all about that."

Tipsy did, as aside from her children, she hadn't gotten anything from Ayers but a last name she couldn't seem to ditch.

May Penny went on. "I'm not worried about his finances, but I am worried about the children."

"So am I," said Tipsy. "I don't want anything adding to their stress."

"Is that why you stopped…seeing Scott Brandt?" asked Mimi.

"Ah. Ayers told you," said Tipsy. "Yes. That's the primary reason I stopped seeing him. Ayers and I have been getting along lately. The idea of me and Scott…upset him."

"That's putting it mildly," said May Penny. "It was the one thing he and Kate agreed on during the trip."

"We were in the Atlanta airport," said Mimi. "I was beside Ayers in the Chipotle line when he got a text from…" A longer than usual pause, as if Brad's name might bring on an asthma attack. "….Brad Humphries, about you and Scott. He immediately dropped a few f-bombs. Traumatized the burrito makers."

"Kate was in tears, and Ayers's face was like an overcooked beet. I made Mimi take the kids down the terminal to get ice cream. Told them both to get it together."

"I shouldn't have gone out with Scott," said Tipsy. "It's weird and makes everyone uncomfortable—"

"Who does it make uncomfortable, besides Kate and Ayers?" asked Mimi. "I don't think it's weird. If anything…it's kind of cool, if everyone's getting along. Only one set of parents and kids."

"Scott said that—but wait. You *really* don't think it's weird?"

"This is Charleston, Tipsy. *Everyone* does weird things. If you like him, I don't see any problem with it. Except for Ayers freaking out. But that's his issue…and he should get over it. So should Kate. Y'all are all adults. We're not talking about a spouse-swap, because both couples were already divorced." She shrugged. "Dating post-divorce is hard. I don't blame you for going for it if you find a good guy."

"That was my initial thinking. But everyone else—"

"Everyone else can blow it out their pie hole," said May Penny.

"You agree with Mimi?"

"You seem to be awful concerned with who agrees with who, and not concerned enough with your own personal business."

"But...what about Ayers? When he found out, he went off on me like a high school fire alarm. He even sent Little Ayers some texts with nasty insinuations about Scott—"

"He did what?" May Penny's sunglasses fogged up in irritation. "He's taking it too far."

"I agree, and thank you, but—"

"Tipsy. I love my son. You know how I love his foolhardy ass. But are you going to let him run your life forever? I was under the impression that's one reason you divorced him. At least make all the drama worth it."

Tipsy sat in stunned silence.

Mimi slurped down the rest of her frosé. "Oooh...brain freeze." She paused and let the ice between her ears melt. "Mama's right, Tipsy. You gotta do what's best for you."

"But you still have to deal with my darling Ayers. And that, ladies, is where I'll exit this conversation." May Penny stood and sashayed to the golf cart. She sat in the passenger seat and whipped out her phone. She traded her sunglasses for reading glasses and started scrolling Facebook.

"I'm in shock," said Tipsy. "Y'all just told me to go for it with Scott, even though Ayers is about to start World War III in the family court."

"That bad, huh?" said Mimi.

"Worse. In the two days between him screaming at me in my front yard, and me breaking it off with Scott, he sent me at least a hundred texts. A whole slew of them included Clark Middleton's name."

"Mama and I figured as much, but what can he do in court? Y'all are divorced. You can date who you want."

"I don't know. But I'm just getting ahead financially. I could probably hire a lawyer to defend myself this time, but I don't want to spend the money I have on legal fees."

"That's why you need to...hit Ayers himself where it hurts. I learned a bit about all this stuff when I was...*you know*."

"Thinking about leaving Jimmy," said Tipsy.

"Right. Talked to divorced friends. Even met with a lawyer. First… child support is *always* modifiable. Either upward or downward. If I recall, yours was set during Ayers's great financial rut."

"Correct. After he lost all our savings in that land deal. Technically, he still owes me money from our settlement."

"You didn't go after him when he bought the new house?"

"No. Again, I don't have the money to fight him in court. Besides, Kate makes a lot of money herself. I figured she made a big contribution."

"Maybe she did, but Ayers ain't in his version of the poorhouse anymore. Daddy made a nice announcement on the Disney Trip. Ayers finally got the promotion…he always wanted. He's now VP of Operations for ColSouth. You can bet it came with a pretty raise…and a fat bonus."

"So you're saying—"

"Fight fire with fire. It's not even an idle threat. You can legitimately get more money out of him. At the very least, what he already owes you."

Tipsy's head spun like Little A's skateboard wheels. No wonder Ayers was turning his backyard into an aquatic oasis. The idea of getting more money out of him appealed to her, but she had her own big payday coming, if she sorted out the irascible spirits of the Bonneau House. She was making ends meet okay, and she truly didn't want to spend her hard-earned money—whether from her artistic or her exorcism endeavors—on an attorney.

Ayers, however, knew none of that, and despite his recent confessions, she had no plans to share personal details about her life with him. That revelation smacked of deception, and true to form, she felt a twinge of guilt. Before Granna started howling, she reminded herself that Ayers had stood by while she teetered on the verge of financial ruin for two years. The idea of roasting Ayers in a financial firestorm didn't totally change the equation, but it offered a novel path to an answer.

Mimi handed her a business card. Tipsy read the name. *Lisa "LeeLee" Moretz, Attorney-at-Law, Donnelly Family Law, LLC.*

"I met with LeeLee…*back then*. She's a Pinegrounds mom. A total badass. I told her about you. She'll meet with you if you have questions. Waive her consult fee." Mimi tapped the card. "She works for Darlene Donnelly. One of the only lawyers in town…who doesn't take a lick of BS from Clark Middleton."

Again, Tipsy had no words. She took Mimi's hand and squeezed.

"I'll get going…and you didn't hear any of this from me." Mimi pointed at May Penny. "Not from Mama, either."

"I understand. Thanks so much, Mimi. To both of y'all."

"You'll keep us in the loop if you hear anything else significant about Ayers and Kate's blissful marriage, right? We really need an inside ear. Mama is *truly* worried."

Mimi and May Penny had provided Tipsy with insider information and moral support, and they expected the same in return. A fair trade. "Yes, absolutely," said Tipsy. "Y'all please do the same."

"We will. He's a fool, but he's my brother and Mama's son. We love him. I hope they can make it work. If only Ayers knew…he has a battalion of women working behind the scenes to keep him marching in a straight line."

"He's gotta think he's in charge, bless his heart."

"Bless *your* heart—like really bless it, not in our passive aggressive southern lady way," said Mimi. "I want you to be happy. Mama wants you to be happy, too. Since you and Ayers divorced, she sees you for who you are."

"In the past I wouldn't have believed you, but I do now."

"Do what's right for you."

"I'll try to figure out what that is."

"Either way…doling out more cash will chap Ayers's ass just as much as you dating Scott Brandt. Make him choose what chafes him."

———◆✕◆———

Tipsy tossed and turned that night. Her brain hummed between her ears, as if she'd slurped down a couple shots of espresso and a supersized McDonald's Coca-Cola. If she harnessed Ayers's stinginess to make him yield, she could potentially rethink her decision to end things with Scott. She clung to purported red flags, as if she'd tied them together and hung them out a window. She was dangling above a shark-infested moat and relying on weak knots.

The first loop on her makeshift escape ladder: Scott's potentially unrealistic awesomeness. Old adages endure for a reason, but as Granna had suggested, if Scott did something shitty, would he be redeemed? That made no sense at all. Henry had made his own good points. Every male relationship in her life had been fraught with complications. Maybe fear of making another mistake and her own dysfunctional patterns had created complications where they didn't exist, while simplifying Scott's kind, attentive, communicative demeanor into something slyly duplicitous.

Next came Whitney's ad hoc mission of mercy at the GQB, along with Kate's unsolicited secondhand advice. It seemed far-fetched that Whitney and Kate cared much about Tipsy. They had a common nemesis in Scott.

What about Ayers's theory that petty vengeance drove Scott's interest in Tipsy? That one didn't stand up to scrutiny, either. Scott had openly acknowledged both the emotional strain of fighting with Kate and his presumption that she would not accept a Tipsy-Scott union. From Tipsy's stories, he knew Ayers to be a ferocious opponent in his own right. No vaguely reasonable person would call down such wrath upon himself to spite the likes of Kate and Ayers.

One by one, red flags let loose and fluttered down into Tipsy's imaginary moat, where they sunk like soggy tissues. Soon she gripped the last one for dear life. The voice in her head that reminded her of her past mistakes. She'd married Ayers Collins, and fallen in love with Will Garrison. She'd thought they were both right for her. Between Ayers and Will, she'd floundered through the Saint Dave debacle. While she had the wherewithal to avoid getting trapped in Clarice Andrews's fishing net, she'd still ignored Lindsey's good advice to swim around him.

Clearly, her picker was off.

She finally passed out in the blackest hours of the night. The technological gong of her phone's alarm woke her at six, and she stared blearily at text messages from Ayers.

AYERS: I HAVE THE KIDS SLEEPING BAGS AND HIKING BACKPACKS FOR CAMP. I ASSUME U HAVE THE REST OF THEIR STUFF SORTED OUT.

TIPSY: YES. I WILL HAVE EVERYTHING PACKED UP THURSDAY EVENING.

AYERS: OK. I WILL PICK THEM UP AT 6AM SHARP FRIDAY.

TIPSY: THANKS. I'LL HANDLE PICKUP AT THE END OF THEIR SESSIONS.

Ayers didn't reply, so he must have been in agreement. She stared at the ceiling. Last summer, she'd taken advantage of extended kid-free time to stay at Pamella's place. Proximity to Ivy had helped move the mystery along. With the kids at camp and Jillian and Sophie on Kiawah, a stay at the Bonneau House was in order. She got up, brushed her teeth and hair, put on a bra. She FaceTimed Jillian, who immediately answered from her oceanfront balcony at The Sanctuary with her open laptop on the table in front of her. She looked as if she'd already run a few miles.

"I thought you'd be up," said Tipsy.

"The early seagull gets the best trashcan pickins." Jillian sipped her iced coffee. "What's up?"

Tipsy explained her impending lack of parental responsibilities and asked to bunk up at the Bonneau House. "It will be easier to yank Thomas into the here and now if I can flop into a bed and recover."

"Sure," said Jillian. "Plenty of space. Choose a room. The cleaning people change the sheets regularly even if no one sleeps in the beds. You'll look for my sister?"

"I already found her. We had a nice chat. As nice a chat as can be had with a paranoid, manic, unintelligible ghost."

"Hmm... so, what did y'all talk about?"

"What came after is more important than the conversation." Tipsy decided to lay it out there. "I observed one of her memories. An altercation between you and your mother that she overheard. I get the sense it happened a couple weeks before you left for camp, and she died."

Jillian looked as if Tipsy had recited an embarrassing diary entry. Her air of effortless command abandoned her. She said nothing. Her phone's speaker grumbled its secondhand embarrassment as the ocean wind whipped past.

"It wasn't your finest moment," said Tipsy, "but you were only seventeen, and I could tell you'd reached your wits' end with Catherine. Your mother had no interest in how the situation affected you. You said some nasty things—"

"I said I wished Catherine was dead," Jillian whispered. "I said those horrible...horrible words, and she heard me."

"Yes. She did. When I'm...inside...one of those memories, I can usually feel the source's emotions. Your words did hurt her."

Jillian rested her elbows on the table and covered her face with her hands. Her shoulders shook. Despite her frustration over Jillian's lack of forthcomingness, Tipsy felt for her. "Jillian, don't beat yourself up. Like I said, you were a kid who had lived in a terrible situation for a long time. Can you...tell me what happened after the argument? I can try to see it in Catherine's memory next time I find her, but—"

"The next two weeks before I left for camp were hell." Jillian wiped her eyes and sat up straight. "Mama balked at sending her away. Kept calling the family doctor over to knock her out with drugs, but as soon as they wore off, she was roaming the house again. Talking to herself. Yelling. Then she'd race outside and hide in the greenhouse until Daddy dragged her back in. She tried to climb the walls around the estate and cut herself on the iron spikes. I started getting genuinely worried something would happen to her. Maybe she'd fall out of a tree, or jump off the piazza. I wondered if...if what I said..." She grabbed her nose.

"If what you said made her worse?"

She nodded and released her sniffer. "The day before I left, I went into her room and sat with her for an hour or so. I apologized. Said I loved her and I'd take her shopping with me and my friends when I got home. I begged her to try to get better."

"So y'all worked it out?"

"No. She was so drugged up, she slept through it. I have no idea if she even heard me, let alone rationally forgave me. Then I left for camp, and she died a few days later."

"Ugh. That's terrible."

Jillian leaned toward the phone. "I denied having anything to do with her death, because I didn't want Sophie to know I agree with my mother."

"What do you mean?"

"I *was* involved. I said terrible things, and she went through the worst spell she'd ever had, and then...she killed herself."

"Huh? You said a car hit her."

"She stepped in front of the car on purpose."

"How do you know that?"

"The police investigated. The driver and his passengers all testified that she was standing on the side of the road, and jumped in front of the car. Given her...problems...it was easy to surmise a suicide. When I got home, my mother made me read the police report. Dragged me to Catherine's grave in Magnolia Cemetery. She wanted to bring me home from camp for the funeral, but my father wouldn't let her. He thought it cruel of her to blame me, but she was right."

"Jillian, you can't take all the blame. You said she got worse when y'all moved to Legare Street. She had so many problems, and I've already explained that living with a ghost is stressful for a clairvoyant. It was one overheard argument. You blurted out one nasty sentence."

Jillian chuckled. "A sentence, alright. The death sentence of my family. Funny how none of us could see Cathy, but she haunted us anyway."

Jillian's grief made Tipsy feel bad for chastising her, but she had to make sure she wasn't hiding anything else. "In the memory, you also admitted she told you she saw ghosts, but you didn't tell me."

"How could I admit my sister had confided in me about ghosts, and I didn't believe her, and then my daughter confided in me about the same thing, and I didn't believe her, either? I thought Sophie would never forgive me if it took a third party—you—to convince me she was telling the truth. Are you going to tell her I knew?"

"I don't feel like it's my place to tell her."

"Thank you. I'm sorry I lied to you. I *really* am."

"It's okay. I understand why. But moving forward…"

"I'm an open book." Jillian maniacally swiped her face and looked at her fancy runner's watch. "I have to go. Sophie and I have massages this morning. Enjoy the house. There's a ton of frozen Trader Joe's food in the freezer. Please, have at it. Think of it as your personal B&B."

Tipsy thanked her, and said goodbye. She hung up and rubbed her stinging eyes. She opened them to Henry sitting in the chair beside her dresser. "Hey, Mott," she said. "Any luck finding Thomas?"

"No, I'm sorry. I've been to the house several times, and he hasn't appeared. My feelings are rather hurt. I thought we hit it off quite well."

"He doesn't want to interact with me, so he's avoiding you, too. I wish I understood *why* he's avoiding me. I can't help but think he knows I'm on to him. I'm more and more convinced he's *not right*."

"I hate to be wrong, but maybe your instincts about him are correct."

She smiled. "If I convinced you *and* Granna, I must be on the right path. It's all connected somehow. Thomas. Patience. Even Catherine. She dislikes him so intensely, and his demeanor in her memory struck me as… smarmy. Even her damn dog hated him. Maybe *he* contributed to her death."

"There we disagree. He's bound to the house. She killed herself by the lake. I don't see how he *could* be involved."

"Yeah…either way, the two of them are a terrible influence on Sophie. She's doing better, but I have to get rid of them before she comes back, or she might go downhill again. Then what do we do? I don't think she can be *proactively* admitted to the hospital."

"It's too bad you don't have connections in the psychiatric ward."

Tipsy sighed. "Scott."

"You can reach out to him and see what he thinks about everything."

"You mean about Sophie."

"No. *Everything.*"

Chapter 17

Tipsy finally took Henry's advice to heart. She tucked her kids into bed, and then sat on her front porch in a rocking chair and waited for Scott. His black Yukon pulled into her driveway and she rocked harder. The chair's frenzied swaying coupled with her anxiety nauseated her. The Yukon chirped like a giant raven as he locked the doors and walked toward the house.

"Hey." He stopped on the top stair, as if waiting for permission to take that last step into her presence.

"Hey. Come…in." She motioned to the haint blue ceiling. "Or out."

He sat in the wicker chair beside her. A small end table between them added distance. She'd eschewed the loveseat in favor of her own rocker. If they were on the same piece of furniture, the temptation to touch him would overpower her.

"Do you want a beer?" she asked.

"Nah. Work tomorrow."

"Good. I don't want one either, and if you had one, I'd feel obliged."

He leaned on his elbows and looked up at her from beneath his long, dark eyelashes. "It's good to see you."

"It's good to see you, too."

"I still don't know why you wanted me to come over. I'm kind of hoping it's about—"

"Sophie Yates."

"Oh." He sat back. "Yeah. How's she doing?"

"Okay, for now. Jillian took her out to Kiawah for a week or so, but I'm worried about her return. She's improved since she left the hospital, but I've also come to understand how…complicated…her situation is."

"What do you mean?"

"Her living situation…" She sighed in frustration over all the things she couldn't tell him. "If we don't rectify the underlying problem…when she gets home, she'll lose it again."

"I don't know how I can help without *understanding* that underlying problem."

"I know…but…hypothetically, how bad off would she need to be to be admitted again?"

"We can't admit someone based on what *may* happen. Especially not a legal adult who isn't exhibiting signs of psychoses or threatening to harm herself or anyone else."

"That's what I thought, but…I feel like Sophie is a tube of biscuit dough. She might explode at any moment. There's so much going on there."

"Believe me, I've seen it all. Even when we brought Sophie in, she wasn't in nearly as bad shape as many of our patients."

"But her situation is…unique."

He raised one eyebrow. "Because she's a rich girl with depression, anxiety, and an overbearing mother? This is Charleston, remember?"

"It's not that. I wish I could explain it—"

"It sounds to me like you *can* explain it, but you *don't want* to explain it." He reached across the end table and brushed her hair off her shoulder. His fingers lingered for a second. "You can tell me, Tipsy. You can tell me anything."

"I can *really* tell you *anything*?"

"Yes. You can."

In that moment, Tipsy's mind and heart connected with her mouth. She couldn't stop if she tried. This conversation would tell her everything she needed to know about Scott, and allow her to help Sophie, too.

"Sophie sees ghosts," she said.

"Ah, okay. Sounds like hallucinations to me."

"No. She *sees ghosts*. I know she sees ghosts because I see them, too."

He stared at her without speaking. Her stomach retreated into her ribcage and trembled like a trapped mouse.

"Can you tell me more?" he finally asked.

"Are you going all Sigmund Freud on me?"

"No. You told me something that's obviously a big deal to you, but you gave it to me in one sentence. If I'm going to understand, you have to explain further."

So out it came. She started with the little boy who haunted her childhood church, then moved on to Granna's wisdom about keeping her powers a secret and avoiding ghosts. The strain of hiding her abilities from her peers and the sense of lonely alienation. Next, Henry and Jane and John, et al., and her connection with the Yates women. She finished with her efforts to kick Catherine and Thomas out of the Bonneau House for good. Through it all, Scott watched solemnly, asked a few clarifying questions, and nodded in all the right places.

After almost an hour of talking, Tipsy ran out of words. "Now you know everything. More than any other living person has ever known."

"You said you told your old boyfriend."

"I only told him basic information. My friend Henry gave him a demonstration to make him believe me. But I've never talked to anyone about it like this." She laughed, and then choked on a sob. "You really got this therapist thing down."

"I'm not your therapist, Tipsy."

"No. But now you'll be my referring psychiatrist, since you surely think I'm crazy."

"Why did you tell me, if you had such a bad experience with Will?"

"Maybe between Pammy, Jillian, and Sophie—living people I've talked to—I'm *a little* more comfortable with it now. But it's not just that. I *had* to tell you." Her mind added an afterthought. *So I can understand what's between us and if I can trust you.* But she didn't say it. Such assurance would only come if he didn't know she sought it.

"Can you give me a second? I should be sure about what I want to say, so I can say it right."

"Uh. Okay. I'm going to get some water. You want some?"

"Sure."

Tipsy walked into the house. She paused in the foyer with a hand over her chest. If she pressed down hard enough on her lungs, she might stop herself from hyperventilating.

"Are you unwell?" Henry appeared at the bottom of the staircase.

"I told Scott Brandt my whole life story. Including the parts about death."

"Good gravy. How did he take it?"

"Not sure yet." She walked into the kitchen and ran some water into two glasses.

"Would you like me to move some things around, to prove my existence to him?"

"Not yet. I need to see his genuine reaction first. Without you backing me up."

"If he acts like an ass, I'll blast him off the porch."

"Thanks, Henry."

"Good luck, Tipsy. I hope he's worthy of you. Oh, and by the way. I'd like you to come with me to visit my mother."

"When did you have a change of heart?"

"I don't know that my heart is any different, but something is compelling me to go." His pale cheeks colored. "I'm afraid to go alone."

"Of course I'll go with you. If I don't have a heart attack tonight."

"Go talk to that man. He's waiting for you."

"If he's still sitting there, I guess it's a good sign."

She walked back to the porch and handed Scott his water. She sat down in the chair beside him and resisted resuming her violent rocking.

"I'm a scientist," he said. "You know that."

"I do." *There's no way he believes me.*

"Psychiatry is science to me. Neurology, too. Pathways in the brain. Chemicals like dopamine and serotonin. Genetic predispositions and outside environmental factors. Controls and variables."

"Yup. Got it." *He thinks I'm nuts.*

"I told you I went into psychiatry to help people, and I did. But I could have chosen other ways to make a difference. The mystery of the brain drew me in. It's the center of who we are, and yet we understand so little about it."

"Clearly, you think my brain is screwed up."

"Not necessarily. We talk all the time about neurodivergence. What if your brain diverges in a different way? Allows you to tap into things, forces, we don't understand?"

"Are you serious?"

"Listen, Tipsy. I told you I'm not really religious—but I was raised Catholic. We have a deep belief in the mystical and mysterious. I believe something bigger than us drives the workings of the universe. Maybe certain people can access that force in ways others cannot."

"You're saying you believe me?"

"If only you saw these things, I might not. But you already told me your grandmother had this ability, so that speaks to my experience with predispositions. You and Sophie have seen the same things, too, right?"

"Yes. We've had conversations with Henry, together."

"Then there must be something there." He smiled. "It's fascinating. I'd love to learn more. I'm honored you told me."

Tipsy covered her face with her hands. She heard him get up. He gently pulled her to her feet and led her to the love seat. They sat and he wrapped his arms around her. "It's okay," he said. "I'm here. I believe you."

"Thank you," she whispered.

"I think it's pretty cool, actually. Now you're going to have to put up with me asking you a ton of questions about it. If you never talked about it before, get ready to chat now." He cleared his throat. "That is, if you want to talk to me regularly."

"Scott. I want to talk to you every day, all day. But I'm so scared, of everything. Now that I told you, I'm even more scared. What if I trust that you believe me, and then you stop?"

"You're going to query yourself into a good old mental breakdown. One that has nothing to do with ghosts and everything to do with the emotional baggage you're lugging around."

"Can we start out slow? Talk about Sophie's issues?"

He hugged her. "We can talk about whatever you want to talk about."

So they did. Until almost two in the morning. While they didn't reach any great conclusions about Sophie, Tipsy reached one about herself. If she didn't give Scott Brandt a chance to prove he was imperfect in the best way, she would always regret it.

◆──◆✕◆──◆

On Thursday morning, Tipsy dropped Little A and the twins at their volleyball and soccer camp, hit Target for last minute sleepaway camp supplies, and then spent the day wrangling tourists at the GQB. The kids were unusually quiet when she picked them up after work. They stared out the windows, perhaps contemplating their first stints away from home with no Mom, Dad, Gigi, or BopBop.

She watched their blinking lashes and twitching noses. They were separate human beings, while simultaneously being bits of Tipsy residing outside her body. She pondered the maternal need to keep one's children close, lest you lose a part of yourself. With each passing year, she would have less control over M.P., O-Liv, and Little A. The thought made her want to cry and scream and trap them in the safety of her embrace, forever.

They arrived home, and she grabbed each one in a hug as they got out of the car. O-Liv compliantly returned her embrace. Little Ayers tolerated it, and didn't complain when she pushed his hair out of his eyes. "We should have gotten you a haircut," she said. "You'll be a sheepdog by the time you get home from camp."

M.P., her little firecracker, was last. Tipsy grabbed her arm as she went past, and squeezed her against her side.

"*Maaa-aaam*," said M.P., but she put her own arm around Tipsy's waist.

"You okay, buddy? You seem spaced out."

"Yeah. I'm okay. But Coach Amy yelled at me today for talking too much."

"Ah, honey. Sometimes you gotta zip your lip."

"I know, but sometimes I don't anyway. Coach never yells at O-Liv. She likes her better."

Tipsy stopped. "Coach always tells me how much she likes both of y'all."

"Then why do I get in more trouble?"

"Why do you think?"

She sighed. "Because O-Liv zips her lip when she's 'sposed to. How can we be twins, but be so different?"

"You're your own person, and so is O-Liv. With strengths and weaknesses. We all have them."

"Sometimes I feel a little…jealous of her. Because everyone likes her all the time and she doesn't even try."

Tipsy bopped M.P.'s nose. "That's natural. Sometimes she's jealous of you, too. Because you tend to be the star of the show."

"Oh. I never thought of that."

"Everyone has always lumped y'all into one person. But as you get older, that will change. Make sure what doesn't change is y'all loving and being honest with each other."

"Okay, Mama." M.P. hugged Tipsy, hard, and ran up the steps.

She paused before she went inside herself. She never had a sister, but she always wanted one. She would have welcomed any combination of three children. All boys; all girls. Whatever fate had seen fit to send her. Still, she believed she had the best kind of threesome. Her boy wouldn't grow up with brothers beating on him and competing with him. A gentler upbringing would lead to a gentler nature. That hadn't worked for Big Ayers, but Little A was a ten-point buck of a different color. Her girls would have a built-in best friend, all the closer for being twins.

Although sisterhood didn't work out so well for the Porcher girls, Granna.

If Little A is a different version of his daddy, said Granna, *your girls are just as far off the mark from Jillian and Catherine.*

It's so sad. The two of them, all tangled up in hurt and misunderstanding. She removed her phone from her pocket and opened a new text box. As soon as she typed the letter *S*, Scott's name appeared. Not even Shelby beat him out, as if her phone had been waiting to send this message. *I don't want to be defined by unresolved issues.*

Plenty of time to resolve them, sugar.

Tipsy started typing.

⸺✦⸺

After the kids were asleep, Tipsy waited for Scott on the porch once again. This time, she sat on the loveseat. She no longer feared being close to him, and besides, if she chose a rocker, she might gyrate herself right off the porch. She'd decided she wanted to be with him. Naturally, she now feared he'd reject her.

Henry appeared on the loveseat beside her. "To quote Little Ayers, you're giving off weird vibes."

"I'm freaking out, Henry. What if he's coming over for the satisfaction of telling me to go to hell for jerking him around?"

"Such behavior is outside the male wheelhouse. I assume he's had a long day at his place of employment. He has a free night without his children. He won't want to don shoes, leave his house, and appear face-to-face with a woman, just to tell her he has no interest in her. He'd rather recline on his sofa with a glass of bourbon and a book." He shrugged. "Or, to modernize, watch Netflickers."

"*Flix.* I hope you're right." Headlights lit up her yard. "Here he comes."

"Relax, my friend. All will be well."

Henry disappeared, and within moments, Scott replaced him beside Tipsy. "Loveseat this time, huh?" he asked.

"You noticed?"

"It's pretty obvious you don't want to be close to someone if you choose a rocking chair over the loveseat."

"It's not that I didn't want to be close to you. Quite the opposite. I wouldn't have been able to help myself from…" She elbowed him. "You know."

"I don't know, darlin'. But I'm sitting here waiting for you to explain it to me."

"I *do* want to be with you, Scott. You're right. I'm scared shitless. Getting hurt. Making another mistake. Facing the wrath of Ayers."

He took her hand and laced his fingers through hers. "At our age, with kids and entire lives we've spent decades building and then tearing down and then building up again, there's a problem if you're *not* scared."

"You're scared, too?"

"Hell, yes. I haven't exactly made the greatest relationship choices. And Hurricane Kate is in the same category as Hurricane Ayers."

"Every relationship I've had has been… *forced*. I had to wrestle them into submission. Squeeze myself into too tight clothes, or wallow in something five sizes too big. My whole life has been like that. From my family to fighting for my education to my professional life. Oh, and don't forget my freakish secret psychic powers. I'm not used to things being easy."

"I understand what you mean, but it worries me when you say how *perfect* we are. Don't get me wrong—I feel the same kind of euphoria. But it's a lot of pressure. I don't want to let you down."

"I'm sorry I kept harping on that. Neither of us is perfect, and of course we'll have challenges in our relationship. Life is complicated at our age. We have kids and jobs and impossible exes. But the *relationship* part has always been a struggle for me, too. *You* and *me*…seems oddly… *natural.* I didn't know how to handle it."

"When you're not breaking up with me, you make perfect sense."

She gently thumped him with an accent pillow. "You truly believe me about the ghosts?"

"It's wild, Tipsy. How can I say it's not? But it's also fascinating for me to contemplate the existence of those kinds of abilities. Like I said, it opens up a whole new perspective for me in the way I perceive not only my day-to-day existence, but my work. So yes, I believe you." He smiled. "If you have a way to prove it, I'd be happy to witness that, too."

"I'll call Henry if you want me to. The guy who haunts my house. He'll come out if I ask him."

"Soon, sure, but I'd rather have you to myself for a bit, if that's okay."

"It is." She gently turned his face toward hers. "I'm in. *Again.* If you can forgive me for being a crazy person the past couple weeks."

"I see crazy people every day, and you are not one of them. I'm in, too." He kissed her, and then rested his forehead against hers. "I never really left the building. I was waiting for you to find the door again."

Chapter 18

Ayers appeared in Tipsy's driveway at ten minutes till six on Friday morning. He loaded trunks and suitcases into his truck while she said goodbye to the kids. They were excited, but even M.P. seemed on edge. "Two weeks is a long time," she whispered, as Tipsy kissed her cheek.

"It will fly by for y'all," she said. "Your dad and I will be the ones sitting at home, bored and missing you!"

"Will you write to us, Mama?" asked O-Liv.

"Yup. Y'all have your stationery to write your own letters, right?"

"Yeah," said Little A. "I'll feel like I'm living in the prairie days. Writing on actual paper and sticking it in an envelope."

"Positively historic," said Tipsy.

"Y'all get in the truck." Big Ayers held up a white and red paper bag. "Who wants a Chick-fil-A biscuit?"

Nothing like fried comfort food to make kids forget their nerves. They piled into the truck and started arguing over who had to sit in the middle.

"Gotta get on the road," said Big Ayers. "Kate is already past Summerville. I want to drop Little A and Tristan at the same time."

"Good idea. Drive carefully." She stepped back as Ayers got into the truck. O-Liv rolled down the window. Little Ayers had agreed to sit in the middle, and all three kids laughed and bounced in place.

"Greystone and Falling Rock, here we come!" yelled O-Liv.

Hands waved and endearments were exchanged, and Ayers backed down the driveway. Tipsy smiled around biting her lower lip. Her twisted grin probably turned her into a female Pennywise the Clown, but she didn't cry. As the truck disappeared, her phone dinged in her pocket. With an audible sigh of relief, she read a text from Scott.

SCOTT: HOW ARE YOU HOLDING UP?

TIPSY: A FEW NERVES, BUT A SUCCESSFUL DEPARTURE. MY PAINED FACIAL EXPRESSION WOULD HAVE TRAUMATIZED THE KIDS IF THEY'D BEEN LOOKING OUT THE WINDOW, BUT THEY WERE EXCITED AND DISTRACTED BY CHICK-FIL-A.

SCOTT: AWESOME. I WENT OVER THERE TO SAY GOODBYE TO MINE, TOO. SIMILAR ANXIOUS GIDDINESS ☺ KATE WAS CIVIL. I DIDN'T SEE AYERS. HOW WAS HIS EARLY MORNING DEMEANOR?

TIPSY: NEUTRAL, WHICH IS FINE WITH ME. I'M HEADING TO THE GYM, THEN I'M PACKING UP TO MOVE INTO THE BONNEAU HOUSE. IF YOU'RE INTERESTED IN HAPPY HOUR ON THE PIAZZA OF A HISTORIC MANSION.

SCOTT: SIGN ME UP.

Tipsy left out one key part of her daily plan, because it would be too complicated for text. She planned to meet up with Henry at his parents' old house to get information about Thomas Bonneau from the lingering spirit of Henry's dead mother. *That* story, if it proved fruitful, would be better discussed over piazza beers.

After her workout, she drove downtown to the Bonneau House, where she perused the third floor bedrooms. She picked the smallest one, across the landing from Sophie's room. A patchwork quilt-bedecked queen bed squeezed in beside a white dresser. Some fake plants, a beveled mirror, a framed print of three rabbits dancing around a maypole, and a 1998 Spoleto Festival poster rounded out the cozily dated décor. She'd feel safer in the huge house with all four walls within easy reach.

She opened the GQB, but as lunchtime approached, she flipped the sign from *Open* to *Closed*. She stuck a handwritten note on the door (*Closed for lunch, back soon!* ☺) and rode Shelby's bike to Bull Street. She leaned the bike against a tree in front of Henry's parents' house. Her phone dinged, and she swiped over a text front Shelby. NURSERY FEVER AGAIN...I AM SO NOT CUT OUT FOR THIS. MAMA IS COMING OVER AND I'M GOING TO THE GALLERY FOR A FEW HOURS.

TIPSY: I UNDERSTAND! GOD BLESS THE MAMAS WHO ARE CUT OUT FOR IT. I
RAN OUT FOR LUNCH. BE BACK IN ABOUT AN HOUR.

SHELBY: ALL GOOD! TAKE YOUR TIME!

The orange cat was still there, bless his fat furry heart. Tipsy sat on
the warm pavement with her phone by her ear and scratched his head.
"Hello, Garfield," she whispered, as Henry appeared on the stairs.

"Hey," she said. "You ready for this?"

He shifted uncomfortably. "Meh."

"Should you go inside and find her, or call out for—"

"Henry. You're back." His mother looked over the railing of the
second floor piazza. She disappeared, and then reappeared on the steps
beside him.

"Yes, Mother. I'm back."

"And you brought your friend."

"Hi, Mrs. Mott." The cat spit at Patience again, then crawled into
Tipsy's lap. His tail irritably swatted the sidewalk.

"Intolerable creature," said Patience. "If I were alive, I'd give him
the boot in his fluffy little rear end."

"How...are you doing...Mother?" asked Henry.

"About the same as the last time you saw me, dear. The same as I've
been for...eighty-some years." She wrung her hands. "I don't *want* to
quarrel with you. You're my son. The first person I've spoken with in
years. I hate that our reunion resulted in an argument."

"Did our squabble surprise you?"

"I suppose not. We never got along very well."

"No. We did not."

Patience smiled. "Let's talk about other things, shall we?"

"Sure," said Tipsy. "How about Thomas Bonneau?"

"Oh, Thomas again. I'd rather not discuss him." She looked at Henry.
"Not because of anything *inappropriate* about my acquaintance with
him. I simply don't like to think about that time, or things I saw."

"What did you—"

301

"We can go inside and reminisce about the good ol' days. Wouldn't you rather talk about those happy memories?"

Henry closed his eyes, as if praying for strength from whatever higher power he believed in.

"Mrs. Mott," said Tipsy. "We're not here to reminisce with you about anything. We *need* to know more about Thomas. Something about him feels...unnatural, and—"

"You're not as simple as you look."

Tipsy took her first Patience Mott insult in stride. At least the woman was on topic. "A young woman lives at the Bonneau House. She's like me. She can *see ghosts*."

"A young woman with seer's powers?" She frowned. "Living under the same roof as the dead Thomas Bonneau?"

"Yes. She's having a difficult time. It's a long story, but...I'm worried about her being around him. You said you don't remember how he died, but if you remember anything at all, it would be so helpful—"

"I didn't want to talk about him, so I *claimed* I didn't remember," said Patience, with a shrug. "But if it will convince your young lady to avoid him, I'll tell you the story. A winter night in 1883—"

"Wait. How about if you show us?" Tipsy quickly explained how they might see Thomas's death. "So if you focus on the memory, and we touch you, all should be revealed."

"If you know how Thomas died, he can *move on?*"

"Yes. That's the idea. If he wants to go."

"Can you do the same for me?" Her eyes widened. "I don't remember my own death."

"Yes. But I'll have to come back another day. Seeing these memories—especially the traumatic ones—takes a lot out of me."

"I've waited this long. Thomas should be gone from this world, and whoever that girl is, she should understand his true nature."

"How...*nice* of you," said Henry.

Patience turned to her son. "I've done some thinking since you appeared, Henry. Perhaps I *was* too hard on you as a child. I've watched enough of your television programs over the decades. Donna Reed. Mrs. Brady. Even that silly yellow woman with blue hair."

"Marge Simpson?" offered Tipsy.

"That's the one. By the standards of today, I suppose I wasn't a good mother. But I'm not as heartless as you've always believed. I tried to *do right* by you. Make you strong. Successful. *Normal.* Even if I went about it in ways Mrs. Simpson would poo-poo." She brushed imaginary dirt off her skirt. "Anyway, if I can help this girl, I will. But y'all promise you'll come back and help me?"

"I promise," said Tipsy.

"Yes, Mother. We'll…both…come back."

Patience stood and descended the stairs, then sat again on the bottom step. Henry gingerly touched her back, and Patience reached one gnarled hand toward Tipsy. The cat looked up at Patience and mewed, but this time, he didn't hiss.

◆✕◆

Tipsy doesn't recognize the space, because she's staring at a blank, exposed brick wall. She stands on roughly hewn plank boards and thick wooden beams crisscross the slanted ceiling.

"Here we are again." Henry is close to her, but she cannot detect his minty smell or feel his perpetual chill. Strangely unnerving, like he suddenly spoke in a foreign language.

"Where is here?" she asks.

"Turn around," he says. She follows his line of sight, and the location makes sense. The Bonneau House's unused fourth floor bedroom. The young Patience Lewiston—Patty—rustles around the room. A gas lamp casts flickering light over her small bed. Sweat has darkened the edges of her blonde hair, and longer pieces escape her single braid in wisps. She alternates between forcefully swiping strands behind her ears and stuffing her belongings into a valise. She pauses and stares at a pile of sewing supplies and a loom. A shaking index finger drifts to her mouth and she chews her fingernail.

Emotions appropriately soak this memory. Or more accurately, a solitary emotion. Overpowering, panic-inducing fear.

The door behind her gently opens, and Thomas Bonneau appears, framed in the darkness. His fair skin glows, but his black clothes and hair blend in with the darkness behind him. He's a disembodied, cavern-eyed face and two floating pale hands. Patty doesn't notice him. She's too busy deciding what to do with the loom. It's expensive, but she can't carry all her belongings at once, and she has to leave, now. She considers asking one of the servants to meet her somewhere, but she'd be putting that person at risk. Can she handle the guilt if Thomas were to—

"Where are you going, Patty?" he asks.

She spins around. When she has control of her breathing, she tentatively smiles at him. "I'm preparing to leave. I'll move to Mrs. Wilson's boarding house, like you suggested."

"I'm glad to hear you talk sense. Mrs. Wilson's will be a much better place for you. It's a ladies' boarding house, after all. Better company. Better customers than a bunch of grimy old men."

Her smile flutters. "Thank you so much for arranging it."

"You've been a good housekeeper, Patty, but you're much more likely to find a suitable husband with your own kind."

"Yes. Of course." *In her desperation to get away with him, she'll agree to anything he suggests—absent marrying him herself. She cannot believe she'd entertained that fantasy mere hours ago. Marry Thomas Bonneau, live in this big fine house, hobnob with the fancy neighbors. She'd hinted around that the house needed a mistress, but once he caught her drift, he suddenly wanted her to move out.*

His passive rejection had been embarrassing, frankly. So she'd come up with an idea which proved to be both a disaster and a deliverance. She decided to follow him and see exactly what his late night carousing entailed. She knows he's a habitual gambler—she's figured out that young men with money to spare use said cash to create more cash—but she's always suspected his involvement in more salacious activities as well.

Given what her spying revealed, she doesn't want to know anything else about him. Not where he gets his pocket money or how he spends it. She doesn't want to know him at all. She wishes she never stepped foot in this God forsaken house.

"Tom, will you please step out? I need privacy to pack my personal items."

"So modest." His low chuckling puts Tipsy in mind of a growling wolf. "It's nearly three in the morning. Why don't you leave all this until daytime? I'm sure you're particularly tired. Long walks in the moonlight will do that."

"Who's been walking in the moonlight? Not me."

"Patience," he says. "Don't make me lose mine. I can't abide a liar."

"I've been here all evening. You can ask one of the boarders—"

"Let's see." Thomas meanders into the room. Lamplight reveals his death outfit—black trousers, old boots, his claustrophobic overcoat. "Mr. Frank is visiting his mother in Orangeburg. Mr. Petty had business in Walterboro. Mr. Richards is staying with his colored mistress, as he does most nights."

"Please don't speak of such things to me. It's not proper. None of this is. You're right. This isn't a good place for me and now I'm going. I've been here all evening, packing." As she babbles, she tries to think of someone who might vouch for her. Kindly old Mr. Reilly, who lost his entire family in the war and lives alone on the second floor. "Mr. Reilly—he's been here all night, too."

"Reilly has been asleep for hours, as he tends to drink himself into a stupor before sundown. He's also hard of hearing. I doubt he can clarify your whereabouts. The other rooms are not let, as you well know, since you're the housekeeper. No one can confirm you didn't follow me this evening."

Patty raises her chin. "So what if I did? Were you doing something you shouldn't be doing?" She's bluffing, but she hopes his fear of discovery will make him leave her alone.

"That depends on what you saw."

"I saw nothing. If you were doing something, I didn't see it."

He darts at her with surprising speed, as if he's accustomed to sneaking up on people. He takes hold of her arm and she pushes against his overcoat-covered chest. He doesn't flinch. His feet remain planted on the floorboards.

Although Thomas isn't built like his father, she might as well have been shoving Dr. Legbone himself. "I don't know what I saw—"

"Spit it out, before I break your arm."

He twists and she gasps. "Alright! I saw you—with a red-haired woman—on Chalmer's Street and I—let go! You're hurting me! I'll scream!"

"Scream all you want. These walls are thick."

"I saw you walk down Unity Alley and you pushed her against the wall. I thought you were going to do—indecent, manly things to her—but then... you did even indecent-er things. You put your hand on her throat and—"

He covers her mouth with one hand. "Enough."

Patty's head thrashes. "Just let me leave. I won't say anything. I'll be gone and you'll never hear from me again—"

"Why couldn't you have gone to Mrs. Wilson's like I asked? What did you possibly think you'd gain from spying on me?"

"I...well..." Her dark blue eyes bulge like overripe blueberries about to burst.

"Did you think you might find out something scandalous? Some great secret you'd dangle in front of me to make me marry you?"

That's exactly what she had thought as she followed Thomas Bonneau out of the house that evening. If she held something unsavory over his head, maybe he'd suddenly see her as the ideal bride. Like a dalliance with a Chalmer's Street whore. Preferably one of the negro ones, or even the famous yellow China dolls. No simple sin, like gambling. Something truly distasteful she could threaten to tell the minister at the Huguenot Church under the guise of trying to save his soul, but offer to withhold if he agreed to marry her. She hadn't expected to see him strangle the life out of one of those girls on the streets.

Patty Lewiston wanted to be mistress of this house, but not bad enough to blackmail a murderer into marrying her.

"Have you followed me before?" he asks. "What else have you seen?"

"Nothin'! I ain't seen nothin'! I swear'n my mama's grave!"

He laughs again, but the growl morphs into a snarl. "There's the country girl you've been hiding." He shoves her, and she stumbles. Her ankle twists and she slams against the chest of drawers. A sharp corner slashes her cheek.

"My mother had a scar, there," Henry says to Tipsy. *"On her face."*

Patty scrambles to her feet and backs away from him. He lunges at her, but she climbs across the bed. She pushes the bedframe, and it whacks against his knees. She grabs a broom and brandishes it at him. Her desperate, ineffectual swiping reminds Tipsy of Shelley Duvall's character in The Shining. *Like a determined courier with a message to deliver, that damn movie follows her from mystery to mystery.*

"I hate that it's come to this. Your father being an old family friend and what not. But you brought it upon yourself by forgetting your station, and meddling in my affairs. Things don't turn out well for people who meddle in my affairs."

Patty swings the broom again, even as she frantically tries to distract him. "Did that poor girl meddle in your affairs?"

"Ginger? Nah. Nosiness wasn't her fault. Unfaithfulness was her failing. What is unfaithfulness, but weakness? Women. All of you. Weak, inconstant creatures. Look at my own mother. Dying, and leaving me to suffer under the saw-wielding hands of Doctor Legbone."

"Your mother didn't leave you—she died bringing you into the world. What greater love is there?"

"Bah! You know nothing about anything. Yet your mouth runs wild, like all your sex. Didn't we talk about this very issue on your first day in this house? I thought you were learning to shut up and listen. That's what you're meant to do. To have sons and listen to their joys and sorrows." He looks as if he might stomp his foot, like a petulant child. His eyes are fierce, jittery, maniacal. *"I never had anyone to listen to me! Not ever!"*

"All I've done is listen to you!" She's getting mad. Tipsy can feel it. "Never met a bigger blowhard in all my born days!"

"At least Ginger kept her mouth shut if she got drunk enough. Still, she betrayed me. She was a whore, but I thought, what manner of woman would be more faithful than a whore with the promise of monetary security? But she was no different from the others."

"What others?"

He wags a finger at her. "Your father was right about your mouth, honey. No matter. It will be quicker if you don't fight me. My father didn't fight me. But then again, he didn't have much of a chance."

Her brow furrows, and the broom momentarily sags. "You told me your father fell down the stairs."

"He did. Oops!"

"You pushed him. Your own father!" Fear again overpowers righteous anger. If he killed his own father, he'll have no problem knocking off Patty Lewiston from Edisto Island.

"Yes. I did. Not as exciting as squeezing the life out of him, but it got the job done." He smiles. "Now that you know so much…we must get on with this business."

She tries to dart past him, but he grabs her braid. She jerks backward, and they crash into one another like orchestral cymbals.

Thomas still has hold of her hair, but Patty Lewiston is a country girl. She understands the physical vulnerabilities of bulls, stallions, and men. She spins around, reaches down, and grabs his crotch. She grits her teeth and squeezes.

He gasps and doubles over. She runs into the hallway, with Tipsy and Henry right behind her, and a hobbling Thomas bringing up the rear. She starts toward the stairs, but Thomas once again grabs her by the hair. He flings her across the landing toward the attic door.

She grabs books from a crooked bookshelf and throws them at him with surprisingly good aim. When he covers his face with his arms, she wrenches the attic door open and darts inside. Once again, Tipsy and Henry follow and Thomas Bonneau lumbers after them.

As Tipsy's eyes adjust to the darkness, she picks out old furniture, wooden crates, and piles of household tools. Strips of moonlight stream through the dormer windows, and she catches the pale glow of Patty's hair. She beckons to Henry, and they approach Patty's hiding spot.

Tipsy and Henry can move through the obstacles in their path, but Thomas must pick his way around them. He grunts and curses as he trips over tables and boxes. "Patty, damnit. Come out, honey. No use dragging out this agony."

Patty huddles in a heap beside a broken bureau. Her fear is so powerful Tipsy can almost smell it, like sweat and blood and urine-soaked underpants. She squirms, and swipes at her neck. A squeak of pain escapes her.

Thomas follows the sound. Patty rubs her neck. She looks up, and her eyes widen. Tipsy and Henry follow her gaze. "Dear lord," mutters Henry.

The largest beehive Tipsy has ever seen has wrapped itself around the rafters. The low drone emanating from it reminds Tipsy of Miss Callie's outdated washing machine struggling through a spin cycle. Patty peers around the corner at Thomas as he picks his way across the attic. Then she looks up at the beehive again.

"Oh, damn," says Tipsy. "Thomas is allergic to bees! In his memory, he said he had a terrible reaction to a bee sting as a child. He sends the servants up here to clear out the bees and wasps—"

"Honeybees can build hives faster than you can remove them," says Henry. "We had one under our porch on Bennett Street. Over three days, a few swarming bees became a colony. It was—"

Patty abruptly stands. She still grips a book in one hand, and grabs an old vase with the other. "Get away from me, you murderer!"

Thomas is within ten feet of her. "No place to go now, Patty, but promise me you'll look me in the eyes. It's so much more... intimate...that way. You wanted to be close to me, didn't you?"

"I did. And I was a plum fool." She backs up until she stands directly under the hive. Agitated bees float down from the ceiling, but Thomas isn't in their line of moonlight. He doesn't see them. Patty chucks the book at the beehive. A well-flung vase follows it. The buzzing becomes a furious roar.

Thomas winces, and smacks his neck. He squints at the dead insect in his hand. "Oh.....dear."

Patty scurries around the bureau. She swats at the bees swarming her own head. The bees lose track of her and go for Thomas. His jumping and flailing would have been hilarious if Tipsy wasn't watching his face swell in real time. Patty hoists her skirts. She plows over everything between her and the attic door.

Thomas collapses in a writhing heap. He yells after her. "Patty, the bees!"

Tipsy and Henry are right behind her, but Patty opens the door, takes one astonished look back into the attic, and slams it in their faces.

———•✕•———

Tipsy woke to Henry's impatient glare. "I'll finally be an old man by the time you wake up," he said. Henry and Patience still sat on the steps. They watched her through the same dark blue, deep set eyes.

"Sorry. It's more taxing on me. The minor issue of my physical being." As usual, observing a violent death made Tipsy's stomach flop around like a beached fish. She still sat on the warm sidewalk, so she leaned forward and let her head hang between her knees. The orange cat twisted around her legs and meowed his sympathy.

"You okay, miss?" An older lady in a straw hat stood on the front porch with a watering can in her hands.

Tipsy glanced up at her, and scratched the cat's arched back. "Yes!" she called out. "Just saying hi to this guy."

"That's Peach," said the woman, who must be the current owner. "He's orangish, and round, and fuzzy."

"What a cute name. Hi, Peachfuzz," said Tipsy, as she stroked him.

"He's our welcome wagon. You certain you're alright?"

Tipsy had handled such concerned bystanders before. A smile would work wonders, so she grinned up at the woman, even as her eyeballs pulsed in their sockets. "Yup! A little lightheaded. You mind if I sit on your stairs with Peach and make a call?"

"Sure. Take your time and wait until you feel up to walking."

"Thank you, ma'am." She put her phone to her ear again and spoke to Henry and his mother. "So Thomas was…a murderer?"

"Yes," said Patience. "I saw him kill a woman in an alley off Chalmers Street. Strangle her with his bare hands. Walk away and leave her there, like dropping an apple core."

"He admitted to killing his own father, too," said Henry. "Pushing him down the stairs."

Patience nodded. "Thomas and Dr. Bonneau were not close, but I never imagined Thomas killed him. Y'all heard tell of Ted Bundy?"

Her relatively modern reference surprised Tipsy. "Of course. He killed dozens of women in the 1970s."

"Barbara up there on the piazza—she's a lovely lady—Barb and her husband watched a program on their television about him. I watched, too, as I do sometimes when I'm lonely, or sad. Mr. Bundy's charm and good looks drew those poor women in. Made them trust him. Thomas hadn't entered my mind in decades, but when I looked into that Bundy devil's face, I thought, *I've seen such eyes.*"

"What happened after he died, Mother?" asked Henry.

"His maid, Rachel, found him the next morning when she came upstairs to open some windows and let the breeze in. I heard her scream, and pretended to be as surprised as she was, but I did go to Reverend Dupre at the Huguenot Church. The Reverend knew Thomas his entire life, and his parents, and the rest of the Bonneaus. I told him what happened. He was shocked, but wanted me to keep it to myself, because of his affection for the family. I promised I would, and he asked the lawyer who handled the estate to let me manage the house until it sold. I stayed on for a couple more months, then I moved to Mrs. Wilson's."

"The Reverend covered it up." Tipsy shook her head. "So much for justice for that poor woman and Thomas's father."

"He did insist Thomas be buried somewhere else. He's in Magnolia Cemetery."

"That's why he isn't at the Huguenot Church with the rest of his illustrious relations." Tipsy's phone rang. It was Jillian, but she sent it to voicemail. She had a few more things to sort out before she gave Jillian this news.

"Do you know if he killed anyone else?" asked Henry.

"I don't, but I've wondered," said Patience. "He did mention *others* the night he died, and he seemed rather comfortable with it all. The Yankees had only left town a few years before, and there wasn't much rule of law. It was every man, or woman, for themselves. There were always whispers of people going missing and unidentified bodies found. Usually poor people, but even the upstanding citizens disappeared or turned up dead now and then."

"There is *no way* Jillian will let her daughter step foot in a house that's haunted by a serial killer," said Tipsy. "We should—"

Her phone dinged. Once, twice, three times. She looked at it. Jillian, again. She swiped over three texts.

JILLIAN: WE CAME TO TOWN FOR SOPHIE'S THERAPY APPT. STOPPED BY THE HOUSE TO GET SOME STUFF. SOPHIE IS IN HER ROOM AND SHE'S MELTING DOWN AGAIN. SHE'S TALKING TO PEOPLE AND CRYING AND ARGUING

JILLIAN: THE DOOR IS LOCKED AND SHE WON'T LET ME IN

JILLIAN: ARE YOU THERE PLEASE COME TO THE HOUSE ASAP. PLEASE HURRY MAYBE SHE WILL TALK TO YOU

"Oh, hell," said Tipsy. "We're too late."

"For what?" asked Henry.

"Sophie stepped right back into that damn house. It sounds like she's already having a run-in with the serial killer in question."

"Thank God you're here. I thought about calling the police." Jillian paced the landing outside Sophie's room. Tipsy heard muffled arguing through the door. She turned to Henry, who sat in an ornamental chair beside the staircase like a director sizing up auditioning actors. Tipsy spoke to him in her mind. *No way I'm mentioning serial killers right now. Jillian will probably break the door down with an ax.*

Henry nodded. "I don't recommend mentioning my presence, either. I doubt she'd see how I add value."

Tipsy grabbed Jillian's hand as she passed. "Let's see if she'll open up for me."

"Okay." She squared up and faced the door. "I'm right behind you."

"You won't be able to see what's happening. It will confuse you, and distract me. I won't let anything bad happen."

Jillian eyed the door as if considering ramming it with her thin shoulder.

"*Please*," said Tipsy.

"Fine. I'll be sitting on the bench outside Mama's room."

"I'll get you once we sort it out. Don't be alarmed if you hear…a crash or two."

Jillian sighed deeply, but she backed toward the staircase. She spun and clipped down the steps, as if she might change her mind if she lingered. Once she disappeared, Tipsy put an ear to the door.

A snappy male voice, and then a shrill female one.

"You cannot believe anything this lunatic is saying!"

"At least *I* never killed somebody. Stay *away* from him, Sophie Rose."

Tipsy knocked on the door.

"I said *go away*, Mom!" yelled Sophie.

"It's Tipsy, Sophie," said Tipsy, as Henry left his throne and ambled across the landing. "Will you let me in? Maybe I can help y'all sort this out."

"Right on! Let her in," said Catherine. "She'll say I'm right!"

"You don't know a goddamn thing about me, and neither does *that* woman!" Thomas sounded nothing like his usual congenial self.

"Y'all. If I come in, we can talk—"

The doorknob shook and the door opened. "After you," said Henry.

Tipsy stepped over the threshold. Sophie sat on the bed with her arms around her knees. Thomas stood beside the fireplace, and Catherine was by the piazza door. Tipsy motioned for Henry and he followed her into the room. He waved his hand and the bedroom door shut. The presence of three ghosts turned the air-conditioned room into a well-furnished igloo. Sophie grabbed her KZ sweatshirt and pulled it over her head.

"Well! Here we are," said Tipsy, with a strained smile. "Catherine, this is my friend Henry. He haunts my house."

"Hi," said Catherine. She pointed at Thomas. "*He's* a murderer."

"Lies!" said Thomas. He scratched his neck, and then swatted at his ear.

Sophie scooted off the bed. "Aunt Catherine, you're confused—"

"I am not confused! Not one *eenie-weenie* bit!"

"No, Sophie," said Tipsy. "Unfortunately, she's not confused at all."

"But she said he's a murderer. That can't be." Sophie blushed furiously. "We're…friends."

"He may claim to be your friend. He may even *think he is* your friend," said Henry. "But he's also a *murderer*."

Thomas sputtered like a fire trying to grip a wet wick. His mouth opened and closed. He hissed his rage, a cornered snapping turtle.

"Your father was wrong to treat you so poorly," Henry continued, "but regardless, you were wrong to shove him down the stairs to his death."

"He wouldn't have—would you, Tom?" asked Sophie.

"Of *course not*. Where would anyone get such a *ridiculous* idea?"

"From my mother," said Henry.

"Impossible. Patty must have died long ago—"

"All of y'all died long ago, yet here we are," said Tipsy. "Lucky for us, Patty-Patience is also a ghost, and she has a good memory."

"I deny any connection to my father's death." He scratched each thigh with the corresponding hand. "I deny it all."

"Do you deny Patience saw you kill a young woman in an alley off State Street?"

"*Denied!*" he shouted, like a judge overruling a pushy prosecutor's objection.

"When you tried to kill my mother, she got the impression you killed others. In addition to an unfortunate prostitute and the esteemed Dr. Legbone Bonneau."

"Thomas tried to kill *your* mother?" asked Sophie.

"He did, but she outsmarted him. If she hadn't, I might never have been born. I wouldn't have thought her capable of such quick thinking, but in an inspired moment, my darling Mumsy lured him into the attic and set a swarm of bees on him."

"*Darling?* You said you couldn't tolerate the woman." Thomas pointed at Henry. "Don't believe him, Sophie. He's a liar, too."

Tipsy approached Thomas with narrowed eyes. She waited for recognition to dawn on his face as he remembered his own demise. "I won't call Patience a *murderer*, because she killed you in self-defense. But she killed you, via those bees, just the same. *Because she discovered the truth about you.*"

Thomas turned in a slow circle. By the time he faced them again, he wore his usual beguiling, reasonable expression. "Perhaps she misunderstood me that night. Or maybe…she was bitter!" He grinned, as if they were at trivia night, and the right answer had suddenly come to him. "I never showed the slightest romantic interest in her. I told you two that she'd gotten improper ideas about her station in life. Those ideas included thinking *I* should marry her. Henry, you acknowledged Patty's spiteful social climbing."

"She was a social climber, and she could be spiteful. But she showed us *exactly* what happened that night. We watched it in her own memory, like Sophie watching The Gossipy Gals."

"*Gossip Girl,*" Sophie muttered, and Tipsy hushed her.

"Did you see her memory when you *looked into* her head?" asked Catherine.

"In a manner of speaking," said Henry, "but it's more complicated than a simple peek over the fence."

"No, it's easy! The backup singers get super loud, and a ghost's head looks blurry, and I can see right into it! Like looking into a kaleidoscope! When *I* looked into Thomas's head, I saw it all. Thomas confessing to killing those people, him chasing the girl called Patty, a zillion bees, the whole kit and kaboodle."

"That explains why you don't like him," said Tipsy. "You realized he was a murderer."

"Yes. I may have been crazy. I probably still am. I hear voices even other ghosts don't hear. I always feel like something is coming after me, even though I've become the boogeyman myself. But I don't *make up* things like what I saw in Thomas's head. I wasn't going to be friends with a murderer. Not then, and not now. So I cut him off. And I don't want him in my house! Near my family!" She yanked on her hair. "Get *out*! Get *out*! Get—"

"Oh, please," said Thomas. "You didn't *cut me off* anything. I did the cutting. Tell them how you drove me mad following me around and running your mouth, until *I* began ignoring *you*!"

"It doesn't matter who cut the other off, or out, or up," said Henry.

"It does! It explains why she detests me and she's trying to blacken my name with Sophie, and now the two of you."

"Thomas, you talked my ear off from the first time I met you," said Tipsy. "In the memories I've seen, you did most of the talking. You admitted running off at the mouth and Patty-Patience called you a blowhard—"

"Uppity bitch!"

"—so if you hadn't talked to anyone in decades, I find it hard to believe you'd voluntarily return to chatting up the azaleas."

"Fair point," said Thomas. "When Catherine first came to the house, I'd been alone for so long, the idea of a resident companion thrilled me. But then…the constant hysterics and nonsensical blathering. And sweet Jesus, the complaining. *Your mother sent you away. Your father ignored you. Your snobby sister didn't listen to you.* There was no *resting in peace* for me. So I stopped talking to her. Then it got worse when she came up with this…this…insulting delusion!"

While Tipsy had ignored ghosts most of her life, she'd never considered that a *ghost* might have to ignore someone *living*, too.

"Fine. I'll admit it," said Catherine. "I'm not a liar, like you. You did hide from me. All the sudden, you just stopped coming out to visit with me. You were so…mean." Her lower lip stuck out. "You made me think you were my friend. You even made me think you… *cared* about me."

"You have no sense, and you misunderstood my intentions. I never—"

"He only wanted to talk to me as long as I listened to *him*. He only liked me if I agreed with him and said nice things to him. You don't care about anyone but yourself. You're...you're a vacuum cleaner sucking up other people's feelings! Now he's doing the same thing to Sophie! He's buttering her up like a stack of pancakes! Don't believe him, Sophie. He's a terrible boyfriend."

"Boyfriend? What...uh. I never..." Sophie had gone as red as one of her own long stemmed roses. Jillian's worst fear had come home to roost. A dead guy was trying to seduce her daughter, and given her reaction, he was succeeding.

"Sophie," said Tipsy. "If you've developed a romantic attachment—"

"No! *N-No*. Not like... that."

"You're young and full of tortured feelings. I get it. But a ghost is *not* boyfriend material!"

"See? See?" said Catherine. "She needs to stay away from him—"

"Damn all this feminine bickering!" Thomas smacked his neck, as if to squash a creeping insect. Perhaps a *honeybee*. A reasonable explanation for his perennial itchiness. "Catherine is demonizing me because I rejected her! Patty did the same! Henry, don't you see? Women! Hysterical, conniving, deceitful women—"

"You seem very angry with the fairer sex," said Henry.

"I have every reason to be angry! From my own damn mother who died and left me, to your damn mother who killed me!" Thomas pointed at Henry. "Yet somehow, I'm the monster! Patty Lewiston spied on me, then set the bees on me and left me there, knowing I'd die in agony!"

"So you *do* remember," said Tipsy.

"Of course I do. I've felt their little legs crawling all over me, and their poison pulsing through me." He scratched frantically at his neck and ears. He reached into his overcoat and raked his fingers down his chest. "Ever since Catherine told me the story."

"Wait—since Catherine *told you*—" Tipsy turned to Catherine. "When did you tell him?"

"Many years ago," said Catherine. "Before I died."

"If you know…can you move on?" Tipsy asked Thomas.

"Catherine gave me the means to move on years ago, without even realizing it!" Thomas crossed his arms over his chest. "I can *move on* anytime I choose. But why would I?"

"Okay—hold on." Pieces started locking themselves into place in Tipsy's head, as they had with John and Ivy's deaths. "You've been able to move on for years, but you've chosen to stay here. You also know Catherine somehow figured out how you died, so you're aware that the story of your death and moving on are connected. You've been avoiding *me*, so…" She looked up at Thomas. "You don't understand *how* Catherine learned the truth about your death."

"How can I possibly understand what oddballs like Catherine—and *you*—are capable of?" he asked. "She came to me, jabbering on about *seeing into my head*. She's talking about it again, here and now. What in tarnation does that *mean*?"

"Maybe if you *asked me*, I might have told you," said Catherine.

"Ha! You can't string thoughts together any more than I can string a fiddle. Still, somehow your blathering revealed all manner of experiences of which I had no memory. Opened up strange portals to places I have no desire to see." He sneered at Tipsy. "I sensed *you* messing about in my head, too. But I refuse to let you in. I'm the man of this house. You can't *make me* do anything. I'm staying *right here*."

Another puzzle piece found a matching partner. Thomas's questions about Jane moving on, his avoidance of Tipsy, and even the strange end to the Chalmers Street memory finally made sense. Thomas might not fully understand *moving on*, but he wanted to understand, and he had indeed sensed Tipsy knew what was up, supernaturally speaking. Whatever he assumed she knew scared the bejesus out of him. "You've been avoiding me because you're afraid I might *force* you to move on," said Tipsy.

"When Henry mentioned his wife moving on, I knew you had something to do with it." Thomas pointed at Catherine. "She never managed to unseat me from this house, but I'll give you credit for being less of a fool. Another freak, yes. But you have a shrewish intelligence about you."

"If Tipsy and Catherine are freaks," said Sophie, "then what am I, Thomas?"

Thomas turned to Sophie as if he'd forgotten her presence. "Oh. Ah…I don't put you in the same category as these two, honey."

"Why? We all share this talent. Catherine and I have the same blood." Sophie turned to Tipsy and Henry. "You two are sure he's a murderer?"

"Yes," said Tipsy. "I said I'd explain all about how ghosts move on, and I will, but right now, you have to trust us. We *saw* him confess."

Sophie glared at Thomas. "You…*asshole*."

"Sophie, you believe whatever they say—after all our talks— special friends—"

Thomas kept sputtering denials and affirmations, but Tipsy turned to Catherine. "Did *you* know Thomas can move on? To the next plane?"

"You mean, like, at the airport?"

"No, sugar. Like escaping his haunting. Going to the next world. The *afterlife*. Heaven. Hell. Whatever you want to call it."

"No. How would he? *Far out!* I *want* to do that. I want to get on the next plane right out of here."

"A healthy way to think about it." Tipsy turned back to Thomas. "That's what *you* need to do, too."

"Never. I'm not going *anywhere*."

"You have to. Sophie cannot stay in this house with a dead murderer she has a crush on."

"*Hello!* He's an evil, coldblooded killer!" said Sophie, as if she'd revealed Thomas's malevolence and homicidal tendencies to Tipsy, rather than denying Tipsy's attempts to inform her of the same. "Crush literally over!"

"I'm not leaving," said Thomas. "*Catherine* should be the one to leave. This house was peaceful until she resurfaced. She's the problem! She can hurt Sophie, not me!"

"I would never!" Even as Catherine said it, Sophie's framed photos and her computer skittered off her desk. The white lights on her mantle flashed, and at least fifty tiny glass bulbs shattered like exploding popcorn.

"You can't control yourself even if you want to!" shouted Thomas. "You senseless bitch!"

"You *both* should go," said Henry. "If either of you cared about this young woman, you would."

Catherine's long hair floated around her head, auburn spiderwebs looking for a spot to anchor. "Get out of this house! Thomas Bonneau, can you dig it? Get *out*! Get *out*! Get *out*!"

Perfume bottles shot across the room. They struck the wall, sending a cacophony of sweet scents into the increasingly cold air. Without another word, Thomas blinked out, but Catherine kept raging. A magazine smacked Sophie upside her head.

"Catherine!" yelled Tipsy. "Stop it before you hurt—"

The cyclone of Catherine's rage sucked Sophie's heavy KZ water bottle into its vortex. Tipsy swatted it with her own power. The top came loose when it hit the floor. Frigid water splashed up Tipsy's bare legs. Jillian's voice carried through the door, over Catherine's yelling, Tipsy's beseeching, and Sophie's crying. "Sophie Rose! Honey! Let me in, please!"

"Mom. Mama. Help me!"

Jillian banged on the door. "Open this—"

Henry held out one hand. The door flew open and Jillian lunged for her daughter. She tackled Sophie on the bed and engulfed her in a fierce embrace. Clothes, binders, nail polish bottles, and a couple empty Coke cans swirled around them.

Tipsy pictured herself as a human magnet, pulling the detritus out of a tornado. Her stomach rolled. Her brain rattled around in her skull as if in the throes of her own personal earthquake.

The wind stopped as if it had hit a brick wall. Airborne objects clattered to the floor.

"I don't mean to be one of those jackasses who belittles the emotions of women," said Henry, as he raised his hands. "But this time, Catherine, you must *calm down*."

Henry curled his hands into fists before his chest, and then let fly like Merlin casting a powerful spell, or Thor throwing his hammer. Catherine stumbled backward. Her ankle rolled and she fell to her knees. Her hair flopped into her face as if exhausted by its own levitation. Colors undulated from her socks to her head, like the grip of a rainbow python. The snaking light squeezed, and her back arched. She gasped, and disappeared.

"I'm going to throw up," said Sophie.

Jillian gingerly removed her arms from her daughter, as if she might fly away. "You sure, sweets? Do you need a—"

Sophie slunk off the bed and retched into the trash basket beside her desk. Jillian looked to Tipsy, as if the rules for holding a friend's hair or patting her back were different when ghosts caused the yacking instead of alcohol.

"Let her get it out," said Tipsy.

Sophie eased away from the trashcan. She sat on the floor and leaned against the bed. "It's so stuffy," she said. "I...I can't breathe."

"Do you want to go outside?" asked Jillian. "On the piazza?"

"No. I want to get out of here. I need to walk."

"Uh, okay. Can I come with you?"

Sophie nodded.

"Your flip-flops are in the foyer." Jillian looked at Tipsy as Sophie stood and trudged toward the door. "Can you come? I want someone else with us who can see *everyone* who might be hanging around."

Tipsy's own queasy tummy and throbbing head would benefit from some fresh air. "Sure. I'll come." Jillian went after Sophie, and Tipsy turned to Henry. "You look a little peaked, too. You okay?"

"I am, but I need to rest. Interfering with another ghost taxes me more than handling a living person."

"I bet. Easier to make Ayers ice skate on my driveway than blast Catherine into the crevice between this life and the next. Go home. We'll reconvene later."

Henry disappeared, and Tipsy texted Shelby. Shelby confirmed she'd hold down the GQB fort, so Tipsy followed Sophie and Jillian down the stairs, out of the house, and off the property. They walked down Legare Street and took a left on South Battery, where the homes were mostly early twentieth-century, squarish brick mansions on wide, spacious lots. The houses aged as they approached Whitehall Gardens. Less brown brick, more pastel stucco. They crossed the intersection of King and South Battery and grabbed a bench across from One King Street, the old Fort Sumter Hotel, which had been converted into luxury condos in the 1970s.

Sophie sat between Tipsy and Jillian. "Before y'all ask, yes. I feel better."

Jillian took her hand. "Good, sweets."

"You'll feel even better if you fess up and give us the whole story of what's been happening at that house."

"I guess," she said, but she stared out at the harbor, as if waiting for her ship to come in. Behind them, a group of children got through an entire round of red light, green light, and she didn't say anything. Jillian looked too scared to ask questions, so that burden fell to Tipsy.

"Okay....you said you were *friends* with Thomas, but I gather you think of him as more than a friend." Jillian's eyes widened, but Tipsy held up her hand. "We're not judging you. Are we, Jillian?"

"Uh. No. Definitely not."

"You got this handsome guy in your house. Appears about your age. Tragically lonely. I see the appeal." Tipsy remembered Sophie's romanticism of Henry and Jane's joint haunting. Given her feelings about Thomas and her depression, it was even more disconcerting. She didn't want to further alarm Jillian, so she tried to address it subtly. "But you know it could never, *ever* work, right? Not in any…state of existence?"

"Of course I do. I thought…I don't know *what* I thought, except I thought *about him* all the time. I've never had a boyfriend."

"You went on some dates," said Jillian.

"My sisters set me up with fraternity guys, Mom. I was so nervous, I barely said anything. One guy tried to kiss me and I freaked out and turned away. He got a mouthful of my hair. He probably told the whole frat I'm a lame prude. But I could talk to Thomas. I mean, *he* talked most of the time. But I loved listening to his stories. When he asked me questions, I could answer without having a panic attack."

"Maybe it's easier to talk to him, and like him, because he's an impossibility," said Jillian.

"Good point," said Tipsy. "For the past couple years, sometimes ghosts felt safer to me than living people."

Sophie wiped her eyes. "You're both right, but he seemed so… it was…"

Tipsy hurt for her. "He killed at least two people, Sophie," she said gently. "Tried to kill Henry's mom. He's the freakin' Legare Street Strangler."

"I meant what I said in my bedroom. *Crush over.* I'm socially awkward, but I'm not stupid. Even if he wasn't a murderer, I heard how he talked about you and Aunt Catherine. If he thinks you two are freaks, he thinks the same thing about me."

"I'm sorry you couldn't tell me about all this when it started," said Jillian.

"It's okay, Mom. I know you tried. I'm sorry I was so rude and mean for months. I was…overwhelmed. When I first started talking to Thomas, I noticed headaches. Felt queasy. No appetite. But it wasn't too bad. If I took a nap or left the house for a while, I felt better. When I found Catherine, it got worse, and when they started fighting, it was *awful.* I started feeling…*really* depressed. Anxious all the time. I never knew when they'd start screaming at each other. Both of them trying to convince me the other was a terrible person."

"But you stuck it out," said Tipsy, "because of your…feelings… for Thomas?"

"That had something to do with it, but it's also about Aunt Catherine. I can't *exactly* relate to her, but I related to her more than anyone else I'd ever known. I truly wanted to help her. Thomas seemed to want to help her, too. He said there was a way to release her from her haunting. He wanted *me* to help *her* escape."

"Ah," said Tipsy. "So you knew about *moving on*, too, because he confided in you—"

"Now that I know the truth, I wouldn't call it *confiding*. He told me so I'd figure out how to get rid of Catherine. He didn't want anyone to know she visited the house, either. He said we had to keep it a secret so Mom wouldn't make me leave. I thought he wanted me to stay for… me…but…" She shrugged. "I guess not."

"Did he ever tell you *he* can move on?"

She shook her head. "He told me he didn't know anything about his own death, and didn't care to find out. Except for dealing with Catherine, he said he was happy in the house. I sensed he wanted to be rid of Catherine for his own peace, too, but I thought if I freed her, I'd be helping both of them. He wasn't sure *exactly* what we needed to know, but it had something to do with understanding how she died."

"I'd told you about the car accident," said Jillian.

"You did, and Thomas overheard people talking about the accident in the house over the years. But Thomas thought we had it all wrong, since she was still hanging around, so I asked her about it directly. She verified that BeeBee talked about the car accident, too, but I never got anything else out of her." She winced. "Except the stuff about you, Mom. I thought…maybe you being involved was, like, the missing link. I'm *sooo* sorry."

Jillian hugged her and kissed the top of her head. Like all good mamas, she knew that hugs and kisses often say more than words.

"When you started coming around, Tipsy, I thought about asking *you* about ghosts moving on, but I figured it would raise your suspicions." Sophie smiled ruefully. "Jokes on me, because you've been trying to get Thomas to move on all along, right?"

"Yes, she has," said Jillian. "I'm paying Tipsy to rid our house of ghosts. Especially that psycho Thomas Bonneau, but if my sister is also a troubled spirit, I want to help her be at peace. We can't keep living there, with your abilities, if we can't…remove…both of them."

"I'm sorry we didn't tell you," said Tipsy. "I've been on y'all about secrets this whole time. Now Sophie knows mine."

"I understand. I would not have handled it well, even a week ago. Now it's obvious Thomas was *using me* to get rid of Catherine. Maybe he liked having me around to listen to him blab away, but nixing her was his real goal."

"He's screwed up," said Tipsy. "Thomas believed his poor mother, who died giving birth to him, was a weak person who abandoned him. Then there's his run-of-the-mill misogynism. He claims to want peace and tranquility, but he also craves an audience. That's where women come in. We're supposed to hush up and raptly listen to him, but get out of his way when he's not in the mood."

"And somehow predict which of those moods he's in," said Jillian. "Maybe that worked in the 1880s. Maybe even the 1950s. But today the professionals would call it psychological abuse."

Tipsy nodded. "He hates us, unless we're serving to pump up his ego."

"I can't believe he sucked me in, but he was so nice to me. I'm an idiot."

"No. You were having a hard time. You don't have a lot of experience with guys. Men like Thomas sense vulnerability like bats using echolocation," said Tipsy. "He couldn't give himself away as a controlling, chauvinistic psycho right away. He was really convincing. My friend Henry liked him. So did his mother Patience, until she realized what he was. Sounds like even Catherine liked him before she discovered he was a murderer."

"You recognized something weird in him," said Jillian.

"Yeah, but I'm still learning to trust my instincts. Given all the questionable decisions about men I've made in my life, I wasn't sure." She chuckled. "A lot of guys I thought were *good* turned out *not good*, although none of them were serial killers. Then the guy I convinced myself was *not good*, is probably the man of my dreams. So I'm not judging anyone's choices. All you can do is try to listen to your heart. My heart told me something was off with Thomas."

"Did your heart tell you something is *not off* with Dr. Brandt?" asked Sophie.

"Oh, jeez," said Tipsy. "How did you know about that?"

Jillian smiled. "We speculated when we were buying Sophie's roses from a wholesaler. Anytime he came up, you started glowing."

"Same with him," said Sophie. "At my last appointment, I mentioned you, and he blushed right through his beard. But then you've been sort of *sad* recently, so I wondered."

"We're still figuring it out. It's complicated."

"At least he's not a dead serial killer," said Sophie.

"What now, Tipsy?" asked Jillian.

"I have to understand how and why she died." Tipsy glanced at Sophie's hand in Jillian's on the bench. She didn't want to strain the zipper of their tentative understanding by postulating that Catherine had committed suicide due to Jillian's unkind words. "We have some... theories...but there's got to be more to it. Thomas understood one thing. If Catherine overheard Betsy telling the whole truth, she'd already be able to move on."

"Really?" asked Jillian. "So you think she died...some other way?"

"I assume she *was* hit by a car. I can't imagine BeeBee making up something so gruesome. But the reasons are as important as the mechanics, and Catherine doesn't have the whole story." Tipsy shook her head. "At least she *wants* to move on. Thomas is the hum dinger, as my Granna would say. I've yanked ghosts out of hiding when I wanted to talk to them. I've made them disappear by shoving them, in a supernatural sense. But I've never yanked or shoved one into the *afterlife*."

"We're not going back into that house until he's gone," said Jillian. "We're getting right into the car."

She looked at Sophie, as if waiting for an argument, but Sophie shrugged. "Okay. But I gotta pee, Mom."

"We'll stop at a gas station." Jillian stood. As usual, she was all business. "Fill 'er up, potty break, then back to The Sanctuary for some... sanctuary."

"Y'all go on. I'm going to sit for a few minutes and breathe the harbor air, then I gotta get back to the gallery."

Tipsy watched them go. Jillian surely wanted to power walk, but she adjusted to Sophie's wobbly stride. They linked arms, and Sophie let her mother support her. A different kind of sanctuary, but no less of a safe haven.

Chapter 19

J illian and Sophie retreated to their ghost-free beachfront oasis, and Tipsy returned to the GQB for a few hours. After she closed up shop, it was back to the Bonneau House to clean up and decompress. As she stepped into the shower in the little bathroom attached to her chosen bedroom, she remembered she didn't have privacy arrangements with Thomas Bonneau. Hopefully his fear of her coercing him into the afterlife would keep Thomas far from her room, but she rushed through her shower anyway.

Before Scott arrived to share a Trader Joe's pizza on the piazza, Tipsy texted Jillian to make sure visitors were okay. Jillian replied with an enthusiastic affirmative—HE CAN STAY AS LONG AS HE LIKES!—and a heart emoji. Nice of her, but Tipsy wasn't sure if Scott would be ready for that. It had only been a few days since they reconciled.

She put a couple pizzas in the oven and gave him a tour of the house. Given the size of the place, the oven timer started dinging before they returned to the kitchen. They set up their feast on the second floor piazza. Scott sipped a glass of red wine, but Tipsy's lingering nausea disavowed alcohol. Her queasiness could only tolerate—and be squelched by—the pizza gods. She warned him that she might eat an entire pie herself.

"What do you think of someone like Thomas?" she asked, once they were settled around the table. She spoke around a bite of thin crust pepperoni. "From a psychiatric sense."

"There's something wrong upstairs with anyone who commits those kinds of crimes. But remember, mentally ill people are more likely to be victims of crimes than commit them." He set his wine glass on the table. "It's difficult to diagnose someone like that, but probably extreme personality disorders. Anti-social? Narcissistic? Schizoid? All of the above?"

"How would you *treat* him?"

"Unfortunately, medications don't help with personality disorders the same way antipsychotics stabilize schizophrenics and SSRIs pull people out of depression. People with those kinds of disorders don't acknowledge their faults and weaknesses. They don't want help. When someone shoots up a high school, politicians scream about mental health access. My response is, *it's not so simple*."

"Whatever disorder he has, he hides it well. Ironically, his winning personality ultimately gave him away. He was too damn rational and content for a ghost."

"You understand normal ghost behavior, not me. But it sounds like he should not be around an emotionally vulnerable person like Sophie Yates."

She leaned toward him. "I love it when you use phrases like *antipsychotic* and *mental health access* and *emotionally vulnerable*."

He laughed. "I love that you love it. How about...ECT?"

"What's that?"

"Electroconvulsive therapy." He held a finger to his temple. "*Zzzzt*."

"Y'all still do that?"

"Yes. Nowadays, it's done in a controlled hospital environment under anesthesia. It's the best treatment we have for major depression. Sometimes bipolar disorder. It eases mania. It can even bring people out of a catatonic state. Basically, the more acute your illness is, the better response—"

"*So hot*." She leaned in and kissed him. He kissed her back, and made her laugh whispering psychiatric lingo in her ear.

They finished their food and moved to a wicker sofa. Scott laid down and pulled Tipsy onto his chest. The ceiling fan whirred above them. It ineffectively sprayed hot, muggy air over the piazza. "It's hot as blue blazes. I'm going to sweat my ass off, but this feels good."

"Mmmm." She ran her fingers over his chest. "I hate to bring up unpleasant business, but can we talk about Ayers and Kate?"

"Sure. As long as we get it over with and move on to a less stressful topic, like serial killers."

"This will be a brief strategy meeting, not a drawn out complaining session." She explained Mimi's idea about child support and her settlement agreement. "I can take him back to court and get more money out of him. From the research I've done, it's pretty straightforward. If he makes more, he pays more in child support. The money he owes from the settlement hasn't gone away. I've never pursued it because I didn't think he could afford it without risking the kids' home."

"You want to go down that path?"

"I'm considering it. I wish I didn't have to take *anything* from him. Maybe if he wasn't paying me, I wouldn't feel obligated to be his therapist. But…he *does* owe me the settlement money, and it *would* give me leverage to make him leave us alone."

Scott laced his fingers behind his head. "Kate makes her own money, but believe me, she didn't marry Ayers solely for true love."

"If *he* has to pay me more, it's more money out of their collective pockets."

"It's worth a shot. You going to text him about it? Or confront him in person?"

"I haven't decided yet. With Ayers, everything requires careful contemplation." She rested her chin on his chest and looked up at him. "That's it. Strategy session over."

He ran his hands over her back. "What's next on our agenda?"

"A whole lot of nothing. I'm pretty tired." She rested her cheek on his chest again and listened to the *thump, thump, thump* of his heart.

"Sounds perfect."

"By the way," she said. "Jillian and Sophie figured out we're an item."

"Yeah? How perceptive of them."

"They're both big fans of you. So they're onboard. Jillian even said you can stay here. With me. If you want to. If it's not too soon."

He looked down at her with a furrowed brow. "Too soon?"

"Since we just made up. I thought maybe you wouldn't want to… *you know*. Yet."

He started laughing. She pushed herself to her elbows and stared down at him. Her hair formed a curtain around their faces. "What's so funny?"

"You, darlin'. Believe me, it is *not* too soon."

"I don't know! You men—y'all think differently from us."

"Do *you* think it's too soon?"

"Hell no, but—"

He laughed again. "Not so different after all!"

She swatted him and sat up, but she was laughing herself, her tiredness forgotten. He stood and tugged her to her feet. He walked her backward toward the piazza door. "We got this giant house to ourselves. How many bedrooms in this place?"

"Seven? Eight?" She fumbled on tiptoe to kiss him.

"Perfect. Let's drag out this ghostbusting business for at least eight days."

Tipsy woke to the welcome sight of Scott's broad back. She threw an arm over him and he rolled over. He smoothly tucked her under his arm. "W'time is it?" he muttered.

She reached for her phone on the bedside table. "Sixish," she said, as she rested her cheek on his chest.

"Ummm." He promptly went back to sleep.

She held up her phone in one hand and swiped over her text messages with her thumb. Her head rose and fell with his deep breathing as she read.

SHELBY: IT'S MIDNIGHT AND I'M STILL AWAKE EVEN THOUGH LOTTIE IS ASLEEP. I'M LITERALLY GOING STIR CRAZY. GOING TO DROP BAMBINO WITH MY MOM IN THE MORNING AGAIN AND COME IN FOR A FEW HOURS. SO NO NEED FOR YOU TO RUSH.

TIPSY: OKAY! I'LL RUN SOME ERRANDS, ETC.

She let Scott sleep for another thirty minutes, before poking him and reminding him he had to go home, get ready for work, turn around, and drive back downtown to the hospital.

"I'll bring my stuff over tonight," he said, as they walked downstairs. "I can get ready here tomorrow."

Tipsy replied with a happy kiss and sent him on his way.

She went to the gym in Mount Pleasant, then drove to Ayers's house to pick up some old baby clothes she'd promised Shelby. The plastic bins she'd neatly organized were in storage in his attic. He told her he'd leave them on the porch before he left for work, but to her surprise, his truck sat in the driveway. She looked at the clock. It was almost ten.

Maybe being a VP comes with flexible hours, said Granna.

Tripp Collins is at work before seven every morning. If Ayers starts slacking, his promotion might quickly turn into a demotion.

Kate's Lexus wasn't there. All five kids were at camp. She wouldn't get a better opportunity to inform Ayers about her reunion with Scott. In a moment of indecision, she texted Scott and gave him the scenario.

Scott replied right away. I'M IN BETWEEN PATIENTS AND ONLY HAVE A COUPLE MINUTES. BUT YOU THINK IN PERSON IS BETTER THAN TEXT?

TIPSY: IF I CAN GET UP MY NERVE AND GET THE WORDS OUT, YES. AYERS IS A BULLY, AND BULLIES DON'T LIKE TO LOOK YOU IN THE EYE.

SCOTT: IF YOU THINK SO. BUT IT WORRIES ME. I'D BE MORE COMFORTABLE IF I WAS THERE, TOO.

TIPSY: I HAVE TO DO THIS ON MY OWN. HE'S MY PROBLEM.

SCOTT: OUR PROBLEM. THEY'RE BOTH OUR PROBLEM. KATE MIGHT SEND NASTY TEXTS, BUT SHE'S TOO PASSIVE AGGRESSIVE TO SCREAM IN MY FACE. I DON'T THINK I CAN TOLERATE THAT JACKASS SCREAMING IN YOUR FACE.

TIPSY: YOU'RE SWEET FOR WORRYING, BUT I CAN'T LIVE MY LIFE BEING INTIMIDATED BY HIM ANYMORE. I MADE A DECISION, AND I HAVE TO DELIVER IT TO HIM. BESIDES, HE MIGHT NOT CARE WHAT MY NEIGHBORS THINK, BUT HE CARES ABOUT HIS. I THINK HE'LL KEEP A LID ON IT.

SCOTT: OKAY, BUT PLEASE TEXT ME AS SOON AS YOU FINISH TALKING TO HIM.

TIPSY: WILL DO. ♥

SCOTT: ♥

Tipsy parked in the driveway. She climbed the steps like she was doing the walk of shame crossed with her last stroll toward the electric chair. Her mouth dried out faster than a drop of water on hot cement. Several neatly labeled plastic bins (*Girls 6-12 mos., Girls 12-18 mos.*) sat beside the door. She rang the doorbell.

No movement from the house, so she rang again. She heard pounding feet, but still no Ayers. She rang a third time, and he yelled from inside. "Damnit! I'm coming."

He walked down the hallway in a pair of ripped shorts and an old Governor's Cup fishing tournament tee-shirt. He opened the door. "Sorry. Figured you were the Amazon guy. What's up? You want the bigger clothes, too?"

"No. Just want to talk."

He leaned against the door. "*Okaaaaay.*"

"You're not at the office?"

"No. I got wi-fi. I'm working from home some these days."

"Nice. Perk of the new job?"

His jaw clenched. "Modern life. Who told you about the new job?"

"Small town, Ayers. Congrats, by the way."

"Thanks. I gotta get on a call—"

"I've reversed my decision about Scott. Thought you should hear it from me directly."

"What do you mean?"

"When you went ballistic in my yard, I told Scott I didn't want to see him anymore. I have decided I *do* want to see him. Date him. Be with him. Whatever you want to call it."

Ayers's face reddened as she talked, but he glanced at the neighboring houses. Two young women with toddlers in strollers had stopped to chat beside his driveway.

"Tipsy." He spoke through clenched teeth. "I told you. That guy will not be around my kids—"

"Yes, he will. When I think it's appropriate, he *will* be around them. And you will not disparage my significant other to them—"

"Now he's *significant?*"

"—in an attempt to dictate my choice of partner."

"I have a right to tell you what I think. You told me what you thought about me marrying Kate—"

"That had everything to do with your choice to *marry* your girlfriend of two months, and nothing to do with Kate personally. Although, from what you've told me, maybe she does have some personal problems."

"Don't you disparage my wife!"

"I'm not disparaging her. You're the one who came to me with complaints about her. I've been nothing but supportive and tried to give you insight. Because unlike you, I care about your happiness!"

"I care about your happiness, too! That's why I'm warning you to stay away from him—"

"What do you know about him, huh? Other than what Kate has told you."

"That *is* what I know. She was married to him. She's the one who knows him."

"You told me she can grip a grudge like a sloth hanging from a tree branch. You ever considered she might have a grudge against Scott? You even *felt sorry* for Scott, for putting up with her for so long!"

"I was upset with her! We were in a rough spot! But we're working though it and—"

"I'm glad you're working through it. I want you to stay married. If me and Scott gave y'all are reason to unite and forget your own bullshit, that's an added bonus!"

"But Scott—"

"I'm done, Ayers. I'm dating him."

"Stop interrupting me—"

"Hell, no! You've interrupted me for the past eighteen years!" She leaned toward him. "Scott and I are together. And you're going to stop harassing us. Kate is going to stop, too."

"Like I can control Kate."

"If you both value that big raise you got, you will. I'm here to make a deal. You owe me one hundred and fifty thousand dollars from our settlement. I'll take a hundred, and forego the fifty."

"I, uh…what the hell…If you—we…" Try as he might, he couldn't come up with anything else.

"And I won't take you back to court for more child support."

"What? You can't. We decided all that years ago—"

"Everything related to children is modifiable based on a change in circumstances. I don't know exactly how much you're making now, but back then, we downplayed your salary and ignored your trust fund. I accepted it, and overlooked the outstanding settlement money, out of guilt. But those days are done."

"How is *this* a deal?"

"It's a deal because it saves you fifty thousand bucks, plus legal fees and whatever a judge decides you owe in child support for the next ten years. On my end, you back off me and Scott, and you make sure Kate does the same. A win for everyone."

His breath came in whistles, like a bull before a highly experienced matador. "I'll call Clark."

"Go ahead. This kind of situation is cut and dry. I don't need someone as fancy as Clark Middleton to get more money out of you."

"You're willing to take less, and let the child support stand as it is, if I give you my…blessing…with Scott Brandt?"

"I don't need your blessing, but if you agree to leave us alone and be civil, yes. But Kate has to agree to stop harassing him, too. I assume she's pretty happy with your big raise."

He backed away. "This is bullshit. It's exploitation."

"It's a negotiation, Ayers. It's *my life*. And I'm not letting you control it anymore."

"You. They. I….*Whatever!*" He stepped behind the door and slammed it.

Tipsy turned toward the street, but she paused before descending the stairs. They were steep, and she felt lightheaded. She wondered if she'd breathed through the whole interaction.

When she got into her car, she texted Scott. I SAID MY PIECE. NOW WE WAIT.

Her phone dinged as she stopped at an intersection.

SCOTT: ARE YOU OKAY? HOW DID HE TAKE IT?

TIPSY: I'M OKAY. HE WAS PISSED. BUT HE DIDN'T SCREAM LOUD ENOUGH TO MAKE THE NEIGHBORHOOD MOMS CALL THE COPS.

SCOTT: I WISH I HAD BEEN THERE TO SUPPORT YOU.

TIPSY: YOU'RE SUPPORTING ME RIGHT NOW. I TOLD HIM KATE IS INCLUDED IN THE DEAL. THEY BOTH LEAVE US ALONE. I WON'T TAKE HIM TO COURT.

SCOTT: DID HE AGREE? EVEN IF HE DOES, IT REMAINS TO BE SEEN IF SHE WILL.

TIPSY: HE'S GOING TO STEW FOR A WHILE. BUT I'M GLAD I LAID DOWN THE LAW. I'VE PUSHED BACK AT HIM A FEW TIMES OVER THE PAST COUPLE YEARS, BUT TODAY, I WAS REALLY IN CONTROL. ON ANOTHER NOTE, YOU MIND IF I ASK A FRIEND OF MINE TO JOIN US TONIGHT? HE'LL ONLY BE ABLE TO STAY FOR A WHILE.

SCOTT: IS THE FRIEND DEAD? SURE. SOUNDS INTERESTING.

TIPSY: YES. WITH ME AND MY GHOSTS, THINGS ARE ALWAYS INTERESTING!

She sat there for a moment with the engine humming. The street sign in front of her read *Grand Oak Avenue*. When Tipsy and Ayers bought their first house on this street, Grand Oak Avenue seemed like the perfect name for a Lowcountry thoroughfare. Now, the rows of cookie cutter houses and the street's generic Old South moniker were a cliché. Kind of like her marriage to Ayers. Scratch the surface, and reveal cheap construction.

She'd always known something was not right in her relationship with Ayers. Looking back, she'd *always* known.

She felt none of that with Scott. She was still learning about him, of course, but the deepest part of her core told her this was *very, very* right. True craftsmanship built on a strong foundation.

A honk jolted her out of her daydreaming. She stepped on the gas and put Grand Oak Avenue and Big Ayers in her rearview, but as she passed her old house, a memory stirred.

Granna's brownies. The smell of chocolate, and another slamming door.

———— ✴ ————

Tipsy sits on the kitchen floor with her four-year-old twins. She's looking for Granna's brownie recipe in her recipe box. It's Friday evening, and the girls are fired up to bake and watch a Barbie movie with their mama. Little Ayers is having a sleepover at Mimi's, and Big Ayers is hunting. He'll be home late, so it's a girls' night in the Collins household.

"Here it is!" Tipsy removes the dogeared card from the box and hands it to Olivia Grace. "My Granna wrote this herself."

"Her words are so swirly." O-Liv points at the looping letters of Granna's classic penmanship.

"That's old-fashioned writing. Sometimes it's even hard for me to read it."
Mary Pratt takes one side of the card. "What does it say?"

Tipsy gently retrieves the card before they unintentionally rip it. "It lists the ingredients we need, and how to mix them together. Some big words on here, ladies, like chocolate and vanilla extract!"

"Do we need eggs?" asks M.P., as she gets to her feet. "I'll get 'em!"

Tipsy stands and tucks the other cards back in the box. "Be careful y'all—"

All three of them jump when the door leading to the detached garage flies open. Big Ayers plows into the kitchen. "Damnit. Such a pain in my ass—"

"Ayers…hi?"

"Don't start, Tipsy! Don't!"

"I'm not starting—"

"Daddy! Are you done hunting? Do you want to watch Barbie with us?" asks M.P.

"We're making brownies!" adds O-Liv. "Granna's brownies!"

"No, y'all. I'm not done hunting. I haven't started yet."

"Brownies are more fun!" says M.P.

"Brownies, brownies—"

"Girls, shush," says Tipsy, before Ayers really flips out. "What's the mat—"

"Dad wants me to call the foreman at the Summerville Library site and I left the project file here." He storms through the kitchen. Tipsy hears him stomping around in the little office across from the dining room. "I was past Awendaw!" A drawer whacks shut. "I had to backtrack!" The chair scrapes across the floor. "Where the hell is it?"

Both girls drift across the kitchen and wrap themselves around Tipsy's legs. She rests a hand on each one's head. Another drawer whacks, and then Ayers pounds back into the kitchen with a bulging manila folder under his arm. He already has his phone in his hand. "Call Carlos Rivera!" he barks into the phone.

"Calling Carlos Rivera, mobile," Siri demurely responds, as Ayers slams the garage door behind him.

"Where were we?" asks Tipsy.

"Uh, eggs," says O-Liv.

"Great. Two eggs. Can y'all each crack one?"

The girls go to the fridge and gingerly remove the eggs. They wash their hands and mount their stepstools. Tipsy sets about gathering the rest of the ingredients. She's made the recipe so many times, she knows what she needs, and doesn't need to think until she gets to the measurements.

She contemplates her feelings about Ayers's performance as she opens and closes cabinets and drawers. Other than frustration about her kids listening to such ridiculousness, she feels…a whole lot of nothing.

She isn't angry, or worried, or confused. She isn't hurt that he didn't say hello or goodbye. She doesn't care that he came home, and she doesn't care that he left again. She doesn't care what happens while he's gone, and she doesn't care when he'll be back. A strange revelation. The man who has borne her every emotion on his own fierce current for so many years has no effect.

An interesting question arises in her mind. What would happen if he didn't come back?

That sneaky thought has all kinds of implications. She shakes her head. Good lord, what is that all about?

But the questions keep coming. Would she be upset? Would she be relieved? Would they be okay? She has his life insurance policy. Tipsy and the kids would be fine. It would be…easier.

Jesus, Granna! What am I thinking? I'm a terrible person.

Tipsy, you're not—

No. No. No. I will not think like that. That's my husband. I love him. He's my children's father.

He's also a tyrant.

He can be…draining—

Haha! Like a Roto-Rooter, that man!

—but still, the idea of something happening to him should make me feel terrified, not…relieved? Good lord. What is my problem?

Sugar, I know you don't want anything bad to happen to Ayers—

No. No. Never!

But you might want to consider why those thoughts popped into your head.

Tipsy nods to Granna, and herself, and starts measuring flour, but even though she'll make brownies with the girls many times over the next year or so before she asks Ayers to move out, she'll never forget this particular baking session. The day she realizes something is terribly wrong with her marriage. The first time she acknowledges her life might be better without him.

Chapter 20

S helby was still ensconced in bills, P&L statements, and inventory spreadsheets at the GQB, so Tipsy stopped by her own house and asked Henry to meet her at Colonial Lake. She drove downtown, found a parking spot on Broad Street, and walked half a block to the corner of Rutledge and Broad. As she stepped onto the lake's cement promenade, she shaded her eyes until she found Henry's bright red hair. Like a proud teacher observing a kindergarten Halloween parade, he sat on a bench and benevolently observed passersby. She waved until he noticed her.

He disappeared and reappeared at her elbow. "I'm still amused by everyone's modern clothing," he said. "Especially the shoes. I don't know how y'all walk in your flop-flips."

Tipsy let that cute mistake slide. Maybe she'd start calling them *flop-flips* herself. "Better than wearing a starched collar or a petticoat in a hundred degree heat. Now, how do we find her? I can't imagine her haunting allows her to roam around the entire lake."

"I gotta stay close to the road. Even though it's *so loud*. Cars, cars, *trucks*, cars."

Tipsy and Henry turned toward that sullen voice. Catherine Porcher shimmered in a blob of rainbow air near the trees lining the Broad Street side of the lake.

Tipsy and Henry joined her in the shade. Between the tree limbs and the two ghosts, the temperature dropped to the pleasant chill of a spring morning. "Hey, Catherine," said Tipsy, as she took her phone out of her pocket. "Don't mind the phone. Helps me look normal when I'm talking to you."

"Hi." She slid toward them with her bright eyes on Henry. "Who are you again?"

"Henry."

"That's a *grandpa* name."

Henry looked mildly offended, so Tipsy cut in. "It's popular again nowadays. Many little Henry's running around the playgrounds. Would you still like to move on, Catherine?"

"I'd like to leave right away. On a jet plane!"

"I'll take that as a yes," said Tipsy. "We need to understand your death—"

"I killed myself because of Jillian."

"How do you know?" asked Henry.

"Mama said it in the greenhouse. Jillian said I should die. I remember. She *did*. She did say it."

"Yes, but she also apologized to you," said Tipsy. "Before she left for camp. Do you remember that part?"

"Nope." Catherine swayed on her feet. "Mama said I ran away because of what Jillian said. Stepped right into the street and got *blasted* by a car."

"That can't be right. Or at least, it's not the whole story. If you understood, you'd be able to move on already."

"That big ol' jet airliner will carry me far, far away."

Tipsy'd had enough of Catherine's Top 40 Countdown. She sat in the pine straw. "Catherine. Cathy? Can you sit here with me? I'm going to help you…catch the plane. Okay? Sit."

To her relief, Catherine sat, and Henry joined them. "Why don't you *relax*, Catherine," said Henry. "Just…rest. Maybe even…take a nap. A peaceful…bit of…repose. You must be…sleepy."

Tipsy thought Henry's incantations might remind Catherine of pushy doctors and unwanted Valium. Surprisingly, instead of raising her hackles, his amateur hypnotist routine did the trick. Her eyelids drooped. "I do get sleepy. So tired. Really…really…tired."

She closed her eyes, and Henry nodded at Tipsy. He reached for her shoulder. Tipsy touched one of her multicolored socks.

———•✕•———

Tipsy wakes up to the 1970s version of Sophie's bedroom. Yellow paint on the walls instead of pale pink, and yellow and brown shag carpet under a bed with a green and orange daisy bedspread. Henry points at a girl-shaped lump under the covers. Auburn hair cascades across the pillowcase.

Thomas Bonneau stands beside the window, doing his best Lord Byron impression. His black curls cascade across his forehead. Catherine stirs, and her three visitors—one she can see, and two who are hidden from even her clairvoyant eyes—approach the bed.

Catherine sits up and wipes her face on her orange Clemson sweatshirt. She peers around like an owl caught in bright sunlight. "It's...quiet. It's quiet now. Thank you. Shhhh."

"Catherine? Are you awake?" asks Thomas.

"Shhhh. No. It's quiet."

"We haven't spoken much lately—"

She looks up, and scrambles back against the bedframe. "Murderer! Don't touch me."

"You know I can't touch you. I can't hurt you one bit." He sits on the edge of the bed.

She covers her face with her hands. "You're not real. Doctors say you're not real. Jilly said you're not real—"

"I'm as real as you are. Realer than the other voices you heed so dutifully."

"But I don't want you to be real."

"What we want to be real is of no consequence. You of all people understand that."

"I saw what happened. You told the blonde girl you killed people, then tried to kill her, but...I saw the bees come for you. They buzzed so loud. All of them, crawling all over..."

"Yes, yes. We've already discussed it. Very unfortunate, but it was a long time ago."

She shook her head. "Go away or I'll scream."

"If you scream, your mother will come back with more medicine. The stuff that makes you cloud up like a fog bank on a winter morning. You've been sleeping for days."

"How many days?"

"Let's see…it's been almost two weeks since the fight between Jillian and your mother. You haven't been right since. You've been increasingly hysterical."

"I remember Mama and Jilly fighting." She rocks in place. "And Jilly said…she said some real mean stuff."

Thomas speaks in a low, soothing voice. "It's been three days since Doctor Boone paid a visit and gave you something. Some concoction that made you sleep like…well, as they say, like the dead."

"Jeepers creepers. Three days." Catherine licks her lips. "No wonder I'm so thirsty."

"You mother came in and made you drink. But you barely opened your eyes."

"I think I remember…oh. Jillian came, too. She…wait a darn minute!" Catherine smiles. "She told me she was sorry for being so mean! She cried. Asked me to forgive her." She swings her legs over the edge of the bed. "She's leaving for camp. I want to say goodbye to her, too. She said when she gets back, she'll help me in the garden and take me shopping with her and Amanda—"

"Do what now?" says Thomas. "Your sister, Jillian, said all that?"

"Yes. I was so happy. But I don't think I told her!"

"Told her what?"

"Why, I forgive her, of course." She puts both feet on the floor, but when she stands, the room spins. She grips the bedframe. "I have to catch her before she leaves."

"She left yesterday, Catherine."

"Oh. Drat. I can write to her—"

"*I hate to be the bearer of bad news. Jillian never came in here and apologized about anything.*"

"*Yes, she did. I remember—*"

"*I've been sitting here, watching over you. She never came.*"

"*Thomas is lying to her,*" Tipsy says to Henry. "*He doesn't want her to know Jillian asked for forgiveness.*"

Henry nods as Catherine rambles on.

"*No. I'm sure she did. She apologized for saying…what she said. She said we'll go shopping—*"

"*You want that to be true, but it simply isn't. No one has come in here but your mother. Not Jillian. Not your father. Only your mother, and she cried each time.*" He sighs. "*It must be awful, being such a burden on your family.*"

"*Jilly didn't come in here? Neither did Daddy? Just Mama, being sad?*"

"*Just Mama, and me. I wanted to be here when you woke up.*"

Her eyes narrow, and for a moment, she doesn't look crazy. "*Why? I thought we were friends, then you started hiding from me. Now you're nice again. You don't make sense.*"

"*I'm sorry. But everything gets so loud, don't you know? It makes me short tempered. Makes me want to be alone.*"

She nods, because she sure does know. The murmuring is already getting louder in her brain, like the audience chattering before the start of a movie.

"*You've been upset with me,*" says Thomas. "*I did things…when I was alive, that weren't…kind. Sometimes, it's like some other person takes hold of me. Like when your backup singers get a hold of you. You understand that, too.*"

She nods again.

"*We share so much understanding. I know the ghosts are real. I also know what it's like to have…forces…you can't escape.*"

"*But my backup singers don't tell me to hurt other people—*"

"*They may someday.*" He walks around the other side of the bed. "*They may tell you to hurt your mother. Or your father. Probably your sister first, since the voices hear how cruel she is to you.*"

"I would never! Don't say those things."

"Your sister, she deserves death after being so mean to you. If I could, I'd do her just like I did my father. A quick bounce down the stairs. Or if you'd prefer something more frightening but less painful, I'd put my hands on her throat and squeeze—"

"Don't you dare. You stay away from my family!"

"We've already established I can't hurt you or anyone else. I'm teasing you, Cathy. Having a laugh. Giving a yank on your leg."

She puts her hands over her ears and closes her eyes. "You're as bad as the backup singers. Confusing me. Stop it. All of you. Talking at once. Stop!" She hums, and then starts singing. "The door was open and the wind appeared. The candles blew and then disappeared!"

Thomas walks right through the bed until he's standing in the middle of the mattress in front of Catherine. "Catherine, shut up!" he yells into her face. "The voices are quiet!"

She flinches, but she opens her eyes. He glares at her. "Do you have any inkling of how frustrating it is to listen to you? No wonder your sister hates you. If she's cruel to you, it's because she has to live in this house with you. With your ranting and terrible singing. Poor girl can't even invite her friends to call."

"Uh—but you just said Jilly deserves to die and—"

"What? Absolute nonsense. I said no such thing."

"If he's trying to confuse and befuddle her, it's working," says Henry to Tipsy. "I'm confused and befuddled myself. What's he playing at?"

"I have no idea," says Tipsy. "Is he trying to help her calm down, or get her worked up?"

Back on the bed, Catherine starts rocking. "I don't understand what you're saying. Any of you."

"You claim to care about your family, yet you make them miserable every day. Your poor, sad mother, and your father, slowly drowning himself in bourbon. Your sister didn't apologize to you. She has nothing to apologize for. You deserved whatever she said."

"She said they'll all be better off without me."

"Why don't you leave? Run away. Jillian is right. They'll all be better off without you."

Her rocking slows, and a lone tear creeps down her cheek. *"You think?"*

"Who cares what I think? Listen to the backup singers. What are they saying?"

The backup singers are partial to the power of suggestion. A hundred judgmental opinions command Catherine to get away from here and spare her family the misery of her.

"Where should I go?"

"Far away. As far away as I am."

"You mean, become a ghost?"

"If you were gone, their lives would be easier. Your mother and father wouldn't worry all the time. Jillian can have a normal life. It would be a mercy."

"I could—the piazza is high enough—"

"Oh, no. If you're going to do...that...you must leave this house. It would be cruel to leave a mess for your mother to discover. Best to...disappear. Somewhere else. Anywhere else."

"He's telling her to kill herself, but not to do it here," says Tipsy. *"He's trying to get rid of her, and he doesn't want her haunting this place with him!"*

Thomas has struck manipulation gold by twisting Catherine's fragile brain into a knot and playing on her love for her family. She jumps off the bed. She mutters and sings to herself as she yanks off the Clemson sweatshirt. Underneath it, she wears a Rolling Stones tank top. She retrieves a pair of rainbow striped socks from the drawer and pulls them on. She pauses at her vanity mirror, grabs a lipstick from a decorative dish, and slathers coral across her lips.

"We have to follow her, Henry," says Tipsy, as Catherine walks toward the bedroom door. *"We have to—"*

A disorienting jerking sensation, as if Catherine's memory took Tipsy's arm and swung her around. She fears the memory is ending prematurely, but when she blinks, she's standing beside Colonial Lake in the middle of a thunderstorm. Despite the heavy rain, Tipsy feels neither wet, nor cold. No *sting of raindrops on her exposed skin. The unnaturalness of it all unnerves her. "Henry? Henry!"*

"Here," says Henry, as he moves into the glow of a streetlight. Passing cars on Broad Street wade through flood water. Their spinning tires displace the rain in spraying liquid sheets. Henry points at the lone human figure beside the lake. Lightning flashes around her as Tipsy and Henry approach. Her toes in her striped socks grip the promenade's cement ledge. Tears mix with rain on her face as she sings a hodgepodge of songs. She talks to Sharona and Mary. She sends out an SOS, because it's clear she can't go on.

Catherine can't swim. The black water below frightens her, but she's fixing to jump in. Thomas is right. Jillian had been right, too. Her family will be much better off without her. She just has to get up the nerve to do it. For once, she wishes the backup singers would start screaming at her, but they're oddly subdued. The thunder's constant grumble and intermittent crashing overpowers them. As the seconds tick on, she realizes the thunder isn't drowning them out. They're retreating. Getting quieter. Going…mute.

"Ah, Tipsy," says Henry. "I can't watch this young woman take her own life."

"It's awful, but you have to help me learn exactly what happened."

"Whatever happens, it's as much Thomas's fault as Jillian's. Probably more."

"Just watch and listen. Her thoughts and feelings are all there, like our version of the voices in her head."

Henry nods grimly, and Tipsy refocuses on Catherine. Her arms hang at her sides. She doesn't blink at the whipping rain, nor flinch when lightning streaks the sky. A non-schizophrenic person might be so agog if she suddenly had to interpret a hundred voices in her head, but for Catherine, shock and awe is the result of silence.

In that quiet clarity, the last of her Valium fog lifts. The voice of her sister Jillian fills the empty space in her head. Jillian's real voice, not the snark of a judgmental backup singer. Jillian's true words, from a memory.

The memory of Jillian sitting on her bed. Crying and saying she's sorry. Saying she'll take Catherine shopping with Amanda as soon as she returns from summer camp.

"She was there. She did apologize." Catherine smiles into the rain. *"I forgave her. I told her I was sorry, too, but only in my head. It never came out of my mouth."*

"She remembers!" says Tipsy.

"But Thomas…he lied to me. Why, Sharona?" She swipes at her eyes. *"Who cares. He's the evil one. He's a murderer! I let him talk me into coming out here and—"* She jumps back from the edge. *"Good grief! I'm not listening to a murderer tell me to kill myself. My mother would—oh, my poor mama! She'd be…so…and I have to write a letter! A letter to Jilly. Right now!"*

To Tipsy's dismay, even though Catherine steps away from the literal edge and her emotions are manically happy, her thoughts start stirring up her typical toxic mental witch's brew. Now the backup singers demand she run home. Run, run, run, right away. Images of stationery and stamps dominate everything.

She spins around and sprints toward Broad Street. Tipsy knows what will happen, but she goes after her. Henry disappears and reappears in the middle of the street. Out of instinct, she screams at him to get out of the way, but the Cadillac bearing down on him can't hurt him.

It can hurt Catherine, and it does. She runs straight into the street without pausing. The car doesn't pause, either. There's no squeal of brakes. No hydroplaning in the flood water. Just the slam of Catherine's body against the hood. Tipsy catches a glimpse of flailing limbs in a flash of lightning, and then she wakes up.

———◆)(◆———

A million tiny somethings were pricking Tipsy's rear end.

Bees? Bees! Visions of Thomas's disturbing demise accompanied the mental warning, but when she opened her eyes, she wasn't stuck in an attic with an angry, buzzing hoard. She sat on her butt in a pile of pine straw beside Colonial Lake. She eased onto her knees, and the world and her stomach rolled. She swallowed the spit that built up in the back of her throat and waited for the trees to stop spinning. Once she was sure she wouldn't hurl, she picked at the pine needles stuck to the back of her thighs. Something tickled, and she swatted her calf. A half dozen voracious bugs crawled over her legs.

"Fire ants! Damnit." In her panic, she forgot she was on the verge of puking. She frantically itched and swiped, in a passable impression of Thomas Bonneau warding off imaginary bees. She jumped. She shimmied. She did the Fire Ant Jig.

"Uh, Tipsy—"

"Hold *on*, Henry. These things are about to crawl into my—"

"You must look."

Tipsy immediately forgot the fire ants when she looked up. Catherine Porcher floated above the lake, arms akimbo. The sunlight behind her shaded her face and hid her expression. Despite the still air, her long hair undulated like a banner in a high wind. The bible studies of Tipsy's childhood returned to her. Drawings in her *Jesus Loves Me—and You!* coloring book. Catherine was a levitating angel in rainbow striped socks.

She put her phone to her ear and approached the lake with one hand shading her eyes. The sickening lump in her throat had retreated back into her belly, but her pounding head reminded her that she'd just witnessed a violent death. "Catherine? Come down, okay? So we can explain to you what we saw—"

Catherine swooped toward Tipsy like Supergirl coming in for an emergency landing. "You don't need to do that. I saw *it all*."

"You did? Usually we at least have to clarify the details."

"Not always," said Henry. "You didn't need to explain to me and Jane, or Camden and Ivy."

"But with y'all, I forced two ghosts to show me the same memory—"

Henry shrugged. "Maybe it's different for her. The same way she doesn't need to touch ghosts to see into memories."

"I can see straight into the heads of other ghosts." Catherine pointed at Henry as she lit on the sidewalk. "If I want to, I can look right into your mind like I look through a window after a spring cleaning."

"You don't have to touch the ghost?" asked Tipsy.

"No. That would be so *lame*. Touching ghosts and getting cooties."

"Okay…well, you're the only schizophrenic clairvoyant I know. Maybe it's different for you."

"Just now, I saw into *my own mind*, too."

"So you understand what happened?" said Tipsy.

"Yes, I also understand what *didn't* happen. I didn't kill myself. I ran out into the road. Very *lame* of me, but the backup singers were screaming, and that's what I did. I remember Jillian, asking me to forgive her for being cruel. I did forgive her." She scowled. "If anyone was at fault for what happened, it was Thomas. Not my sister."

"I looked into that car," said Henry. "There were several men inside. One had a liquor bottle. They were laughing and carrying on. Not paying one bit of attention to the road in front of them."

"Blaming Catherine for jumping in front of the car made for a nice alibi for drunken manslaughter," said Tipsy. "Do you feel like you can move on, Catherine? Henry said it's like—"

"Like you can feel again," said Henry. "Warmth. Tingling."

"I do feel that. I feel so light." She levitated again. "So *clear*. My own mind is as clear as looking into yours, Henry. In fact…I don't hear anyone. No one at all. Only myself, talking to y'all."

"No backup singers?" asked Tipsy.

"No. Nothing!" She spun like an excited hummingbird. "Sometimes they quiet down for a while, but I can always sense them lurking. Hiding in the corners of my mind. It seems like they're…*gone*."

"Maybe by remembering, you can finally silence them forever," said Henry. "If you move on to the next plane, they won't follow you."

"I hope so, but…I can't move on anywhere until I made amends with my sister."

"I'll tell her what really happened, that you forgive her for what she said all those years ago, and you want to make amends." Tipsy smiled. "Sophie can be y'all's interpreter!"

"Cool beans. I'll tell Sophie the awful things Mama said about Jillian were misplaced."

"They're staying at a hotel. Jillian won't come back until we figure out how to get rid of Thomas."

"Yes. Sophie cannot be around that *terrible* man. He claims he can't *hurt anyone*, but he sure did hurt me. Do you know how to remove him?"

"No. But I promised Jillian we'd try."

"I'll help you, if I can."

"Wonderful," said Henry. "I'm sure you will prove very useful."

Tipsy smacked a dogged ant on her thigh. "As they might say, the more supernatural firepower, the better."

"Who says that?" asked Catherine.

"I do," said Tipsy. "We good?"

Henry and Catherine nodded and agreed, and they broke up to allow the ghosts to rest and Tipsy to get to the GQB. She checked her vital signs when she got into her truck. It had been years since she'd cleaned up puke in her vehicle. The days of carsick toddlers and uncontrollable little kid stomach bugs were behind her. She didn't plan on revisiting that nastiness with her own vomit.

Settled tummy, check.

Mild, manageable headache, check.

All systems were go, so she cranked the engine. Jillian Yates would have appreciated her bossiness, with her ghostly friends and her internal organs. Tipsy was in charge, and the more she was in charge, the more she liked it.

Tipsy and Scott moved to the first floor piazza that evening to enjoy the blossoming hydrangeas. Whoever had planted them, be it Catherine, Betsy, or a professional landscaper, had done a fine job. Over the past few weeks, the lush bushes had bloomed with an almost aggressive enthusiasm. Bees and butterflies capered from one fragrant purplish-blue cotton candy cluster to the next. Tipsy and Scott shared a bowl of Cheez-its. "I forgot how good these things are," said Scott, as he tossed them back.

"They're addictive. I buy them for the kids, but I eat most of them."

"That's me with peanut M&Ms."

"Jane kept a dish of caramels by our front door," said Henry, as he materialized on the joggling board across from them. "She claimed they were for guests, but I think she kept the dish filled for me. I always grabbed a handful as I headed to the warehouse."

"Surprised you have any teeth left," said Tipsy.

"With my OCD? No way. I floss twice a day."

She chuckled. "Sorry. I was talking to Henry. No fluoride treatments in his day."

Scott looked around. "Is he here?"

"Right there." Tipsy pointed at the elegant man Scott couldn't see.

"Give him my regards, Tipsy," said Henry.

"He said to give you his regards."

"Uh…same? Can you give him mine?"

"He hears you."

"Oh. That simplifies things. On his end, anyway." He rubbed his arms. "It's chilly out here all the sudden. And it smells like…Altoids?"

"Both temperature and perfume courtesy of Henry. He's a natural AC unit, and he's got that minty fresh feeling, even without Colgate." She crossed one leg over the other. "Most ghosts have a smell. Jane was lemony. My friend Ivy smelled like an apple pie right out of the oven. Catherine smells flowery."

"Sounds like the candle aisle at Target."

"The smells are usually pleasant. Except Thomas Bonneau. He's kind of…musty."

"Tipsy, this man bears no resemblance to the portly old doctors I knew," said Henry as she peered into Scott's face. "He's quite…well-formed. I see why you and Shelby found him so heated."

"Hot," said Tipsy, but before Scott asked for clarification, she said, "Thanks for fitting us into your busy schedule, Henry. I hope we can have a nice chat about the human brain."

"I wonder if it's accurate to talk about my brain," said Henry. "Since it moldered away a hundred years ago."

"Even if you don't have a brain, you still have a mind. Your powers sprouted from your mind in life. What are ghosts but remnants of the power of those minds?"

"How do you know it comes from our minds? What about souls? Ghosts are supposed to be *souls*. Not disembodied brains."

"Sorry, but getting one side of the conversation is kind of weird," said Scott.

"I know. Henry, try to just listen. Scott can give us insight into how our minds work. He deals with the brain as…a kind of map of electrical pathways. He believes me about ghosts because he believes those pathways are different for different brains. Is that accurate?"

"Basically. Should I talk…like…that way?" Scott pointed in the general direction of Henry. She nodded, and he went on. "Some mental illnesses include heightened sensitivities—"

Tipsy held up a hand. "Hold on. Sometimes I have to clarify modern stuff. By mental illness, he means—"

"A sickness of the mind, not the body," said Henry. "Like Catherine, hearing voices. Or hysteria. Melancholy. I understand, Tipsy. People have had mental illnesses for as long as they've had brains. I knew plenty of mentally ill people. I arguably was one myself."

"Touché," said Tipsy. "Take it away, Dr. Brandt."

"Mental illnesses can be the product of a particular brain's reaction to emotions and stimuli. Schizophrenia is your brain on overdrive, interpreting—and even inventing—stimuli. People on the autism spectrum experience sounds, colors, and tastes more intensely. Anxiety and depression are normal emotional reactions—worry, sadness—taken to unhealthy levels. According to my hypothesis, supernatural powers like y'all's originate in brains that are uniquely susceptible to specific stimuli. *Supernatural* stimuli."

"So you're saying the stimuli—the ghosts—exist around everyone," said Tipsy, "but only our brains can detect them?"

Scott nodded. "Catherine's abilities vary from yours, and Henry's, correct?"

"Yes. From what I can tell, she doesn't even have to touch ghosts to see into their memories. She says she looks right into their heads."

"Catherine had schizophrenia during her lifetime. Her brain was wired differently from even y'all's."

"I approve of your approach," said Henry. "It's comforting to know it's a deficiency in ordinary people, instead of a flaw in us."

"That doesn't necessarily mean everyone else is *deficient*, as Henry just said," said Tipsy. "But the idea that our brains are *different* makes sense."

"By accepting the difference, and actively exploring it as you have the last few years," said Scott, "it's almost like you've been giving yourself cognitive behavioral therapy."

Tipsy nodded. "I have more control over my powers than ever. I'm confident I can make Thomas come out, and I can hold on to him. But I have no idea how to force him to *move on*."

"I suggest utilizing the differences between you, and Henry, and Catherine," said Scott.

"You mean me being alive, and they're both dead?"

He nodded. "Your brain is still a swirling mix of electrical impulses. I can't say what's happening in Henry and Catherine's minds, because like we've established, there are no brains firing in their heads. But Tipsy said y'all can both utilize telekinesis, right?"

"Teleka-what?" asked Henry.

"Telekinesis," said Tipsy. "The ability to move objects around with your mind."

Henry waved his hand, and Cheez-its levitated from the bowl. They arranged themselves into a floating smiley face.

"Holy shit," said Scott. "Is that really—"

Tipsy grabbed a few crackers and handed them to him. "It is indeed," she said. "Teleka-what-sis."

Scott shook his head. "Well knock me down and steal my teeth, as my granny used to say. Anyway, Tipsy has a connection to this physical world. Henry and Catherine have a connection to the next plane. Right? They can both *move on* if they want to."

"Yes, they can. So can Thomas," said Tipsy. "He's got a door waiting for him, but he hasn't stepped over the threshold. We have to *force* him through it."

"Can Catherine and Henry push him the same way they use telekinesis?" asked Scott.

"Perhaps," said Henry. "But I don't understand how I move things. I just do it."

Tipsy repeated Henry's musings to Scott, and then said, "The first time I pulled Henry into the here and now, helping Jane was my primary motivation. Somehow, I knew I could do it, *and* what had to be done."

"When I first learned to leave the Bennett Street house," said Henry. "I *believed* I could, and I did it. But what about your altruism angle?"

"Hmm. It's really Thomas's fault Catherine died. He's also responsible for all the guilt Jillian suffered. His manipulative ass is dangerous to Sophie. If we can't get rid of him, Jillian and Sophie will move, no matter how badly they'd like to keep this house. Making him move on is an act of justice, and Jillian and Sophie will be able to stay here, to boot."

"Sorry again, uh…y'all," said Scott. "But this unilateral convo is killing me. Can you fill me in?"

Tipsy squeezed his hand. "While I'm holding on to Thomas, Henry and Catherine will think good thoughts, and *believe* they can push him. Hopefully, that will be enough."

"Now I must leave you," said Henry.

"'Kay. Henry's got to go," she said to Scott.

"Thanks for stopping by. And, uh…have a nice night?"

"And y'all." Henry bowed with a flourish, and then walked through the wall.

Tipsy turned to Scott. "You okay?"

"Sure. My first time saying goodnight to a ghost, but all good." He smiled, and draped an arm around her back. "You think he likes me?"

"Yup." Tipsy smiled back and snuggled against him. "Believe me, if he didn't, you'd know."

Chapter 21

ipsy asked Shelby to hold down the fort at the GQB for the third morning in a row. She hated shirking her art-slinging responsibilities, but General Shelby Patterson Callahan had retired too early. She happily resumed command in the hope of earning another star.

TIPSY: I'M AS UNRELIABLE AS A C OF C POTHEAD THIS WEEK.

SHELBY: NO PROB. MAMA WILL WATCH LOTTIE. THE MORE I'M BACK AT WORK, THE MORE I REALIZE HOW MUCH I MISSED IT. YOU'VE BEEN A LIFESAVER THE PAST FEW MONTHS. I HAVE TWO INTERVIEWS FOR SALESPEOPLE THIS WEEK, AND I WANT YOU TO PAINT! WE CAN LET YOU OFF THE HOOK SOON. MAYBE PERMANENTLY OFF THE HOOK???

TIPSY: WE'LL SEE. BUT TODAY THIS FISH NEEDS A CATCH AND RELEASE. THANKS! XOXO

Kind of unusual for a boss to be encouraging her best employee to quit, said Granna. *But she's right. If she hires someone decent, the time has come! Tipsy Collins, full-time artist.*

Tipsy repeated her milquetoast reply to Granna. *We'll see.*

Scott left for work, and she went for a short, hard run down South Battery and past Whitehall Gardens. She passed John Huger's childhood home, the Joseph George Huger House. She compared it with the Doctor Legbone House. John's house was larger, but it sat on a comparably small parcel of land. When it came to the configuration of their estates, the antebellum Charleston gentry had faced tough choices. Big, huge, or gargantuan houses? Sizeable, expansive, or sprawling lots?

She hit the harbor, ran up a few steps to the promenade atop the seawall, and slipped past the controversial Confederate Defenders of Charleston monument, where activists regularly faced off with the kind of angry, rebel-flag waving, closeted racists who gave Southerners a bad name. She pushed hard along waterfront Murray Boulevard, and sprinted the block between Lenwood Boulevard and Limehouse Street. As she slowed to a walk and her breathing returned to normal, she pondered last night's theoretical conversation with Scott and Henry. Plausible hypotheses, but would speculations be enough? Henry would do what needed to be done, but if Catherine's mental clarity proved temporary, she wouldn't be much help. She might even unintentionally interfere.

Guess we'll find out, Granna, said Tipsy, as she approached the Bonneau House and punched in the gate code. By now, Tipsy and the gate were old friends. It honked a welcome. "You need a WD-40 touch up," she said, as she gently shut it. The gate agreed with a creaky sigh.

She went inside, took a shower, and put on fresh gym clothes and a BROCo baseball cap. She laced up her running shoes again. This endeavor required sturdy footwear, not flop-flips, although Catherine would have to make do with supernatural socks. She checked her phone.

Almost ten. Henry and Catherine should be here.

Not quite high noon, replied Granna. *But good timing for a psychic shootout.*

She went downstairs and entered the study. Henry sat behind the desk, and Catherine stood beside the bookshelf. To Tipsy's relief, Catherine had tucked her wild hair behind her ears, and her blue eyes were clear.

"I explained the process to her as best I could," said Henry.

"Great. It's confusing, but it's the best we have."

"I'm not *confused* at all," said Catherine.

"I'm glad one of us feels confident." Tipsy pointed at the threadbare rug. "Should we sit—"

Catherine melted to the floor. Henry followed her. He fastidiously wiped the rug, although no dust would stick to him. Tipsy joined them, as if they were children playing *duck, duck, goose.* "How to start?"

Henry held out his hands. "I apologize for the familiarity, Miss Porcher, but you and I should have a connection."

Catherine wincingly offered her hands to Henry, but when his big fingers folded around her small ones, she seemed to relax.

Suddenly, this idea seemed ridiculous and premature. "This is a crapshoot," said Tipsy. "We don't know what we're doing. It might be a disaster. If it doesn't work…or if anything bad happens…like the windows blowing out—"

"We won't know until we try," said Catherine, "or something explodes."

Catherine was right. They had to give it a shot and hope all glass stayed in the windowpanes where it belonged. Tipsy remembered Henry's peaceful voice guiding Catherine into a state of meditative serenity. She slowly inhaled and exhaled. Once, twice, three times. She closed her eyes.

Without the distraction of sunlight streaming through the window or shadows swaying on the floor, her mind offered to take her on a tour of the house. She started on the fourth floor, beside Patience's old bedroom and the attic where Thomas met his demise. She flowed down the stairs, past Sophie's room and her own temporary lodgings, and then descended another staircase and perused Jillian and BeeBee's rooms. She checked both upper piazzas, and the kitchen and dining room, but she did not see Thomas, nor sense his hidden presence. She returned to her own body in the study, but still felt no hint of him.

Her imagination allowed her to pass through the study door and the brick walls of the foyer. On the far end of the first floor piazza, near the azalea bushes, the air shimmered.

Come out, Thomas, she said in her mind. *Save us both the trouble.*

She sensed his surprise and his fear, as she always did when she drew ghosts out of hiding. He pulled away from her.

She reminded herself of the reasons why Thomas Bonneau had no right to exist in this house. She thought of him purposely confusing the permanently befuddled Catherine. How he'd pushed her buttons until they cracked. Next, she recalled the arrogant, unrepentant way he'd described his crimes to Patience Lewiston, and his disturbingly nonchalant attempt to kill her. If Patience had died, the world would have been robbed of Henry Mott's enigmatic presence. He'd preyed on Sophie Yates's vulnerability to serve his own desire to rid himself of Catherine's harassment. He'd indifferently pursued the means to his desired ends, even as Sophie sickened, dropped out of school, and had a nervous breakdown.

No wonder she couldn't read his feelings in his memories. He didn't have many, except selfishness, arrogance, and entitlement. Her intellectually ambidextrous nature rebelled against the idea that people were all good or bad, but even his sad backstory couldn't make up for his poisonous evolution. She intensely empathized with the other ghosts she'd met. They'd all had started out questionable—irritable, suspicious, secretive, irrational, cantankerous—and proved to be interesting, intelligent, well-meaning, lovely people. Except for Proctor James, who turned out to be an absolute hypocrite. Still, even he showed genuine remorse for his terrible actions in life.

Tipsy didn't know what the universe had in store for someone like Thomas Bonneau. As she'd told Scott, she didn't believe in heaven and hell. But if the next life included retribution, Thomas certainly deserved it.

She seized him, like she'd grab a priceless family heirloom as it fell off a shelf, or a baby sliding off a diaper changing station. He was a baseball whizzing past her face, and she snatched him out of midair.

Tipsy gripped Thomas with her mind, and all her desire to rid the Doctor Rene Bonneau House of his malevolence. He'd get what he deserved, and Sophie and Jillian would get some peace. They'd live in this beautiful place and repair their relationship. Jillian could focus on giving away her fortune to the less fortunate, while Sophie built her flower business and regrew her aunt's gardens. Catherine Yates would have justice for a life she never had a chance to live.

She dug her proverbial claws into him like an osprey clinging to a fish. Thomas tugged and thrashed and floundered—that mullet wasn't going to be breakfast without a fight. Terror made him strong. She held on.

Tipsy opened her eyes. Catherine and Henry still held hands, but they were watching the ceiling. Tipsy looked up. Thomas Bonneau writhed above them. The dusty chandelier hung still, even as Thomas's flailing limbs passed through its unmoving metal arms.

"Let me go!" said Thomas. "Let. Me. *Go!*"

"No," said Tipsy. "Normally I'm all for leaving the moving on to the ghost, but not in your case."

"I won't move on! I don't want to see them!" He frantically tugged at his overcoat and swatted the air around him. He groaned. "The bees. Patty, the damn *bees!*"

"Keep him talking, Tipsy," whispered Henry, through clenched teeth. "If he's fighting *you*, he's not fighting us."

Catherine's hair whipped back from her face. She blinked and winced as if bits of hail peppered her.

Tipsy looked up again. "You don't want to move on because they'll be waiting for you. A big crowd of people you murdered. Do you even remember how many you killed?"

"I can't—it was too long ago—"

"Just confess. Maybe whatever doles out judgment—God or karma or a bunch of Jedi warriors—will be easier on you."

"I...uh..." Even as he writhed, he kept up his incessant scratching.

Tipsy bore down, and he yelped. "Adele Coming! Her parents were friends with my father," he said. "He thought I might marry her. She snuck out of her house to meet me one night. I kissed her...and her neck looked so...I put my hands on it...and—"

"You strangled her?"

"Left her in Washington Square. Getting close to women of my own class...was too dangerous. So then there was... the farrier's daughter."

"Who else?"

He kept struggling. She pictured herself taking him by both arms and shaking him.

"A mulatto girl! Her mother sold vegetables from a cart. Two others... or three...from the hothouses on Chalmers—"

"That's where Patience Lewison caught you killing a prostitute. You somehow found time to push your father down the stairs, too!"

"My father always hated me! *You're stupid too scrawny too lazy you killed your mother.* Then after Adele and the farrier's daughter, he started asking questions—now let me go!"

He squirmed, and Tipsy adjusted her grip. Her brain was sweating. "Henry, y'all got to hurry up."

"We're getting there. A little…more…."

Tipsy turned back to Thomas. "But why *kill* those poor young women?" she asked.

"Because they were just as disappointing as my mother. The rich girls expected too much of me. The poor girls weren't any better. And always, the harping, nagging, grousing. When they wouldn't shut up, I silenced them."

"You rarely shut up yourself. You *enjoyed* silencing them! You got some gross thrill from it!" Name calling is the least intelligent form of argument, but Tipsy was getting desperate. She'd never held a ghost for so long. "You weird ass…freaky…pervert!"

"After I died, at least I had peace. Until *she* came along." He pointed at Catherine. "I thought she might finally be one to *listen to me*, like a woman should, being that she was daft. But *no*. She was the worst of them! Then she somehow looked into my head, and she screeched at me like a harpy day and night. I couldn't sit on the piazza. Couldn't look out the window of my own study. That *shrew*, bombarding me, in my own house!"

"She saw through your act…called you out." Sweat dripped from under the brim of Tipsy's baseball cap. "But you couldn't get rid of her… not forever. *She* came back to haunt *you*."

"I got rid of her once. She was never supposed to come back, yet here she is, more maddeningly nettlesome that ever! I've existed in this house for a hundred years. I never felt like I was losing my mind until she returned!"

So Henry was right—Thomas was afraid of Catherine. Not because she could harm him in any way akin to pain. None of her projectiles would damage him. She could, however, destroy his fragile, precarious sanity.

"You wanted to be rid of me, but I'll get rid of *you* instead." Catherine stood and pulled Henry upright. She let go of one of Henry's hands, and pointed at Thomas. Henry raised his own arm. They reminded Tipsy of Granna and PopPop, standing on their porch in Martinville in the long gone days before PopPop's death. Holding hands and waving as Mama backed down their long dirt driveway.

White light flowed from Henry and Catherine and surrounded them like a cocoon. Thomas slipped from Tipsy's grip. "Henry! Catherine! Do something!"

"I *see* it," Henry whispered. "The…next…plane. Oh, my lord." He sighed, as if looking upon the face of his firstborn child.

The white light solidified into something vaguely resembling a corridor. Depth should not exist amidst such blinding white, but somehow, it did. Tipsy experienced no fear. That unexplainable place was warm and pleasant, and smelled like the ocean. It pulled at her heart and her mind, equally.

How can a ghost resist this? she thought. *I couldn't if I tried.*

Thomas did not share her sentiments. The brighter the light, the more he thrashed. Tipsy imagined a straightjacket around his midsection, and his arms conveniently flattened against his sides.

He kept yowling. "*It itches itches itches…too cold no it's too hot too bright too dark…I won't go you can't make me this is my house my house my house—*"

Henry's eyes rolled in his head, but he pulled Catherine's hand as if on the losing side of a tug of war. "Push," he said. "Push. *Push.*"

Despite the glare, Catherine stared into the corridor of light. She smiled, and nodded, and smiled again.

"Catherine! Push!" Henry was a father trying to assist his pregnant wife. The baby was coming, and she expected him to do all the work. "Don't just *stand there.* You have to help me *push.*"

"Shhhh. I can't hear the voices when you talk."

"Oh, no," said Tipsy. "She hears voices, *now?*"

"Thomas, there are *lots* of people who want to talk to you," said Catherine. "Set things straight."

Thomas clawed at his face. "*Nononono*—"

"They're not only here for *him*. There are so many of them. *So. Many. Voices.* But they're nice voices. I like listening to them—"

Tipsy had to make Catherine act before she lost her mind again. She kept her mental grip on Thomas, but she reached for a dry fireplace log with her physical hand. She chucked it through the window.

Catherine jumped at the sound of shattering glass, then refocused on Thomas. She grinned at him; the handsome, charming killer of an unknown number of people, including herself by proxy. "You're going now."

He snarled down at her. "You lunatic wench—"

"I'm no lunatic anymore, thanks to Tipsy and Henry showing me the truth. *You're* the wacko. The nutjob to the max. A complete crackpot." She turned to Henry. "Now?"

Henry nodded. "Now."

"Three. Two. One. Push!"

Light blasted from their hands. The corridor trapped Thomas Bonneau in the afterworld's tractor beam, and there was no turning back. The light had called him home years ago, and he'd rudely ignored it for too long.

Thomas shrieked as if his own father was sawing off all four of his limbs without morphine. His face darkened past slate gray to a sickly purple and split like a rotting plum. Spectral detritus vibrated and scattered, until he was only a violent black scribble.

No matter how much he deserved it, Tipsy could not watch. The gruesomeness of his end superseded all the grisly deaths she'd witnessed over the past two years. She covered her face with her hands. When she peeked through her fingers, the light was gone, and so was Thomas Bonneau.

◆—◆✕◆—◆

Henry stretched his fingers and shook out his hands as if he'd been dangling from a pullup bar. "Is he truly gone?" he asked.

"Yes," said Catherine.

"How can you be sure?" Henry's alarmingly blurry edges made his mouth and his words appear out of sync. He flopped into the chair behind the desk with an uncharacteristic lack of grace. If he'd had any weight, the chair would have tipped over backward.

Likewise, their intense supernatural effort and its macabre result left Tipsy with a roiling stomach and a boiling head. Only Catherine seemed unaffected by the exorcism of Thomas Bonneau. She stood firmly erect, her edges crisp and sharp. "In my life and death, I've never been certain of anything," she said, serenely. "But now, I absolutely understand what's real and what's not. The light—the afterlife—was *real*. Thomas has moved on, and he's not coming back."

"I must return to Bennett Street," said Henry. "I feel as if all my appendages have detached from my body. Arms, legs. Head floating above my neck like a balloon on a frayed string."

"Henry, wait," said Catherine. "The voices said something about you."

"Your backup singers?" asked Tipsy.

"No way. I've heard *true voices*, and I'll never mistake the backup singers for real voices—or listen to them—ever again. I have a message from Jane."

"A *message*…from Janie?"

"Is she your wife? She must be, from the way she spoke about you. She's *so pretty*, like a porcelain doll. I can see y'all together."

Henry stood and walked through the desk. He grabbed Catherine's hands again. "Yes. *Yes*. My beautiful wife. Jane Robinette Mott. Black hair, shiny like a raven's wing. Eyes like bits of sky trapped in her face." Diamond tears filled his eyes.

"That's her." She squeezed his hands and let go.

"What did she say?" His fuzzy edges threw off little sparks, as if his emotions were electrocuting him. "Tell me everything—damnit—" He punched the side of his head. His fist passed through his own cheek and came out the other side.

"Henry, stop it!" said Tipsy. "You need to go home."

Catherine reached out and eased his fists away from his face. "Come back tomorrow and I'll tell you everything she said."

"But don't you want to move on right away?"

"I can wait another day. I want to speak to my sister, remember? Catch up on the last forty years."

"I'll go, and return in the morning, if you promise to wait for me," said Henry. "Please don't leave without telling me Jane's message."

"I swear I won't," said Catherine.

Tipsy breathed a sigh of relief when Henry disappeared. His agitation made her headache worse. She could only tolerate Zen spirits, and Catherine was as peaceful and content as a yoga instructor on Xanax. Tipsy held up her phone. "I'll tell Jillian and Sophie that Thomas is gone and it's safe to come home."

"That would be real nice of you."

Tipsy tried to focus on her phone screen and the room spun. "I feel so *out of it*. Don't you?"

"A bit tired and achy, like I slept on a hard mattress, but the quiet is invigorating. I'll sit outside and listen to the softness."

"Okay. I'm going to lie down after I text Jillian. I need a power nap."

Tipsy texted Jillian—HEY! WE DROP KICKED THE SERIAL KILLER INTO THE AFTERLIFE, AND YOU DIDN'T CAUSE YOUR SISTER'S SUICIDE, BUT I'LL LET HER EXPLAIN THE DETAILS LOL—and then went upstairs to her temporary bedroom. She remembered her work responsibilities and called Shelby to let her know she couldn't come in. She claimed PMS exhaustion and a headache. Not a total fib, as she was absolutely knackered and she felt like a thorny rose bush had sprouted between her ears. Shelby seemed happy to stick around for the afternoon, so Tipsy kicked off her shoes, drew the blinds, and collapsed on the bed. She fell asleep as soon as the quilt touched her shoulders.

In her dream, she walked down a wooded path with Granna. The path would soon turn into the tantalizing white corridor, so she wanted to run. *Slow down, sugar,* said Dream Granna. *Not nearly time for you. So much good coming your way.* Dozens of blank canvases of different sizes, propped on easels, lined the trail. A paint rainbow ran across the dirt forest floor. She reached for a paintbrush, but her shoes slipped in the slick, colorful mud.

Tipsy jerked, and woke up. She blinked her dry eyes and smacked her tongue around her parched mouth. Her head still hurt when she sat up, but the room didn't spin. She looked at her phone. She'd been asleep for over three hours.

She got up and went to the kitchen, where she found some Tylenol and downed two glasses of water. As she walked through the dining room, she heard jolly laughter. She peeked through the window at Jillian, Sophie, and Catherine on the piazza's wicker furniture. A pitcher of sweet tea sat beside Jillian, and Sophie had a Coke. Catherine's socked feet were propped up on the coffee table and she'd twisted her messy hair into a knot around itself.

Tipsy walked to the porch. "Hey, there," she said.

"Our hero!" Jillian jumped up and hugged Tipsy, and Sophie was right behind her. They showered her with thanks.

"You're welcome, y'all. I had a job to do, so I did it."

"That was the most complicated job I've ever managed," said Jillian, "and I navigated corporations through major acquisitions. You're sure he's gone?"

"Catherine believes he is. If she says so, I believe her. If Sophie feels better, that's a great sign."

"I'm so *grateful.* I got my house back, but more importantly, I got my little girl back, and my sister." Jillian wiped at her eyes.

"Don't cry, Jilly," said Catherine. "Sophie, tell her I said—"

"Aunt Catherine said don't cry, Mom."

"Now *that* is something I never imagined I'd hear. I'll try to keep it together." Jillian picked up two boxes of Girl Scout cookies. Thin Mints and Samoas. "Want one, Tipsy?"

Tipsy took a couple Samoas. She's always loved their unique combination of chocolate, caramel, and coconut. "My Granna kept these in the freezer."

"Cathy and I loved them when we were little." Jillian removed four Thin Mints from the sleeve and started munching. "We were in Brownies together. Once she couldn't participate anymore, I made sure Mama bought a bunch of boxes."

Catherine leaned toward the cookies. "I love that smell. Mint and coconut. Takes me right back."

"I love the smell," said Jillian. "Mint and coconut. Like childhood."

Tipsy smiled. This would be an evening Sophie and Jillian would never forget.

"You want to sit with us?" asked Sophie.

"Nah. Y'all catch up. I'll pack up my stuff and head home to check on Henry."

"Thank you, Tipsy," said Catherine. "For *all* your help."

"You're welcome, Catherine." She took a last look at Catherine's pale, youthful face and bright, intelligent eyes. She seemed so blissfully *aware*. Of her surroundings, her family members, and herself. "Safe... travels. Goodbye."

There was a finality to it. Catherine would move on as soon as she cleared up things with her sister and niece and revealed Jane's message to Henry.

Tipsy hadn't gotten to know Catherine very well, as Catherine was just getting to know herself. Still, she felt a little blue, knowing she'd never see the fragile, pretty ghost again. Every ghost she helped inspired a sense of responsibility in her, like an animal shelter volunteer guiding puppies to their forever homes. She was happy for them, but felt a loss, nonetheless.

I put so much energy into these mysteries, Granna, Tipsy said, as she gathered her toiletries—and Scott's—and packed them into her weekend bag. *Once I solve one, I have to adjust to normal life again. What do I do with myself now?*

You see if another mystery comes up. Paint. Take care of your kids. Hang out with Scott Brandt, the sexy shrink.

Tipsy laughed out loud, even as she felt old childhood mortification. *Granna! You never use that word.*

What? Sexy? I'm human, Tipsy. Your grandpa, now, Lord have mercy... that man was sexy. When he mowed the lawn, all the ladies would slow down on the state road. Gawk like Robert Redford himself was zooming around on a John Deere. I didn't worry, because Donald McNair never once looked at another woman—

Even as Tipsy cringed, she let her grandmother ramble on about her sexy PopPop. She enjoyed hearing a story about her family involving love, not dysfunction. Hopefully, someday she'd have her own such stories. Tipsy listened, and looked forward to embarrassing her own grown children.

Chapter 22

Tipsy's supernatural hangover demanded more pizza. She asked Scott to pick up a large pie on his way to her house. He came through the door with a pizza box under one arm and a work suit for tomorrow draped over the other. She was on the sofa in her taco PJ bottoms and an old USC hoodie, but the pizza smell got her up lickety-split.

Tipsy set out plates and napkins in the kitchen while Scott hung his suit in the hall closet. She poured herself a Coke and poured a glass of water with no ice for him. His teeth were sensitive to cold, and he couldn't tolerate ice cubes. She relished learning such tiny details about him. His disdain for ice and his love of scrambled eggs. The way he meticulously folded every item of clothing—even his boxer briefs—as if he'd spent years working at Banana Republic.

The room spun as she walked to the table with the glasses. She stopped and blinked until the walls settled into place. He walked into the kitchen and took her elbow to steady her. "You gonna make it?" he asked.

"I think so. But I should lie down again after we eat."

"Take a nap if you need to." He slid around behind her, wrapped his arms around her waist, and brushed her hair aside. His beard tickled her neck when he kissed her. "I can rub you down later, if that sounds good."

She leaned into him. "If someone asked me to choose between a lottery win and your rub down, I'd choose the rub down."

He took the drinks and sat at the kitchen table. "What was it like, kicking a ghost into the afterlife?"

She described the whole bizarre experience as best she could. The light. Thomas's fear. The sense that something had consumed him.

"None of the other ghosts I've known were afraid like *that*. Then again, they weren't murdering psychos with zero redeeming qualities and no remorse. Once we had hold of him and dangled him over the abyss, the abyss saw its chance, and swallowed him."

"Reminds me of the pit with the teeth in *Return of the Jedi*."

"Exactly. He's being slowly digested for a thousand years." She shivered. "He seems like your typical serial killer. No empathy. Huge ego. Wanted attention and validation. Got some perverted thrill from killing. I hope he has to look into the faces of his victims. His own father included. He had a tough time growing up, but it's no excuse."

"A lot of people have difficult childhoods," he said. "Why do some of them end up like him, and some don't? A combination of nature and nurture? A predisposition sparked by some extraneous variable? On the flip side, what about people who have blissful childhoods, and still end up like him?"

"Your rhetorical questions are as hot as your psychiatric lingo."

"Your fabulous psychic powers are even hotter."

Tipsy laughed, and her phone beeped. It was Shelby.

SHELBY: HEY! HAVE TWO EXTRA TICKETS TO ZAC BROWN ON DANIEL ISLAND SATURDAY NIGHT. BRIAN'S BOSS AND HIS WIFE HAVE TO GO TO A FUNERAL. YOU WANT TO COME? MAYBE BRING... SCOTT?

Tipsy looked up at Scott. "Shelby wants us to go to Zac Brown with her and Brian on Saturday. What do you think?"

"Shelby approves of me, right?"

"Yes. She's been your biggest fan from day one. Even *before* day one, when I pretended I didn't have a crush on you."

"Let's do it."

"I haven't been to a good concert in years, and I'm always looking for an excuse to break out my cowboy boots. The Daniel Island stadium is an awesome venue." The more she considered the idea, the more it excited her. "This will be *so fun*. Even more fun because we're going together."

"Agreed." He took her hand and kissed it. "Where you go, I go, cowgirl."

———◆※◆———

Daniel Island is visible from the Ravenel Bridge, but despite its as-the-crow-flies proximity to downtown Charleston, inaccessibility relegated DI to a quiet farming community until the 1990s. With the building of Interstate 526, Charleston's eternally incomplete semicircular beltway, Daniel Island became a feasible development location. Investors dreamed up a self-sufficient new urban community, framed by the Wando and Cooper Rivers, and built from the cornfields up. Charleston County and Berkeley County fought over the lucrative new tax base, which resulted in DI being located in Berkeley County, while simultaneously being subsumed by the City of Charleston. Over several decades, the community diverged into two *sides*, the hyper-exclusive, golf course dominated Park Side, and the Other Side. The Other Side was only slightly less exclusive, with picture perfect neighborhoods organized around well-maintained parks and community swimming pools, as well as DI's shops, churches, schools, office buildings, restaurants, a county library, and a pretty waterfront district on the Wando River.

The outdoor stadium basked in the shadow of the hair-raisingly tall James B. Edwards Bridge like a giant cement crown, graciously hosting big-name concerts and a professional women's tennis tournament. Every few years, a new corporate sponsor resulted in a name change. When Tipsy and Scott met Shelby and Brian to see the Zac Brown Band, Volvo held sway over the party.

Tipsy and Scott parked behind an office building half a mile from the stadium. Tipsy wore a short, flowery boho dress and the comfy cowboy boots she'd had since the days of Gamecock football Saturdays and KZ Game Day pins. She didn't mind the walk on an unusually balmy night, especially with Scott's hand in hers.

The two couples met in the courtyard outside the stadium. Shelby glowed on her night out. She had on her own cowboy boots, jean shorts, a beaded tank top, and a cowboy hat. Her wavy blonde hair hung over her shoulders and reddish lipstick outlined her pretty smile. She bounced through the crowd and hugged Tipsy. "Tips! We're out in the world!"

"We are indeed!" Tipsy hugged Brian, and introduced them both to Scott. She laughed, because Scott and Brian were both wearing khaki shorts, flip flops, and pale blue polo shirts.

Scott smiled. "We got caught being basic Charleston dads."

Brian offered a fist bump. "But we'll be basic Charleston dads having a damn good time."

Shelby gave Scott the once over, and wagged her eyebrows approvingly at Tipsy. Scott took Tipsy's hand again and the four of them walked toward the security staff and their waving metal detectors.

"Sooooo," said Shelby. "How many familiar faces will be in this huge-ass crowd?"

"Too many," said Tipsy.

"Really?" asked Brian. "There will be like ten thousand people here."

"We will know approximately eight thousand," said Shelby. "Baby, you haven't lived in Charleston long enough to understand how it works."

"Neither have I," said Scott.

"Since we're relative newcomers, we should be safe," said Brian. "But be prepared for drama. When my girl runs into people, it might be good, or it might be *bad*."

Shelby elbowed him. "I grew up in this town and I got a long memory. What about you, Tipsy?"

"I didn't grow up here, but I have my own history. But no drama tonight, Shelby."

"Of course not! I'm grown, sister. I'm a *mom*." She danced in place to the opening act's distant fiddle jam.

"Uh huh," Tipsy said fondly, but a hint of foreboding accompanied Shelby's speculations. Zac Brown wasn't from Charleston, but with his beachy Southern ditties and his SEC vibe, he had honorary local status. Year after year, his perennially popular music provided the soundtrack for Charleston's boat and beach days. He hadn't played a live Charleston show in a few years. Such a celebrated event would bring people out of the woodwork like termites fleeing the Orkin man. She wanted to enjoy herself, not look over her shoulder the whole evening.

"Anyone in particular you're *not* looking forward to seeing?" asked Scott.

"A few candidates come to mind, like Ayers and Kate."

"They went to her cousin's wedding in Nashville."

"Ah. Perfect. He didn't tell me." She stuck her arm through his. "Thus proving our theory about the convenience of our unusual arrangement. You brought me into the loop, and now I won't worry about seeing them."

"Our arrangement is perfection," he whispered, "and if we eliminate that torturous option, who cares who else we see?"

Tipsy and Shelby hit the ladies' room and then waited while Scott and Brian stood in the beer line. Tipsy inhaled the pleasant scents of popcorn and fry grease. The opening band banged toward an epic finale in the background. Between their guitar riffs and the audience's cheering, Tipsy had to read Shelby's lips to understand her.

"Our social media stalking *did not* do him justice. And he seems really nice!"

Tipsy watched Scott casually chatting with Brian. Shelby's comment inspired giddy pride, as if she'd complimented a figure in one of Tipsy's paintings. "He's something else."

"Finally, a guy who measures up to *your hotness*. Ayers and Will…" She grimaced, as if Tipsy had poured straight fry grease down her throat. "*Please.* Remember Saint Dave? Gag!"

"Don't kill my buzz before I get one, sister!" She shook her head at her friend's convenient forgetfulness. Shelby had crowed about Will's good looks when she convinced Tipsy to go out with him. She'd also acknowledged that while Ayers was no fine wine, he'd been a looker in his prime. As for Dave, everyone acknowledged both his douchebag-ery and his hotness. Scott left them all in the dust. Superior handsomeness aside, he was also smarter, and kinder, and more compassionate, and funnier, and more interesting, and—

"Hey! Tipsy!"

Tipsy turned, and smiled at the sight of Sophie Yates and two pretty blonde girls. "Sophie!"

"This is Avery and Josie," she said, pointing to her two friends. "Y'all, this is Tipsy. She's…ah, friends with my mom. Tipsy is a KZ, too!"

"Oh, fun!" said one of the girls. She made a K and Z out of her outstretched fingers.

Tipsy once again tried to remember how to return the gesture without spraining her wrist or jamming a finger. The girls were little Charleston Dress Code Blondes in the making, Gen-Z version, so she couldn't differentiate between them. "Nice to meet y'all. I'm so glad you're here, Sophie."

"I decided I need to start socializing again since I'm feeling better."

"Everyone in the chapter missed Sophie, like, *so much*," said Avery-Josie. "A bunch of us had tickets for this show, so when she finally got in touch again—" She poked Sophie. "—she had to come with!"

"That's so nice of y'all."

"We've all been through tough times," said Josie-Avery. "Mental health is nothing to be ashamed of."

"Her sisters are here for her!" said Avery-Josie.

"Well…y'all are awesome." Many grownups bemoaned the next generation, but not Tipsy. These young people never failed to impress her. At their age, Tipsy and her compatriots had been clueless, while Sophie's cohort struck her as worldly, self-assured, and accepting. If they talked so openly about mental health and supporting one another, humanity wasn't doomed.

"We're gonna get pretzels," said Sophie. "And, ah…Cokes."

"Good idea." Tipsy bet a year's worth of sorority dues that Sophie's sisters had a few White Claws stashed up their sleeves.

As Josie-Avery lined up and Shelby messed with her phone, Sophie said, "I'm going back to school in the fall. Declaring my majors. Botany and small business. Mom is going to help me form an LLC for my floral design company. It's all really happening!"

"Great! I'll start sending clients your way." She glanced at Shelby, but she was FaceTiming her mom, who held a goggle-eyed Baby Lottie up to the phone. "Everything... *quiet*...on Legare Street?"

"Yup. All uninvited house guests have *moved on*. Mom and Catherine made amends, and Catherine left. No sign of...the other guy."

"All's well that ends well."

"Sophie!" said Avery-Josie, who balanced two Cokes and a bucket of popcorn. "Can you get this popcorn?"

"Go on," said Tipsy. "Have an amazing night." *Enjoy this time, sugar. It's priceless, and it doesn't last forever.*

Sophie looked up at her with a baffled expression. *I...will? And thanks for the advice?*

You heard me?

Yeah. What the heck? You talk to your grandmother in your head, but this is wild!

Granna and I communicated like this during her life. You and I are both clairvoyants, and we have a connection now, so....welcome to my head, I guess!

Oh, my gosh. What else am I going to learn about this crazy power we share?

You got your whole life to figure it out. I'm here if you need me.

Thanks so much. She grinned as she backed away. "Say hi to Dr. McHotty for me."

Tipsy laughed. "Will do."

———◆)(◆———

"I saw Sophie," said Tipsy to Scott, as they found their seats. "She's feeling much better."

"Great," he said. "And now you've broken the seal."

"I haven't even had a drink yet."

"No. I mean you saw someone you know, and it was positive."

"You're right!" She gestured toward the stage. "These are great seats!"

"Hey, look. There's Lindsey and P.D.!" Shelby pointed into a nearby box. "*Linds!* Lindsey!"

"Holy hell, Shelby," said Tipsy, but she laughed. "You're gonna blast my eardrums out before the amplifiers even start up."

"She sees us! Girl! *Whaaaaat's up!*"

Tipsy turned in the direction of Shelby's frantic waving. She found Lindsey, enthusiastically waving back. She lifted her own arm, but just as she got in a good wave, it froze.

"They're in the BROCo box," said Shelby. "Isn't that—"

Tipsy elbowed her, smiled, and finished her wave. The shaggy-haired blonde man beside Lindsey and P.D. raised one hand and waved languidly. It was Clarice Andrews, P.D.'s boss. The notorious player Tipsy had gone out with last summer, who had unwittingly incited the Windjammer Incident.

"Hey, Linds!" Tipsy yelled. "Y'all have so much fun!"

Once she got over the initial surprise, it was simply funny to see Clarice. She scanned the crowd in his box, but she didn't see Kim Nowak, the woman who'd bitched her out at The Windjammer, or Shelby's neighbor, another member of his fan club. Maybe he'd taken last summer's lessons to heart and dissolved his harem. Regardless, none of her business. Just another drama-free sighting of a known entity.

She linked her arm through Scott's again and started to ask Shelby if her mom had managed to get Lottie to sleep, when the stage lights came on.

"I'm so excited, y'all, oh my—*whoooooooooo!*" Shelby screamed as Zac Brown and his band walked on the stage.

Tipsy yelled along with her, as Scott and Brian whistled.

"*You know I like my chicken fried…*" sang Zac, and the crowd went ballistic.

"He's starting off with a bang," said Shelby. "*Cold beer on a Friday night!*"

After thirty minutes, Tipsy's first beer went through her. To her annoyance, she had to use the bathroom again. Scott offered to go with her.

"It's okay. You don't need to miss any of the show," she said.

"I'll get another round." He leaned around and poked Brian, who said something about a Mich Ultra and a Coors Light.

"You sure?" Tipsy asked Scott, but he was already dragging her through the crowd. He rejoined the beer line and she ducked into the bathroom. The potty queue seemed several miles long. She shifted on her feet as the industrial hand dryers whirred. With each set of cowboy boots leaving the bathroom, she crept closer to sweet relief. She texted Scott to cheerfully vent about the wait.

"Tipsy, right?"

Tipsy about wet herself as she stared into Whitney Morrison's sweaty face. Her black eyeliner was running, and she wore a tight, lacy black shirt, black jeans, and black cowboy boots. A black cowboy hat rounded off her vampirical ensemble. She looked like she was on her way to Hank Williams Junior's funeral.

"Hi…Whitney," said Tipsy.

"What a great show, huh? A bunch of us have floor seats! Where are you sitting?"

The question caught Tipsy off guard, and she answered without thinking. "First floor balcony." *Shit. That was dumb. Now she knows our general vicinity.*

"You here with Scott?" Her eyes narrowed. "I heard you're still with him."

"Ummm, hmmm." Tipsy assessed the line. Six more people in front of her, but there were a lot of stalls. She wanted to get away from this woman before she got a repeat of the Windjammer Incident. *The Zac Brown Altercation,* whispered her frazzled mind. *The Volvo Car Stadium Skirmish.*

If they were in the same bathroom, Whitney's seats were on this side of the stadium. She needed to warn Scott and get back to their seats before Whitney tried to track them down.

"That's your problem," said Whitney. "Don't say I didn't warn you."

The comment was as irritating as Tipsy's painfully full bladder. "I won't have to."

"Aren't *you* sure of yourself? If he screws you over, you'll deserve it."

Tipsy had gotten into a regretful catfight in a bathroom last summer, but she couldn't let that one go. "You pretended like you showed up at my job out of concern for me. That was BS."

"I don't even *know you*."

"My point exactly. Enjoy the show."

Whitney scowled. "I will. I'm having a *great time*."

"Ummm, hmmm," said Tipsy, once again.

"I'm with a real man now. Actually…you know him. He's friends with your old boyfriend, Will. Will is *so nice*, by the way. So is his current girlfriend. So *young and pretty*."

"Yup. They're a match made in heaven."

"We see them all the time. *We,* meaning me and Glen."

Tipsy snorted. She should have predicted as much after her glimpse of Whitney on Glen's boat. "Glen. *Right*. He's a peach."

"He's amazing. And he's not…*gay*."

"You don't have to worry about Glen being gay. Still married, yes. Unattracted to women, no."

"What's *that* supposed to mean?"

"I guess you'll find out."

"Like you'll find out Scott is—"

"I'm already finding out who Scott is." It was *so not like* her, but she leaned toward Whitney. "In all his *obviously heterosexual* glory."

Whitney's scowl indicated a logical deduction. Scott's lack of randyness around her might have been the result of her sexuality, not his.

The line crept forward, and to Tipsy's relief, three doors opened at once. She shot into a stall, peed at lightning speed, and exited to wash her hands. She thought about texting Scott, but it seemed faster to run out of there.

She exited the bathroom in time to see Whitney stomping away from a befuddled Scott, who held four beers in a drink carrier.

"Oh, lord," said Tipsy, as she approached. "She cornered me in there and then I had to pee and I didn't have time to warn you and—"

"I wasn't expecting her to swoop in out of nowhere like The Bat in the Cowboy Hat and read me the riot act, but it's all good."

"Ugh. I may have...provoked her. With reference to our amazing sex life."

He guffawed. "Ah, that makes sense. She advised me to stop trying so damn hard to convince you I'm straight."

Tipsy joined him in laughing. "Promise me you'll disregard her suggestion!"

"I've never had worse advice in my life."

She leaned on him and he grabbed for the wobbly beers. As their laughter trailed off, she put a hand on his arm. "I'm sorry. Seriously. I'm sure I riled her up."

"She hasn't had the chance to scream at me in a couple months since I blocked her on my phone. Everyone stared. It was her shining moment. She also made sure to tell me she's found someone new who is *amaaaaz-ing*. Hopefully it lasts so she forgets all about me."

"With the guy she's talking about, it's doubtful." Tipsy shook her head. "But she can't say I didn't warn her."

They made it back to their seats in time for Zac to slow it down. The band played *Sweet Annie* and *Oh, My Sweet Carolina*. Scott stood behind Tipsy and they swayed with his arms around her.

"I love this song," she said, as Zac broke into *Colder Weather*. She had to lean in close, and her lips touched his ear as she spoke.

"Me too," he said. "*I'm with your ghost again.* That was me, even before I knew you saw ghosts. When I was walking around, missing you."

"I'm so sorry I hurt you. I hope you know I felt the same way. I wish—"

"Shhh." His own mouth close to her ear made her shiver. "We're here together now," he said.

When the song finished, the people in front of them took a bathroom break, giving Tipsy a clear line of sight to the floor seats below them. To her chagrin, she immediately noticed Whitney scanning the first floor balcony. Their eyes met, and Whitney tugged on the arm of the guy beside her. Tipsy recognized Glen's blond hair, but the band (and whatever he was smoking) transfixed him, and he paid Whitney no mind. Whitney leaned around Glen and tapped the next guy's shoulder. He turned and—chagrin, part two—Tipsy recognized Will's profile. Beside him, Julia's petite, dark-haired form.

Whitney gestured to the balcony. Will looked up, and Tipsy's gaze flicked back to the band. She pulled Scott's arms tighter around her, as if to hide in his embrace, and he kissed her neck.

As the song ended, she looked down at the floor again. Will was watching her, and they made the briefest eye contact. Julia bounced in place and put her arm around his waist. He smiled at whatever she said, and kissed the top of her head.

Watching Will and Julia, Tipsy felt…*nothing*. She once experienced a similar nothingness in her kitchen, when she realized she didn't give a hoot whether Ayers Lee Collins, IV, came or went. This *nothing* held none of the complications of an impending divorce, and she welcomed and embraced it. She smiled to herself, like Catherine enjoying the newly discovered silence.

Tipsy turned away from them, and focused on the smell of Scott's cologne, his scratchy beard, and his warm arms. Zac's wistfully hopeful words came back to her. *Soon we'll be together, and I can't wait till then.* She no longer had to wait, and it was sweet.

◆〉〈◆

After the concert, Tipsy spent the night at Scott's house. She checked her phone one last time after she washed her face and donned the cute pajamas she'd stashed in Scott's dresser drawer. She had a text from Shelby.

SHELBY: OMG SO MUCH FUN. I'M NOT LOOKING FORWARD TO LOTTIE'S EARLY MORNING WAKE UP. IF SHE SLEEPS TILL 6 I'M LUCKY! BUT SO WORTH IT! WE LOVE SCOTT BTW.

TIPSY: I DO NOT ENVY YOU THAT WAKE UP! SO GLAD Y'ALL LIKE HIM. I THOUGHT BRIAN MIGHT BE WEIRDED OUT BECAUSE OF WILL.

SHELBY: WILL AND BRIAN ARE BUDDIES, BUT BRIAN KNOWS Y'ALL ARE NOT RIGHT FOR EACH OTHER AND HE WANTS YOU TO BE HAPPY. BESIDES, LET'S FACE IT, MY BABY IS A LITTLE TOO BRAINY FOR WILL GARRISON AND P.D. STARKEY.

TIPSY: I HAVE NO COMMENT! GOING TO SLEEP. NIGHT!

As she hit send, another name appeared on her phone. WILL GARRISON. *Oh, lord, Granna. What the heck does he want? To give me a lecture? Only one way to find out.*

Meh. I'm tired.

She almost ignored the text, but the idea that Whitney might have riled him up made her check it.

WILL: HEY TIPSY. I SAW YOU TONIGHT AT ZBB WITH SCOTT. I WANTED TO SAY YOU LOOKED PRETTY HAPPY AND THAT'S GOOD TO SEE. I'M NOT JUST SAYING SO TO BE THE NICE GUY. I AM A NICE GUY OF COURSE. HAHA. BUT I MEAN IT.

On one hand, a nice message. On the other, kind of presumptuous, as his comment insinuated a need for his approval. She considered what she knew of him. When he couldn't get away with true sarcasm, he disguised his feelings with double-edged pleasantries. She would not allow him to goad her.

TIPSY: THANKS, WILL.

As she hit send, another text came through.

WILL: GUESS WE'RE BOTH WHERE WE'RE SUPPOSED TO BE.

There it was. Passive aggressive central. She replied again. YUP. HOPE ALL OF Y'ALL HAVE A FUN NIGHT. TAKE CARE.

She pondered as she twisted her hair into a side braid. Will believed he was a *nice guy*. The nicest. But true nice guys didn't need to remind everyone of their own amiability. With truly nice people, others are the ones describing them that way.

More power to you, Mr. Nice Guy.

A certain passive aggressive southern phrase can be the cherry on that thought, said Granna.

Tipsy smiled at her own reflection in the mirror. For a moment, it seemed as if a young Granna smiled back at her. *Bless his heart, Granna.*

Exactly. Bless his emotionally unintelligent heart.

Scott was already in bed, in his boxer briefs, reading news headlines. She crawled across the sheets and snuggled beside him. Any thoughts of Will immediately left her mind like so many chickens abandoning a cramped coop. She trailed her fingers over his chest. "A classic Charleston night of unpredictable positive and negative interactions," she said.

"Twenty points for Sophie. Negative ten for Whitney. That still makes the evening a ten out of ten."

"Agreed. So fun." She yawned. "And now it's past mama's bedtime."

"Don't fall asleep yet." He gently tugged on her braid. "I got some advice tonight. I still need to ignore it."

She flopped backwards, laughing, and he rolled on top of her.

Chapter 23

Tipsy eagerly awaited more information about Jane's message from the beyond, but Henry retreated into conspicuous reclusiveness. His normal routine included appearing in her presence at least once a day, either to chat or offer his telekinetic assistance with some household chore. When the kids were home, he enjoyed observing their play or watching movies with them. Three days of Henry-less-ness passed, and she started worrying.

After a long day at the GQB and no time to eat lunch, a prickly, hangry Tipsy returned home determined to flush Henry from his hiding spot. She scarfed down a banana and a turkey sandwich, and then walked the house from top to bottom with a box of Cheez-its.

No Henry on the first floor, or in any of the bedrooms. No Henry on the front porch, or the little stoop leading into the backyard. No Henry in the gardening shed where she stored her painting bench. She returned to the dining room and attempted to move the mahogany table. She grunted and groaned with effort, but no Henry showed up to magically shift the table.

Finally, she went into the parlor, where Henry and Jane had died. She planted her hands on her hips. "Henry? What's up with you?"

No response.

"Come *out*. Let's catch up."

As the silence stretched on, anxiety beat out frustration. If Henry had moved on without saying goodbye, she'd be terribly hurt.

"Henry Mott!" she said. "Get your ass out here!"

Still nothing.

"Good lord. Don't leave me hanging, or I'll have to—" She braced to pull Henry into her presence. She balled her hands into fists and gritted her teeth.

"Don't strain yourself." Henry appeared on the sofa in his signature professorial position; one leg crossed over the other and his big hands engulfing his knees.

"Henry! Thank goodness." She plopped on the sofa next to him, her irritability forgotten. "I thought you moved on without saying goodbye."

"I would never. You're my bestie."

His use of that feminine endearment amused and touched her. "Aw, thanks. But why have you been hiding out?"

"I've had so much to think about. I get as overwhelmed as…as…"

"Sophie, managing Thomas and Catherine?"

"An apropos analogy. Forgive me for leaving you swinging—"

"*Hanging.*"

"—but I didn't know where to begin. You're curious about Jane's message, but first…let me address the second most important woman in my life."

"Oh, right! I forgot about your mom. We have to go downtown and set her free—"

"I already did."

"Damn. That's the second time you've tackled a Patience-related challenge without me. I'm surprised you haven't insisted on moral support."

"Once the urge seized me, I had to act before I changed my mind."

"What did you find out? Can she move on?"

"She… I…" He held up his hand. "My mother always rendered me speechless. Can we try it this way?"

Tipsy was an old hat at all this. A time-hopping version of Granna's Easter bonnet. She didn't reply. She tucked her legs underneath her, and held up her own hand.

"A memory within a memory," said Henry, as the darkness fell.

———•✕•———

There's something different about this vision. It's like she's looking through the antique windows of the Bonneau House. The thick glass warps the image on the other side. Or maybe she's staring into a swimming pool and a breeze stirred up the water. Tipsy is seeing the memory Patience showed Henry... through Henry's own memory.

She's standing in a square kitchen. A few rudimentary appliances sit on black and white checkerboard linoleum—a small steel icebox, a stove with an l-shaped exhaust pipe, and a farmer's sink. Simple wall-mounted shelves house blue and white china dishes. A vase of yellow and white daisies adorns a wooden kitchen table. Patience Mott sits at the table in her brown calico dress, so it's her death-day. The man who sits across from her looks to be about forty. Tipsy squints through the haze, and recognizes Edward Mott.

She blinks and rubs her eyes. The vision sharpens, as if she scrubbed away the layer between Henry and Patience's recollections.

"Do you like how the kitchen turned out, Edward? It has all the modern conveniences a good cook wants in 1934!"

"Mother," says Edward. "You avoid cooking—"

"I bake sometimes, and Sally appreciates it."

"—and since Father passed away, you need to be careful with your spending."

"You're doing a fine job running Mott & Phipps."

"We talked about this a few days ago. You know my plans."

"Don't be silly, Edward. Y'all aren't moving to California and taking my only grandchildren with you!"

He takes her hands. "We are. Mary's brother has a position for me in San Francisco—"

"Mary this. Mary that. Why is her family so important?"

"It's not just about her family, although her parents will be moving out there soon, too. Roger's new department store is going gangbusters—"

"I don't like that talk. What do you even mean?"

"It's an opportunity, in the middle of a depression. I'm hoping Roger will make me a partner. Aiken & Mott has a nice ring to it, don't you think?"

"Mott & Phipps is much *better."*

Edward tries another angle. "I told you, you can come with us. We can set up you in a little house—"

"I have a house! This beautiful place your father worked so hard to procure for us, and I've worked so hard to make into a treasured family home. And besides, who would Sally work for, if I left?"

"Sally is a fabulous cook and a firecracker housekeeper. She'll find someone to take her on. You don't need all this space. You're like a single grape rolling around an empty bowl."

"That's because you don't visit. Don't bring Eddie and little Henrietta to see me."

"Listen. We need to discuss your finances. I'm selling my ownership in M&P to Clyde Phipps. Do you remember?"

"Stop acting as if I'm going dotty. I remember what you told me two days ago."

"Good. I want to make sure you're taken care of. I'll use some of the money from the business sale. Set up an account for you—"

"I can't manage that, Edward! I'm an old woman, all by myself!"

"You managed the household ledger, and you helped Father with the M&P books in the early days. Still, I can have Lamboll Middleton set up as a trustee. I trust him emphatically—"

"No. I won't let some Broad Street lawyer dole out my own money to me like I'm a charity case."

Edward throws up his hands. "Do you want someone to help you, or not?"

"I want my son to stay in South Carolina, where he belongs, with his wife and children. I want them to know this house—"

"Your whole life, you complained this house isn't South of Broad. The address wasn't hoity-toity enough for you. Now it's become the church of Saint Patience the Martyr."

"How cruel, Edward. You don't care about me at all."

"You're the one who doesn't care," says Edward. "You don't care about us having a new start in a new state where everyone looks forward instead of mooning around over the glorious past and the Lost Cause. Everyone white, anyway. It's no wonder any negro who can is moving to Chicago and Baltimore and Detroit. Less likely to be strung up from a tree in those places."

Patience looks as if she might tip over backward and land on her head on her state-of-the-art linoleum. "Good heavens, Edward Mott! How dare you talk about such vile things in my kitchen! No one we know would do anything like that!"

He laughs. "I don't believe for one minute you're so naïve. You know exactly what our friends and neighbors get up to in their white sheets."

"I think you should leave. Come back tomorrow, when you're not so… agitated."

"We're leaving tomorrow. We have the train tickets. Our house is let and the renters move in on Friday. Just because you don't want to hear me, doesn't make it not true." He tries to take her hands again. "I'll bring Mary and the children over here this evening to say goodbye. But you must promise me you'll act appropriately. Can you do that?"

"Hell's bells. I know what I'm saying. What I'm doing. It's you who have made an awful decision."

"I'm making a decision for my—no. I won't justify myself to you one more time. I'm tired of your selfishness."

"Selfish, me? Why, Edward—"

"You cared more about the neighbors' opinions, than about me, or Father. You certainly never cared about Henry. Any kind word is covered in barbs, like pretty roses sprouting dangerous thorns. Only Henry saw through your charade."

"Don't talk to me about your brother."

"You still embarrassed by him? By his odd mannerisms and quirks? His eternal glowering? Or the fact that he finally succeeded in appeasing you by marrying Jane, only to dash all your hopes of social grandeur by murdering her?"

"Keep your voice down!"

"*Who will hear me? There's no one in this house but the ghosts of a family that never existed!*"

"*You lived a charmed life, whether you care to admit it or not, as did Henry. Neither of you boys had to scrounge through blackberry bushes or shoot squirrels. You never got sick from brackish water. You didn't watch your mother shrivel up, or your daddy die from a broken heart and rotten lungs.*"

"*That gave you an excuse to treat me and Henry like rungs on your social ladder? Climb right up and over us with your pointy shoes? Then abandon Henry, to boot?*"

"*When you've given your children everything and they turn out like Henry, you'll understand.*"

"*We don't even know for sure that he did it! Don't you remember how quiet and soft-spoken he was? He wouldn't hurt a fly. He cared only for reading books and writing stories.*"

"*He had a temper on him. You were embarrassed by him yourself when y'all were children.*"

"*I was, and I'm ashamed to admit it, because he was more than all of us, Mother. If we'd loved him better when he was small, God only knows what he could have done.*"

Patience is struck dumb for a moment. Then she starts sputtering. "*I don't—what are you—*"

"*I got my own children now. God willing, I'll have more. I see how my Mary adores them. I see how she kisses and hugs them and cheers them on. How she listens to them and reminds them every day that she's proud of them and loves them. What happens to a fragile child, like Henry, when he doesn't get such love?*"

"*Well. Well…now.*"

"*If Henry really was a murderer, it's in no small part your fault.*" *Edward stands and grabs his hat.* "*Now goodbye. We'll write to you.*" *He takes a few steps toward the door, then stops. He returns to his mother and squeezes her shoulder.*

He stuffs his hat on his head and leaves the house. Even when the door slams behind him, Patience doesn't move. Tipsy senses her deep regret, and a curious realization. She hasn't thought of Thomas Bonneau in years, but she recalls that no one loved him as a child. In a roundabout way, he'd said so many times, with stories of his grim father's heavy hands and the mother who died and left him all alone.

Thomas was a fragile, unloved child, and look how he'd turned out.

Her Henry was an odd boy, but a sweet one. She remembers him hanging on her leg when he was frightened, and how he was frightened so often. Once, at maybe five years old, Henry told her he saw dead people. A figment of his imagination, of course, but he'd seemed genuinely terrified.

At the time, she only thought of his annoying clinginess. A little sissy boy! He embarrassed her in front of the people she desperately wanted to impress. If she befriended them—the South of Broad people she'd first met when she lived in Thomas Bonneau's house—it meant she and her family were safe. Such people always managed to get by on connections and good breeding, even if they were as broke as a sprung carriage axel.

When Patience met tall, ginger-haired Frederick Mott, she saw the gumption in him. True to her prediction, he'd made sure they never had to worry about money. When Henry married into the Robinette family, Patience's safety had finally seemed assured.

But then Henry died, and his lovely wife with him, under such horrible circumstances. At the time, she wondered if he could have committed such an atrocious act, but it was simpler to brush it under the rug than take the rug outside and beat the dust out of it. Henry's death made Edward grow up, and he'd married Mary Margaret Aiken, another daughter of an old family. Patience forgot Henry, and when she didn't make a fuss, most everyone else forgot him, too. The Robinettes remembered, but Pierre was dead, and Theresa Robinette had moved to the country with her remaining daughter and her Yankee husband.

As she sits in her fancy kitchen, Patience Mott isn't sure if Henry killed Jane and himself, but if he did, maybe Edward is right. Maybe her own indifference had turned that gentle, quirky little boy into a coldblooded killer. Someone like Thomas Bonneau.

She'd lost Henry either way. Now she was losing Edward, too, and she wouldn't let that happen. She couldn't apologize to Henry, but she should apologize to Edward right quick while she had the chance. She'll admit he's right about Henry, and she'll tell him she'll go to California with him and Mary and the children, if they'll have her. This big house is of no consequence if no one she loves is in it. As she gets older and lonelier, it will be a prison, not a home.

Edward will be walking to his own house on nearby Pitt Street. If she hurries—if her sore knees will let her—she might catch him.

Her head starts ringing as she stands, and pain shoots through her skull. She stumbles, and clutches at the base of her neck. A moan escapes her. It sounds like the beginning of a call for help, but it melts into the lowing of a frightened cow. Her mouth sags as she grabs for the edge of the table.

Patience Mott hits the linoleum with a splat, like a wet sack of flour, and the memory ends.

"I wasn't sure it would work," said Henry, as Tipsy opened her eyes.

"At first it was a little…muffled. But I saw everything. The fight with Edward, then it looked like she died of an aneurysm. A burst blood vessel in her brain."

"Yes. Like Catherine, she never knew what hit her."

"A Cadillac, or a stroke. Fast and hard, out of the blue, with the same result. But in this situation, her emotions seem more important than how she died. I got a lot of guilt over how she treated Edward. But mostly…you."

He nodded. "She didn't remember any of it. Not her feelings or revelations, or Edward telling her about California, or deciding to go with him and his family. She didn't remember me telling her about the ghosts, or wondering if I really killed Jane."

"That means she also didn't remember wondering if she inadvertently turned you into another Thomas Bonneau." Tipsy shook her head. "How sad. Unresolved guilt could lead to a haunting."

"By the time she woke up as a ghost, whatever funeral proceedings Edward arranged were over, and he must have been in California. She's been resenting both of us for eighty years. Me for being an embarrassing murderer. Edward for abandoning her and that house."

"But *now* she remembers. Did y'all…come to peace?"

"I believe we did. We talked about my childhood confession about the ghosts. She cried, because even when she became a ghost herself, that conversation didn't come back to her until now. She apologized for not believing me." He smiled. "I explained the true story of my death, and Jane's. Thoroughly scandalized her, of course."

"What else did y'all talk about?"

"So many things. Old family stories. My father. It pleased her to know Thomas Bonneau got what he deserved. I told her Jane moved on, and that made her happy. She asked me questions about my supernatural talent and my existence with you. She seemed…proud of me for looking after you. She said she raised a gentleman, after all, and she lamented never getting to apologize to Edward. And…she asked me to forgive her."

"Did you?"

"I did. If Jane forgave me for how I treated her, I can forgive a sad old woman with less understanding of her own behavior than even I had. Besides, all these memories have helped me understand her. She had her own fears and struggles."

"I assume she's moved on."

"Yes. She has."

"So you moving on, too?"

"No."

"Henry…you don't have to look out for me! You can go home, to Jane. I hope Catherine's message included such a request." She twirled a finger at him. "And speaking of…"

"Ah, the message. I'm not quite ready to discuss it with you."

"What? Now you're really leaving me hanging."

"I'm not. I truly don't understand it myself. I will tell you. I promise. But I need time to think about it."

"You just want something to brood about." She scowled. "Always gotta be so mysterious, huh?"

Like cocoa powder mixing with hot water, his earnestness always dissolved her annoyance. "I don't know how to be any other way."

———◆✕◆———

Over the next week, Tipsy made the most of her kid-free time. She spent three days at the GQB, training Shelby's new salespeople. The first young woman reminded Tipsy of herself. A recent graduate of C of C, she was a talented studio art major who relished the idea of setting up her own easel in the gallery and working Shelby's professional connections. The second woman—a middle-aged transplant from Chicago with a retired heart surgeon for a husband. They'd purchased a condo near Waterfront Park. She didn't need to work, but she loved art, and wanted to be productive while her hubs played golf. Shelby always had trouble finding reliable help, but Madison and Christina (respectively) were her best candidates in ages.

In the evenings, Tipsy painted like the ghosts of Mary Cassatt and Frieda Kahlo possessed her, either at her own house, or Scott's. He'd go for a run, or hit the gym, and then cook them dinner, while she frenetically transferred paint from palette to brush to canvas. On Wednesday, two days before she picked up her kids from camp, she finished Catherine's portrait. He whistled when she revealed it to him in her kitchen when he stopped by her house during lunch.

"Amazing." He pointed at the bike basket full of roses. "Those flowers are an optical illusion. I want to grab them before they spill out all over the floor. Or grab *her*, before that giant bike tips right over. Her face— did she really look like that?"

Tipsy made eye contact with the smiling auburn-haired girl in the photo. Her wild eyes kept secrets Tipsy would never understand. She'd known unbearable noise and experienced the deepest silence. She'd carried messages from one plane of existence to another. "That's her," said Tipsy. "But it's a combination of her living self, and who she became before she moved on. Who…she might have been."

"I have no idea what that means, and yet somehow…I do." He rubbed her shoulders. "You need a break. Why don't you see what the girls are up to this evening?"

"I don't feel like going out, but I can see if anyone wants to come by for a glass of wine. I *do* have to give Jillian this painting."

"I think you should."

"Only if you do something fun, too."

"Brian asked me to come by and try his homebrew."

Tipsy laughed. "I'll trade you a Brian for a Shelby."

"Perfect. But I have one request. Promise me you'll make a little *retirement announcement* to Shelby after you unveil your masterpiece to Jillian."

She gently shoved him. "You're as bad as my Granna in my head."

"No excuse, darlin'," he said.

She spent the rest of the afternoon tidying up her house and creating an amateur charcuterie board. As she arranged cheese and sausages and jars of fig spread, she ran numbers in her head. Expenses. Budgets. Potential profit depending on the number of paintings she sold. By the time she showered and wiped out some wine glasses, she'd almost convinced herself she had a feasible plan.

She set up her tarp-covered painting and her entertaining spread on the front porch and popped the top on a Bud Lite. Before her butt hit the rocking chair, a blue BMW pulled into her driveway. Pammy waved through the windshield as Jillian applied lipstick.

Pamella got out of the car, and Tipsy assessed her latest outfit. She wore flat sandals with giant bows on the toes, red and yellow striped overalls, and a designer plain white tee. She accessorized with parrot-shaped earrings and a jangly ankle bracelet. Jillian looked positively sedate beside her in white shorts and a pale green linen blouse. Her tiny tennis shoes matched her top, and her boulder-sized diamond studs adorned her ears. Tipsy did detect Pamella's influence in her giant pink sunglasses. Or maybe she'd started hanging out with May Penny.

"Hey, lady!" yelled Pammy. "Thanks for having us. Perfect evening for a pre-dinner drink."

"Hey, y'all," said Tipsy, as they walked toward the porch. "Out on the town later?"

"We are! Trying to get Jilly to agree to Red Drum for dinner. Jillian is single, and you know what they say about *Wednesdays* at *Red Drum*."

"I do," said Tipsy, in reference to the popular Mount Pleasant restaurant's fabled cougar night. According to urban legend, Wednesdays at Red Drum meant single older ladies on the prowl.

Jillian scowled. "Hell to the no."

"If you change your mind, I got the perfect shirt," said Tipsy, as she pictured her *COUGAR MOM* tee.

"Wherever we go, I gotta change." Pamella pointed at her outfit. "So basic."

Jillian laughed. "If you're basic, then I'm positively rudimentary." They joined Tipsy on the porch. The three of them sat on Miss Callie's old wicker furniture.

"I can't go to dinner in flats, Jilly! And neither should you. Although, if I'm getting you out of the house, I'm not complaining."

"I gotta start socializing sometime. Can't play tennis, work on my house, and hover over my daughter twenty-four hours a day."

"I saw Sophie the other night," said Tipsy, as she handed Jillian a glass of wine. "So nice to see her out and about."

"She told me. I can't believe the change in her. She's seeing her friends and filling me in on all their escapades. Excited about school and her sisters visiting from California. She's got some floral events coming up, too. Starting small with a baby shower and a housewarming, but I think she's on to something."

"It's all thanks to you, my exorcist pal!" said Pammy.

"Not *just* me. I have a whole cadre of helpers these days. My undead honcho, Henry. Scott as my moral support—"

"You hold on to that man," said Jillian in a girlish, gossipy voice. "He's a GD saint, doing what he does for a living. I didn't think they made men like him anymore."

Tipsy smiled. "Believe me, I know what I got."

"Don't sell yourself short. *He's* got something special, too," said Jillian. "You're a gem. And so... *capable*. I pray my Sophie grows up to be as well-adjusted about her supernatural powers as you are. I hope y'all keep in touch."

"We will. But like I was saying, I had help. From Catherine, too." Tipsy stood. "Speaking of...you ready to see her again?"

"Uh...I thought she was gone for good—"

Before Jillian finished, Tipsy removed the tarp from her painting with a flourish. Jillian covered her mouth with her hand, but her fingers were drawn to her snout as if she had magnets up her nostrils. She squeezed her poor nose until the tip went bright red. "You're a genius, with the ghosts, and with the paintbrushes. So now, I need a check from you."

Tipsy faltered. "A check?"

"A *blank one*, sweets. I need your bank account information for the wire."

"Oh, gosh. Right. I figured you'd write *me* a check."

"A check, for two hundred thousand? No, my dear. Much simpler to have my accountant wire it to you."

"Wait, what? *Two hundred?*" Granna would tell her to *zip that lip, sugar*, but lip-zipping is impossible when one is so flabbergasted. "We agreed on one—"

"Tipsy, we had a deal. Remove a ghost for a hundred-k. Turns out there were *two* ghosts, and you got rid of both of them. You also provided me with *that* amazing memorial to my beautiful sister. Put it this way, if you get audited, it's $150,000.00 for home design services, and $50,0000.00 for the painting."

"I don't know what to say. I've never sold a painting for so much—"

"I paid my Palo Alto interior designer more to pick out furniture and paint colors. My house out there contains at least five paintings worth that much. Talking about money is gauche, but what you did for me is priceless. So please, take the money. And for the love of God, start charging more for your paintings."

"Thank you. Thank you, *so much.*" Tipsy sat back in her wicker chair. Her budget numbers recalculated themselves in her head. She fought the urge to get up and retrieve the notebook where she'd been scribbling notes and storing printed-off Excel spreadsheets.

I cannot believe this, Granna. I truly cannot.

It's hard for me to fathom, too, but Jiminy Cricket, I ain't complaining. You wished upon a star, and made it all happen.

"Pammy," said Jillian, "there is no reason people in San Francisco and Atlanta wouldn't pay big money for Tipsy's work."

At that moment, Shelby's new minivan pulled into the driveway. Shelby honked, and hopped out of the car. "Sorry I'm late!" she said. She swept up the stairs in a floppy yellow cotton sundress with a bluish stain on the skirt, flip-flops, and a salt-encrusted COCKS baseball cap. "I barely escaped. No time to shower. No time to brush my hair. Toothpaste drying on my dress, so my breath is tolerable."

"At least you're here," said Pamella. She pointed at herself, Jillian, and Tipsy. "We got eight kids between us. We all remember those new baby days."

"Lindsey can't make it," said Shelby. "P.D. is still fifty miles offshore, chasing fish."

"Eek," said Tipsy. If P.D. didn't get it together soon, Tipsy sensed a massive blowout coming. And not from one of Baby Paul's diapers.

Tipsy introduced Jillian to Shelby, and made sure to mention Jillian's interest in art. Shelby knew Jillian was, as Granna said, *a gazillionaire,* so she eyed her with keen interest. They chatted about California artists for a bit, and Tipsy could tell Jillian's knowledge impressed Shelby.

"I was just telling Pamella it's time Tipsy goes nationwide," said Jillian.

"I couldn't agree more," said Shelby, "so I'm officially firing you."

Jillian and Pamella looked horrified, but Tipsy laughed. "You can't fire me, because I quit," she said.

"You do?" Shelby hugged her. "I'm so glad!"

Now Pamella and Jillian appeared both confused and distressed, so Tipsy filled them in. "Shelby has been encouraging me to paint full-time for months. Thanks to Jillian, now I can."

"Yes!" said Pamella. "You create, and between me and Jilly, ATL and the Bay Area are locked up."

"She needs New York, too," said Shelby. "I know NYC pretty well, but there are other key cities. DC.

Miami."

"I know people in DC," said Jillian. "I used to go there for work..."

Tipsy stared into the butterfly bushes as they chattered away about their plans for her national artistic takeover. She did more rough math in her head. She relished the idea of a nest egg, so she'd be as frugal as ever. Maybe with time, patience, and good planning, her egg would grow, not shrink.

It's what you always wanted, sugar, said Granna. *To paint for a living. A real, true living. Share your talent with the world.*

This is amazing, Granna. Scott will be so excited for me. I can't believe I have someone to share it with. She thought her heart would burst with happiness. *How is my life suddenly falling together, when it's been falling apart for so long?*

Life changes, sugar. We go around fearing change. Hiding from it. But sometimes, if we're brave enough to face the fallout those initial changes can bring, life swings the other way just as fast.

———◆✕◆———

Tipsy's last day at the GQB included a ceremonial after work toast at the Blind Tiger with Shelby, Christy, and Maddy. Afterward, she walked past the darkened gallery on her way to the garage. She'd spent countless hours in that musty old building in the past few years. She'd shed tears and laughed her ass off. She and Shelby has screamed at each other. She'd worked on multiple paintings, all of which had found their way to the right spot on somebody's walls. So many customers from so many cities, states, and countries had come and gone.

She paused on the corner of State and Queen and looked over her shoulder. The sunflower painting had sold earlier in the week. She had no GQB inventory, but now she had ample time to rectify that problem. At the sound of clopping hooves, she looked up. There was her old buddy, Creamsicle, pulling a private carriage. His guide faced backwards and gave his historical shtick to an attentive, well-dressed couple. The guide didn't need to keep his eyes on the road. Creamsicle knew the way. The horse pricked his ears in Tipsy's direction. She waved to him, and decided his painting would be her first venture as a full-time artist.

Tipsy drove home with visions of Creamsicle dancing in her head. She hummed as she climbed the porch stairs and stooped to pick up a UPS envelope. The door opened of its own accord as she juggled envelope, keys, water bottle, purse, and files from the GQB.

"Thanks, Henry," she said, as she entered the house.

"Not a problem," he called out, from somewhere on the second floor.

She plonked her stuff on the console table in the foyer, adjusted her ponytail, and turned to the envelope. She hadn't ordered anything from Amazon, and the envelope was flat. The kind that held important documents, not face creams or cheap socks. She squinted at the return address. *A.L. Collins, IV, 605 Grand Oak Avenue, Mount Pleasant, SC 29464.*

Legal papers, Granna? FML!

Huh?

It means... But Granna would not approve of that euphemism. Tipsy twisted the envelope into a tube, as if to crush it into oblivion. *Forget it. I'm saying, this is a potential problem.*

Wouldn't one of them process servers have to give you legal papers? Like last time?

Maybe?

Well, open it! Look the problem in the face.

I...have to take a shower. As she had the last time Ayers dumped legalese on her, Tipsy dropped the envelope on the console table and tried to ignore it for the next few hours. She showered, did some sketching, and made a salad for herself and Scott for dinner. As she chopped tomatoes and cucumbers, the envelope whispered slyly to her from the foyer. She yelled for Alexa to play Zac Brown. She drowned her anxiety in Zac's ode to cold beers and perfectly fitting jeans.

She didn't bring up the envelope until she and Scott were sitting on the front porch with a post-dinner glass of red wine. His chin jutted, but he wordlessly got up, went into the house, and retrieved it. He returned to the porch and tried to hand it to her, but she waved it away. "I can't. You open it."

She sensed his burgeoning anger. If the envelope contained bad news, she'd go inside, retrieve her Swiffer, and let him aggressively mop the porch floorboards until he calmed down. He broke the seal and removed two sheets of paper from the envelope. Last time, the legal papers had arrived in a fat packet. Ayers's list of complaints to the court couldn't be too serious if two pages could explain them.

Scott shook his head, and the grim line of his mouth twisted.

"What is it?" she asked. "Is that a smile of relief, or a grimace of pain?"

"You read it." He handed her a piece of plain computer paper. Ayers had scrawled across it in black Sharpie.

I AGREE. KATE, TOO. -ALC

"He agrees to what?" she asked. "What's the other—"

Scott gave her the other piece of paper—a cashier's check for one hundred thousand dollars.

"Holy. *Hell.* No. Freakin'. *Way!*"

"You said he'd need to stew over everything. Does this mean they're willing to—"

"To leave us alone! This is a hundred thousand dollars of the one hundred fifty thousand he owes me. I offered to take hundred-k and let the rest go, and not address the child support issue. Hallelujah!" She stared at the check, and Ayers's familiar illegible signature. "But…do you think he can control Kate?"

"Hmmm." Scott rubbed his chin. "She'll find little ways to gouge me, but as long as she's not blowing me up day and night, no worries. I've been dealing with her for fourteen years. But it's not only about that, darlin'. That check—"

"I know. With Jillian's money, and this…I'm not just okay. I'm… *rich*."

"Not Kardashian rich, but you'll be very comfortable while you build your artistic empire."

"I'll be able to—and then I can—" She burst into noisy tears.

He put an arm around her and squeezed. He held her as she blubbered away until she cried herself dry. "I'm sorry—"

"Tipsy…."

"Okay. Not *sorry*. But I want to make it clear I'm sobbing my eyeballs out because I'm *so damn* happy."

"I know how hard the past few years have been for you. I had my own challenges, but they didn't include having to rebuild my career from the ground up while worrying about paying the bills. If anything, work stabilized me. Now you'll have stability, too."

"The fact that I have it with you makes it exponentially sweeter," she said.

He kissed the side of her head. "You and your sexy vocabulary."

A bluish light at the end of the porch caught Tipsy's eye. Henry sat on the joggling board.

"Hey, Henry." She sat up and turned to Scott. "Henry's here. Can he join us?"

"Uh, sure. Do I need to move over?"

"The rocker is fine," said Henry, as he materialized on the chair across from them. "I won't stay long. Jane and I used to sit on this porch during my good moods. I don't want to ruin the porch ambiance for the two of you."

"If you move on, maybe y'all can sit together on a porch on the other side."

He smiled. "Not quite yet. In fact, I have some news that…you may find exasperating. Vexing, perhaps."

"I've found you exasperating and vexing many times. Just tell me what's on your mind."

"I'm starting over on THE GREAT STORY."

"You're kidding."

"What?" asked Scott.

"You know his book? He said he's starting over." She leaned toward Henry. "Why now, when you're making some progress—"

"I must follow my muse."

"Where is the muse heading?"

"I don't know for certain yet."

"Does this have to do with Jane's message?"

"Perhaps."

"Argh, Henry. You make no sense—"

"I'm sure you'd rather I move on. Especially now that your sweetheart will be here more often."

"I've told you a million times. I'm happy to have you in the house. Scott doesn't mind. He knows you're like my brother. Right, Scott?"

Scott looked around, as if he wasn't sure where to aim his answer. "I don't mind at all. Tipsy told me y'all respect each other's privacy, and you've been a great friend to her through some really tough times."

"Tell him thank you. It's admirable how this man has accepted you, and therefore, me." She repeated Henry's message to Scott, and then Henry said, "Can you teach me to use your lapdown?"

"You mean my laptop? My computer?"

"Yes. The machine where you write things."

"Will you try to type using your powers?"

He nodded. "Every day, I'm more adept at using my abilities. I always imagined my novel written out in my own hand, but your modern ways are more practical."

He raised a hand. A few hydrangea blossoms cracked off the bush on the other side of the porch railing and floated toward Scott. He plucked them out of thin air and offered them to Tipsy.

"I'll do whatever I can to help you," she said. "I hope Jane isn't annoyed with me from the other side, since I *could* expedite the process by pushing you through your own door."

"Thank you. Jane wants me to be at peace. She understands I still have work to do here, even if I no longer need to serve as your protector. Someone else worthy has come along to do that." He stood. "I'll take my leave now. Y'all enjoy the porch."

"Thanks, Mr. Mott," she said, as he walked through the wall and disappeared into the house. She filled Scott in on the rest of the conversation. "So he's hanging around for a while."

"You think he'll finally be at peace when he finishes his new story?"

"I hope so. Although I wonder if a spirit like Henry can ever fully be at peace. Maybe turbulence is too ingrained in his nature."

"I hope not, for his sake. Now that I know what it feels like to be at peace, I wouldn't wish turbulence on anyone."

"Hmmm." Tipsy leaned into his arms and listened to the buzzing cicadas and trilling tree frogs. She touched a hydrangea blossom to her nose and inhaled its delicate yet robust fragrance. The flower's full-bodied pink color could only be described as *rose. Carolina rose*, or better, *palmetto rose*. A rose by any other name might be a hydrangea grown in sandy Lowcountry soil, or an ingenious decorative flower woven from something else entirely. Different hues, myriad blossoms. All part of her own protracted, gradual blooming process. It was finally time to step into the sunlight, and let her artistic talent bloom for all the world to see.

Scott would be there to support her through the inevitable bumps, just as she'd be there for him. He unequivocally *believed* her, and he wholeheartedly *believed in* her. She felt the same way about him. Fear didn't stand a chance in the face of so much steady love, and her astute instincts of late—that Thomas Bonneau was all wrong, and Scott Brandt was so right—had taught her to trust her heart. After all, that complicated metaphorical organ had always told her true. For years, she'd simply chosen to ignore it.

Many evenings, she'd sat on Miss Callie's porch and thought about other people questioning her sanity, but Scott dealt with insane people every day. He knew lunacy when he saw it, and he didn't think her crazy. As for everyone else—including those who said Tipsy and Scott were fools for falling in love with their respective ex-in-laws—maybe they were the crazy ones. Tipsy had never felt saner in her life.

THE END

Acknowledgments

A s I wrap up the third installment in Tipsy's story, and move on to the (anticipated) final book in this series, I find myself repeatedly thanking the many people who have been instrumental to the success of these books. First, thank you to every single reader who has fallen in love with Tipsy and her friends (living and dead). You have spread the word about this series, written positive reviews, and sent messages demanding to know what happens next. Your dedication kept me typing away, even as my day job threatened to consume my creative energy and I battled carpal tunnel syndrome. I hope I'm doing justice to Tipsy's evolution!

Thanks to everyone at Bublish for the behind-the-scenes work, and to Caroline Staley (the Gallavantor) for once again providing the beautiful cover art. The cover for *Palmetto Rose* might be my favorite Gallavantor creation yet!

Always, thank you to my darling mother, Dianne Wicklein, who will celebrate her seventieth birthday on the day this book launches into the world. Thanks, Mom, for cheering me on and for listening to my complaints with equal enthusiasm. Even if they don't always realize it, my children—Eliza, Harper, and Cyrus—keep me motivated. I hope my example will inspire them to put in the hard work that is inherent to the pursuit of any worthy dream. A shout out to my bestie Erica Bogdanowitz, who is always there to lift me up, make me laugh, share frustrations and victories, and, of course, compare outfits.

Many readers have expressed hope that Tipsy will find a man who is worthy of her. I've raked our heroine over the coals in the last two novels, and she's due for some happiness. That happiness comes with the bumps and bruises endemic to middle-of-life love, but I always knew the wait would be worth it, for Tipsy and her legion of supportive fans. I am so fortunate to live under the same roof with a man who makes it easy to imagine and craft the perfect partner for her. Thank you to my husband, my best friend, my confidante, my cheerleader, my kids' stepfather, and my resident comedian and mental health expert, Dr. Jeffrey S. Cluver, MD. From the romantic to the practical, I couldn't do any of this without you.

Lastly, dear readers, as a bit of a teaser, plan to spend a lot of time with Henry Mott in Book 4! Please follow me on Instagram (@stephaniealexanderbooks), TikTok (@stephaniealexanderbooks), or Facebook (/crackedslipper) for updates and news about my work, including Book 4!

With affection,
Stephanie

CPSIA information can be obtained
at www.ICGtesting.com
Printed in the USA
LVHW041610180623
750109LV00001B/99

9 781647 045012